THE MAP OF LOST MEMORIES

BALLANTINE BOOKS

NEW YORK

THE MAP

of

LOST MEMORIES

A Novel

Kim Fay

Published in the United States by Ballantine Books, an imprint of The Random House Publishing Group, a division of Random House, Inc., New York.

BALLANTINE and colophon are registered trademarks of Random House, Inc.

LIBRARY OF CONGRESS CATALOGING-IN-PUBLICATION DATA
Fay, Kim.
The map of lost memories: a novel / Kim Fay.
p.   cm.
ISBN 978-0-345-53134-6
eBook ISBN 978-0-345-53135-3
I. Title.
PS3606.A9524M37 2012
813'.6—dc23   2012004142

Printed in the United States of America
on acid-free paper

www.ballantinebooks.com

2 4 6 8 9 7 5 3 1

FIRST EDITION

Book design by Dana Leigh Blanchette
Title-page and part-title images: © Julie Fay Ashborn (temple);
© iStockphoto (stone woman and pattern)
Map by Janet McKelpin

For my gramps,
Woodrow "Buck" Ethier

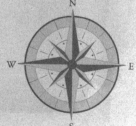

SHANGHAI ↗

China

Vietnam

Laos

Siam

South
China Sea

Cambodia

• Kha Seng

Stung Treng

Angkor •
Wat

MEKONG RIVER

• Phnom Penh

• Saigon

Contents

Part 1

SHANGHAI

Chapter 1	Desperate Weather	3
Chapter 2	The Upper Hand	14
Chapter 3	In Yellow Babylon	30
Chapter 4	A Place Like This	48
Chapter 5	Hope and Futility	57
Chapter 6	The Letter Opener	65
Chapter 7	The Other Side	74

Part 2

SAIGON

| Chapter 8 | The China Sea | 87 |
| Chapter 9 | A Trusted Colleague | 102 |

Chapter 10   The Right Dress   118

Chapter 11   The Butterfly Garden   128

Chapter 12   The Compass Rose   140

Part 3

CAMBODIA

Chapter 13   Not a Mirage   153

Chapter 14   The Revolution   165

Chapter 15   A Great Cambodian
               Adventure   178

Chapter 16   The *Alouette*   193

Chapter 17   Second Chances   205

Chapter 18   Crossing the Line   219

Chapter 19   Complete Certainty   231

Chapter 20   The Sacrifice   240

Chapter 21   The Bullet Wound   253

Chapter 22   The Ravine   263

Chapter 23   Midnight   273

Chapter 24   The Puzzle Lock   290

Chapter 25   The Last Orphan   299

Chapter 26   The Coming Night   315

Part 1

SHANGHAI

From its inception as a foreign enclave,
Shanghai emerged a free city. New arrivals
required neither visa nor passport to enter.
To the dispossessed, the ambitious and the
criminal, it offered a fresh start. Lady Jel-
lico, who was brought up in the city, recalled, "One never asked why someone had
come to Shanghai. It was assumed every-
body had something to hide."

HARRIET SERGEANT,
Shanghai

Chapter 1

Desperate Weather

At the far end of the apartment, a row of shutters opened onto a balcony overlooking the swayback roofs of Shanghai. Beyond the low buildings and down a crooked street, the Whangpoo River shushed against the wharves. A heavy, velvet humidity pressed down on this dark belt of water, a perpetual tension that caused a wilted draft, lifting fumes of jasmine and sewage, coal and rotting river weed, into the thick night air.

Inside, the small living room was crowded with a dozen overheated journalists and revolutionaries, as well as the usual assortment of eccentrics that congregated at parties in Shanghai in 1925: a Persian opera singer, a White Russian baroness, and a gunrunner of indeterminate nationality. There was a priest bright-eyed on cocaine he had ordered from the room service menu at the Astor House, and Irene Blum recognized the Italian fascist she had seen the night before, parading through the Del Monte with a tiger on a leather leash. Shanghailanders never needed an excuse to gather, but tonight they had one: the return of Roger and Simone Merlin from France, where the couple had gone to raise funds for China's Communist party.

The Merlins were late, and a restlessness that matched Irene's stirred among the guests. She overheard the Italian fascist complain, "Bloody hot," prompting the Persian opera singer to declare, "Desperate weather. Did you hear about the Argentine ballerina caught stealing spices in the Chinese market? She wears only Coco Chanel. Every time the peddler turned his back, she dropped another pinch of saffron into her pocket. She swears she doesn't know why she did it. Insists the heat must have addled her brain."

Irene understood. It was unsettling, the way the heat subverted. She had been in Shanghai only one week, but already, each day around the noon hour, when the sun was high and the city lay exposed, she found herself envisioning the most uncharacteristic acts. Stabbing a rickshaw driver with her penknife, or shoving one of the demure chambermaids down the back stairs of her hotel. Of course she did not act upon these impulses, but their eruption harassed her and caused a heat-stricken feeling of agitation that had reached a new level of intensity tonight. She had not expected to have to wait a week to meet Simone Merlin, and she was wound tight with anticipation. She could not stop watching the door. Unable to concentrate on conversation, she slipped out to the balcony, where she leaned against the railing, plucking the fabric of her dress away from her skin, seeking relief from the muggy room.

She was soon joined by Anne Howard. Anne had arranged the party so Irene could meet Simone, and yet she now said, "It's not too late to change your mind."

"Why are you so against this?" Irene asked.

"Darling, I'm looking out for you, that's all. This is bigger than anything you've been involved with before. It's not a jaunt to Phoenix to find out if you can detect a forged—"

"I did detect it. And I saved Mr. Simms a great deal of money on that statue, not to mention the humiliation of being duped by a greasy con man from Arizona."

"I know you did. You're good at what you do. I'm not denying that. But if the wrong person gets wind of this. If anyone finds out what you're searching for. And the jungles! Irene, you don't seem to realize what a different league you're in with this expedition."

"I'm in the same league I've been in for years." Irene scowled at the woman she thought she knew so well.

Nearly sixty, her gray hair cut into a fashionable bob, Anne was the self-appointed head of Shanghai's outpost of the Brooke Museum in Seattle. She and Irene had worked together from opposite sides of the Pacific Ocean for ten years, ever since the Great War broke out and Irene was given a job at the museum by its curator, Professor Howard, Anne's former husband. Anne had helped Irene track down missing relics, providing information that could be gathered only in China.

A friend of Irene's mother, Anne had divorced and moved to Shanghai when Irene was five. Each Christmas, she sent Irene a gift: cloisonné rings, silk slippers, a lacquer jewel box that could nestle in the palm of a child's hand. She was the only woman, after Irene's mother died, who gave Irene the sorts of things she really wanted. Throughout her youth, Irene read every letter Anne had sent her mother, descriptions of foot binding, imperial traditions, and the older woman's affair with a Chinese revolutionary who had two wives. She lost herself in this exotic world the way other girls her age escaped into Jane Austen and Louisa May Alcott. As teachers fretfully noted her lack of interest in domestic skills or other female pursuits, the life Anne was living in Shanghai gave Irene hope. It proved that a woman could do anything she liked as long as she did not care what others thought. Every day, with her maps and books and her dreams of lost treasures, Irene practiced not caring.

It was difficult, though, not to care about Anne's opinion. Anne had always encouraged Irene's dreams, and now she did not want Irene to have this one that mattered most. It made no sense.

Irene took a sip of whiskey. Already she felt a little drunk, and this was unusual, since she was from Swedish stock and could generally hold her alcohol. But there was something about the delayed buildup to this moment, combined with the sweltering climate and its intoxicating effect on the body, that made her cautious with her single malt tonight. She said, "I know the risks."

"You're even more headstrong than I used to be." Anne went back inside.

Irene remained on the balcony, standing apart as she often did at parties, her intense observation hidden behind the Scandinavian coolness of her pale blue eyes. She was twenty-nine, half Anne's age, and taller than most women, but not so tall as to intimidate men. For this she was grateful, since men, when threatened, even if only by the threat of height, were difficult to manipulate. And manipulation was essential in the world of art trafficking.

With her dark blond hair pulled back into a loose chignon, Irene had dressed in an uninterrupted flow of silk that emphasized her slender figure. Fine white Indian embroidery caught the lamplight. This was a gown she had worn often for occasions at the museum, to welcome patrons and collectors. She had been wearing it the night she greeted Rockefeller with a martini, when the Brooke Museum had been her pride. When she had been its pride—or so she had thought. She shook her head. She had to find a way to stop thinking about the museum. She had already wasted too much time on that bitterness. As she lit a cigarette, the warm stones of her carnelian bracelet slipped over the bend of her wrist. She touched them, for luck.

When the front door finally opened, Irene heard the Merlins' names shouted out in greeting. Through the men and women who rose to welcome the couple, she glimpsed damp strands of dark hair. The honey light from an oil lamp reflected off a perspiring brow. Smoke adhered to the air. A chill, seemingly impossible in such oppressive weather, whisked up Irene's spine.

Anne had run out of tumblers, and she descended upon the Merlins with rum sodas in coffee mugs. Drinks were raised in a hearty toast to the French couple whose support was integral to the strikes that were debilitating Shanghai's European government and empowering the Communist party's nationalist comrades, the Kuomintang. The Persian opera singer, whose lavender fedora sat askew on her head, giggled drunkenly and slurred, "It's a miracle you were allowed back into the country."

Clutching her glass, Irene peered past one of the shutters that hung slack against the balcony's mildewing wall. Anne was pressing her way back out toward Irene, towing Simone Merlin by her sleeve. This was it. The moment Irene had been waiting for. Beneath the apartment in the well of darkness, she could hear the tenor of the city. Children laughed. Water splashed into dishes being washed while a woman mewed a melancholy folk song.

Irene had seen Simone in photographs, but details had been hard to make out. In person, the young woman was afflicted with the cadaverous complexion of many Europeans who were raised in the tropics. Her floor-length dress was nearly colorless too, as if she had emerged from a landscape by Turner. Irene could not fathom how someone so washed out and small had the stamina to raid a temple and support a Communist revolution, but the contradiction intrigued her. She had no interest in people who could be summed up in a single sentence.

"Ma chérie," Roger called after Simone from the cluster of his admirers. "Why are you dashing away from me?"

Simone did not look back. "There is someone Anne insists I meet."

Roger took a few steps after his wife. He appeared to be in his forties, much older than she. He too was slight in build, but he held his chin arrogantly high, and his stern intellectual's eyeglasses deflected attention from his insubstantial physique. "Are you sure?" he asked.

It was an odd question, and Simone paused at the threshold to the balcony while Roger waited for a response. She stared stoically past Irene into the night. When it was clear that she was not going to answer, he turned to Anne's lover, Song Yi, whose handsome face was flushed from the praise he had been receiving throughout the night for his recent translation of Karl Marx's Communist Manifesto into Mandarin.

Gently, Anne asked, "How was the journey?"

"We fought the entire time. You know Roger. He doesn't believe in compromise. I told him I intended to succeed in leaving him this time, and he tried to throw me overboard." Simone smiled, but there was no humor in her tone as she said, "I'm lucky I'm not feeding the fish at the bottom of the Arabian Sea."

"He sounds like a horrible man," Irene said.

"He is," Simone confirmed.

Irene could scarcely believe that this was her first exchange with Simone Merlin as she asked, "Did he hurt you?"

"I'm alive, so no, I suppose not."

Anne clasped Simone's hand. "He's going to help us save this country." She said this as if it were a consolation.

Although Roger and Song Yi were inside and speaking only to one another, Roger's resonant voice carried to the balcony, as if to emphasize Anne's words. "The next stage in the strikes is a necessary evil. Men will die; it's unfortunate, *bien sûr*, but if we are not willing to accept the sacrifices, then we do not truly want change." Louder, he added, "Are you listening, my dear wife? Do you hear what I'm saying? Are you ready for the sacrifices needed to achieve what you think you want? Do you have enough conviction? Strength?"

None of the guests showed any sign of embarrassment as Roger hurled this challenge at Simone. They merely watched as if the couple were characters in a favorite film serial.

"Do you?" Roger barked.

The drunken Persian opera singer leaned forward. Irene was repulsed by the greediness of the onlookers, and moved by the exhaustion in Simone's expression as she stepped all the way out onto the balcony and slipped behind the shelter of a louvered door.

"You can't hide from me!" Roger shouted.

Simone sighed. "Song Yi is lovely. I'm always envious of how calm he remains. With Sun Yat-sen's death and these latest strikes, everyone else is on edge. And now that Roger has come back, the city is going to erupt, I can feel it. The mood is like it was in Saigon, right before the authorities burned our press." Wistfully, she added, "I envy you, Anne."

The conversation was straying too far from where Irene needed it to be, and she hoped she did not seem unsympathetic as she guided it around. "Has Anne told you why I want to meet you?"

"She said you're going to Cambodia."

Irene waited for more, but Simone was silent.

Finally, Anne spoke. "That's all I revealed. The details aren't mine to tell."

Simone perked up. "Had I known I was in for a mystery tonight, I would have dressed for the occasion."

With the woman's attention triggered, Irene quickly introduced herself. "I'm Irene Blum, of the Brooke Museum."

"I know the Brooke well. It has quite the layered reputation."

Irene was pleased. That reputation was her doing, even though she had not been rewarded for it. Had not even been acknowledged, in the end. "Like you," she went on, "I specialize in Cambodia and its ancient Khmer people. Of course, not exactly like you. I've never been to Cambodia, and my father wasn't an Angkor scholar. He was the night watchman at the museum. I grew up in it. You could say I was its student. Your student too. Your monograph about celestial imagery in Khmer art is masterful."

"Are you trying to flatter me?"

"I'm being truthful. Your life . . . it's the life I always wanted."

"Unhappily married to a scoundrel? I find that a strange aspiration."

"I'm talking about—"

Anne interjected. "Simone, when Irene was nine, her mother died. Her father had the good sense not to hand her off to the first pie-baking matron who waddled along. He took her to the museum with him every night instead. She spent her childhood sleeping in the Hall of the Apsaras. He gave her a calling. A woman with a calling, now that is a thing of beauty." She sighed. "Great beauty and great danger. Tread cautiously, my dear," she warned, before going back inside to her guests.

"The mystery deepens," Simone murmured.

"It *is* an honor to meet you," Irene maintained, thrusting out her hand. She could feel the range of calluses on Simone's palm, and she considered their source: the ruins Simone had spent her childhood scaling, the bas-relief she and Roger had stolen from the temple of Banteay Srei. Irene had seen the sculpted stone for herself in Seattle, and it awed her to think of Simone prying it from the temple's wall.

Simone opened her handbag and removed an enamel compact. Her fingertip fluttered into a pad of lip rouge. She applied a thin stain, and when she finished, her reddened mouth reminded Irene of the women in the Chinese district who spat rusty betel nut juice into the street. "Are you going to tell me what you want, or do I need to make tiresome small talk for a while?"

"I'm not usually this nervous," Irene admitted.

"Is it because you have a secret?"

"A remarkable secret."

"If it helps, you're not alone. Everyone who comes to Shanghai has something to hide."

Irene contemplated the room. "That's not how it seems. It feels as if everything here is on display. Communism, opium—"

"Cleavage and heartache? How many woe-is-me stories have you already heard of fat English husbands stolen away from their families by nubile Chinese prostitutes?"

"Too many, considering I've only been here a week." Eased by Simone's candor, Irene asked, "Would you tell me something about your life in Cambodia? Anything you like."

"So, tiresome small talk it is."

"Not to me."

Blinking in the direction of her husband, who was declaring that the Chinese needed foreigners to show them how to rid themselves of foreign rule, Simone reached for a rattan fan that had been left on the railing. As she waved it, stirring the air, the scent of boiled ginger floated across the balcony. "I was a girl when I left. Only eighteen. I couldn't predict how hypocritical Roger's version of a revolution would become."

Irene was not political, but she wasn't ignorant either. She knew about Communists, and not just how they raided the tsar's palaces, scattering Botticellis and Rembrandts to pay for their rebellion. She also knew they controlled the Kuomintang and wanted to take over Shanghai, and China altogether if they could manage it. But this did not interest her, despite the role she knew the Merlins played in this situation. "Do you want to go back to Cambodia?" she asked.

"I miss it."

"What do you miss most?"

"To stand in Angkor Wat is to be humbled," Simone said. "A temple that served as an entire city, the pinnacle of Khmer civilization, abandoned for centuries, but still, it is . . ." She eyed her husband warily through the slats in the louvers. "It is . . ."

As if facing a mirror, Irene recognized Simone's guarded expression. "You can trust me."

"It is holy."

Irene heard this, *holy,* as if it were a password. "I'm going to Cambodia in search of a lost temple. I'm going to search for the history of the Khmer." She had not planned to blurt this out, and she paused, rubbing her collar between her thumb and forefinger.

"Go on," Simone urged.

The inquisitive look on Simone's face was encouragement enough, and Irene continued, "I have a diary that belonged to a missionary. It indicates that he found a written history of the empire."

"Anyone who has ever studied the Khmer talks of such a finding."

"Dreams of it," Irene corrected her. "Do you dream of it?"

"I'm not sure anymore." Simone shifted, and with her back to the yellow light shining down from a torch at the end of the balcony, her face was hidden by its own shadow.

"I want to hire you to help me find the scrolls."

Simone's voice lurched. "Scrolls?"

"You've heard of them, haven't you?"

"I've heard the rumors, like everyone else."

"This is more than a rumor. I have a map."

Simone grazed the fan against her cheek. "Why did you come to me?"

"You took the bas-relief from Banteay Srei. You know how to do this sort of thing."

"How do you know about . . . Oh yes, you would know. You work at the Brooke. Are you going to take the scrolls for the museum?"

"Actually, I *worked* at the Brooke. There was a . . . a falling-out. So no, I won't be taking the scrolls back there. I want them for me, to study, and I don't plan on taking them anywhere." This wasn't true, but Irene could not tell Simone so. She could not risk anyone knowing that she was going to take the scrolls to America as the centerpiece for a new institution—

one in which she was in charge. "But I'll still need secrecy. You know what would happen if a single word of this got out. If anyone knew we'd found the key to a lost civilization, we'd have every archaeologist and treasure hunter out there after us."

"Naturally."

"I've heard so much about you. How you learned Sanskrit from temple rubbings while you were a girl. That you read fluently in Pali and Khmer." Irene could not hide her envy, for the only other language she knew was French. "I want you to translate the scrolls for me. I want you to tell me what happened to the Khmer Empire." Her fingers clenched the balcony railing. "We will be the first Westerners to know."

"When I was a child," Simone said, "I wrote stories about how I was going to discover new temples. My father thought I should be a novelist. I wrote the lectures I would one day present to geographical societies around the globe, and I even designed the dress I would wear on my tour. It would be made of Khmer silk, with ivory buttons carved into the shape of the rosettes that are found on the temple walls."

The wistful moan of a conch horn rose from a junk down on the river. Irene's beloved job was gone. Her father was dead not even a year, and Henry Simms—the man who had sent her on this quest—was dying. Soon she would have no one left, no one who understood her. But she felt this woman understood. "Then you will come with me?"

Simone looked out at Roger, slouched on Anne's old chaise, his shoes digging insolently into a red velvet bolster. He raised his glass in the direction of the balcony. She said, "I'm sorry, Irene."

"What do you mean?"

"You cannot begin to know how sorry I am."

"Sorry about what?"

"I can't go. Not now." Disgusted, Simone said, "Especially not now. Not on the eve of my husband's revolution."

"But you sailed all the way to France to raise money for the strikes. I'm authorized to offer you fifty thousand dollars, but I can get more. Name your price."

"If only this were about money."

"Fifty thousand dollars is not *only* money. It's a fortune."

"I told you what happened on the ship. Roger will not let me leave him. He's on the cusp of making history."

"How long will it take?"

Simone tossed the fan on the chair beside her. "Irene, this is a revolution, not a barroom brawl. Sun Yat-sen is dead, and the parties are splintering. The power struggles alone are enough to drive Roger mad, and if he goes any madder than he already is—"

"You want this revolution more than you want the scrolls?" Irene asked. "Is that what you're saying?"

"What I want has not mattered for a long time." Quickly, Simone walked back into the apartment.

Simone had called Angkor Wat *holy*. She called her husband's revolution *hypocritical*.

"Wait," Irene said. "I don't understand."

But rather than explain, Simone returned to Roger, perching on the arm of his chair and affectionately setting one hand on the nape of his neck.

The night seemed to shift, as if Shanghai were settling down into its foundation. A fitful cool struggled to press in from the distant East China Sea. Irene heard propellers thrashing against the black Whangpoo River. And she wondered what in the hell had just happened, while below in the dark a melon had been split, its sweetness clinging to the humid air.

Chapter 2

The Upper Hand

Six months earlier, in January, Irene sat in her office at the Brooke Museum of Oriental Art in Seattle, looking around at the objects that had accumulated over the years. She ran her hand lovingly along the edge of the drafting table that served as a desk, laid flat and stacked with her latest assignment, an inventory of John Thomson's 1866 photographs of Angkor Wat. She admired the three French oak filing cabinets, hand-me-downs that had drifted in from other parts of the building as her need for more space in which to store correspondence and collection catalogs grew. Above them on the wall was her favorite item in the room, the first thing she had put in this storage-space-turned-office when she claimed it for herself a decade ago: a framed watercolor her mother had painted of the filigreed stone walls of the Khmer temple of Banteay Srei.

Irene remembered how it had hung in such solitude back when she was starting out, before her passion for Khmer studies outgrew the room, dominating all other projects she worked on for the museum's various departments. Out of necessity, she found herself pinning her maps of Cambodia with one edge over the top of the other, and cramming statues of deities from Khmer archaeological sites wherever she could fit them on the pair of overflowing bookshelves, until one day she walked in and noticed that the office resembled a neglected curio shop. Usually, she was organized, meticulous, and every night as she left for home, she told herself she would tidy up the next day. But with each new day at the museum there was always something more important to do.

Now she would have no choice, for soon she would need to gather up all of her belongings and move them into Professor Howard's spacious office at the end of the museum's second floor. She smiled at the thought of this prospect, and it was the first time she could recall smiling since the day after Thanksgiving, when she had found her father slumped on their sofa, his gaze viscous, his speech slurred, his memory of her already gone, two excruciating weeks before his body was finally destroyed by the stroke that had annihilated his mind.

Even though the office was steamy with warmth from the overheated radiator in the corner, Irene shivered against this recurring vision. Then she banished it. Her father had been so proud of all that she had achieved, and he would have hated for her anguish over his death to mar this one thing she wanted more than any other.

It had been a year since Professor Howard turned seventy and began discussing his retirement. A year filled with anticipation and meetings as he and Irene planned her transition into his place. He had met with the board of trustees no fewer than three times, championing her, as she had hoped he would, paying her back for all that she had done since she'd started working for him. She'd brought the museum to international attention while allowing him to take the credit, to keep his pride—biding her time, satisfied to know that once she took over, her expertise and influence would gradually become public knowledge.

Last week, Professor Howard had formally announced his retirement, and yesterday he'd told Irene that the trustees wanted to meet with her today at three. There could be only one reason for this. It still amazed her, that before the age of thirty she was going to reach her life's goal of becoming the first female head curator of a major American museum. Euphoria gripped her as she heard footsteps coming down the corridor.

Professor Howard leaned into her open doorway. He was, as always, disheveled, his shirt half-untucked and his wispy, grizzled hair in need of a cut. He smiled. "They're here."

Irene grinned back, and when she reached him, she squeezed his hand.

"You've been generous to an old scholar all these years," he said, tightening his fingers around hers. "You deserve this."

Together they hurried up the back stairs, not just out of excitement but to escape the freezing cold of the hallways. In a jersey dress and matching cardigan, Irene was not attired for January. In general during the winter months, she wore heavy wool skirts and sweaters to work, but today it was essential to look the part she was about to take—slightly Continental, with a vague bohemian professionalism she had discovered that men admired in women who dealt in art.

When Irene and the professor entered the small boardroom, the trustees were already seated at the end of the U-shaped table, with their backs to a pane window that revealed the dingy winter gloom over Portage Bay. On the downward side of middle age, the three men were nearly interchangeable, timber and shipping barons who wore the excess of their prosperity in buffed fingernails and plump jowls, their well-tended paunches not quite hidden inside expensively tailored suits. Encircled by murals of Seattle's Klondike gold rush boom, in which they had figured prominently, they rose from their leather chairs and tipped their gray heads to acknowledge Irene's arrival.

"Good afternoon, Mr. Lundstrom," she said, "Mr. Quinn, Mr. Ferber."

It was only as Irene finished addressing the men that she noticed another one standing off to the side. He was tall and broad, with his hair greased down like Valentino's. Even though he was Irene's age, he was dressed in the style popular with boys on college campuses around the country, in a dark jacket that contrasted with his baggy, cream-colored Oxford trousers. What was Marshall Cabot doing here? She glanced at the professor, but he was clearly as surprised as she was by Marshall's presence. Although she had known the trustees since she was a girl, she could not read their expressions.

Carl Lundstrom cleared his throat. "Irene, I believe you know Marshall."

A hint of strain in Mr. Lundstrom's tone turned Irene's curiosity to unease. Indeed, she did know him. Marshall had studied art history at the Sorbonne, and had written his master's thesis on archival techniques. His time at Paris's Musée Indochinois du Trocadéro had been spent researching casts and plans brought back by the de Lagrée mission from Angkor Wat. It was research that Irene had cataloged for him the previous year, when he held a small exhibition of Khmer artifacts at his Cabot Gallery in Manhattan.

"Yes," she said to Mr. Lundstrom. "Marshall and I met last year at Mr. Doheny's estate. During the trip the professor and I took to consult with the Los Angeles museum when it started acquiring Chinese art. Hello, Marshall."

"Dear Irene," Marshall said, with the entitled bonhomie of a man who has made a place for himself in life, "don't forget what a great help you were to me when the war broke out." He told the trustees, "Shipping art to New York through enemy submarines was risky business."

Mr. Lundstrom nodded knowingly. "Irene has always been a great help. I'm certain the two of you will make a formidable team. Irene, we have good news for you. Marshall has done us the honor of agreeing to curate the Brooke Museum."

Irene stared at him. "But that's my job. You can't give him my job." She tried to think as a sound like the sea rushed into her ears. She turned to Professor Howard. "You told me . . ."

"I don't understand," he muttered.

Firmly, Mr. Lundstrom said, "Irene, you must be aware of our position. You have no credentials. And to be fair, as a woman—"

"As a woman?" Fighting to hold back tears, Irene forced the modest, coaxing smile she had employed to her advantage so many times over the years. "As a woman, I was able to befriend Charlotte Grant. That friendship is the reason we are the only museum in America with a complete re-creation of court life in imperial China. Florence Levy," she went on, unable to calm the tremor in her voice, "she has done an exceptional job as director of the Baltimore Museum of Art. And Belle da Costa Greene has no formal training, but ever since she took over the Pierpont Morgan Library, Mr. Morgan scarcely makes a move without consulting her first."

"Before you say anything more," Mr. Lundstrom interrupted, "you should know that this decision is made."

"Carl," said Professor Howard, emerging from his initial bewilderment to address Mr. Lundstrom, "you and I spoke about this just last week."

"We spoke about Irene's value to the museum, Thomas. There's no denying that. You're essential, dear girl," Mr. Lundstrom said to Irene. "Marshall will surely benefit from your assistance as he settles in."

Suddenly, Irene felt as heavy as the granite clouds outside. Hanging low over the charcoal water, they pressed down on the last of the day, crushing the evergreen trees on the hill that rose from the bay's opposite shore. Dear God, what had she been thinking? Only now—looking at Marshall Cabot, whose nonchalance made it clear that he had been prepared for this scene—could she see how naïve she had been, maneuvering in the background, trusting that she would be rewarded for her hard work and expertise, not ignored for her lack of prestige. But even if she too had gone to the Sorbonne, published monographs, and owned a gallery, Marshall Cabot would still have one advantage, and with this understanding, her distress became desperation.

Around her, the room began to quiver, and the ship laden with Yukon gold on the wall behind Marshall sputtered on the outskirts of her blackening vision. She pressed one hand down on the end of the table as the floor rolled beneath her. "I was grateful to you during the war," she said urgently to Professor Howard, as if he were the one who could fix all of this. "I really was, for giving me a start. For giving me the chance to work here. I knew why you did it, I never once deluded myself, I knew it was because the men were gone, but I didn't care. I was happy doing anything just to be here. Filing, typing letters. But soon I was doing more than that. Tell them I did much more than that."

Professor Howard's face was so pinched that he seemed to be in physical pain. "I did, Irene. They know. They've always known."

"They can't have known. If they did, they wouldn't have . . ." Appealing to the trustees, she said, "I spent every spare second of my time sorting things out. You must remember what it was like before I came here. Artifacts were just piled in the corners of galleries. I went through every piece of paperwork, I tracked down provenances and past sales, I put it all in order. I've given my life to the Brooke Museum, to its reputation."

Irene's throat burned, and it took all of her strength to resist the insistent push of tears. Was that what they were waiting for, as they watched her so impassively, for her to break down and prove their point, that a woman was too emotional for a job of such importance? "You told me what a fine curator I'd make. You let me think . . ." She could hardly believe it, that after all she had accomplished, these men had so little regard for her. Who did they think they were, sitting there pretending they didn't damn well know the Brooke Museum had been wallowing in obscurity until she came along? Ashamed and angry at being pushed into betraying the professor in such a way, she declared, "I'm the only reason this museum has a reputation. I put it on the map."

"Irene, that is why I've so looked forward to working with you." Marshall spoke in a tone of conciliation. "Let me take you to dinner tonight at the Olympic. We can discuss all of this reasonably over a bottle of wine. Colleague to colleague."

"That's a fine idea," Mr. Lundstrom said, sounding relieved.

The other two men nodded, and Irene was horrified to realize that they had assumed she would accept this situation.

Her words came out in a rush. "I couldn't agree with you more, Marshall." And although she knew she should stop talking, she recklessly went on. "We have so much to discuss. For example, I'm sure you still wonder how forty Duanfang ritual vessels could have been put on a ship in China and then disappear without a trace by the time that ship reached America. I believe they were intended for your gallery, isn't that right?"

Marshall looked confused.

"You see," Irene continued, "along with his interest in Chinese servant boys, Mr. Quinn here has a great interest in Chinese art."

Mr. Quinn's ruddy face went white.

"Irene," the professor cautioned, "don't do this."

But Irene's eyes narrowed, and she felt herself hardening, the callus of comprehension forming as she understood so clearly in hindsight not only how naïve she had been but also how stupid. "That, in fact, is what I was doing in Los Angeles when we met. I had an appointment with C. T. Loo. You didn't even know he was in California that week, did you? No one knew. No one but me. I'd arranged to buy your Duanfang bronzes for Mr. Quinn's private collection." Sure that she would lose her courage or be cut off at any moment, she finished quickly. "Each of the trustees has a fine private collection, but keep in mind that you must be discreet about this. As well as expertise, this job will require your great discretion."

Though she sounded confident, Irene could feel her defenses dissolving, and she knew she had to get out of the room as fast as possible. "Excuse me," she said.

As she fled, she could hear the professor trying to find his footing. The words *deceptive* and *disgraceful* followed her along the shadowy corridor, where the air was so chilled that the white cloud of her unsteady breathing made it seem as if the overcast day had stolen indoors. Her chest tightened as she walked down the stairs, passing the Japanese, Siamese, and Burmese halls, until she reached the Khmer wing and stood shaking beneath the arch leading to the Hall of the Apsaras.

As Irene stared into the gallery, the brittle frame of her defiance collapsed, and she wept. She had wanted to be the one in charge of this museum for so long, but this was about more than just her job. The Brooke Museum was her home. She had grown up in this small, narrow room. Catching her breath and wiping her eyes with her sleeve, she entered it now and approached the first of the ten sandstone pedestals that lined the walls. Each held a single bronze *apsara*, and she picked up the celestial goddess in front of her, the way she had when she was a girl, cradling it in her arms. Tenderly, she traced the flowered crown that rose high above the statue's distant, enigmatic expression.

Such magical days, those days that went as far back as Irene's memory would take her, when her mother had bundled up food as if they were going on a great expedition and brought her into this hall for picnic dinners with her father. After he began his rounds, her mother would take out her sketchbooks and let Irene choose a statue from one of the pedestals. Side by side they would draw, the honeycomb pattern of a decorative collar, the teardrop shape of an eye, the willowy, outstretched arms of an *apsara* captured mid-dance for the pleasure of a king.

Then her mother died, and each night her father spread out a bed of quilts beneath the *apsaras'* passive gaze. It was more than a decade since Irene had slept on the museum's floor, but she could still see the statues above her, swaying in the low caramel light that glazed the air from an oil lamp in the corner. She remembered the longing she had felt as she waited during those days and weeks and months after the funeral for her mother to return. How many times had she closed her eyes, desperate to hear *mon petit chou,* "my little cabbage," whispered into her ear as she fell asleep?

The only thing from those days that Irene had forgotten was the futility of her longing, the inevitable realization that she would never hear those words again. But she recognized the same hopeless feeling as it washed over her now, as she stood amid the dancing goddesses in a world she had thought would one day belong to her.

Irene walked slowly away from the museum, her impractical, thin-soled shoes unable to find traction on the frozen slopes of the campus paths. Her face tingled in the icy air, and she pulled the lapels of her father's peacoat over her mouth. Classes were done for the day, and winter's somber dark encased the early evening hour. With her eyes bloodshot from crying so hard, she did not want to run into anyone she knew, and she was thankful for the piercing cold, which had pushed everyone indoors, where wood fires burned, releasing a smoldering promise of comfort into the night.

As she passed the buildings on the far north side of the campus, a row of white houses—half a dozen tiny two-bedroom cottages provided for the university's watchmen and their families—came into view. Irene's house was in the middle, and she had almost gotten used to it being the only one in the row without a porch light on or signs of life stirring from its chimney. Once performed by her father to welcome her home from work before he left for the museum, these small rituals, like so many others she had taken for granted, had perished with him. But tonight, from the distance, she saw a glow in the front window and, as she got closer, a haze of smoke above the roof.

A membrane of frost slicked the metal doorknob, and she had to wrap her hand in her sleeve to turn the handle. Opening the door, she was not surprised to see Henry Simms, her father's oldest and closest friend, standing at the fireplace. He didn't say anything as she came in and took off her coat. Irene saw that his hair had been trimmed and smoothed into place, and she guessed that he had spent the afternoon with his barber at the Hotel Washington. He must have come to celebrate what they had both assumed would be good news, and she felt queasy at the thought of what she had to tell him, especially after he had gone to such effort. How deceptively healthy he had made himself appear, even though, at sixty-eight, he had been warring with cancer for almost a year.

She saw a decanter of wine on the coffee table. Beside it were two glasses, and the sight of them arranged so neatly emphasized the room's disarray, a reminder of the full extent of her loss.

Once lined with books, the shelves were bare, and there were dark patches of wallpaper where her mother's watercolors had hung. Everything Irene owned—plates, glasses, clothing, *National Geographic* magazines, phonograph records, and her father's brass sextant—was piled on the floor. Empty crates lay about; they had been sent over by the university, which had also out of sympathy allowed Irene to stay through the holidays, even though the museum's new night watchman had been hired within a week of her father's death.

Irene had been born in Manila, but by her first birthday her parents had moved into this house. It was cramped and smelled of damp northwest forests all year round, but as with the museum, she had considered it hers. She knew every groan in its floorboards, every crack in its porcelain sinks. Now, she had to leave it. But whenever she tried to pack, she found herself standing helpless in the middle of the room, holding one of her father's cowboy novels or the toaster that made two slices at a time, given to him by friends one Christmas because he liked gadgets and they were always able to find something new from the Sears catalog to amuse him.

Taking in her surroundings, Irene's eyes became damp once again. She told Mr. Simms, "I didn't get the job."

"I know." His expression was solemn. "Lundstrom told me this morning."

"Why didn't you warn me?"

"You needed to hear it unarmed."

"Why?"

"To know how you truly feel about it."

Irene sat down on the sofa, in the wavering light of the fireplace. This made no sense. Then again, nothing about today made sense. "What did you say when he told you? Did you tell him that you wouldn't let him do this?"

"Now that I'm dying, my influence with the museum is diminishing."

"Don't say things like that."

Physically, Mr. Simms was not an imposing man, but he was nonetheless one to whom others felt compelled to give their attention. When he spoke, there was a quiet confidence in his voice that conveyed his power. Despite his sickness, that quality remained, and he sounded easily capable of following through on any threat as he said, "My dear, if you want me to make your curatorship a new condition of the Brooke's endowment, I will. I'll call Lundstrom right now and tell him I'll withdraw my money tomorrow, and my collections too, if he doesn't give you the job."

Scratching her finger back and forth across a worn patch on the sofa's tufted velvet arm, Irene thought this over. "Why didn't you make that threat this morning?"

Rather than answer this question, Mr. Simms half-filled the two wineglasses and handed one to her. "Drink this."

She took a sip.

"More," he instructed. "You need it."

She did as she was told, and as the warmth flowed into her limbs, she felt something coming loose deep inside her. *"A great help!"* she declared. "That's what Mr. Lundstrom called me. As if I've been nothing more than an able assistant all these years." The insult was despicable, and she turned away, staring beyond the crystals of frozen white mist that varnished the window.

"Do you intend to stay on?" Mr. Simms asked.

Her outburst in the boardroom flashed back to her, and she could see the flame of her words engulfing the bridge she had painstakingly built over the past ten years. The trustees' shock would surely turn to wrath, if it hadn't already. "I can't." As she said this, she glimpsed her reflection, the swelling around her eyes blurred against the dark pane. Between her father's death and the loss of her house and job, she felt as if she were vanishing. "What am I going to do now?" she asked.

"Just as we planned when you learned that you were losing the house. You will come and live with me." Mr. Simms took a drink of his wine before adding, "Now that I have your undivided attention, we can finish cataloging my collection. This will give us the opportunity to complete it before I'm gone."

Henry Simms was a formidable collector. Irene had assisted with his purchase of the Villeroy Collection when it came up for sale in Paris, and she'd overseen his acquisition of a portion of first-century Roman silver that was recovered from the ashes of Vesuvius. She had full access to his collections, those he loaned out to museums or displayed at private events, and the ones he kept shuttered away from curators, historians, and the rest of his fellow connoisseurs. She alone knew that he had Titian's *Venus with a Mirror*, which had disappeared in the art world skirmish that followed the murder of Russia's Tsar Nicholas. It was logical that Irene would be the one to prepare his final reckoning, but she was aware that by making this suggestion now, when she needed it most, Mr. Simms was also doing what he did best—saving her.

The first time he rescued Irene, she was not even born. Her father had been a sailor and curio trader in the Orient when her mother, eight months pregnant, was kidnapped in Manila and held for ransom. Irene remembered how Mr. Simms and her father had talked about it, nine years later, during the weeks after her mother's death. Sitting together nightly at the museum, playing chess on a Ming dynasty *xiangqi* set in the Chinese hall, the old friends would relive the kidnapping—*that damn book . . . never seen so much blood*—as if Irene weren't there. Always, the conversation began with the mysterious book, the reason her mother had been kidnapped, and ended with the two men Mr. Simms had killed and the gunshot wound that had nearly taken Irene's mother's life.

Then after her mother died, Mr. Simms stepped in again, distracting Irene from her pain by cultivating her fledgling interest in the Khmer. Alongside plates of gingersnaps made by his cook, he left maps out for her in his kitchen, clever drawings that led her on hunts through the three levels of his Italian Renaissance manor on the top of Queen Anne Hill. With one of these maps clutched tightly in hand, she would follow its trails through greenhouses cared for by a man poached from Kew Gardens or secret passageways enveloped in Pannemaker tapestries, to find the bronze incense holder or glazed stone lime pot that Mr. Simms had hidden for her on any given day—so she could start a collection of Khmer relics of her very own.

Years later, when the war ended and soldiers returned from Europe to take back their old jobs as elevator operators and traffic policemen, Mr. Simms recommended that Professor Howard keep Irene on at the museum. But by that point, the professor had discovered her value. He was pleased by the way she tended the exhibition halls as if each were its own temple. He took pride as the museum's reputation spread around the globe. Curators, gallery owners, and archaeologists started contacting him, asking for information and advice, and Irene let him be the one to give it—certain of her future, certain of her strategy, and certain that the days of needing Mr. Simms's help were long in the past.

In her anxiety, Irene had picked a hole through the fabric of the sofa, and the stuffing popped out, wiry and rough. She told Mr. Simms, "It's not enough."

"What do you mean?" he asked.

"Managing your collection." Beneath her exhaustion, a new train of thought was taking over. "It's not enough to give me the upper hand."

"Are you talking about revenge?"

"I simply want what I have earned. I enjoy tending your collection, you know that, but the Brooke's collection—I've done everything I could to make the museum a showcase for Khmer art. That's the one thing I really love. I actually thought that once I took over, I could turn the Brooke into the foremost museum dedicated to the Khmer. Everything I've worked for is there. I can't imagine my life without it, and I have no idea how to prove to them how wrong they are about me."

Crouching, Mr. Simms picked up her father's electric percolator from among a pile of kitchenware. He examined the tarnished metal, as if in the dull surface he saw back to all of the conversations it had fueled. When he spoke, he had a strange smile on his face. "If there was ever a time to believe in providence, this is it."

Smoothing the sofa's torn fabric, Irene asked, "What do you mean?"

"The box your father left me. Irene, did you look inside it before you gave it to me?"

A few weeks earlier, when she emptied her father's room, Irene had found a pine box the size of a small travel trunk, bound in twine that was tied with her father's distinctive hitch knots. The label pasted on top bore Mr. Simms's name. "No, of course not."

Mr. Simms wrapped the frayed electrical cord around the percolator and placed the appliance with his hat and overcoat on the sideboard, as if he intended to keep it. Shuffling in the pocket of his coat, he removed a small book. He held it out to Irene. "This was in the box. Have you seen it before?"

The slim, calfskin-bound volume was soft from handling. She turned it over, examining the front and back covers before opening it to a faded inscription.

Property of:
Reverend James T. Garland
Boston, Massachusetts
Beginning on the day of our Lord 1 April 1825
Finishing on the day of our Lord 15 August 1825

"No," she said. "What is it?" When Mr. Simms didn't reply, she thumbed through the onionskin pages to one marked with a grosgrain ribbon. Its margins were lined with sketches of stone spires sprouting through feathered palms. The handwriting was firm and masculine.

24 June 1825

I have spent the past 27 days traveling north and east away from the awesome relic of a city called Ang Cor. The weather has been a source of misery. There are hours when it feels as if we are floundering through a seabed. Svai does not seem to notice. He perseveres as if he is a slave and not a paid guide. Yesterday we reached a malarial trading village on a tributary of the Me Cong River. Svai calls it Stun Tren. I calculate that we are within six days of the Lao border.

"But the first recorded sighting of Angkor Wat occurred in the eighteen sixties," Irene said. "If this man was there in 1825, why—"

"Keep reading."

This morning Svai woke me before daybreak and said he wanted to share a secret. We walked through the jungle for at least a mile before we came upon his goal. My first sight was of crumbled stone, akin to the debris found in the foliage around Ang Cor. I observed a sloping stone wall with a white fromager tree growing through it. Svai patted a fragment of wall and announced, "Musée." He led me through a precariously stabilized archway into an untidy courtyard surrounding a collapsing stone temple. When we walked into its center, it was dark. Svai produced a lantern. The reek of bat caused my eyes to water. I was reluctant to go farther, but Svai insisted.

The lantern's flame rebounded inside the sanctuary, and I discerned a metallic glow. Svai plunged into the temple and returned with a flat metal scroll no larger than a sheet of writing paper, scored with the elaborate hybrid cuneiform of Sanskrit and Chinese characters I had seen on stone steles at Ang Cor. Svai said what I can only crudely translate as "the king's temple" and then proudly declared that this temple contained the history of his savage people on ten copper scrolls.

Irene looked up, astounded. "Is this what I think it is? This man saw the history? It exists?"

"It seems so."

"What if it's still there? But it would have to be there. If someone had taken it, we'd know. If anyone would know, we would. Oh, my God, we have a clue. The first real clue to finding out what happened to the Khmer civilization!" Irene was disoriented by the severe pounding of her pulse. Not just in her chest and wrists, it beat its wings into the corners of the room like a trapped bird. "You've had that box for two weeks. Why haven't you shown the book to me until now?"

Mr. Simms refilled their glasses. Together they drank while she stared at him in wonder, and he—a man who always knew what to say—seemed to be at a loss for words.

"And why did my father leave it to *you*?" she persisted. "He knew how much something like this would mean to me."

But Mr. Simms did not answer, and Irene's attention was drawn back to the diary. "All this time I've let the Khmer come to me," she said. "Whenever I thought about going to Cambodia, it was as a curator. I would visit Angkor Wat and then spend time doing research at the museum in Phnom Penh. I've been waiting for so long for their history to be found, but I never dreamed it might be found by me. Unearthing the Khmer's history could buy me a place, a position that could never be ignored." Standing up, she declared, "I want to go. To Cambodia."

Still, Mr. Simms was silent, but Irene saw the rapture that shone in his clear blue eyes, the same look that crossed his face whenever he was preparing to make one of his illicit acquisitions.

"I want to be the one to find it," she told him, "and you think I can do it, don't you? That's why you didn't force Lundstrom to give me the job. You knew if I got the curatorship, I might not go. You want me to search for this history."

"I have thought of nothing else since I opened that box," he finally responded. "The scrolls are going to be the summit of my collection. My swan song. And you, my dearest Irene, will be the one to bring them to me." In the firelight, Mr. Simms's age and illness slipped away, and he was a young man again, vigorous, ready to conquer the world. "If you are lucky, you experience one great adventure in your life."

"Have you had yours?" she asked.

"I have been very fortunate. I have had several incredible adventures," he assured her, his eyes focused on the diary. "May I give you some advice?"

Irene nodded, eagerly.

"The one thing to remember about an adventure is that if it turns out the way you expect it to, it has not been an adventure at all."

Chapter 3

In Yellow Babylon

While waiting for Simone Merlin to return from France, Irene had fallen in love with Shanghai. Occupied by the French, British, Americans, and Japanese, each with their own self-governed district, it contained the entire world. Walking among its rickshaws, trams, and Buick touring cars, its Tudor manors and Spanish-style villas, she might come across a haggard Russian prostitute fighting with a pair of Chinese singsong girls over an English sailor. And a few steps farther on, she could encounter an old Cantonese man dragging a wheelbarrow full of pink baby bonnets, or Japanese courtesans dancing to a German-Jewish band in front of a nightclub in broad daylight.

Although Shanghai was a heady concoction of

the unfamiliar, Irene was attracted to more than its vitalizing jumble. She was also captivated by the challenge it presented. As she explored, she found herself cataloging all that she saw, the way she had done with the artifacts at the Brooke Museum and in Mr. Simms's collections. Files opened in her mind, and within them grew lists. From Sikh policemen with their dark hair bound in crisp turbans to Chinese ladies wearing cut-work leather pumps from Italy, the inhabitants of the city could fill a volume. And the shops, selling theater costumes and Hershey's cocoa and lotus root. What a pleasure it was to group them into categories by what they sold: canaries chrysanthemums larks mice chopsticks dice incense mangoes inkpots flies. Every day her lists grew as she moved through the wide boulevards of the French Concession, fertile with peonies and magnolia trees, or the Chinese quarter, with its narrow lanes of dumpling stalls, fortune-tellers, and toddlers peeing in gutters through the slits in their pants.

Shanghai was a worthy test for Irene's skills. It felt as if the city were a scrambled, unbounded collection that she had been commissioned to sort, put there to help heal her injured belief in her talent. For ten years she had been doing more than just classifying objects known. She had been pursuing and locating and systemizing objects lost or stolen and hidden away. She had taught herself to analyze rumors as if they were scientific evidence. She had learned how to track the sales of art and the travels of men, and to use calculations to fill in the blanks. She worked with the laws of probability. She put pieces together, every way possible, over and over until they fit. She used her instinct. She had exceptional instinct. Mr. Simms admired this about her.

More than any expert Irene had met, Mr. Simms had mastered the intricacies of dealing in art. He understood an object's worth, not solely its dollar value but how that value could be manipulated into emotional currency, and he shared this knowledge with her. It was under his tutelage that Irene learned how to appraise an owner as well as an artifact, and to use her appraisals to round up information and sort through it until she found an answer, most often the location of an object that had gone missing. It was what she did best—figuring out—and it was what she was doing now in Shanghai, the day after Anne's party. If she could collect enough information, she would be able to deduce what Simone wanted, what she needed, and how to convince her to come to Cambodia.

Because Irene always paid attention, subtly eavesdropping wherever she was, she already knew which bars in Shanghai were good for what: French wine, the best jazz, White Russian bodyguards, Siamese virgins. To build a foundation on which to construct theories, local gossip was essential, and for Shanghai's gossip, the Yellow Babylon was the top choice. As she made her way to this nightclub, dusk faded, leaving the streets burnished, lit by lanterns since the electricity had been cut because of the strikes.

It was the cocktail hour. The room felt sullen with heat, Shalimar, and the masculine reek of cigars. Candles hung like pendants in glass jars from the ceiling, above a dozen tables bunched up at the rim of an empty stage. Irene surveyed the crowd. She dismissed those who regarded her with disinterest. She sought the one—there was always one—who eyed her, a newcomer, greedily. The house rumormonger. A watering hole staple.

She approached the table in the back corner, occupied by an older woman who had fair European skin and tilting Asiatic eyes. She wore loops of pearls, and her hair was powdered, as if she had traveled to Shanghai from the eighteenth century. A blue macaw was perched on the back of her chair.

"May I join you?" Irene asked.

The woman smiled, as if she had been waiting all day for a stranger to come along. "Please, my dear, have a seat."

"I'm Irene Blum."

"Countess Eugénie. A pleasure to meet you. What would you like to drink?"

"Scotch."

"Excellent." This too was said as if an expectation had been met. Signaling to a waiter, she asked, "What brings you to the Yellow Babylon, Irene?"

"The revolution," Irene said. "Communism in China." There was nothing to be gained in tiptoeing around. As she had long ago discovered, the more candid she was, the more callow and less suspect she seemed. "I'm wondering why a foreigner would want to be involved in it. Why would he care?"

The countess laughed. "Good Lord, darling, I have no idea."

"Is it a romantic notion?"

"Romantic? Chinamen are murdered in the streets in the name of the cause. The cause! What a ridiculous term. Factories are burned to the ground to make an ideological point. If you ask me, it's a nuisance more than anything else."

The waiter brought a decanter. His pour was generous, but Irene did not pick up her glass. She asked, "Does this revolution need Simone Merlin?"

The countess clapped. "Oh dear, you're not a very good spy."

Irene let this remark stand, unchallenged.

The countess winked, and Irene knew the story would travel around Shanghai, about the American spy asking after the wife of Roger Merlin. But as Irene also knew, tales spread by women like this countess were always taken with a grain of salt. While this meant that few would believe the countess, it also meant that Irene must be judicious in acting on anything she confided. "How delightful. I assumed this was going to be another dull night of opium and jazz. Do you smoke? Would you like a pipe?"

"Another time," said Irene, not letting on that she had never smoked opium before. She didn't want to seem *that* callow. "Do you know Simone?"

"Everyone in Shanghai knows of her."

"What do you think she gains from this revolution?"

The countess was nearly giddy with this distraction from her usual evening out. "To the Chinese, Simone is a queen. It must feel quite satisfying to be treated like royalty."

"What else?"

The countess rolled her eyes. "I suppose she could have some innate sense of justice."

"Altruism?"

"The average Chinaman does live a miserable life in this city," the countess said, as if this were a secret. "I treat mine well, but I'm an exception."

"Do you think Simone's beliefs could have anything to do with loyalty to her husband?"

"Daggers to that detestable man!" The countess leaned over the table conspiratorially. "Last year she tried to leave him. She headed overland, poor ninny. He caught up with her in Wuchow and nearly beat her to death. Officially, she was kidnapped and attacked by Municipal Government thugs. It was terrific fuel for the cause. The riot lasted almost two days. Lily, over there at that table with the colonel, she's a nurse. She's the one who treated Simone. Lily," she called out. "Lily, dear, come over here and meet my new friend, Irene."

Lily was at least fifty, and her efforts with makeup could not hide her jaundiced skin—a distinguishing feature, Irene had learned, among alcoholics in the city. Her tight dress did not suit her barrel of a body. Her ankles were beefy, and she stumped toward them on stilt-heeled shoes, carrying a glass of champagne in one hand and a cigarillo fitted into an amber holder in the other. "Well, well," Lily drawled dramatically. "What has the cat dragged in?" From her pursed expression, it was evident that all other women were competition.

"Oh, Lily, behave. Irene has come to perk up the evening. She's a spy."

"Who for?"

"The enemy, of course." Irene answered and gave her best light-hearted grin.

"Who cares?" said the countess. "Sit down and tell her about Simone Merlin."

Lily slowly raised an eyebrow. She eased into the chair beside Irene and reached her arms across the table for the macaw. The macaw snapped at the cigarillo, but Lily pulled back, giving the bird a sip of champagne instead. "Don't be naughty, President Coolidge. I haven't forgotten what you did to my Persian carpet. So, what would you like to know, Irene the spy?"

"Did Simone's husband nearly beat her to death?"

"She told me he did. Having been in such a situation myself, I believe her. Women lie about many things, but that is rarely one of them. It's too humiliating to make up. Besides, Roger Merlin is a cur."

"Why do you say that?"

"He doesn't care about the Chinese people."

The countess was amused. "You don't care about the Chinese people, Lily."

"True," Lily said, "but I don't go around pretending to help them. If I feel like kicking one, I do it. And I never feel bad about it afterward."

"You think he's a phony?" Irene asked.

"I think his ego puts Napoleon's to shame."

"Why would he care if Simone left him?"

Lily studied Irene as if she were stupid. She leaned toward her, and the stench of spoiled gardenia perfume leaked from her pores. "He is a man, darling."

"Still, she's not his prisoner," Irene said, annoyed.

"I think after she lost the baby, she gave up any hope of getting away from him."

"There was a baby?" the countess asked. "Darling, you never told me about a baby."

"Really? I thought I had."

"You know you didn't tell me."

"My dear countess, I wouldn't keep something like that from you."

"Just as I would never keep from you that your colonel has a predilection for lithe young factory workers."

"What happened?" Irene asked, turning the conversation back before it could detour.

Glancing unhappily at the colonel, Lily said, "Simone was pregnant when she tried to leave Roger."

The countess gasped.

Stunned, Irene asked, "He beat her while she was pregnant?"

"I sat with her in the hospital for six days," Lily said. "He hit her to rid her of that baby girl. You can be sure of it by the way he did it."

"How awful." Irene's thoughts grew dark with this gruesome vision.

Sickened by the helplessness and pain Simone must have felt, she had to force herself to continue. "Do you know where she was going?"

"I'm not enjoying this conversation anymore," Lily said. "It's too depressing for a Sunday, even in Shanghai." She flicked her cigarillo onto the floor.

The countess sighed. "I must admit, I have never cared for Simone. But a baby changes things. Poor, dear girl."

Lily stood and said to Irene, "Cambodia, my fair-haired American spy. That is where Simone was going when he caught up with her. But I have a feeling this comes as no surprise to you."

"I don't care about anything else," Simone declared. "You can talk to whomever you want about whatever you want, except my baby."

Irene looked up to see Simone standing in the doorway of Anne's office. It was late Monday morning. After her evening with the countess and Lily, she had not slept well, and she was now attempting to clear her head by helping Anne grade a collection of Yangshao pottery.

"This is my city," Simone continued. "How dare you come into it as if it's yours for the asking. As if my life is yours for the taking. If you wanted to know more about me, why didn't you walk down the hall and ask me? My office is always open."

Irene was caught off guard by how rapidly gossip traveled through Shanghai, so much faster than she had expected. The electricity was dead, the air was sopping, and she spoke as she rarely did, without thinking. "How did you end up at the mercy of a man like that? How could you let such a thing happen?"

"Let such a thing happen?" Simone's anger disintegrated into bewilderment.

Seated in the open window, Anne reproached, "Irene, that's offensive."

"You're right, I'm sorry." Irene realized that she was allowing her feelings about what the museum trustees had done to her overlap with what Roger had done to Simone. She smoothed the documents on the desk in front of her, rubbing her palm across the top sheet, smearing the ink with her sweat. "But, Simone, will he really chase you down if he knows someone is watching? If you're with me?"

Simone stepped into the room, her face shielded by the shadow of her wide-brimmed black hat. Her green Chinese-style blouse was paired with black stovepipe trousers that might have come from a man's suit, making her look as if she had just walked off a vaudeville stage. "It won't matter who is there."

Behind Anne, sunlight reflected into the alley's chasm and glanced off scraps of faded laundry drying on a railing opposite. "Darling, if Simone doesn't want to go, let her be."

"Let her be?" Irene asked with disbelief. "How can you of all people say that? You left *your* husband because you no longer wanted to be a housewife. This is so much worse!"

"My reasons were far more complicated," Anne rebuked. "You know that. You have always known that. In any case, Thomas was not a threat to my life."

"That's all the more reason for you to leave him," Irene said to Simone. "You shouldn't have to live with such fear. I can help you. This could be your opportunity to escape him."

"Let's change the subject," Anne said. "This is far too complex a problem to discuss in this kind of heat. Summertime in Shanghai makes things seem worse than they actually are."

Simone frowned as she crossed the room to the settee. "You blame everything on the heat."

"People are far less volatile in cooler climates."

"Hardly, Anne," Irene said. "The Wobblies are rioting in Seattle."

Simone took off her hat and rested her head on the arm of the settee. She moved deliberately, tipping her head to one side to reveal her right earlobe, split into a V. A bruise bloated her jaw and cheek. "Irene, I think you should know, I did tell my husband about your offer. A frying pan makes quite the weapon. He is resourceful, *n'est-il pas?*"

"Oh, darling." Anne was on her feet, making her way to Simone.

"I told him I have an opportunity to go in search of a lost temple.

Then I made the mistake of telling him how much I want this." Her fingers trembled over the scab on her ear. Perspiration beaded on her face. "I never knew I could be this lonely."

"Hush." Anne folded Simone into her arms and stroked her hair. "It will rain soon, I promise."

As Irene watched them, it occurred to her that loneliness is not about what happens when you are alone but about what happens when you are with others. It is about how willing you are to open your heart and allow another to get close to you. At least Simone was letting Anne hold her and console her. Irene could not remember the last time someone had held her that way. Not even her father or Mr. Simms.

Anne said, "Irene, please fetch the thermos on the shelf behind my desk."

Simone smiled. "To sleep, perchance to dream."

Irene handed the thermos to Anne, who removed the lid and filled it with a soupy, gray liquid. Simone drank, and then Anne filled the lid again and offered it to Irene, saying, "I will lay out some cushions for you."

Irene took the cup. Its contents smelled vile. "What is it?"

"I make it myself." Anne retrieved a pair of pillows and a blanket from the cupboard. "I buy the poppies from the one-eyed mandarin behind Jardine's."

As Anne spread out a knitted afghan, Irene's mind was drawn back to her childhood, to her bed of quilts on the Brooke Museum's floor.

"It does wonders," Anne said. "Every ache, every pain, every melancholy thought inside you, gone, faded away. Better than Bayer. Much nicer than a psychoanalyst. For some reason I always feel worse when I leave a session with mine."

A candle had burned down in a jade ashtray on the desk, and the still blades of the fan cast an indolent shadow on a patch of wall near the ceiling. As attractive as it was, the idea of escaping into such an easy sleep, Irene was more tempted by the thought of Simone's office down the hall. She hoped Simone had left the door open, since she was not adept at picking locks. Handing the lid back to Anne, she said, "No, thank you."

Retreating from the tragedy that was her life, Simone curled onto her side. She was so different from the person Irene had thought she would find, and part of her wanted to send a telegram to Mr. Simms and inform him that he had made a bad decision in choosing Simone to help her. But to fail at what she had come to Shanghai to do would be too painful in the wake of her humiliation in Seattle. Besides, it would take time to find another person who knew Cambodia and the Khmer as well as Simone did. Mr. Simms had trusted Irene to fulfill his dying wish. Time was one thing she did not have, especially since the next available passage from Shanghai to Indochina was sailing in three days.

With the labor strikes, there was no telling how soon another ship would leave the city, and so Irene was going to keep trying to find a solution, starting with searching Simone's office. Busying herself with the task she had begun, she waited for Anne to gulp the foul-smelling tea and stretch out on the blanket, humming a Chinese love song until eventually, along with Simone, she fell asleep.

Just two doors down the hall, Irene felt as if she had traveled halfway around the globe only to end up back in her own office at the Brooke Museum. Simone's cramped office was a shrine to Cambodia, its walls covered from floor to ceiling with yellow survey maps, its shelves an exhibition of statuettes—dozens of *apsaras,* made of bronze, of brass, of silver, of stone.

One was crafted from pounded tin, the kind of cheap trinket sold at souvenir stands. Another was carved from pink sandstone, glossy with handling and age—eight centuries old, Irene estimated from glancing at it. In the russet shadows beyond the reach of the kerosene lamp, a shelf held Étienne Aymonier's archaeological inventory, the first systematic survey of the temples and one of the primary guides Irene had used in teaching herself the skill of classification. She pulled out the atlas from Auguste Pavie's Indochina mission and opened it to the map she had studied back in Seattle when she first learned of the lost temple; it covered the ambiguous border area between Cambodia, Vietnam, and Laos.

As Irene sat down at Simone's desk, where Sappho Marchal's *Khmer*

Costumes and Ornaments was open to the inscription "To my dearest friend. Return home soon, Sappho," a feeling of optimism rose in her. This room was proof of how meaningful Cambodia was to Simone.

Irene trailed her finger through a thick deposit of incense that lay like an anthill within a brass holder. Eager to know more about this woman whose passion for the Khmer seemed to equal hers, she tugged open the top desk drawer. She took out a bottle of Luminal that contained six tablets, and from beneath the bottle three sheets of stationery. She read, "Dear Louis, you are going to" and "Louis, this is" and "Louis, the time has." She did not know who this might be.

Reaching in deeper, she removed a handful of clippings from Shanghai's Municipal Government and Communist newspapers. She leafed through the articles, all of them about Roger. Strikes he had organized and riots he had incited. His attendance at the First National Congress with Sun Yat-sen the previous year, his work with Bolshevik military instructors, and his arrest after a French attaché was killed by a pipe bomb. He was released for lack of evidence, but the editorial tone of the *North-China Daily News* implied his guilt.

In dealing with Roger Merlin, Irene understood how cautious she must be, but still, he was just a man, and men were open to negotiation. They preferred it over ultimatums, as long as they thought they had won. It was easy enough to make a man think that he had won, and from what she had gleaned so far, this was all Roger wanted.

As she was putting the clippings back into the drawer, a headline caught her eye: FIRE DESTROYS SIMMS & CO. FLOUR MILL IN POOTUNG. Startled by the sudden presence of Mr. Simms's name, she skimmed back through the papers, and redirecting her attention, she saw that according to the articles, Henry Simms owned a great many factories in Shanghai. He was mentioned more than any other industrialist, and always in relation to his business interests being under siege by the Kuomintang.

Irene had known that Shanghai had long been Mr. Simms's second home. It had been his base before and after his time in Manila, where he met her parents, and she remembered him traveling to the city when she was a girl. She still had the picture postcards he'd sent of rickshaw coolies, and the petite pink robe he'd brought back for her from one of his trips. She also knew that he had investments all across the Orient, in shipping, importing, and exporting, and in tea and rubber plantations throughout Malaya and Vietnam, but they had never talked about any of this. The details of his financial empire had never extended into the sovereign state of art they shared—not until this moment. Irene felt chagrin at not having bothered to speculate about Mr. Simms's dealings in Shanghai, and what these dealings could mean: that he and Roger Merlin were enemies.

Henry Simms had sent her to hire the wife of his enemy.

Mr. Simms's story was as familiar to Irene as her own father's. He had not gone from being a wheat farmer's son in eastern Washington State to being one of the wealthiest men in the world simply by figuring out a few sharp business moves. He was a strategist, a mastermind. He did nothing that was not thoroughly planned, and as she clutched the brittle newspaper clippings, the possibility of something bigger than she had anticipated swelled, unformed, into the room.

Irene thrived on secrets and mysteries. She thrived on finding answers, and Mr. Simms knew this about her. It was not improbable that he had planned on her learning about his stake in Shanghai. He could even have known what he was getting her into with Simone, although if he did, Irene could not comprehend why he would have her seek out Roger Merlin's unstable wife. But she was intrigued, as she felt sure she was meant to be.

Back in Anne's office, Simone was still asleep, snoring softly. Near her on the floor, Anne gazed drowsily at the ceiling. "Tell me honestly why you don't want me to do this," Irene said, keeping her voice low as she stood in the doorway.

"It's shameless to ask me questions when I'm in this state," Anne protested.

"You won't answer me if you're sober." The sun had passed the meridian, and the office was now layered in shade from the buildings across the alley. Still, the heat was ripe and full. Only one candle remained lit, its low flame sputtering in the pooling wax. "You've never opposed me before."

Anne tipped her head to look up at Irene. "You're going to steal the scrolls."

Irene dropped her voice even further. "I've never said that."

"Henry is financing your expedition. You didn't have to."

"Did you tell Simone about Mr. Simms?"

"If Roger finds out that Henry is involved . . . Even if she does make it to Cambodia with you . . . The scrolls, she'll be devastated when you take them to America."

"What about me? You know how much I need this."

Anne's movements were lethargic as she propped herself up against the base of the settee. "You're crossing a line." Her attempt at a firm tone was undermined by the effects of the poppy tea.

"I didn't know that you believed there was a line. There didn't seem to be one when you wanted me to help you find the empress dowager's ring."

Anne lifted her wrinkled hand into a crease of dusky light, illuminating the ring whose braid of gold framed a cinnabar carving of the character for Puyi, the name of the empress's chosen successor, her great-nephew, the last emperor of China. The ring had disappeared upon the empress's death, most likely spirited away by one of her handmaids. Irene recalled with pride how she had tracked it to a Serbian collector, Murat Stanić. Leveraging her request with knowledge about the location of Caesar's Ruby, a pendant that had gone missing from the Romanov crown jewels, she'd convinced Stanić to deliver the ring to her rather than to Puyi, who was offering a sizable reward for it after his expulsion from the Forbidden City. "Irene, we're not talking about a piece of jewelry," Anne said. "This isn't another statue or vase. This is a country's history. Its heritage."

"And I will make sure it's protected. If I don't discover it, it might be lost forever. If someone else discovers it, who knows what might happen to it? I'm not going to take the scrolls just for me, Anne. I have plans for them. They'll be safe."

"You've created a convenient argument."

"It's a true argument! I won't hide the scrolls away in a private gallery. I intend to establish a museum around them. A place that will give them their due *and* give me mine. Can't you understand why I need this? Why

I need something bigger than a statue or vase? After the board of trustees—"

"Sweetheart, I know how hard this has been on you, but you need to—"

"I deserve better. I deserve *this*. I need it."

"Enough to jeopardize her safety?"

Irene studied Simone, who looked like a child, her knees pulled up to her flat chest. Despite the low light, the bruise on the side of her face was visible, a gray-green welt running the length of her jaw. Irene did not want to see anyone hurt, but she was almost thirty. She could not start over. She had worked too hard. She was too good at the life she had crafted for herself to let it slip away. "He hit her with a frying pan. If I can get her out of here, I'll be doing her a favor."

Alone in her hotel room, Irene took her map case from beneath the mattress, where she had tied the brown leather bag to a wooden slat for safe-keeping. The stitching around one of the brass buckles was rubbed away, and the flap was stained with a water mark that looked like a continent drifting in a brown sea. She unhooked the buckles and removed the collection she kept inside. Carefully, she unfolded the topmost map, its creases as soft as old flannel. It was the first map her father had given her after her mother died. She laid it on the floor and beside it another, and then another, until she was standing in a patchwork sea of Cambodia, its landscapes embellished with indigo tigers and crimson Hindu gods.

As dusk passed quickly outside her window, the Cardamom Mountains lay partially hidden beneath the tangle of cotton bedspread that had slipped to the floor. Tonle Sap Lake streamed into the darkness beneath the writing desk. The thick vein of the Mekong River fractured the countryside, and tassels from the shade of the oil lamp cast patterns, like the frayed shadows of storm clouds, over the saffron fleck that marked the town of Stung Treng. Irene's girlhood had been a succession of journeys, coursing through her imagination into this faraway country. She gazed down on those adventures, layered in a pentimento of remembrance.

Finding the lost temple was about more than taking back what was rightfully hers, and Irene was angry with Anne for not acknowledging this. Since she had left her job at the museum, she could see how her entire life had been leading her to the moment when Mr. Simms showed her the missionary's diary. Now, in her hotel room in Shanghai, she sat down on the bed with it and skimmed the pages she had memorized and nearly worn through with rereading:

> *I have spent the past 27 days traveling north and east away from the awesome relic of a city called Ang Cor.*

These words had been written one hundred years to the month before Irene's arrival in Shanghai, and thirty-five years before Henri Mouhot, a French naturalist, claimed to be the first to have discovered Angkor Wat and announced it to the world. It was incredible to think that this missionary, Reverend Garland, had seen it—*Ang Cor,* he called it—before Mouhot and not mentioned it to a soul. Nor had he disclosed what he came upon a few days afterward.

> *Svai patted a fragment of wall and announced, "Musée.". . . said what I can only crudely translate as "the king's temple". . . proudly declared that this temple contained the history of his savage people on ten copper scrolls.*

Irene had laughed the first time she read the words: *savage people.* The Khmer were as far from being savage as the ancient Romans. More so, since the Romans had their gladiators and the practice of throwing Christians to lions. During the Khmer's reign, from the ninth to the fifteenth century, they ultimately commanded a region of more than one thousand temples that spread from Siam into Laos and down to the South China Sea. Their bas-reliefs held up to the Greeks' and Persians', and they were masters of engineering with their massive system of public waterworks. Most important to Irene, they built the largest temple in the world, Angkor Wat, which alone encompassed five hundred acres. A million people had once lived there.

Then, after centuries of high civilization, the empire vanished. But even at its height it was unknown to the West, and by the time Mouhot came along, not a shadow of its brilliance was said to remain among the Cambodians, as the descendants of the Khmer were now called by the outside world. All that was left were miles and miles of temples, abandoned except for the monks who inhabited them.

When he first saw the ruins of Angkor Wat, Mouhot had written, "It is a rival to the temple of Solomon, and erected by an ancient Michelangelo. It is grander than anything left to us by Greece or Rome."

What had happened to cause the entire Khmer civilization to disappear? Scholars devoted their lives to this question, and Irene had pored over the possibilities. Theories abounded, but the answer was still a Holy Grail, one that many, including Irene, feared would never be found, given the impermanence of Khmer record keeping.

The Khmer had chronicled their world using mulberry bark paper and stacked cords of palm leaves. These pages had disintegrated or had been destroyed in the hundreds of years since they were written. But copper scrolls. Irene could envision them, as Reverend Garland must have seen them, for she had studied such documents in the course of her career: metal scrolls that had been unrolled and flattened into the thinnest of tablets. Such objects could easily survive. They could still exist. And if these particular scrolls did, and if they contained Cambodia's history, Irene was closer than anyone had ever come to discovering them.

From the pocket stitched into the back cover of the diary, she took out another map. Reverend James T. Garland's map, drawn with the precision of a cartographer. Each distance on his route was noted, neatly penned along the jungle trails of northeast Cambodia, from the town of "Stun Tren" to a destination, marked with a blue *X*, near a village that he called "Ka Saeng" not far from the Lao border. Irene had reviewed the reverend's calculations exhaustively, in Seattle and on the *Tahoma* crossing the Pacific Ocean and in this hotel room while waiting for Simone to come back from France, using her own maps for comparison. The starting point was the trading town of Stung Treng, at the confluence of the Mekong and Sekong Rivers. It was reachable by steamer from Cambodia's capital, Phnom Penh. The end point near Kha Seng lay in uncharted territory, but the reverend had recorded the names of villages on the way to it. The path was so clearly designated that it made Irene laugh. Could it really be that easy?

As she folded the map back into the diary, she removed a calling card that she had put into the pocket for safekeeping. It had the name of a business on it, "Rafferty's Nightclub," and printed in the corner was "Marc Rafferty, Prop." She turned it over and once again read Mr. Simms's cramped, back-slanted script: "If you need assistance of any kind, this is your man." When Mr. Simms had given her the card, it was no surprise that he knew whom she should go to for guidance in Shanghai, considering his relationship with the city. Later, adrift on the ocean, she gave it little thought. But now, in light of what was happening with Simone . . . Mr. Simms did nothing without a purpose, no matter how incidental it seemed.

Looking out the window, where the haphazard angles of Shanghai's rooftops were indiscernible in the blackout, Irene considered how nonchalantly Mr. Simms had first mentioned partnering with Simone Merlin, during the early stages of the planning for Irene's journey. One evening he had summoned her to the study that nestled in the center of his manor's top floor, a vault of a room where they had spent countless hours deep in discussion over the years. When Irene arrived, a fire was burning, mellowing the deep hue of the cherrywood walls into a rich rosy amber. Mr. Simms stood with his back to her, facing the only ornament in the room: three slabs of golden pink sandstone, fitted together one atop another, nearly six feet tall.

Their border was sculpted with sinuous florets that coiled around a carving of a divine *apsara* from Banteay Srei, the tenth-century Khmer temple known as the Citadel of Women. The goddess had arrived at the manor two years earlier, shrouded in secrecy since word had spread so quickly of her disappearance. Irene had been with Mr. Simms in the middle of the night when the *apsara* was delivered and pieced back together in this room. He had given no explanation as to why this antiquity, and only this one above all the others he owned, deserved to occupy the most secret space in his home, and she knew better than to ask. So there the carving resided, undisturbed, chiseled into her sandstone alcove.

Standing beside Mr. Simms, waiting for him to explain why he had called for her, Irene gazed on the *apsara*. Despite all the time she had spent studying it, she never grew bored admiring the serpentine limbs, the placid set of the mouth, the flat cheekbones revealing the Hindu ancestry of the Indian traders who once trespassed through the Khmer territories on their way to China.

Finally, Mr. Simms asked, "Did I ever tell you how she was taken out of Cambodia?"

Irene nodded. "In coffins."

"Clever, so very clever. And you know who took her?"

"Yes," Irene said, easily playing her part in this conversation they'd had so many times before. "Roger and Simone Merlin."

"I have been thinking about this woman: Simone. She might be just the right person to help you find the scrolls. What do you think?"

It had been as simple as that. But thinking back on it, Irene wondered if it really had been that simple. Picking up her maps and folding them with care, she slid each one into the case. She weighed new possibilities as she bathed and washed her hair, combing it out but not tying it up. It felt too good, cool and damp over her shoulders. She put on a sleeveless linen dress and a new pair of sandals she had bought at the Wing On department store, and then she went out into the city, to see if she could find out why Mr. Simms had so casually suggested that she might need assistance from Marc Rafferty.

Chapter 4

A Place Like This

It was dark among the quiet streets of Shanghai's French quarter. With the calling card as her guide, Irene stood in front of a metal gate and sought an indication that she had come to the right place. Candles lay along the rim of the high brick wall, but the descent of thin, flickering light did not reveal any kind of sign. Suddenly, shrieking and jazz swelled from within, and the gate crashed open. It was as if a bomb had exploded, catapulting people onto the sidewalk. Women in high-heeled evening sandals stumbled against one another. A swarthy man fell and was crushed as the crowd trampled over him. But everyone was laughing. The men wore tuxedos. A woman tripped past, peacock feathers sprouting from her gem-encrusted hair, howling as if she had heard the world's dirtiest joke.

"Bosch would have loved painting this city."

The man who spoke was tucked into a fold of shadow behind Irene. He must have been standing there all along.

"Did you say Bosch?" she asked.

"A Flemish artist," he said.

"I know who he is. Fifteenth century. Temptation and morality."

He nodded appreciatively. "Don't forget deadly sins."

"And the torments of hell."

"So you can understand how well Shanghai would have suited him." The man's accent was European but not traceable to a specific country, as was the case with many who had lived a long time in the Orient. He squinted at the chaos of people bursting out of the nightclub. "A riot has broken out in the Chapei district. The damn fool Chinese are torching their own warehouses. I hear that the view is spectacular from the roof of the Palace Hotel."

A teenage Filipina shoved through the crowd. She yanked a spangled leash, and an Italian greyhound skittered over the cobbled walkway behind her. "I stole a bottle of Veuve," she squealed to the man as she waved the champagne above her head. "I'll make it up to you later, sugar. Boy, oh boy, will I!"

A burgundy Rolls-Royce led a parade of cars toward the British Settlement and the rooftop view from the Palace Hotel. Only Irene and the man remained behind. He stooped down, picked up a purple feather boa, and carried it into the courtyard. As she followed him, he asked, "You're not going to join the fun?"

Willows draped their leaves over pools of candlelight. A yellow ginkgo had been overturned, and its ceramic pot was shattered. Jade ashtrays littered the wrought-iron tables. Irene noticed a sign hanging from a post: RAFFERTY's. She said, "It doesn't seem like much fun to me."

"A smart woman. I like that." The man smiled. "Actually, I started the rumor. I don't have the patience I used to. I'm leaving Shanghai, and everyone and his mistress wants to bid me bon voyage. Each of my patrons

likes to think I'm his best friend, simply because I don't divulge the re-
pugnant secrets he lets slip when he's acting as if he's too tight to know
better. I am tired of these people."

"Are you Marc Rafferty?"

He paused, examining her, taking in her perspiring skin and her pale
blue dress, which seemed loose at first but would be discovered to deliberately skim the slight curves of her body if one looked closely enough.
"I am. And who are you?"

In the light filtering down from an upstairs window, she returned his
appraisal, taking in his unconventional collarless shirt and loose Oriental
trousers. He was tall, and his body had substance without being heavy.
His eyes were deep set, and his dark blond hair curled over his ears in the
humidity. He would have been too handsome if his face had not been
hardened by a look of tired reproach. Worried that she had chosen a bad
time to come to him, she said, "My name is Irene Blum."

His expression instantly softened, and he laughed. "How about that?
And I thought I'd lost the ability to be taken by surprise."

"You know who I am?" she asked.

"What brings you to me?"

"Henry Simms gave me your name."

Marc considered this. "Why?"

Irene held out the calling card.

He stepped closer and read the note on the back of it. "Do you? Need
assistance with anything?"

"I must, if he anticipated it."

"This is true."

"Then you know him well, I take it?"

Marc looked as if he did not understand the question. But he merely
said, "Well enough," as he swept the boa across a tabletop, clearing the
debris of ash and cigarette butts onto the ground. "It's going to rain soon.
It's one of the few things I will miss about Shanghai. The way the air
grows static like this right before a storm, and then when you think you
can't bear the tension any longer, the rain comes and you're rescued,
again. Come in. Have a drink."

He led Irene into a room tentative with candlelight. The walls were built of rough gray stone, like those in a cellar. In one corner five band members slouched around their instruments, obscured by the smoke of their cigarettes. A gaunt greyhound, identical to the poor creature dragged by the Filipina, was tethered to a microphone stand. Pacing, it drew its leash tight each time it reached the front row of tables. The air smelled of hot wax and citrus perfume, cardamom and sweat.

Marc brought a bottle of whiskey to a table scarcely large enough for two. "I don't have ice," he apologized. He waited for her to take a drink before raising a candle and holding it near her chin. "You don't look like a temple robber," he said.

This was the last thing Irene had expected Marc Rafferty to say. "Why would you think I'm a temple robber?"

"Henry told me. Are you denying it?"

She was astonished that Mr. Simms would confide in this man about her expedition, and at the same time, she was thankful that he had anticipated how much she would need someone to confide in. "No," she said, "I'm not."

"That's a bold thing to admit."

Irene was aware of his leg near hers beneath the table. "I've kept a lot of secrets," she said, "but never one as big as this. And never in a place where I didn't have someone to talk with about it." She remembered what Simone had said in Anne's office about being lonely. "It catches me off guard, how alone it can make me feel. I don't know you, but for some reason it's comforting that you know what I'm doing. I *am* going to raid a temple," she said, recklessly, savoring the words spoken aloud.

"Loneliness," Marc murmured. "It's a funny creature here in Shanghai. There are so many people, and everyone is poking into everyone else's business all the time, and still no one really knows anything about you. You don't realize how alone you've been until a rare moment when you aren't."

The room was a cocoon, muggy and impermeable. It flustered her, how familiar the low tenor of Marc's voice felt. "You said that you're leaving. Where do you plan to go from here?" she asked.

"First, Saigon, to visit my aunt."

"I'm going to Saigon too. I'm on my way to Cambodia."

"I'll be en route to Amsterdam. My cousin owns a coffeehouse on the Keizersgracht. He's asked me to run it for him. It's time for me to go home."

"How long have you lived in Shanghai?"

"All my life."

"But you call Amsterdam home?"

"My mother was born there. Her family is still there." He rolled the bottle of whiskey between his palms. "Shanghai hasn't been home to me since my wife was killed."

"I'm sorry." It was only as Marc shifted his leg away that Irene realized how drawn she was to him. She shouldn't have gulped the entire glass. She should have had dinner. She felt light-headed. Clearly it had been too long since she had been with a man. The nearness of Marc's leg, that was all it had taken. Self-conscious, she stood. "How much do I owe you for the drink?"

"Stay," he said, smoothing out a cigarette paper. He took a pouch from his pocket and dropped a pinch of tobacco into the center of the paper, working it into a narrow spine. "My life in Shanghai, it has made me ill-equipped for normal conversation." He lit the cigarette and handed it across the table. The tip was moist where he had held it in his mouth. He lit another for himself. "You can't know what a place like this will do to a person until it has done it to you. It deceives, and then it corrupts, and then it's too late." He inhaled, harboring the smoke deep in his lungs. The reddened ash reflected in his pupils. "What if I'm not satisfied serving coffee to gray-haired shopkeepers and plump housewives in a neighborhood café? What if I miss the need to keep a gun hidden beneath my pillow? I have four bodyguards, Irene. Four thugs whose sole job is to protect me from being kidnapped or worse. What the hell kind of life is that for a man to have grown accustomed to?"

Irene was surprised to find her thoughts drifting to her first boyfriend, a ruddy university student who had sprinted around athletic fields and confused it with achievement. And then there had been the aging art critic when she was twenty-three, with his sea captain mustache and predictable attempts to seduce her with mah-jongg and chop suey. Even her brief affairs, when the solitude of her heart had gotten the best of her, had never stirred this kind of lightning-quick emotion within her. "You're asking the wrong person." She sat back down. "I'm a temple robber, remember?"

He smiled. "So you say."

"Stranger still, so you've been told. I wonder, why would Mr. Simms tell you that about me? And why would he give me your name unless he really believed I would need something from you? What kind of help could I need?"

"I know Shanghai well," Marc said. "Information is my stock-in-trade. Perhaps there's something you need to know about the city. Or . . ." Irene's hand was resting on the table. He reached out with the lightest of touches, as if he was making sure she was real. "Maybe if you tell me about Henry and you, tell me how you ended up here, I can figure it out."

She gazed around. The bartender was napping on a stool. Inside an orbit of smoke, the band members continued to puff on their cigarettes. After being discarded in Seattle, after being rejected by Simone and disapproved of by Anne, Irene was eager for this attention Marc was giving her. "Mr. Simms never kept secrets from me," she said. "Even when I was young, I knew about the hidden rooms in his manor. I knew how he acquired the objects in them. I knew about the clandestine deals and the crates arriving in the middle of the night. His trust meant everything to me. So many people thought it was their right to tell me what was appropriate for a girl without a mother. I hated it. *Irene, that is not appropriate!* But Mr. Simms, he didn't think of me as a child, and by the time I became an adult, I couldn't imagine my life without him." The memory of Mr. Simms's rapid deterioration in the month before she left Seattle nearly brought tears to her eyes. Softly, she said, "I can't imagine what it's going to be like . . ."

"Can't imagine what what's going to be like?"

Outside, the rain pounded as if it were being dragged down by an underground force. Wind blew leaden raindrops through a broken window, and the storm was cold, metallic in the air. Candlelight trembled on the walls. The bartender wound the gramophone, as if *Rhapsody in Blue* could even out the ragged tempo of the storm. Keeping her eyes on the table, Irene turned her palm upward, so that her fingertips brushed Marc's.

He did not pull away. Quietly, as if it mattered to him that they were not overheard, he asked, "Why did he take such an interest in you?"

Shaking off thoughts of Mr. Simms's illness, she said, "He has no children. No one to pass his legacy to."

Marc's hand tensed against hers, and she felt the heat in her face, the skip in her pulse where his fingers lay over her exposed wrist. "There must be more to it than that," he said.

"I'm like him. I have always loved the chase. The unattainable. I'm too intense, I can't help it, I know that about myself. And I have the heart of a thief." She laughed because it sounded so cloak-and-dagger. "*Thief* is too dirty a word, though. You can't just go into someone's home and take a painting. You can't just go into a museum and walk away with a statue. But the painting, the statue, it has to get into the home or museum somehow. That's where it interests me."

His cigarette burning down in the ashtray, Marc leaned forward. He was absorbing her words the way Mr. Simms did, and she felt as if she could tell him, as she could Mr. Simms, anything.

"Who does it all really belong to anyway?" she asked. "Whoever gets to it first. The natives don't care. They have no idea how to preserve their own antiquities. Look at the state of Angkor Wat when Mouhot found it. A complete ruin. It's the French who are restoring it. It's because of the French that it will survive. And the French! They're grabbing everything in Cambodia that they can for their mansions and museums back in France. Art, artifacts, they don't hold still. That's what's amazing. They never have. They never will. Borders shift. Allegiances shift. Think about the spoils of war. Spain ransacked Peru. England plundered the Summer Palace during the Opium Wars. Audacious," she murmured, shaking her head with admiration.

Marc removed his hand and took up the stub of his cigarette. Irene felt dizzy. She had never talked like this, so openly, with a stranger. But he did not feel at all like a stranger, and it disconcerted her, how at ease she was with him. She watched him refill their glasses. The Scotch soaked in the gleam of the candle's flame. "This temple you're after," he said. "Did a border shift? Is it the spoils of a war? How did it come your way?"

"My father wasn't old, not even seventy. I knew he wouldn't live forever, but I never thought—" She had nearly finished her second drink, and although she wanted to blame the alcohol, she knew it was not the reason she was verging on maudlin. Clearing her voice of the emotion that inevitably overcame her when she spoke of her father, she said, "When my father died, last December, he left a box for Mr. Simms. It contained the diary of a missionary who wrote about finding a temple in Cambodia. A temple containing the history of the Khmer people on a set of copper scrolls. If what he writes is true, and if it's all still up there, it could be the greatest discovery of this century."

"What was your father doing with the diary?" Marc asked.

"That's a part of the mystery. He was a bit of a treasure hunter before I was born. He spent years traveling around the Orient. He could have come across it in any number of places."

"Do you think he knew what it meant?"

"He had to."

"How do you know he didn't already try to find it?"

"I don't."

"He could have gone and found nothing."

Irene nodded. "That's possible. But why wouldn't he have told me?"

"So you don't know for certain if the scrolls are still there?"

Irene fingered the smooth beads of the carnelian bracelet that had also come from the box her father left, and that she'd been wearing ever since Mr. Simms fastened it on her wrist. "They have to be there."

"Have to?"

"If I can bring him this one last treasure before he dies, then I can repay him for—"

"Dies?" Marc asked. "Who's dying?"

"Mr. Simms. He has cancer."

A gust banged a shutter closed, and the greyhound spooked, leaping toward the bandleader. A kerosene lamp sputtered, its flame expired, and the light collapsed around them. "I didn't know." Marc sounded as if the wind had been knocked out of him. Irene reached to take back his hand, but the greyhound barked, and the door swung open. The Filipina stumbled in, bedraggled, clutching a leash. Her dog was not with her. "The rain must have put out the fires," she complained. "We were too late.

But the champagne was divine. How can I make amends for being so naughty?"

Two men in wet tuxedos pushed past her, followed by others. One called out, "Brandy for everyone!"

For a second, Marc seemed annoyed. Then he stood up and called jovially to the bandleader, "Gregor, how about a tango for our friends?" He rounded the table and leaned over Irene, holding the room at bay as he pressed his mouth to her ear. "There is one thing you didn't tell me. What are you doing in Shanghai if you're on your way to Cambodia? It's not on the path between Seattle and Phnom Penh."

If Marc had asked Irene to go home with him right then, she would have gone. But the bar was filling up again. That moment had passed. Catching her breath, she said, "I'm here to recruit Simone Merlin to help me find the temple. Maybe that's it. Maybe that's the problem you're supposed to help me with. If you know this city so well, tell me, why has she refused to go with me?"

Marc's brow furrowed with concern. "Because her husband is the most dangerous man in the Orient."

Chapter 5

Hope and Futility

The following morning Irene waited for Simone in her office for nearly two hours, but the younger woman did not appear. Anne had told Irene that Simone often spent time out at the racecourse or in the layette section of the Sincere department store on Nanjing Road, but she was in neither of those places either. Irene even tried the Huxinting teahouse, a pagoda set on pilings in the center of a small man-made lake in Shanghai's Chinese quarter. It was known for its gatherings of Kuomintang. Sitting at an upstairs table at one of the windows hoping that Simone might show up, she sipped her tea and tried to pass the time categorizing the peasants on the paths encircling the water—old matrons grilling flakes of silver fish over beds of coal, grandfathers writing their life stories on the pavement in chalk for money, and middle-aged women hobbling on their bound "lotus feet." All around the lake, scraps of laundry hung limp from wooden poles that extended from the open windows of the tenement houses. Irene sorted through the faded shades of blue and brown fabric, but her heart wasn't in it. There was no sign of Simone, and the day was drawing to a close.

Finally, as the wet late afternoon heat wrung itself out of the soupy sky, and the chance of simply happening upon Simone dwindled, Irene admitted to herself why she was wasting such valuable time. She was afraid of Roger Merlin. After hearing the stories of his violent temper and Marc Rafferty's warning, and having seen what Roger had done to Simone with a frying pan, Irene wanted to avoid him.

If she'd had weeks at her disposal, she would have relished the challenge of maneuvering around him. As it was, there were only two days left until the *Lumière* sailed to Saigon. She'd already bought the tickets, the day after she arrived in Shanghai. She had to get Simone on that steamer, or else leave the city on her own and work out a new plan along the way.

She took a taxicab to the Merlins' apartment on the Quai de France, a narrow street that paralleled the Whangpoo River. Reaching the top landing, she checked once again for the bulk of her map case tucked inside her jacket. In a sconce on the wall, an oil lamp burned, and its light cast a distorted phantom of her silhouette down the stairs. She put her ear to the door and listened for voices but heard none. She knocked.

Simone called out, "The door is open."

Irene stepped inside. The room stank. She recoiled and raised her sleeve to cover her mouth against the odors of food and closed heat that had fermented in layers so thick they seemed visible. The stench of decaying lilies overpowered all else, their stems decomposing in a large glass vase filled with slimy water.

A circle of kerosene lamps hung from the center of the low ceiling, radiating ocher shafts onto four shuttered windows that spanned the length of the sitting room. Directly beneath them, on a teak chair, Simone sat in a blue kimono, draped open, its obi loose around her waist. She lifted her eyes and tilted her head sluggishly.

Irene thought of Anne's opium tea and the bottle of Luminal in the desk in Simone's office. She looked around. "Is he here?"

"No."

Released from the strain of bracing herself to face Roger, Irene stepped toward Simone. She reached inside her jacket for her map case, and as she did so, she felt the merging of hope and futility that comes with taking a last chance. Simone watched her unclasp the buckle. The calfskin cover of the diary was warm to Irene's touch as she opened to the page she had marked with the ribbon. Without prelude she read, " 'I have spent the past twenty-seven days traveling north and east away from the awe-some relic of a city called Ang Cor.' "

"When was this written?" Simone interrupted. Her voice was not slurred, as Irene had expected it to be.

"In 1825."

Simone pressed her fingers against her jaw. The swelling had gone down, but her skin was still discolored.

Mindful of how hungry she was to win Simone over and of how easily she could fail, Irene continued to read aloud, guiding Simone from Ang-kor Wat to the trading town of Stung Treng and out into the jungle. " 'Svai plunged into the temple and returned with a flat metal scroll, no larger than a sheet of writing paper.' " She looked at Simone, who had closed her eyes. " 'Svai said what I can only crudely translate as "the king's temple" and then proudly declared that this temple contained the history of his savage people on ten copper scrolls.' "

While Simone remained motionless, Irene fumbled to release the latch on the nearest set of shutters. The river was so close that she tasted its dampness when she inhaled. She worked her way down the length of the room until every window was open and a breeze stirred the air. Turning to find Simone staring at her, Irene could feel their shared knowledge fill-ing the space between them.

For a time it had been believed that the spectacular Khmer kingdom was built by the Romans or Alexander the Great, by giants or heavenly angels or a lost tribe of Israel. Its builders were once even thought to have been the same despots who ordered the pyramids of Tikal. Then, after existing for six hundred glorious years, their civilization had been devastated, whether by a catastrophic flood or plague or earthquake or comet or infuriated gods, no one knew. Those were the ancient rumors underlying the modern theories that were bandied about in archaeological digests, lecture halls, and museum offices—and Irene was certain Simone knew of every one of them, just as she did. As for facts, as for a history that could be written, indelibly, both of them also knew that it was waiting to be discovered.

"May I see it?" Simone asked.

Rather than read the diary, she examined it, fingering its pages, reaching into the empty pocket at the back. Irene had not brought the map. That would come only when she knew that Simone could be fully trusted. Simone said, "Roger will come after you too."

Irene's gaze caught on the only attempt at adornment in the disorderly apartment, a painting by Rodin of a Cambodian dancer, hanging in solitude above a cabinet. The woman's hand evaporated into a sepia wash of watercolor, as if she were a work in progress. "I've considered every argument that can be made against this expedition," Irene said. "Is the diary authentic? What if the scrolls were taken years ago? What if the reverend was wrong about what he saw? What if he misinterpreted his guide? But I don't care. It's worth any risk to me to find out the truth."

The sound was frail, so soft at first that Irene did not recognize it. Simone was weeping. Irene found a water pitcher and a glass, and waited as Simone drank thirstily. "But you don't have to take *this* risk. You're an idiot for having anything to do with me," she said.

"Time will tell."

Simone wiped her face with the sleeve of her kimono. "Where did you find the diary?"

"It was my father's."

Startled, Simone said, "Henry Simms is your father?"

Irene was taken aback by the question. "Mr. Simms? My father? No." She stumbled over her words. "Mr. Simms and my father were friends. What did Anne tell you about him?"

"Nothing."

"Then why bring Mr. Simms up?" Irene asked. "What does he have to do with this?"

"Do you think I don't know? I'm a fool, but I'm not stupid. You've come from the Brooke Museum. You've offered me fifty thousand dollars. You're going in search of the most important archaeological relic of our time. After the auction for the bas-relief that Roger and I took from Banteay Srei, we were told Simms bid twice its value. He had to have known he was lining my husband's pockets. My Communist husband, whose goal is to destroy Simms's enterprise here, and all because he wanted to own a piece of the Khmer temples. Because he couldn't bear the thought of Mellon or Stanić owning it instead. Simms would take Angkor Wat to Seattle stone by stone if he thought he could accomplish it. Who else would be backing you on this?"

"Does it matter?" Irene asked.

"It depends on what he wants."

"He wants what I want. Once I've found the scrolls, I will be invaluable to every museum that has ever had anything to do with the Khmer—even the Guimet! But this time they will know who I am. Me, not 'I.B., on behalf of Professor T. Howard,'" she said disdainfully.

"What does that mean?"

"I spent years corresponding with the curators at the Guimet Museum, acquiring photographs and prints of documents from explorations in Cambodia. I created a catalog more thorough, more evaluative than even their own. But every letter, every single letter, that is how I signed it—'I.B., on behalf of'—out of respect for Professor Howard. Never once did I sign my own name. It never occurred to me that I wouldn't be given my due."

"Forget about the Brooke," Simone said. "Forget about the Guimet. It doesn't matter what anyone thinks about you in Paris. It's an irrelevant city. Europe is irrelevant. It's dying. But the Orient!" Sitting up straight, she pulled her robe together and secured the sash. "Once you've stood among the stones of Angkor Wat, once you've seen and touched the home of the Khmer, you won't care about anyplace else. You definitely won't care what fusty old scholars halfway around the world think of you. I admit, I didn't believe your story about having a map when you told me at Anne's party. I couldn't let myself, not after everything I have suffered. If I do this, if I leave him, I need to know: What gives you such confidence?"

Irene had never told anyone, aside from Mr. Simms, about her methods, but Simone seemed close to making a decision. For the first time since entering the apartment, she felt that Simone could be convinced to make the right decision if she was guided skillfully enough, *and* if she was given a good reason to have faith in Irene. Irene glanced at the collection of decanters on the cabinet. "May I have a drink?"

"Help yourself."

As Irene poured just enough whiskey to liberate the last of her hesitation, she asked, "Would you like one?"

"I've already taken some pills." Simone laughed. "If I have whiskey, I'll throw them up. But a splash of sherry would be nice." She accepted a cordial glass filled with sweet yellow liquid and took a sip. "Thank you," she said, relaxing in her chair.

Irene leaned against the sill of the nearest open window, her back resting on the cushion of muggy evening air. "I've created systems," she said. "Ways to gather and cross-reference materials. It amazed me at first how easy it was to request a ship's manifest. Travel schedules were trickier, but assistants are eager to help other assistants. It's as if we're our own secret society, and many of us are women. That helps. Maybe that's another reason why I have always been so discreet. I've never really thought about it before. But it has made it easy to get whatever I want. After all, what could someone in my position possibly do with Rockefeller's Ottoman travel plans? Or Hearst's or Morgan's?"

"And what *do* you do with them?"

"I make grids, mathematical grids, and I fill them in. One with the names of collectors divided into those partial to ancient Greece or Persia or China—every area of expertise. Another with the names of dealers, and others with schedules, missing objects, dates of disappearances, dates of acquisitions. When I fit it all together, you cannot believe how obvious it is where all of the missing Vatican sculptures and Flemish tapestries have gone."

"Grids," Simone said, contemplating this.

"As soon as I read it," Irene said, waving her glass toward the diary still sitting in Simone's lap, "I went back through everything I'd compiled. Copies of letters and journals, books and monographs, anything I could get my hands on written about the Khmer. Mr. Simms cleared an entire room in his house. I covered the floor with graphs and charts I'd filled in with any information that correlated with the diary. I started to see, bit by bit, that it was possible. It really was possible. Simone, you know the accepted hypothesis as well as I do. Khmer society was essentially confined to the area along the Royal Road running northwest out of Cambodia. But think about your father's own research on trading routes. He's the one who figured out that the Khmer sent trade expeditions into the northeast."

"And Wat Phu," Simone murmured.

"Exactly! A Khmer temple complex in southern Laos. Nowhere near the Royal Road, but almost directly north of where Reverend Garland claims to have found his temple. The Khmer could have expanded into northeast Cambodia. Perhaps as the Siamese were invading. Maybe they were preparing some kind of new kingdom based around this temple the reverend writes about."

Simone looked from the diary to Irene. "Your theory makes sense."

Irene felt a trickle of relief as she heard the shift in Simone's voice, the approval.

Simone continued. "There is something I need to know, Irene. Have your hands ever been dirty? Have you ever had to fight for your life? I'm not talking only about Roger. If I leave Shanghai, my every move will be watched. It may be by someone from the Municipal Government or the Kuomintang, or maybe a thug hoping to profit by holding me for ransom. The amount I know about Roger, about the revolution. Do you know how many times I have eaten a meal in Chiang Kai-shek's home? I'm his wife's confidante, and May-ling is a woman who does not know how to keep her mouth shut." As Simone spoke she combed her fingers through her hair, taming her disheveled appearance. "I'm the one who worked with Shemeshko to set up the *Shanghai Chronicle*. I am the contact for Borodin's arms shipments. I've been shot at twice. I am valuable," she insisted, as if Irene had expressed doubt, "and Roger has made sure that I am entrenched. Even if he doesn't come after me, someone else may find a good reason to. When we go into the jungle, we won't be alone."

Finally, here was the impassioned, self-assured woman Irene had thought she would find in Shanghai. And Simone had said *when*. Not *if*, but *when* we go into the jungle. "One hurdle at a time," Irene said. "First we need to deal with Roger. As I see it, we have two options. Run like hell and hope he doesn't catch us, or go to him."

"And do what?" Simone shook her head, as if she thought Irene were crazy. "Do you know what *face* means? Do you understand its importance, especially here in Shanghai? Do you know the extreme measures a man like Roger will take to save face?"

Irene had been raised among collectors and tycoons, men whose entire lives were guided by presumption, hubris, and their so-called honor. "Then we will make sure he does not lose face," she replied.

Simone held the diary to her cheek, like a cool cloth used to ease a fever. "He's angry that I no longer care about his cause. He can't see what he's become, that he's made himself into the cause. I can't criticize anything about it without criticizing him. I can't want to do things my own way without rejecting his. Honestly, Irene, I won't blame you if you abandon me."

Irene watched with dismay as Simone visibly deflated, slumping into her robe. But Simone's choice of word struck her: *abandon*. It was a word that she had worn out in those days after the museum's trustees disowned her. "Where is he?" she asked. "Do you know if he's alone? We shouldn't approach him unless he's alone."

"Aren't you afraid of him?" Simone asked.

"I'm terrified of him," Irene admitted. "But I'm even more terrified of failing, and my chances of failing once I'm in Cambodia are much higher without you."

"You *can* find this temple without me."

"For some reason, Henry Simms wants me to take you out of Shanghai." Irene did not add her own reason, one which she was only beginning to understand. Somehow, in saving Simone, she was also saving herself.

Chapter 6

The Letter Opener

While Simone drove beyond Shanghai's shadowy
city limits, Irene gazed out the passenger window,
but night was falling, and as the area north of the
city grew dark, she could see nothing beyond the
headlights. It was as if they were traveling through
a tunnel that would bring them into the heart of the
night. They did not speak, but the silence between
them, their fragile new conspiracy, was louder than
the rush of wind through the open windows. After
nearly an hour, Irene felt the car slow. Simone was
leaning over the steering wheel, peering through
the windshield. Irene saw only faint ruts in the dirt.
With no guidepost showing her the way, Simone
turned the car. A side lane appeared, lean trees
gathered along its embankments, illuminated in the

feeble wash of the headlights. Above, their high, broad branches vanished as if fitted tightly into niches in the night sky.

The darkness ahead was punctured by a rusty glint. As Simone drove toward it, Irene made out a lantern on a verandah railing. Slowly, Simone circled a house. The tires pressed into the spongy earth, and tall, marshy grass grazed the fenders. She parked the car in a shadow, with its nose aimed in the direction from which they had come, and shut off the motor. The evaporation of that steady rumbling was like the loss of a companion who had been whispering assurances in Irene's ear.

"Where are we?" she asked.

"A hideout," Simone said. "Roger and I are the only ones who know about it."

"Why is he out here tonight?"

"He likes the silence." Simone laughed. "He's writing his memoir. He wants it to be ready for publication the moment the Communists take power."

They got out of the car and shut the doors softly. The stars were very high, as if this part of the world was farther from the heavens than any other. Holding on to Irene's sleeve, Simone guided her up the steps and onto the verandah. Irene felt anesthetized, and she wondered if this draining of all emotion was a precursor to courage. Simone drummed her fingertips on the door three times. She waited a moment and then did it again. There was no response. When she tried the door, it was unlocked.

Irene followed Simone into the bungalow. They both stopped just inside. Two old armchairs and a scarred teakwood desk stood at the end of the front room. Seated at the desk with his back to the wall, Roger did not take his attention from his writing. With his head bowed over the page, he looked like any ordinary man doing office work, surrounded by a blotter, an inkwell, and a tray containing pens and a brass letter opener that caught the light. His face was pinched, and his arms were thin, and if Irene had passed him on the street without knowing who he was, she would not have taken him for a man who beat his wife.

He paused as if he were contemplating what to write next. Instead, his eyes traveled from Simone to Irene. He blotted his pen, carefully screwed on its cap, and set it in the tray. "You must genuinely want to find this temple," he said to his wife. And to Irene, "She is forbidden to bring anyone here."

He is only a man, Irene told herself, nothing more.

"I have already made it clear," he said. "Now is not the time to leave Shanghai."

Irene said, "I just want to talk to you."

"There is nothing to talk about."

"Actually, I've come to make you an offer."

Scraping his chair along the bare floor, Roger stood up from his desk. "An offer?"

Just a man, and men thrive on transaction. They can be bought, as long as they believe they have the better end of the deal. "I understand this isn't a simple situation. I'm aware of the risks of Simone going where you can't protect her. But this temple, it may be the most important discovery of our time. It will bring prestige. It will bring honor to her name—and her name is yours, after all. Think about what it would do for the reputation of your cause, to have your wife restore the history of Cambodia. Isn't that what you want? Isn't that what your cause is about? Giving these countries back to their own people?"

Taking a pipe from the top desk drawer, Roger asked, "This is your offer?"

Irene laughed lightly, intent on hiding how intimidated she was. "No, this is my prelude."

"It's interesting, I must admit."

"I want this to be worthwhile for you. I can give you fifty thousand dollars."

"That's quite a sum—a good starting point. Come in. Have a seat."

Irene started forward, but Simone grabbed her wrist. "No."

Roger tamped a plug of tobacco into the bowl of the pipe. "That is all you have to say? *No?*" He stepped around his desk. "This generous lady is offering to buy you from me, and you have nothing to say about it?"

Irene remained silent. She did not want to antagonize Roger. She wanted to know what Simone would say, but Simone said nothing.

Roger asked Irene, "Do you really think she is worth fifty thousand dollars?"

Simone whispered, "Stop it."

"I don't think you're in a position to give me orders. Tell me, Irene. That is your name, yes? Irene Blum of the Brooke Museum in Seattle? Are you willing to include a pig in the deal?" The edge of his voice grew sharp, cutting through the stupefying heat of the room. "That's how we barter out here in the Chinese countryside."

Irene retrieved a cigarette from her pocket. Steeling herself, she walked up to Roger until she was no more than a few feet away. She forced herself to stand close to him and keep her hands steady as she held out the cigarette, giving him no choice but to light it. "So," she said, as an idea began to take shape, "it's true what they are saying about you."

Roger was leaning against the desk. He could not move away without pushing past her. "What do you mean?"

"You're becoming a liability."

"What are you talking about?" He glanced at Simone.

Irene's hand started to shake, and she lowered the cigarette to her side. She studied Simone, whose reaction she could not read. She took a few steps back, enough to claim a space of her own, hoping he could not tell from the heat in her face how much she feared him. "I've been asking about you around the city."

Roger said, "Do you think I am concerned with what the government has to say about me?"

Irene's mind was a machine, shuffling through every scrap she had acquired since coming to Shanghai. "I'm not talking about the government. I'm talking about people like Voitinsky."

Grigori Voitinsky was the Comintern adviser responsible for the formation of the Communist party in China. The hush that followed Irene's mention of his name was impenetrable. She was not sure who was more startled, Roger or Simone. Firmly she held Roger's gaze. She refused to break the silence.

"I'm curious," he said, finally. "How would you know what Voitinsky is saying about me?"

It was as if she had reached a clearing within the dense forest of her thoughts, an uncluttered expanse in which the lies simply waited for their turn to be told. "A good friend of mine, Marc Rafferty. Do you know him? An information man."

Roger's expression was taut. "The best. Works for Henry Simms. Of course, yes, of course. The Brooke Museum. Simms. You would know Rafferty."

Irene said, "Your stunt on the ship to Shanghai was noted, and not favorably. Trying to throw your wife overboard. You're irrational. Everyone knows you killed the baby."

Roger glared at Simone.

"Irene," Simone said, faltering, "what are you——?"

"She didn't tell me," Irene said. "She didn't have to."

"So Voitinsky is talking about me."

"He's worried about you, about both of you. Worried about what you might drive Simone to do. What revenge she might take. She could do quite a bit of harm, considering her involvement with Borodin's arms shipments." Irene drew on her cigarette. Her hand was no longer trembling. Roger appeared to be mulling what she was telling him. Perhaps these were not lies. Perhaps—inadvertently, instinctively—she had homed in on the truth. "But what if you send her away?"

"Why would I do that?"

"You could send her home to rest for a while. To recuperate. In the company of bodyguards, whom you will choose and I will pay for. It would be seen as more than a gesture of kindness on your part. It will mean that you put the cause above your personal feelings. This is what concerns Voitinsky the most."

Roger looked Irene over with disdain. "She won't come back."

"I wouldn't if I were her."

"You're smarter than I expected you to be." Roger began walking toward Irene. "But you're ignorant at the same time. Do you know how easy it will be for me to check on your story?"

"Be my guest."

"I do admire your audacity."

"The thing is," Irene said, "we are going whether you like it or not. You can benefit—or not. But if you kill her, you *will* take the blame. You won't have any choice."

He came closer still. "How is that?"

"I can't give away all of my secrets."

Roger was at Irene's side, standing so near that she could smell the oily pomade that slicked his hair. Only now did she see the leather holster wrapped around his belt. He was holding the walnut grip of a Colt single-action revolver. An American cavalry gun. A gun Irene had come across in more than one collection of firearms over the years. "Courtesy of Borodin, with my wife's assistance," Roger said. He slid the cold steel barrel down the length of Irene's cheek. "And if I kill *you?* I can do it right now, bury you here, and no one will ever know. Do you understand me?"

Winter entered the room. Frost coated her throat. She could not speak.

He shifted the revolver, pressing its tip into her cheekbone. "Do you still want me to let my wife go to Cambodia with you?"

The air was phosphorescent. Irene saw darts of light, nothing more. "Yes." Her voice was almost nonexistent.

"This is what is called point-blank range. At least you will feel no pain."

"Let her go," Simone whispered. "Please, Roger." She had made her way to the desk and was propped against it, using it for support. "I will beg you if that's what you want."

"How does it feel?" Roger asked Irene. "To have your life in my wife's hands? If I were you, I would be uncomfortable with such a situation."

Simone's weakness was evident in her every aspect, from her pale skin to her scrawny arms crossed tightly over her chest. But when she spoke, her words were as hard as iron. Holding her gaze steady on the gun in her husband's hand, she said, "Irene, move away from him. Slowly. Take the car and go."

"I can't leave—"

"You can. Please, do what I ask."

Irene took one step backward, certain that Roger would grab her, but for reasons she could not begin to fathom, he did not move. Slowly, slowly, her face slipped away from the gun. She took another step, and another, until she bumped against the door. Then she was outside on the porch, and the door was kicked shut behind her. The kerosene lamp had expired, and she shook as she felt her way down the steps, inching toward the car.

Cicadas seethed in the night. Her head dropped between her knees, and her breath came in rolling heaves, choking her until she was vomiting in the grass. With one hand she pulled her hair away from her face, and with the other she gripped the side of the car, as if it could keep the world from spinning. Finally, she stood up. She went back to the house, because she had no choice. She paused at the window beside the door. The curtain was loose, and through the gap she could see that Roger had shoved Simone against the wall. His hand cupped her chin, his fingers digging deep into the bruise. They were arguing, both of them talking fast and furiously at the same time. Irene could not make out what they were saying. The gun was on the desk. Could she get to it fast enough? And even if she could, she had never shot a gun before. She stepped away from the window, and as she pushed at the door, Simone screamed. Irene saw Roger fall backward, his hand clutching his throat. "You bitch!" he shouted, the words gargled.

"Run! Run, Irene, run!" Simone tripped over Roger, who was up on his hands and knees. He grabbed for the hem of her skirt, but the lace was delicate, and as she kicked out at him, it tore away.

Irene was already in the car with the motor running when she looked back and saw Simone's silhouette fastened into the brightness of the doorway. Then it pulled away, dissolving as she stumbled down the steps. She ran to the passenger side and climbed in, shouting, "Go!"

Soft earth spun from the tires, and Irene cursed the rain-soaked ground, her entire body tense as she put the car into reverse, rocking it backward, then pitching it forward, and then back and forth again until it lurched past the porch. She saw Roger in front of the car at the same instant she felt the collision. She stomped on the brake pedal. The clutch shuddered. The car jerked, and she was thrown against the steering wheel. The engine sputtered out.

"You hit him." Simone gasped. The shoulder of her blouse was dark with blood. She jumped out of the car and hurried around the hood, kneeling, disappearing from view.

Irene caught a flash on the floorboard in front of the passenger seat. She reached for the brass letter opener from Roger's desk. It was smeared with blood. She climbed out of the car.

In front of her, Roger lay on his side, with one arm flung out, as if he had attempted to stop the car from smashing into him. The headlights picked out the wire of his eyeglasses, curving down behind his ear. His face was the color of tallow. She could not see where Simone had stabbed him, there was so much blood running down his neck.

Irene looked until she found Simone on her haunches, balanced in the blurred space that separated the headlights from the darkness beyond. The grasses parted as Simone leaned forward, moving toward Roger on her hands and knees. She crawled cautiously around him as if she had been taken in by his tricks one too many times. She reached out for his face, but her hand dropped and she stroked the ground inches beyond where his cheek pressed against the damp earth.

"Is he alive?" Irene asked.

Simone held her fingers over his open mouth. They hovered there, splayed, searching for the suggestion of life. "There's a hospital near the railway station," she whispered. "It's run by Swiss nuns. They're discreet. It's where I stayed after I lost the baby."

The weary ghost of a far-off breeze crept around the car. It might have foreshadowed relief, but Irene had been in Shanghai long enough to know that the subtle shift in temperature was a promise that would not be kept. "What will we tell them?"

"He was already wounded," Simone said, sounding uncertain. "We didn't see him on the ground when you hit him with the car. It was an accident. We need to hurry. The hospital is half an hour away." She stood. Dew left dark stains on her skirt. "I keep a blanket in the trunk. We can use it to carry him." Focused on her plan, she ran behind the car.

Crouching beside Roger, Irene lifted his wrist. She pressed her fingers into his skin, seeking a rhythm in the limp tendons, clinging to him as if he had thrown his arm out to save her from drowning in a cold, dark sea. Did she want Roger Merlin to live? No, she did not. But that was entirely different from wanting him to die.

She could not find a pulse.

Chapter 7

The Other Side

The night was still dark. It felt as if it had been dark for years, as if the sun was never going to rise again. Using a candle, Irene found an aluminum pail and the pump outside the back door. She heated water on the stove in the small kitchen area, then dipped her dirty hands into the water and scrubbed them with a rag as hard as she could. When she finished, she gave the cloth to Simone, but Simone let it drop to the floor and held out her hands like a child. Irene took one in her own. It was cold and unyielding. She thought of Roger lying in the grass. Retrieving the letter opener from her pocket, she used it to scrape the blood from beneath Simone's fingernails, while Simone's tears dropped silently into the cooling water.

Irene was lying on a cot at the back of the bungalow. She was not awake, nor was she asleep, but somehow she had managed to detach herself from consciousness. She did not know how long she had been drifting or where she had gone, but she wanted to stay there, as far away as she could get from the events of the night. She tried to remain in this suspended place but was drawn out by the smell of coffee, her body betraying her as her stomach growled with craving. She stood. Her neck and back were sore from tension. Stretching, she walked to the coal stove, where a percolator simmered. She poured a cup of coffee and looked around the curtained room, at Roger's desk, at the loose pages of his memoir. His life's story interrupted, brought to an end in a way he could not have conceived. The coffee was gritty and too strong, but she relished it.

She found Simone sitting on the top step of the porch. The bungalow faced an unkempt field that was flanked by tall, leafy trees. The sky was hazy with morning mist, as the muffled rim of sunrise emerged over the horizon. Although Simone was gazing toward the front of the car, where Roger still lay, his body was not visible in the tall, sodden grass.

Irene wanted to offer solace, but she could think of nothing to say that would be of comfort. She could not imagine how Simone must feel, terrorized by her husband for so many years, and now faced with this. Finally, she asked, "Were you able to sleep?"

"I don't want to talk about this."

Irene sat down. "I understand."

"What do we do now?"

"We have to leave Shanghai."

"It will be too suspicious if I go away the day after he dies." Simone sounded so defeated. Was it because Roger was dead, or because she was afraid that now she would never get back to Cambodia?

"Not if no one knows," Irene said.

Simone fingered the torn hem of her skirt. "We're going to have to leave him out here, aren't we?"

The mist was dissolving, and the morning began to brighten. Irene appraised Simone's haggard expression and was sure that her own face was equally revealing. Even if they changed out of their muddy clothes and made themselves presentable, it did not seem that they could disguise their role in Roger's death. She said, "If we go to the police, there will be questioning. You have every reason to want him dead. Good reasons, but that won't matter. You'll be one of the top suspects. There could be a trial, and you know what Shanghai is like. The government will take great pleasure in tormenting you. Roger's put you through enough already. Besides, we don't have time for all that. If we leave him here, it could take days, even weeks for him to be found."

"Still, to buy a ticket to Cambodia on the day after he disappears."

Irene was surprised by how logical Simone was being. Just as she was surprised by how clearheaded she felt. "I already bought two tickets for the *Lumière*. It's leaving tomorrow."

"How could you have known?"

"I didn't. I bought them right when I arrived here. The *Lumière* was the first ship to Saigon I could book passage on." Finishing off the thick, bracing remains of her coffee, Irene said, "We're going to need an alibi for where we've been all night. For why I'm with you and why we're going to Saigon. Anne will help us. Come on, we have to get out of here."

Simone rose to her feet. She had aged a decade overnight. "Start the car," she said. "I just need a minute." When she emerged from the bungalow a few moments later, she was carrying a folder. Irene did not have to ask what it contained. She only hoped Simone would be smart enough to burn Roger's memoir before they left Shanghai.

"She's sleeping," Anne said, returning a syringe to a leather medical case.

"What did you give her?" Irene asked.

"Morphine."

"Isn't that excessive?"

"She's built up a tolerance to most everything else. Would you like something, darling? Song Yi brought back the loveliest hashish from Peshawar." Anne glanced at her jade opium kit set out on the bookshelf among her collection of Qingbai porcelains. "Or I can make you a pipe?"

Irene was too afraid of where a drug might take her right now. Closer, rather than far enough away. "No, thank you."

"How about some tea then?" Anne asked.

"Please." Despite the bristling heat of the day, Irene was freezing. She had been cold from the moment, standing in Anne's doorway, that she'd said the words aloud: "Roger is dead." Anne had simply nodded, as if this was to be expected, and Simone had started crying again. Now, having cleaned up in Anne's bathroom and put on a pair of her pajamas, Irene was suddenly aware of the chill crystallizing in her limbs, as it had when Roger pressed the gun to her cheek. She needed air. Sweltering, thawing air. She walked out to the balcony, followed by the green scent of boiling tea. Anne brought a steaming cup, wound in a napkin, and set the warm bundle on the railing.

"I'm having the hardest time walking back through this," Irene said, keeping her voice low so as not to wake Simone, even though she was asleep in the bedroom with the door closed. "Not just last night but these past days in Shanghai, the last months in Seattle, I'm trying to get back, do you understand, before I lost my job, before my father died. There's a path, there must be a path from here to there, but I can't find it. I can't make the connections." She covered her face with her hands, as if doing so could block out the vision of what had happened. "He held a gun to my head."

"I know you want to make sense of this," Anne said, "but you can't."

The city was achingly quiet, with the soup and noodle vendors in the lanes below idle between the busy breakfast and lunch hours. Overhead, the damp sky hung low and unpolished. "I should feel awful about what we did to him," Irene said, "but I don't. What kind of person does that make me?"

Anne guided her into a wicker chair. "You must let this go."

It seemed impossible to Irene that something like this could be *let go,* yet she felt as if she was going to be sick if she thought about it any longer, so she asked, "Where were you last night?"

Anne gazed beyond the balcony railing, down into the alley, where a shop leaned into the open shack next to it. A thin veil of sunlight reddened jars of snake wine and pickled duck eggs. She sank into a chair beside Irene and tucked her feet up on the seat, covering her toes with the hem of her dressing gown. "Why don't you tell me."

"You were with us," Irene answered.

"What were we doing?"

Irene had the strangest headache. The pain was new to her, a tightness that wrapped around her temples and pushed through to the backs of her eyes. She had to squint to bring the rooftops into focus. She had to breathe deeply in order to harness her thoughts. "Having a bon voyage drink. As far as you know, I came to Shanghai to talk to Simone about her father's work on Khmer trading routes. Digging through the archives at the Brooke Museum, I discovered new research on the subject."

In fact, this last part was true. While analyzing everything she had access to in relation to the reverend's diary, Irene had come across a file of letters from a Swiss botanist. He had casually noted a trail of stone markers that he'd encountered during an exploration of Ratanakiri province. The location of these markers fit neatly into conclusions Simone's father had drawn about commercial roads passing through northeast Cambodia. Because travel in even the most remote areas of French-controlled Indochina required a restrictive number of government-issued permits and requisitions, Irene had used all of this information to create a subterfuge— an expedition disguised as a scholarly search for historic trading routes. She added, "It's your understanding that I came to Shanghai to ask Simone if I could study her father's papers."

"And that's why the two of you are going to Cambodia?"

"Yes. After her parents' death, she left all of his work with the museum in Phnom Penh."

Anne reflected on this and then asked, "Why would Roger let Simone leave this time?"

"He was worried she might break down and do something that could harm the party. He had to pacify her, to keep her in line."

"I assume you want me to let this be known?"

"Roger came to you." Restless, Irene stood and retrieved the teacup from the railing, holding it tightly, savoring its heat. "Sending her to Cambodia was your suggestion."

"No," Anne said. "Roger would never come to anyone about Simone.

Not even me. I went to him because I was concerned about the cause. About the damage she could do if she was pushed too far."

"Is this far-fetched?" Irene asked.

"No more far-fetched than anything else that happens in this city."

Although Anne had put sugar in the tea, Irene could taste only its bitterness. The image of Roger, standing so close that she could smell the pipe smoke woven into the fabric of his shirt, sparked insistently at the edges of her thoughts. "Do you think he would have shot me?"

"Yes," Anne said, with sympathy. "And he would have thought nothing of it."

"Surely Mr. Simms must have known how dangerous Roger was."

"That's a reasonable assumption."

"I can't figure it out. Why is Simone worth putting my life in jeopardy?"

Anne looked back into the apartment. The bedroom door was still closed. "Have you told her you intend to take the scrolls out of Cambodia?"

Irene felt confined, hemmed in by the chairs and potted palms on the small balcony. "No."

"Don't you think she has earned the right to know? She killed her husband to save your life."

"She killed her husband to save her own life," Irene protested. "Anne, I have to get us on that ship tomorrow. I have to get us to Cambodia. I need your help, but if you're about to give me an ultimatum—"

"What if I am?"

"Then I hope we will never need an alibi."

"I only want you to think carefully about taking the scrolls out of Cambodia. If you are fortunate enough to find them, I want to know you've considered everything."

"I might be caught." Irene was frustrated that Anne would not let this go. "I might go to prison. I've thought about all of this."

"That's not what I'm talking about," Anne said, refusing to back down. "How are you going to explain what the scrolls are doing in Seattle? You want this discovery to be yours. You want everyone to know you found the scrolls in a lost temple in the jungles of Cambodia. But if they're in America, then everyone is also going to know you stole them. You might be forgiven. Probably even lauded. But what if you're not? The Great War has changed what is acceptable. You know that. All of a sudden, ethics matter, laws are changing, and the Stars and Stripes are leading the way. You're not thinking this all the way through."

In order to achieve what she wanted, Irene could not just discover the scrolls and then leave them in Cambodia. She had to have them in her hands. Among the many lessons she had learned from her mistakes at the museum: She needed proof. Taking the scrolls back to America was the only way to make anyone pay attention to her. The only way to make the trustees understand how much they had underestimated her. "Don't tell me I haven't thought this through! Thinking things through is what I do best," she insisted. She slammed the teacup onto the railing, and it cracked within its cloth wrapping. She looked defiantly at Anne.

"Oh, Irene." Anne's voice trembled. "I don't want you to leave here angry with me. You know I'll do anything I can to keep you out of harm's way. I have contacts, resources, but I can't protect you—"

"From myself?" Irene asked.

"I can't protect you once you leave Shanghai, no matter how good your alibi." She slipped her hand into the pocket of her robe and withdrew a gleaming object. She offered it on her outstretched palm.

Irene's fingers closed around it, and she felt as if she had captured a small steel bird. She aimed the coral-handled pistol at the distant murk of the Whangpoo River. It felt harmless in her hand. So different from Roger's revolver, the thought of which turned her body to liquid. The air around her had absorbed the river's industrial stink of coal and rotting fish. Across the water she saw the smokestacks of the Pootung district factories. She wondered how many belonged to Mr. Simms. She asked, "Have you ever regretted coming here?"

Anne gazed over the slanting rooftops below. "When I first arrived in Shanghai, I was enchanted by how it smelled of jasmine right before dawn. During the first months, I could barely sleep; I was afraid of missing that perfumed hour. At the same time, I was sure I'd made the biggest mistake of my life. I abandoned a decent husband, a comfortable home, the regard of my family. My father never forgave me. When he died, he had not spoken to me for eight years."

"Has it been worth it?"

"I'm thankful every day for that moment of recklessness. How else would I ever have made it to the other side?"

"What do you mean, *the other side?*"

"The place where one feels truly alive. Too many people surrender to a place of safety. That place where all they do is long to sleep so they can dream about living. Even if you don't find what you think you're looking for, darling, it's the going out and looking for it that counts. That is the only way you can know you have lived."

Irene persevered through the remains of the day, refusing to think about what had happened—what could have happened—with Roger. She returned to her hotel room, gathered her belongings, and paid her bill. Letting herself into Simone's apartment with a key that Anne had given her, she went to the bedroom to try to figure out what Simone might want or need, and discovered two trunks behind a screen. They looked as if they had been hastily packed, piled with the circuslike assortment of clothing that made up Simone's wardrobe. Irene secured the trunks, asked the landlord to send them to the dock, and gave him a forwarding address for the central post office in Saigon. It was important to do things publicly. She did not want it to appear that Simone was running away.

From Simone's she went to Marc Rafferty's. She had begun to wonder if she and Simone should hire a bodyguard, and he seemed the right person for this kind of advice. But the nightclub was locked, and when the Algerian watchman for the brothel across the street told her that Marc had already left Shanghai, she realized that she had not come for counsel. She wanted to see him again. Even though she could not tell him what she and Simone had done, she wanted the reassurance she had felt sitting with him in his bar.

Irene made it through the night with the help of a bitter herb from Anne's tall lacquer jewel case of narcotics, each of its drawers offering its own means of escape. When she woke on the morning of the *Lumière*'s departure, her head was filled with mud. The bungalow, the Chinese countryside, the body in the grass—all were buried so deep that she could not have dredged them up if she had tried.

A smoky drizzle dimmed the city, but it did not, as one would expect, cool the dawn hour. Instead, as Irene stood in line at the customs shed with Simone and Anne, heat percolated through the steaming air. She found it hard to believe that she was already leaving Shanghai. Hadn't she just arrived, standing on the deck of the *Tahoma*, admiring the Bund's massive stiff-upper-lip banks and trading houses? How impressed she had been by the respected names mingling shoulder to shoulder down the waterfront: Jardine Matheson & Co., Asiatic Petroleum, the Hongkong and Shanghai Bank. But that was before she learned how little respectability was valued in this city.

Simone, who had positioned herself between Irene and Anne, was wearing the most outlandish hat Irene had ever seen. Its brim folded and flopped around her face, and she had to hold on to Anne's arm like a blind woman whenever she walked. Occasionally she would lift the brim and peek around furtively, and comment on this man or that. "He's watching me, do you see that? They know it, they all know it, how dangerous I am."

Roger's death was undoing her. Of course people were gawking at her, or rather at her clownish hat with its trim of multicolored ribbons. They couldn't help themselves, the coolies loading cargo and the British soldiers standing guard. Even the beggars, limbs swaddled in strips of ocher-stained cotton, cast second glances, as did husbands saying goodbye to their wives and children, who would wait out the city's latest nuisance—a rash of kidnappings from which even infants were not exempt—in Hong Kong and Singapore.

Irene tried to think of any of these men as a threat, but she couldn't, and she knew that this was her shortcoming. She had underestimated the Brooke Museum's trustees. And she had underestimated Roger, even though everyone from the countess to Marc Rafferty had cautioned her. But it felt safe here on the docks, so routine, with the porters transferring luggage and the odor of roasting garlic seeping through the tincture of

drenched river weed. Even the American destroyers sent to protect Western interests seemed innocuous, drab as the overcast sky, surrounded by
sampans that looked as if they had drifted downriver from a previous
century. Sails the color of damp tea leaves drooped above the domesticity
of bamboo birdcages, sleeping cats, and limp, faded laundry.

Anne pressed a packet into Irene's hand. "Have her take this as soon
as she's in her cabin. If she doesn't want it, dissolve it into her drink."

Irene tucked the envelope in her pocket.

Anne's pale blouse was stained through with sweat, and her gray bob
was uncombed. But although her appearance was unusually careless, her
tone was not as she put her hands on Simone's shoulders and said, "You're
going home, my darling."

Solemn in spite of her hat, Simone said, "I'm going to make you proud
of me."

"If you need anything, anything at all, I will always be here for you."
Anne leaned in to kiss her cheek, and Simone hugged her. Blinking rapidly, trying not to cry, Anne said, "Be careful. I couldn't bear it if anything happened to you. Either of you." She let go of Simone and pulled
Irene to her. Instinctively, Irene stiffened before slowly reaching around
Anne's waist. Anne tightened her embrace. Up close she smelled of nut-
meg. Irene did not move. She did not want Anne to stop holding her.

"That man," Anne whispered into Irene's hair. "Near the noodle cart,
do you see him?"

"Yes."

"His name is Eduard Boisselier. If anyone has been sent to watch Simone, it's him."

Simone went straight to her cabin and took the sleeping powder without
resistance. There was enough left over for Irene, who was grateful to disappear into her own cabin and sleep for the rest of the day. When she
woke, the temperature had plunged. Headed for Saigon via Hong Kong,
the steamer had reached the open sea. Gone were the polluted, oily gray
waters of the Whangpoo, and with them the billboards advertising Tiger
Balm and chewing gum. The air through her open window smelled clean,

of cold water and salt. She wrapped a wool blanket around her shoulders and went outside. Her breathing constricted in the alkaline chill. Waves fanned against the side of the ship, and the gray phantom of a gull paced the wake. She leaned against the railing.

As she stared out at the water, a cloud fled, and a luminous flight of moonlight poured over the vast expanse of the East China Sea. Constellations spread across the sky and were absorbed into the curving retreat of the earth. It was as if while sleeping Irene had entered a new country, an unspoiled landscape invulnerable to the decay that lingered beneath the incense and jasmine of Shanghai. She held the letter opener over the railing and let it go. It sparked as it knifed the water. Marc Rafferty had said that you cannot know what a place like this does to a person until it has done it to you. Irene wondered how long it would take to discover what Shanghai had done to her.

Part 2

SAIGON

Our plan had been a slight affair, and quite vague: we talked about it so much that it assumed familiar shapes—far away in Cambodia there were huge flowers waiting patiently until we should come and pick them. Then suddenly, as though the sky had darkened, the adventure took on another form.

CLARA MALRAUX,
Memoirs

Chapter 8

The China Sea

The following morning, Irene entered the *Lumière's* meandering salon through a mahogany door with a porthole murky from years at sea. The steward greeted her with an invitation to join the day's bet on the ship's speed. She declined and scanned the room. It reminded her of the lobby of a hotel that had once been grand. The burgundy fleurs-de-lis on the carpet had faded, and the scuffed wooden floor showed through in patches. It was not even eight, but tables were already occupied by the ship's middle-aged set, fleshy European businessmen and their wives, who looked perpetually overheated, despite the foggy air. Dehydrated old colonials sat alone, reading newspapers they had brought from Shanghai, and a Chinese man dressed in a neat gray business suit had been seated off to one side by himself, the only Oriental in the room. Having scarcely eaten the day before, Irene had woken up hungry, but her appetite withered at the greasy smell of bacon and frying butter. She spotted Simone at a table tucked in the corner, staring out the window into the thick marine drizzle.

Anne had given Irene enough pills, powders, and vials of hennacolored liquids to keep Simone sedated all the way through Saigon and Phnom Penh and into the Cambodian jungles. But as appealing as that possibility was, Irene knew they must confront what had happened. It would not be easy, for even as she said good morning, she could feel the cold pressure of Roger's gun against her face. She could see Simone's hands coated in blood. There were moments when it felt as if that night would be superimposed on her life forever. She lit a cigarette, and with the timidity that follows the sharing of a profound intimacy, she asked, "How do you feel?"

"I can't say that I'm happy right now, but I no longer feel unhappy. May I?" Looking uncomfortable in her lavender blouse, such a demure item of clothing compared to her outrageous outfits in Shanghai, Simone took the cigarette from Irene. "Roger forbade me to do so many things," she said, inhaling hungrily, as if the smoke was a lost part of herself she was trying to recover. "I think you should know, Irene, that while it was happening, I was thinking about the temple."

Irene had expected Simone to avoid talking about Roger's death, and the bluntness of this statement surprised her.

"I hadn't planned to do it, I'm certain of that. But it was in my heart," Simone said. "I can't pretend I didn't want it. That it didn't feel good once it was done. When I cried, I thought at first it was because I felt regret. Then I realized it was because I had forgotten what it felt like to be free. Even though I knew I could go to prison, I was finally free." She studied the gray haze spiraling off the tip of her cigarette. "I'm not sorry. But you. I'm worried about you."

"Me? Why?"

"I'm afraid of what the guilt will do to you."

"Why would I feel guilty?" Irene asked, unsettled by how defensive she felt.

"If you hadn't come here, I wouldn't have killed him."

"Are you saying this is *my* fault?"

"You don't think you have any blame in it?"

Irene looked outside, at the fog thinning along the deck, revealing the outline of a life preserver secured to the railing. She had been so concerned about Simone's fragility that she had not considered her own. "I didn't mean to hit him with the car."

"And I didn't mean to stab him in the throat. I was flailing. Trying to keep him away from me." Simone opened Irene's cigarette case and examined its contents, even though she was not finished with the one Irene had given to her. "We killed him so we could find this temple. *We*, Irene. And I think that given the choice, we would do it again. *That's* what I need to know if you can live with."

"But we didn't go out there to kill him," Irene insisted. "We didn't plan on it. You said so yourself."

As the sun thawed the last smoky strands of fog, baring deep blue bruises of open sea, Simone said, "Be honest with yourself. It was in your heart too."

The first half of the voyage from Shanghai to Saigon passed with agonizing slowness. Each day Irene sat on a canvas lounge chair gazing out at the distant fringe of the Chinese shore, while Simone strolled idly around the deck, dragging the back of one hand along the railing as she passed beneath the balconies of the first-class staterooms on the level above. Overhead the twin stacks released tufts of smoke that wavered like low-lying clouds before evaporating in the cool air. With the smoke came the smudged odor of burning coal, its residue mingling in the dry white skim of salt that Irene washed from her face every night before bed.

Simone wore floral dresses with modest scalloped collars, a style similar to those common among the other young female passengers. This conformity was an obvious attempt to blend in, and it disappointed Irene, for she had enjoyed that particular eccentricity of Simone's. But she understood the necessity. In this floating bulwark of one-dimensional provinciality, Simone did not need help standing out. Everyone knew who she was and whom she was married to. To the financiers and military officers aboard the *Lumière,* a man like Roger Merlin was a natural enemy. To their wives, because marriage in the tropics is about loyalty—not to husbands but to an idea of civilization, often at risk of collapse from dengue fever or incompetent servants, let alone political upheaval—Roger was contemptible. As his wife, Simone was a blatant reminder of the threat to their colonial privileges and the status they could never achieve or afford in their homelands.

Only one passenger on the steamer showed any courtesy to Simone. Eduard Boisselier was the man Anne had guessed would be watching them. Approaching their table during lunch the second day out, he bowed with the courtliness of an earlier era before addressing Simone. "Bonjour, madame. Pardon this interruption, but I would like to introduce myself." He went on to praise an editorial that Simone had written in the *Shanghai Chronicle* about the frailties of the Comintern. "You have some clever ideas about new directions for the party," he said. "And quite unusual, considering what the paper usually publishes." He then asked if he might have the honor of strolling around the deck with her that afternoon.

In spite of knowing that he might be some kind of informant, Irene liked the way this elderly Frenchman flattered Simone. He made her laugh, and as the days dragged on, he gave her something to think about other than Roger. Simone had been born in Cambodia and Monsieur Boisselier in Senegal, but Irene overheard them comparing stories about France, conversing in the homesick patois common to those who lived in the colonies. Still, they had to be careful; Simone could become too friendly with him and, without meaning to, give something away about their plans or Roger's death. One morning before breakfast, Irene pulled her aside. "You should know, Anne thinks he's been sent to watch us," she warned.

Curtly, Simone replied, "Me. He's been sent to watch *me.* Did you think I wasn't aware of it?"

Simone's hostility was not unexpected. After their conversation that first morning on the steamer, a new tension had grown between the two women as they grappled with the fact that they valued the temple over a man's life. This would take some getting used to, this unrepentant truth—

the kind of truth one should not admit even to one's self, let alone share with another.

So while Simone and Monsieur Boisselier walked round the deck, Irene waited for the images of Roger's death to fade, in the same way the bungalow had receded in the rearview mirror as they drove away from the body stiffening in the grass. She could feel the possibility of going stir-crazy, stuck with her anxious thoughts as she waited out the days on the snail-paced steamer, and she sought the peace she'd felt while sailing with her father, doing her best to give her attention over to the sea. To the horizon, stable between water and sky. To the appliqué of whitecaps pleating the surface, luring the mind toward the calm depths below.

Then, gradually, as the mornings passed into afternoons, punctuated by the steady perambulation of Simone and Monsieur Boisselier, a routine that could have become plodding steadily took on significance. Each orbit made by Simone and her escort, although no different from the one that had preceded it, marked the voyage, taking Irene farther, and then farther still, from the vise grip of what had happened in Shanghai.

On the morning that the steamer was berthed in Hong Kong, Irene woke within the tide of a dream—of discovering a temple's fallen pillar in the scrub of a forest floor. As she sat up in bed, the feel of rough stone lingered on her fingers, and she thought about how, in a matter of hours, they would leave this harbor, and when they did, they would be closer to Saigon than to Shanghai. Saigon, the capital of Indochina and the gateway to Phnom Penh. This fact buoyed her, and perhaps it had infected Simone too. She was in good spirits as they sat down to breakfast, talking about looking up her old family servant Touit when they arrived in Cambodia. Touit, who had been as much of a mother to her as the woman she called "ma chère maman" had been.

It was the first time Irene had heard Simone speak of Cambodia in such a lighthearted way. As she pushed her crepe around her plate, she told Irene how Touit would chase her through the darkening ruins of the Bayon temple in order to give her a bath. "I hated coming in from playing out there. I remember one night, hiding behind the Terrace of the Elephants, listening to old Touit puffing over the stones shouting my name. I thought it was funny, but when she found me she told my mother, who gave her permission to punish me in any way she chose. She forbade me to go to the temples for a month."

Irene twined her fingers around her coffee cup, listening to Simone as she had once listened to her mother or Mr. Simms tell her the myths of the ancient Khmer. To her, the story of a servant named Touit chasing a little French girl around the ruins was equally magical. They were interrupted by a steward making his rounds, handing out newspapers just brought aboard. Irene had no interest in weeks-old news from home, but Simone picked through *The New York Times,* the London *Times,* and *Le Figaro,* claimed a copy of the *North-China Daily News,* and continued talking. "She didn't even allow me out for the lunar new year celebrations. I cried for so long I made myself ill."

Simone laughed at this memory and reached for her tea. It was then that Irene noticed the European woman at the table next to them, young but grown exponentially fat, no doubt from giving birth to the five children seated around her. She was holding her own copy of the *North-China Daily* and staring at Simone. Irene read the headline, COMMUNIST LEADER MURDERED!, and felt the scandal careening through the breakfast tables as faces turned toward them. Simone's downcast eyes were studying the headline on the paper beside her plate. Her face turned white as plaster. It was as if Roger's death had not been real until it was put into words and known by others. Simone grabbed her shawl from the back of her chair, and as she rushed away, newspaper crushed in her hand, the fat woman mumbled, "It's about time."

Irene stood. Everyone in the room was watching. She glared down at the woman. "Disgusting Alsatian brood cow," she snapped. She hurried after Simone, but Simone was faster and had locked herself in her cabin before Irene could reach her.

The optimistic spell cast by Irene's dream had been broken by the announcement of Roger's death. After pounding futilely on Simone's door, she took a copy of the *North-China Daily* to the salon and, under the watchful eye of more than one passenger, read a mélange of journalistic fact, opinion, and creative speculation. Roger Merlin's body had been found by a peasant in the countryside. He'd been stabbed in the neck, but before this happened, his arm and leg had been broken, the result of torture reminiscent of battering techniques used during the Opium Wars. There was a brief paragraph about his wife who was away. *Away.* That was all. This was not noted as unusual, and there was nothing accusatory in the mention of Simone, although the journalist described her as a victim who was "one of the situation's greatest benefactors."

Irene learned that three minor Municipal Government employees had been taken in for questioning, and that riots were seeping into the international districts. Envisioning the turmoil, she glanced up to see a table of mustachioed colonials watching her, and she was unnerved. All that was happening in Shanghai, every truth and lie being told in this newspaper, everything these old men across the room thought they knew but didn't, she and Simone had set it in motion.

The monsoon season was under way, and as the day progressed, a storm enveloped the *Lumière.* Chandeliers swung from side to side like the passengers staggering beneath them. The sea buckled and swayed, and although the worst was over by suppertime, few people came out of their cabins for dinner. The immense dining hall felt like an abandoned stage set. Only three passengers ventured to the captain's table in the first-class section. The White Russian orchestra was given the night off because the trombonist and drummer were seasick, and the vacuum created by the absence of music gave the wooden-floored room a forlorn echo. This, combined with the lack of people, made Monsieur Boisselier all the more unavoidable when he raised his hand toward Irene standing alone in the entryway.

He rose as she approached, and when he held out a chair for her, she saw the grooves where the tines of his comb had been dragged through his thin hair, yellow-gray from a lifetime of pomades. His face was blotched with age spots, and his nose was jagged amid his otherwise refined features. He smelled overwhelmingly of camphor, perhaps used for the arthritis that visibly affected his joints, and Irene was glad when he went back to his side of his table. "How is she?" he asked.

This was the first time Irene had spoken to him alone. "Distraught, as you can imagine. She should have been told before the newspapers were delivered. It was terrible for her to be caught so unaware."

"I must admit, Roger Merlin was a man I considered indestructible."

Irene abhorred secrecy when she was the one being kept in the dark, and she could see no harm in letting Monsieur Boisselier know that she was aware of his purpose. "Does this change things?" she asked.

"What do you mean?"

"Does this change what they think she might do?"

He looked bewildered, as if he were trying and failing to recall a conversation he and Irene might have had at an earlier time. "They?"

"The Communists, the Municipal Government, whoever it is that sent you to watch her."

"Interesting," Monsieur Boisselier murmured. He nodded to his half-eaten scallops of veal, languishing in a sauce of vermouth and cream. "Are you hungry? Shall I call the waiter?"

"No, thank you. Not yet." Determined to guide the old man to the answers she wanted, Irene asked, "Am I right? Are you a private detective?"

He laughed. "I like Americans. Very direct. May I ask why this would matter to you?"

Dismissing his amusement, Irene said, "I'm worried."

"Why?" he asked, as he poured her a glass of Bordeaux from the carafe beside his plate.

"My life's work." Taking a sip, she primed herself to practice the made-up tale she had been rehearsing since the start of her trip. "Khmer trade routes. I'm close to piecing together the major passage between Angkor Wat and Peking. I can't do it without Simone. Without her father's research."

"Well, you needn't worry about me any longer. My job is done."

"I don't understand."

"My employer has been murdered."

"Roger?"

"Now I have caught *you* off guard."

Irene could hear the dominance in his tone. She felt her self-possession slipping, and she tightened her hold on her glass, as if this could provide ballast. "How could he know we'd be on this ship? He was . . ."

"Dead?"

"The newspaper said he'd been dead a week by the time he was found."

"Direct, but so very innocent. You bought a ticket in her name the day after you arrived in Shanghai. Anyone could have told him. The entire city was on his payroll."

"Including you."

He took a swallow of wine. "I never should have agreed to half in advance and half once the job was done. I'm too old for this kind of work. But I needed that money. I have almost paid off a cottage in Dakar, right on the Atlantic. I had hoped to retire," he said, wearily.

It alarmed Irene that when she and Simone went to Roger's bungalow in the Chinese countryside, he had already known she'd bought passage on the *Lumière*. Had he told this old man about the temple? If so, Monsieur Boisselier could pass the information along to someone new for the final payment he needed. "What if I finish your contract?" Irene asked.

"How?"

"I will give you what you're owed if you tell me why Roger wanted Simone watched."

He shook his head at her presumption. "You don't know what I'm owed."

Irene's satchels were lined with cash that Mr. Simms had given her. How dare this man not take her seriously? "It doesn't matter. I can pay it."

Monsieur Boisselier examined Irene. With deliberation, he said, "I can assure you of one thing. He told me nothing about Khmer trade routes."

Irene took a sip of her wine, and then another, fighting her instinct to push him, sensing that one wrong word would shut him down.

He reached into his breast pocket for a gold case. Opening it, he offered Irene a cigarette, but she shook her head, intent on waiting him out. He set the case beside his plate, and his eyes never once left her face. Finally, he said, "He believed she was going to betray him."

"There's another man?"

"He did not mention a name, if that's what you're asking. Only once did he give a clue. He said, 'I always knew she would betray me for her first love.'"

When Irene left the dining room, she took with her new concerns: Monsieur Boisselier's possible knowledge of the temple, and now that Roger's death had been discovered, worry about what officials might ask of Simone once they reached Saigon. Even if they did not suspect her, their investigation would cause a delay.

Irene decided that she would not tell Simone about her conversation with Monsieur Boisselier. They had not talked at all about what needed to be accomplished once they reached Saigon or what lay ahead of them in the jungle, and she needed Simone's attention to focus on that. She would pay Monsieur Boisselier, buying his silence with the house in Dakar and then some, and when they reached Saigon, she would track down Marc Rafferty, who had said he was going there to visit his aunt on his way to Amsterdam. If he was as good at gathering information as he claimed, then he was the only one Irene knew who could help her find out what threat Monsieur Boisselier posed and if anyone else was watching Simone.

As Irene entered the corridor leading to her cabin, she saw Simone sitting on the floor outside her door. The wintry margins of the storm had pushed their way inside, and Simone wore denim trousers and a thick cable-knit sweater. The sweater's large, loose neckline revealed a frayed camisole and her winged collarbones. Its belled sleeves hung down below her fingertips. Despite the days spent strolling in brisk sea air, she did not look healthy. Unlike Irene, whose dark blond hair was streaked with light and skin was tanned, Simone had not benefited from the sun.

"I wondered if I would see you again today." Irene held out her hand to help Simone up. "I went to your cabin to check on you earlier. You didn't answer."

"I was trying to sleep." Simone followed Irene inside and stood next to the writing table. She tapped her fingers anxiously on Pierre Loti's *A Pilgrimage to Angkor,* which Irene had been rereading earlier that afternoon. Beside her, the curtain was drawn back, away from the porthole. The storm had worn itself out, and the sky had cleared of all but a lingering stream of transparent clouds. Moonlight reflected up off the plane of water and tunneled through the thick glass, casting a sheer hoop of light on the opposite wall.

"I want to sleep," Simone said, "but he won't leave me alone."

Feeling as though she were looking through the lens of an enormous telescope, Irene gazed out the porthole. In the distance, she saw the wink of a lighthouse, hovering at the rim of the night like a fallen star. She could feel Simone's emotional fatigue, and she sought to relieve it. "Let's not talk about him. Think about something else. Think about Cambodia. Tell me another story like the one about Touit."

Simone sat down once again on the floor, her back against the wall. "What is there to tell? She cleaned our house and cooked our meals and took such good care of me. She even loved me. And how did my parents reward her? Her salary was less than the pocket money I was given for simply being their child. There are reasons a revolution is necessary, Irene. I didn't believe in it solely because he told me to." Her hands tightened into fists. "I don't care what that newspaper says. It's not true. I am not a victim. I knew what I was doing. I have always known what I am doing."

"Who cares what a government sympathizer wrote about you? In the *North-China Daily,* of all tabloids."

"I have never done anything I don't believe is right. I will never do anything I don't believe is right. You must understand that, Irene."

"A story," Irene whispered. "Tell me a story."

"All right, yes, a story." Simone sighed, heavily. "After I would finish with my tutor, Touit would pack a picnic for me, bundles of rice and chicken wrapped in banana leaves. I would carry it out to the temples, and the best part of my education would begin. Do you know of Monsieur Commaille?"

"I do." Jean Commaille had been the first director of the Conservation d'Angkor, where statues and steles rescued from the temple were taken to be restored and studied. He was also credited with clearing the jungle away from Angkor Wat and Angkor Thom. He had been killed during an anti-French peasant uprising in 1916.

"I was his sidekick," Simone said with a small smile. "Sidekick, yes, that was what Monsieur called me, from the day he met me, when I was only four years old. He gave me my own scalpel, and he showed me how to scrape away the lichen from the carvings. He was like a surgeon, such precision. He could spend an entire day working on a meter of stone. That is such an important lesson for a child. Patience. Not that I was ever good at this. I am still a miserably impatient person. When the day became too hot, we would sit in the shade and eat mangosteens, and he would teach me to read Sanskrit, using the *Ramayana* and *Mahabharata* so that I would understand the legends from the bas-reliefs on the temples.

"I missed him greatly when he died. Monsieur Marchal, who took his place, was good enough at his job, but he didn't have time for children. Though I was no longer a child by then. I was almost fifteen." She pressed her head back against the wall, where it lay in a blue gauze of moonlight. "It was lovely, Irene, being there at the beginning, when it was all being discovered. I remember when France annexed the temples from Siam. My father was so excited he gave me my own glass of champagne. I was six, and as drunk as a sailor. My mother was furious!"

Irene had settled into the chair beside the bed. "I'm envious," she said. "I spent my childhood among fishermen and totem poles."

"What about the museum?"

"It was wonderful. But I don't think it was the same as having the real thing."

"It was enough to bring you all this way. I find your interest far more intriguing than mine. How can a child raised around the temples not succumb to their spell? They are a fairy tale set free from its page. They are the imagination sprung to life. I hate to say that I'm predictable, but aren't my feelings a natural result of my upbringing? But a girl from Seattle, how does she manage to fall in love with the Khmer?"

No one had ever asked Irene this. Not any of the curators or collectors she had worked with over the years. Not either of the two young men who had claimed to be in love with her years ago. She felt an uncharacteristic shyness as she said, "Before I was born, my father was a merchant seaman. Most of the wives stayed home, but my parents hated being apart for long periods of time. My mother came out to the Orient with him on one of his voyages, and she loved it so much, she stayed."

"In Cambodia?" Simone asked.

"No, Manila."

"What do the Philippines have to do with the Khmer?" Simone asked, her head tipped in genuine interest.

Intent on keeping Simone from thinking about Roger, Irene answered, "That's where my parents were based. My mother loved to travel, and my father took her with him whenever he could. Java, Malaya, Formosa, Cambodia. He even took her to Angkor Wat. I have some watercolors she did of the temples. They're beautiful. I can show you sometime if you'd like. When my parents were in Phnom Penh, she heard about the palace dancers. That their ballet was the most elegant in all the Orient. But the king was away and they had gone with him. She was disappointed. Then when I was nine, she read that the troupe was coming to dance in San Francisco. This was a year before the exposition in Marseilles. People speak of that performance in France as if it were the first, but it wasn't. I know. The first time they danced in a Western country, I was there.

"We took the train, the three of us. San Francisco was so loud compared to Seattle. And bright, I'd never seen so many colored lights, flashing everywhere I looked. I'd never stayed in a hotel before either, or gone to a theater. And I'd certainly never heard the words *opium* and *bordello*." She laughed, recalling her mother and father talking when they thought she was sleeping, as they sipped Sidecars from "room service," which was what they called drinks mixed from his portable leather cocktail kit.

"And the dancers," Irene whispered. "I remember how they flowed onto the stage, as if their bodies were the current of a river. There was a sound like seashells tumbling around inside a glass jar. It made it seem as if the entire theater was shivering."

"All of the silver on their costumes," Simone said, softly.

Irene was moved to see the significance of her memory reflected in Simone's expression. "I can still feel it here." She laid her hand flat over her breastbone. "My mother told me the dancers were the spirits of the *apsaras* in the Brooke Museum. They were a link between the human and the divine, and I believed her. A week after we got back from San Francisco, her appendix burst. A neighbor found her on our back porch. By the time I came home from school, she'd already been taken away."

Simone sat forward, wrapping her arms around her knees. "My parents were killed in an automobile accident."

The moon had risen higher, and its circle of light melted into a diffuse glow. The shadows no longer advanced with the reflection of the sea. "How old were you?"

"Sixteen. I had an aunt in Paris. She wanted me to live with her, but my parents were buried in Siem Reap. Whenever I thought about leaving, I would find myself thinking about the temples. About what happened to the stones when they were left to the jungle. How they disappeared and were forgotten. I was sent to boarding school in Saigon instead, and soon after that I met Roger. He saw me sitting in a café one day. I'd escaped from my classes. I was good at that, escaping and roaming around the city by myself. I had no friends. I was a strange girl. I'd begun to dress differently. A soldier's jacket over my school uniform or a derby given to me by a lecherous old man on a tram. It infuriated the nuns and embarrassed my schoolmates, but for me it was a form of camouflage. That's ridiculous, I know, since naturally it made me stand out. But somehow it gave me comfort," she confessed, looking down at her baggy sweater and trousers.

"It wasn't only my appearance that intrigued Roger," Simone went on. "He told me he'd never met such a melancholy girl before. He hated jolly women. And he thought I was incredibly smart. No one had said that to me since my parents died, and the nuns thought I was arrogant and discouraged me. Roger, though—with his brilliance and his refusal to apologize for anything he thought—he told me, *me*, that I was brilliant too." Simone pulled her fingers into her sleeves and tucked her bundled fists beneath her chin. "He shouted about everything all the time, Irene. I was so upset about my parents' deaths, but I couldn't even cry for them. I was afraid of what might happen if I did, of not being able to stop. But when Roger yelled, when he kicked the doors and walls, even when he hit me, I felt as if he were releasing the anger trapped inside me.

"It all happened quickly. By the time I was eighteen, I had left school and we were married, and when he decided to go to Shanghai, I realized that staying near my parents hadn't helped me. I hadn't been to visit their graves, and as time passed, it was too painful to even think about returning to the temples. Once we moved, I was so busy working for the party I was able to not think about them at all, at least for a while. But the party changed. Or maybe I changed. I gradually understood that Roger had never wanted what I wanted for Cambodia. Once I lost my daughter, the way I lost my daughter, suddenly I could think of nothing but returning to my homeland. Then," she said, "you came along."

The time had come. Irene could trust Simone. They were the same, each of them with a passion for the Khmer secured tightly atop her loss and grief. She crossed the room to the cupboard and switched on the lamp beside it. She unlocked the cabinet and then the box inside. "I want to show you something," she said. From the box she took Reverend Garland's map. She opened it on the floor and beckoned Simone closer. As they knelt over the map, Irene's finger followed the meander of the Mekong River from Phnom Penh up to Stung Treng and into the jungle of northeast Cambodia. "This is where we're going. To this village, Kha Seng, right here. This is where we're going to find the temple."

Chapter 9

A Trusted Colleague

On the third day out of Hong Kong, Irene saw the coast of Vietnam for the first time. It was mountainous and unpopulated, and she would not have known that the steamer had sailed beyond China if the steward had not told her. She sat forward in her deck chair, clutching the black coffee he had brought, and tried to tell the two countries apart. From a distance, one was as stark as the other.

The rugged mountains were wrapped in a deceptive haze that looked as cool as an autumn afternoon, but the sea air was hot and stiff enough to hold gulls aloft miles out from shore. The water was flat and seemingly impenetrable, as if saturated with ink. As they continued toward Saigon, Vietnam did not leave the ship's sight, the unbroken malachite fringe of it by day and the flickering of its lighthouses at night, until one morning Irene walked out on deck to see that the *Lumière* had broken free from the clinging embrace of the South China Sea.

The steamer had cruised into the tidewaters of the Saigon River, with its maze of tributaries like the *naga*, the mythological, many-headed snake worshiped by the Khmer. Faded violet flowers dappled the muddy estuaries, and low jungle spread out on all sides from the flat, marshy banks. The day was already hot, and although the steamer churned up a sluggish breeze, Irene's linen dress clung to the perspiration trickling between her shoulder blades. Rice fields, pagodas, and water buffalo gave way to factories, spewing clouds of dingy smoke that darkened the sky. Scattered between the godowns, the native huts hitched up on sapling poles did not appear strong enough to support their thatched walls, let alone the men and women squatting in the shade beneath. Naked children splashed in the water, waving without a hint of bashfulness as the steamer floated by. *"Vive la France!"* one boy shouted as he flopped into the water.

The hours passed, and the river curled around on itself, then back on itself again. It seemed to loop toward Saigon, where heat-ruffled spires approached and receded, shimmering from a new direction with each turn. At moments it was as if they were heading back out to sea, and then the ship would revolve one more time, stitching its way toward the city. As Saigon blazed into view, Irene thought about the camaraderie that had slowly deepened between her and Simone during the past days.

By showing Simone the reverend's map, Irene felt as if she had brought about a détente, an unspoken agreement to not talk about Roger—to not even think about him, for they were finally engrossed in the expedition. Monsieur Boisselier was no longer a necessary distraction for Simone as the two women pored over the reverend's diary, looking for a flaw. They found none. They reviewed their plans, how they would hire a car in Saigon to take them to Phnom Penh, and how once in Phnom Penh they would collect the supplies that Irene had sent ahead from Seattle and obtain permits and boat tickets for their journey up the Mekong River to Stung Treng. They discussed the threats of malaria, pit vipers, and tigers, and what it was going to be like to hold the scrolls for the first time.

Irene had examined dozens of expedition reports, and her list of what was needed was thorough. It contained not only the expected tents, mosquito netting, and quinine tablets but also items to help make their journey more civilized, such as a bucket shower and the kind of earthenware pot that could be converted into a campfire stove. She showed Simone her copy of Galton's *The Art of Travel*. It had been a gift from her father, and she cherished it for its wealth of information, from remedies for blisters and snakebite to instructions for finding one's direction by the growth of trees or shape of anthills. Listening to Irene discuss all of this, Simone declared, "*Très impressive*, and surprising, I must confess. Yes, Irene, you continually surprise me."

The only detail of her meticulous planning that Irene did not share with Simone was the one of which she was the proudest: an inconspicuous leather clothing trunk she'd had customized by Mr. Simms's tailor. It was lined with false panels large enough to hold and hide the ten scrolls. More than once she had wanted to show the trunk to Simone, knowing that she would admire its ingenuity. But although they shared the same dream, to uncover the history of the Khmer, and although they shared the same need, to use that history to take back the lives they had lost, after their time on the ship, Irene suspected that Simone would attempt to stop her from taking the scrolls out of Cambodia. Irene tried not to think about this, for when she did she felt guilty about lying to Simone.

As a tugboat nudged the *Lumière* toward its berth, Irene was joined on deck by Monsieur Boisselier. He leaned against the railing beside her and said, "I haven't seen Madame Merlin all morning. I was hoping I would have a chance to say *au revoir*."

Irene tapped the ash of her cigarette into the humid air. "I doubt she's eager to disembark." She nodded toward the wharf, where in front of the customs shed a thicket of colonials waited, nearly all of them dressed in white: jackets, trousers, and cork helmets reflecting in the sunlight. Vietnam's native Annamites milled around them, and among these barefoot rickshaw men stood a French police officer in a drab brown uniform and two European men with black cameras, hanging back, no doubt, for a better view. She said, "I've heard that reporters and a gendarme have been waiting since dawn."

"I suppose this means everyone is watching her now."

Irene felt sorry for Monsieur Boisselier, fidgeting with his watch, as pitiful as a beggar while he waited for the payment she had promised him. But his palpable concern gave her confidence that Roger had not told him about her temple, for if he knew, he would not need her money so badly. She reached into her map case for one of two envelopes she had put together earlier that morning. She handed it to him. It contained five hundred dollars. "Is that enough?"

As he counted the money, his expression showed that it was more than he had expected.

"Is there anything else you can tell me?" she asked. "Anything at all."

He gazed out toward the ocher buildings along the waterfront, punctuated by the jut of a steam crane into the white noon sky. Areca palms flanked the road, their fronds cutting welts of shadow into the sunlight on its paved surface. "This is only my opinion," he said, "but when Roger Merlin spoke of his wife's first love, I somehow had the feeling he was not speaking about a person."

"What do you mean?"

Monsieur Boisselier ducked his head, perhaps afraid that she would think him a dotty old man. "It's difficult to explain." He tucked the packet of money into his coat pocket before she could change her mind and take it back. Then, as if he felt he owed her at least a bit more, he said, "Do you know of Marc Rafferty? I have heard that he's here in Saigon. If you are looking for information, he's your man. Perhaps he can tell you why Monsieur Merlin was having me watch his wife."

As soon as Irene saw Simone striding toward her, cigarette in hand, a white orchid trailing through her upswept hair, she knew how they were going to do this. They were not going to skulk into Saigon. They were going to arrive with nothing to hide. All eyes were on Simone as she crossed the deck. The Chinese robe she wore over her black shirt and trousers gave her an air of royalty. It was impossible not to pay attention to her, a flash of cobalt among the white, beige, and khaki traveling clothes of the other passengers. But it was more than the way she was dressed that caused people to watch her. They wanted to know what was going to happen the moment she stepped into Vietnam. Would she be accosted by the reporters and asked the question everyone wanted to know the answer to? *Do you know who killed your husband?* Would she be detained by the police? They were longing to break up the monotony of their own dull arrivals and, better yet, to see if Simone would be brought down a peg.

Inside the customs shed, a row of officials sat behind a counter processing documents. The tin roof radiated streaks of thick, rippling heat, and the men were soaked with sweat, their hands so damp that they used scraps of muslin to blot moisture from their fingers each time they picked up a pen or stamped a page. As the Oriental passengers, even those from first class, were plucked from the line to show proof of vaccinations to the port doctor, the eldest of the officials examined Simone's paperwork. The skin around his eyes was furrowed, as if he had been squinting at visas in this gloomy light all his life. Irene watched him over Simone's shoulder. The man seemed to be taking an unusually long time. Then, as if he were holding himself in check, he said, tersely, "So, here you are. Madame Merlin. Already a journalist has offered me a bribe to detain you so he might have the first interview. And it is my understanding that the *commissaire* himself has set aside his day for you. But do not take this to mean you are wanted here."

Simone looked confused, as if she had genuinely expected a warm welcome.

"You *are* a traitor after all."

It was such a bald attack. Irene glanced at the customs agents processing passports on either side. They were pretending that they were not listening, but the nearby passengers were not even trying to hide their interest. The exchange would certainly be dissected over absinthe frappés in the nightclubs that evening.

"And you," Simone hissed so everyone could hear, "are a petty, powerless bureaucrat."

A stately colonial standing in line behind Irene barked with laughter. It was now the official's turn for bewilderment. He had not anticipated this defiant response. "I have power enough to keep you out of this country."

Simone glared at the official. "People like you are the reason I joined the Communists. You are the reason the French are going to lose Indochina. How satisfying it will be, watching you scuttle back to Europe with your tail between your legs."

Although Irene admired Simone's gall, bravado was one thing and stupidity quite another. She stepped forward. "Regardless of what you thought of Roger Merlin, monsieur, he was her husband and he has been killed. Brutally killed. She is distraught. A gentleman like you, surely you can forgive—"

"Distraught!" Simone cried. "I'm not distraught. I'm insulted. How dare this puny man treat me like a pariah!"

The official was furious. He folded Simone's paperwork and shoved it back to her. "Since I am merely a powerless bureaucrat, perhaps it would be best to leave you in the hands of the inspector. Come with me."

"You can't detain us," Simone protested, refusing to follow. "This is my birthplace. What are you gaping at?" The woman Irene had called an Alsatian brood cow was grinning at Simone's misfortune as one of the agents stamped her passport. "This is not a carnival. This is my life."

Simone's voice plunged dangerously, and Irene quickly saw that she was no longer feeling courageous. She was panicking, terrified of not being let in, of being exiled back to Shanghai. Irene took her by the elbow and ushered her after the official, into a hot cubicle of a room that contained only a bench running along one wall. The official stood in the center with his arms crossed over his chest. He said, "I will let you know when the inspector arrives. He should not be more than an hour or two."

Irene was exasperated. Roger was dead. She and Simone had paid their dues. Without even bothering to cajole the man, she held out the second envelope she had prepared.

He said, "I have already turned down one bribe today."

"It can't hurt to have a look."

He raised his chin, refusing.

Irene opened the envelope herself. As she fanned the bills out, the official was unable to hide his interest. This was a small fortune—the amount she would have given Monsieur Boisselier, had he known to ask for it. She could see the man debating. Folding the money back into the envelope, she walked toward him. She slipped the envelope into his jacket pocket. Without a word, he left the room.

"What if it's too late?" Simone asked, fussing with the trim on her robe. "What if this is too much for him?"

Irene was troubled by how easily Simone had fallen into a state of agitation, but there was no time to ask who *him* was or to calm her down. If the official's anger had a chance to smolder, who knew how long he would keep them confined? "Come with me," Irene said.

"Where?"

"Saigon."

Taking Simone's arm, Irene guided her back to the counter, where she smiled politely at a young English couple who had reached the head of the line. "Pardon me, but we weren't quite finished." She set Simone's maroon-covered Union Française Indochine passport down in front of the offending official.

The man lowered his eyes. A bead of sweat slid down his cheek and dropped onto the paper, blurring the ink. Beyond the counter the shed swarmed with coolies, grunting with the effort of lifting and stacking luggage. The air smelled of sweat and cowhide. With measured slowness, the official pressed the black stamp into the page so hard that the approval was illegible.

Before he could retract his decision, Irene grabbed the passport and gave it to Simone. She waited for her own to be stamped, and then she followed after the red phoenix that rose up the back of Simone's robe. As she watched Simone step into the margin of sunlight coming through the open door, a prickle of wet heat swooped over her skin—the quick, voluptuous fever that comes before a person faints.

This is it, she thought. The moment I enter this city, Cambodia is less than a day away.

———

Simone walked quickly past the mounds of hat cases, valises, and Louis Vuitton wardrobe trunks, heading for the fence that separated the customs yard from the waiting crowds. She wrapped her fingers around the timber slats and peered into the street. With relief she said, "There he is, right there."

Simone spoke as if Irene should know what she was talking about. Methodically, Irene examined the crowd. Beyond the cluster of colonials, the border of half-naked rickshaw drivers shifted in expectation of fares to come. Farther out, drivers of Peugeots and Chevrolets smoked and chatted to one another. Irene did not recognize anyone. "Who?" she asked.

"Over there, by the woman in the red hat."

Next to the matron, a man was leaning against the trunk of a plane tree. He was young, in his late twenties at the most, his body lean in a typical tropical suit. He was separated enough from the crowd so Irene could see that below the cuffs of his white pants, he wore heavy boots with thick soles more suited to the wilderness than to the city. "Who is he?"

Simone's face was flushed. "Louis Lafont."

"Really?"

"Yes." Simone laughed. "Really."

The assistant curator of the Conservation d'Angkor, Louis Lafont was an expert on anastolysis, the process of dismantling a structure for study and then returning it to its original form. Without his work, Irene never would have understood the architectural techniques of the Khmer. "My God, what's he doing here?"

"I asked him to meet me."

Heat rose off the pavement, and in places the sunlight was so bright on the sidewalk that Irene expected to hear it sizzle. "Why didn't you tell me?"

"What if he didn't come, Irene? It would have been too embarrassing. You would have thought I was a fool."

"Why?" But the moment she asked this, Irene recalled Monsieur Boisselier's words about Simone's first love. Then she immediately thought, No, too easy. If there was one thing she had learned in the last few weeks, it was that nothing about Simone was easy.

Oblivious to Irene's question, Simone rushed out of the customs shed. The instant she emerged, her blue robe billowing, the two French reporters swung around in her direction. Louis saw her and darted through the snag of cars and rickshaws. Even before he reached her, he was holding out his arms. As she fell into them, the air clicked with a camera's shutter.

"Lafont! Hey, Lafont, over here!" shouted the taller of the reporters, a swarthy man whose tone was as insolent as the tilt of his hat. "Is it true that you threatened Roger Merlin's life when Madame Merlin broke off her engagement with you?"

Simone had mentioned nothing about being engaged, nor had she said a single thing about Louis Lafont the night she and Irene had confessed their lives to each other on the *Lumière*.

"Madame Merlin," called the second reporter, using his compact bulk to push past the first. "Chiang Kai-shek himself has said you once told his wife you wanted to hire an assassin to kill your husband." With an attitude as conciliatory as the other's was impertinent, he asked, "Would you like to comment on this?"

"Who has not wanted to hire an assassin to kill my husband at some time or another, you unoriginal little . . ." Simone searched for just the right word and then spat it out with venom. "Hack!" Although the insult continued, it was muffled as Louis pressed Simone into the backseat of a silver and black sedan.

Cringing at Simone's imprudence in rising to the reporters' bait, Irene struggled against the congestion that was growing around the car. In her attempt to skirt it, she was caught in a flurry of sailors whose voices rang with accents from around the world. Red pom-poms flopped on their military caps as they scurried toward their ships near the barracks farther down the waterfront. Elbowing through them, trying to reach the sedan before the gendarme, whom she had spotted pushing past the two reporters, Irene started to panic. How were they going to slip into the jungle undetected with so many people watching them? Beyond a cluster of nosy onlookers, she saw the gendarme shove a paper at Louis and heard Louis firmly declare, "The *commissaire* can wait until tomorrow. Madame Merlin needs her rest."

Irene managed to get to the car and climb into the front passenger seat, beside an Annamite driver who already had the motor running. As she slammed the door shut, Louis said, "Tuan, take us to the hotel."

The swarthy reporter in the hat noticed Irene. "Mademoiselle," he yelled through the closed window as he grabbed onto the side-view mirror. "For you." He was waving a handful of piastre notes. "For an exclusive interview about your time on the ship with Roger Merlin's widow."

"Ignore that lout. Whatever he offers, I'll double it," bartered the shorter, more mannerly newshound.

"I can make you famous," promised his rival as the car pulled away, wrenching the mirror from his hand.

Despite the inescapable curiosity of the passengers on the *Lumière*, Irene had felt sheltered on the ship. But here on land, it was as if she had become part of an exhibit, captured and displayed. The small triumph with the customs officer faded into exhaustion, and she wanted all of this to go away. The gendarme wielding the summons from the *commissaire*. The reporters with their insistent accusations. The mystery of Simone's "first love" followed by the unexpected appearance of Louis Lafont, who would most certainly want to know why they were going into the jungle. To bluff him with her story about an ancient Khmer trading route would be an interesting challenge, but she did not have the energy to think about that right now.

As the docks receded, Irene rolled her window down, but the air felt as if it were being pushed through a furnace. It was that merciless equatorial hour that circled around noon like a vulture, when no alternative, not even hiding in a dark room with an electric fan, could bring the kind of relief a person needed, a relief that reached one's core.

Beneath the sun-speckled tunnel of tamarind boughs that arched all the way to the cathedral, the Rue Catinat was deserted. In Seattle, midnight to dawn were the silent hours. In the tropics it felt as though the days were turned inside out. Irene gazed at silhouettes of hammocks that looked as if they had been painted into shaded doorways. There was not a single European on the street, and the Orientals seemed to have collapsed wherever they had been standing when the sun reached its apex. In an open-faced shop beside a stack of raw silks, a Hindu slept atilt on his haunches. Underneath a plate-glass window displaying a beaded black gown, a naked child lay sprawled facedown on the sidewalk. He wasn't even on a mat, and if Irene had not become accustomed to such sights in Shanghai, she would have thought the boy was dead.

The car passed the palatial residence of the governor-general and traveled into what Irene knew from having studied the city's maps was the neighborhood of Cirque Sportif. Here, villas were set back from the boulevard, as the homes of the wealthy always are. The chauffeur drew the car up to the Petit Hotel du Cap-Ferrat. Like shoals of amethyst fish, bougainvillea swam up the walls. One of the lower balconies was tangled in the branches of a mango tree, and Irene could imagine the sanctuary of the room behind it.

A soup seller sat near the gates, asleep in a patch of shade. His sloped woven hat shielded his face, and his palm-leaf fan had fallen to the ground. Steam simmered from the clay pot at his side. After more than a week on the *Lumière,* far from the tang of an Oriental street, Irene felt the urge to be enveloped in spice. While Louis helped Simone from the car, Irene walked over to the vendor. Breathing in the scent of fish drifting on a current of lemongrass and star anise, she felt her strength begin to return. And it amazed her that somehow, despite how this part of the world wearied her, it also gave her sustenance—just to stand in the middle of it, sheltered from the midday sun by the flaming petals of a coral tree.

As Irene's and Simone's baggage was delivered to the hotel, Louis apologetically explained that he was obligated to attend a meeting and dinner with Murat Stanić, one of the conservation's patrons. Once he was gone, Irene wasted no time in asking Simone why he had been waiting for her here in Saigon. But as Simone watched him drive away, she refused to answer. For the better part of the afternoon, she brooded on the window seat in Irene's room while Irene tried not to think about the latest delay: having to wait for Simone to be questioned by the police.

Finally, Simone roused herself and declared that she wanted to show Irene the teahouses and gambling parlors in the Chinese district of Cholon, places she had skipped out of boarding school to visit when she was a girl. But all the while, as their electric trolley passed autobuses, rickshaws, and boats stacked with paddy, plying the putrid canals, she complained about Stanić, who had arrived unexpectedly in Saigon the day before.

"That man. Bah! So annoying," she declared, stepping down from the trolley and onto a raised wooden sidewalk where traders wearing red fezzes changed money from open booths. "He *would* appear on the day of my reunion with Louis. He has always been a nuisance. A pedophile too, you know. He gets his girls from the local orphanages."

"I know. Everyone knows," Irene said, as irritated with Simone as Simone was with Stanić.

A Serb, Stanić belonged to the exclusive coterie of men, Henry Simms included, whom every archaeologist and museum curator feared for what they might purloin, but ultimately needed for what they were willing to finance. He happened to be the man with whom Irene had negotiated to obtain the empress dowager's ring for Anne. He was also funding two of Louis's most important restoration projects. Irene knew Louis could not afford to ignore Stanić's dinner invitation. "You seem to forget, Simone, he makes Louis's work possible," she said.

Simone marched around a woman serving pressed pork out of baskets that hung like scales from the ends of a bamboo pole. Indignantly, she said, "There was a time when Louis would not have put me second even if God Himself had invited him to dinner."

"You still haven't answered my question. Why couldn't you have waited to see Louis until after we found the temple?"

"I had my first bowl of shark-fin soup in that restaurant," Simone evaded, pointing across the street. "And I learned how to play mah-jongg right next door." She stopped in front of a shop set into a row of balconied, French-style buildings. Its wooden plaque read OPIUM MERCHANT in six languages. The odor swelling from the open door gave the air a sweet, drunken tilt. Through shreds of smoke, Irene saw an old man, his skeletal chest bare, lying with his head on a majolica pillow as he waited for an ivory pipe that was being prepared above an open flame by a boy no older than ten. Gazing in with longing, Simone said, "Perhaps we should take a little rest."

"Answer my question."

Stubbornly silent, Simone moved on, into a lane that felt narrower than it actually was because of all the men and women, children and grandparents, crowding out of their homes as the sun went down. The air was clouded with a vapor, from incense, fowl roasting on charcoal braziers, and yet more opium dens. Eventually, she entered a pharmacy. Its windows were stacked with dark brown pods and swallows' nests, and in the center of it all rested the jawbone of a tiger. As Irene followed Simone inside, she caught her breath against the rank peat smell of old mushrooms and wet grass that came from the baskets.

Simone reached into one of the containers and held out a scaly tuber that resembled a piece of ginger. "Turmeric," she said. "If you make a paste of this, it's good for the skin. Helpful for jaundice."

Irene took it from Simone and put it back in the bin. "You can't ignore me."

Doing just that, Simone greeted the shopkeeper in Mandarin. He returned her greeting with a slight lowering of his whiskered chin. He was indifferent to her knowledge of his language, and to her odd black suit with its magenta cravat and stovepipe trousers, funneled into a pair of button-up Victorian boots. While she talked he retrieved twigs and petals from jars and basins until a dozen piles lay on the counter, like a collection amassed by a boy after a day spent exploring in the woods.

Simone pointed to one of the piles. "This is for insect bites, for the itch. And it's an antiseptic. This one here, it's for fungus. You will not recognize your feet after the first few days in the jungle, but this will help more than any of the creams you can purchase from a Western doctor." She picked up a fernlike lace of dried leaf. "Sweet wormwood for malaria. Louis has had malaria. He'll take quinine since he doesn't have the faith in Chinese medicine that I have, but I will bring this anyway. He doesn't have to know what I put in his tea."

Irene tried to grasp what Simone was saying. "What are you talking about?"

Simone supervised as the shopkeeper bundled each mound into its own brown paper packet. "Once you've had malaria, it never goes away, but there are precautions you can—"

"Louis is going with us?"

"Of course."

"Absolutely not! No!"

"What do you mean, *no*?" Simone asked with indignation. "We need him."

"What in the hell have you done?"

With her back to the shopkeeper, Simone said, "I thought you'd be thrilled. You have no practical experience. He can make this much easier for us."

"I know what I'm doing."

"Anyone can make lists, Irene."

Ambushed by Simone's scorn, Irene frantically searched for an argument to prove her wrong. "You saw me with Roger. He believed me, Simone. He believed that story I told him."

"Then he pulled out a gun."

"And the customs agent. He took that money. It was easy. I have enough money to buy off every official in Indochina. I can give you an envelope for the *commissaire* tomorrow if you need it."

Simone extended a banknote toward the shopkeeper. She murmured *"xie xie"* and swept her purchases into her leather shoulder bag. Tugging at Irene's sleeve, she hurried outside. "You can't say things like that in public. Half of them only pretend they don't speak English, and half of that lot work for the government. Everyone is watching everyone. And let me tell you something, Irene, each time you give someone a bribe, you create suspicion. If you're handing out money wherever you go, it becomes evident that you have something to hide. Can't you see that Louis will give us legitimacy?"

Irene jerked free and sidestepped a black pool of blood hemorrhaging from the threshold of the butcher's shop next door. She dodged past the lacquered duck carcasses hanging off hooks from the eaves, and looked away from the nauseating sight of varnished pigs, sitting on an outdoor tabletop like children's toys from a horror tale. "Men appropriate everything," she said. "They take it all as if they have a right to it, but not this. Not this time! I won't let Louis have what's mine."

Taking refuge in front of a sundries shop, where sidewalk shelves were stacked with turbans and bamboo calendars, Simone retrieved her Gitanes from her pocket. She held out the blue packet, but Irene's eyes were burning and her throat was singed from all the smoke in the air. "You didn't even ask me," she said, shaking her head.

"I'm asking you now. I'm asking you to be reasonable. Think about our situation. Two women, one whose husband has recently been murdered, traveling alone into the jungle. What would we be doing other than running away? Irene, Louis is respected in Indochina. He's a trusted colleague. He has carte blanche access to every corner of Cambodia. He can come and go as he pleases and take whoever he wants with him. I don't understand your resistance. Did you really think we could do this on our own?"

"Yes," Irene said. "I did."

"What would give you that kind of assurance?"

"You."

"Me?" Simone sounded surprised. "Why?"

Irene was dismayed by the sudden doubt she felt. She coughed against the smoke that surrounded her, but this didn't clear the uncertainty from her voice. "You're an expert."

"I'm an expert on Khmer hydroengineering. On Sanskrit. On the *Ramayana* and *Mahabharata* and Marxism and labor leadership. I'm unquestionably an expert on bad marriages. But on finding lost treasures? Roger and I took a bas-relief *once* because we had the chance to pay off the debts for our newspaper." Simone turned away from Irene and surveyed the wares piled on the plank shelves. She touched the laces on a pair of white Keds tennis shoes and muttered, "Fakes. The Chinese can copy anything. Don't ever buy a Waterman pen in Cholon." She dug her hand into a tub of slippers, a jumbled bouquet of fire red poppies embroidered onto blue silk, and pulled out a pair. "We need Louis more than you can know. I didn't want to tell you this, but I suspect Monsieur Boisselier was sent by Roger. Roger could have told him about the temple."

"I know."

Simone's grip on the slippers tightened. "How?"

"I asked him who he was working for."

Simone laughed. "You don't know how anything is done here. No one asks questions like that."

Irene was slowly regaining her footing. "I did, and he told me that Roger hired him."

"You think you're quite shrewd, don't you? In that case, you should understand why we need Louis."

Unfortunately, Irene could see the logic of including him. She could even see the necessity. But his presence would make it harder than ever to get the scrolls out of Cambodia. "I shouldn't have showed you the map," she said. The trust she had felt in Simone on the ship was dissolving. "Now that you know where the temple is, I have no choice."

She waited for Simone to deny this, but Simone's attention was diverted by a trio of singsong girls trotting past. With their colored stockings, satin mules, and black satin trousers that came barely below the knee, they had drawn the clucking disapproval of the old woman guarding the merchandise. Simone just gave the shopkeeper a few coins for the slippers she was holding. "For you," she said, offering them to Irene without looking at her. Quickly, she began walking back to the trolley.

Chapter 10

The Right Dress

.

The following morning, Irene sat at Brodard's restaurant on the Rue Catinat, drinking café au lait and jabbing at a poached egg. Simone was at the police station. She had insisted on going alone, and there was no telling what she would say or do if she was pushed. If this was not enough to worry about, once this wasted day was done, Irene would be having dinner with Louis Lafont.

Irritably, she thought back on the previous evening. After returning from the Chinese district, she had tried to keep Simone with her. Irene was hoping she could wear Simone down into admitting the real reason why she hadn't told Irene about her plan to meet up with Louis, but she had not been able to stop Simone from retreating to her room. Taking up a post in the hotel salon behind the day's newspaper, Irene eventually observed Louis arrive from his dinner with Murat Stanić, and a few minutes later, as soon as she entered the upstairs corridor, she knew that he had gone to Simone's room. She could hear Simone shouting at him for leaving her all alone to explain things to Irene.

At the sound of her name, Irene grew still, but as if Simone sensed her nearby, her voice dropped, and Irene heard nothing more. She went back to her own room, troubled. She could do no more than guess at what Simone and Louis were to one another. Old flames, if what the reporter on the docks had shouted was true. But what did that mean now? The only connection Irene was sure of was that they were both from Siem Reap and had grown up around Angkor Wat. Lying in bed, she could easily imagine the claim Louis must already be staking as Simone told him about the lost temple.

Now, even the morning air was making her uneasy, lank with a gauze from poppies stewing in the opium factories on the river. Irene watched the Hindus setting up their stalls so they could spend another day selling tobacco, and the dozen or so Europeans at the tables around her, all dressed in white as if they were the chorus in some colonial Greek tragedy. After the commotion at the docks the previous day, she had steeled herself for another intrusion by the pushier of the two reporters, or perhaps a gendarme assigned to keep an eye on her. Instead, she was sitting out in the open, completely unobserved, and this made her uncomfortable, as if something were being plotted behind her back at the police station.

Irene knew she was being paranoid, but she'd been thrown off balance by the past twenty-four hours. She and Simone should have been on their way to Cambodia. Instead, she had the entire empty day ahead of her. She could try to track down Marc Rafferty, but she still wasn't sure why she wanted to see him. To find out what she was up against, or was that an excuse because she had been attracted to him in Shanghai? If the latter, she could not afford the distraction. She was annoyed with herself, for letting her emotions override practical need, and she decided, as she finished breakfast, that the most productive thing she could do was shop. She had sorted through the wardrobe she'd brought with her and had not found a single item appropriate for dinner with Louis. He needed to understand, with no room for discussion, that she was in charge. She had long ago discovered that wearing the right dress was one of the easiest ways for a woman to take control of a situation.

The Rue Catinat, she knew, was Saigon's equivalent of the Rue de la Paix, the most fashionable of Parisian shopping districts. Walking beneath the branches of tamarind trees, heavy with brown pods, she studied windows rich with Delphos tea gowns, strings of Venetian beads, and opera capes of gold lamé. But none of it felt right to her. It all seemed intended to distance a woman from the Orient, where alleys between the marble façades of jewelry and fur shops displayed brass gods and Tonkinese embroidery. The darkened interiors of these side lanes were hung with red paper lanterns that made them resemble small temples. Irene's intention was not to isolate herself from this real Indochina. She wanted to appear as if she belonged to it—deserving of the part of it that would soon belong to her. Finally, she entered one of the shops and hoped that the proprietress would understand her request.

The imperious, slouch-bosomed Frenchwoman in charge of the boutique did not. She insisted that Irene try on the requisite white of the tropics—flared skirts with hems to the ground, daring skirts with hems that quivered at the knee—but they all made her feel like a character in a nursery rhyme, as if she should have been tending a flock of sheep. The madame then pulled out every color of the rainbow, and Irene hated them all, especially the "à la mode" Kelly green. "I look like a wealthy leprechaun," she said, frustrated. "Madame, you are not listening to me. I want something Asiatic. If you don't have anything like this, tell me and I can try somewhere else."

Equally frustrated but unwilling to spurn a sale, the madame ordered her Chinese shopgirl into the back room. The girl scuttled out with a tumble of smoky black silk and unfurled it on the counter. The moment Irene saw the ice-blue beads, fire-polished glass the exact color of her eyes, sewn into the mandarin collar, she knew she had found what she wanted.

"It was made for a *fête costumée,* what you English call a masquerade ball," the madame said with censure, while Irene drew the curtain on the dressing area. "My customer changed her mind once she tried it on. As you will see, it is not suitable for a European."

The costume was not a dress, although the tunic and trousers could be mistaken for one, especially at night. It was a variation on the traditional outfit worn by Annamite women. Instead of long, tight sleeves, the fabric formed caps over Irene's shoulders, like the petals of a lotus bud. The tunic hem fell to her calves and was slit up the sides to a pair of Chinese button knots at the hips, exposing the flow of the trousers with each step she took. As she turned away from the mirror and stepped out of the dressing area, the madame's face bore the kind of disapproval Irene had hoped to see.

This was the sort of outfit that could not be worn by the matronly Western women who frequented this store. It was made for an Oriental woman, or for Irene, whose body was slender and lithe. It gave superiority to its wearer, but only if she wore it with grace. Irene did. This would be Louis Lafont's first disadvantage. "It's perfect," she said.

"It fits you well enough," conceded the madame, grudgingly.

Irene had the costume sent to the hotel, and as she left the shop, she ignored the solicitations of passing rickshaw drivers as she made her way up the Rue Catinat toward Boulevard Norodom. She walked quickly into the whipping tropical wind, in an attempt to fend off the anxiety that was building as the time to meet with Louis approached. Around her, gusts bowed the high branches of plane trees, bougainvillea petals blew against the pocked walls, and the sky began to fade with the daylight darkness that comes right before a storm. As she reached Notre Dame Square across from the post office, she looked up to see dragonflies circling the cathedral spires, streaming under a pair of skyward crosses.

Then came a dying of the wind, trapping a stillness beneath the black mantle of the clouds. The first raindrop fell onto her forearm, a bead of water so heavy it felt as if it would leave a bruise. She began running toward the post office. It was only a dozen yards away, but by the time she reached the awning above its front steps, she was soaking wet. As she stood in the shelter waiting out the storm, the air was drenched with the muddling smell of soggy leaves and creosote. It was as if she could feel the slick scallops of mold accumulating beneath eaves, the woolen rot eating away at foundations of the city. Louis Lafont, of all people to have become involved. How easily he could ruin everything.

When Irene arrived at the Continental Hotel at eight, Simone and Louis were not yet there. As she followed the waiter across the open terrace, a red-faced colonial with a handlebar mustache tipped his head in appreciation while his beefy wife, wearing a puffed satin gown, pretended not to notice. Irene's weakened confidence was bolstered by this evidence that her costume was a success.

Seated at a table near the wrought-iron railing that parted the terrace from the street, she ordered a double whiskey to further shore herself up. Down the sidewalk a pack of coolies milled about, gangly limbs draped over the uptilted shafts of their rickshaws. Native boys hovered on corners, waving newssheets at Europeans arriving at the restaurants, and gnarled men in black robes sauntered by, idly hawking stone Buddhas. An evening wind had scooped the worst of the heat out of the city, and the air was now limpid and almost cool. Beneath the potted palms that surrounded the tables, incense burned in shallow clay dishes. The mild fragrance reminded Irene of the Khmer wing at the Brooke Museum, and at this memory she felt a twinge of nostalgia for how straightforward her life had once been. As she spotted Louis crossing the square, she raised her glass and gulped.

His long stride was quick and purposeful. He wore a linen evening suit, cut to his trim frame and carefully pressed in a way that Irene did not associate with scholars, who usually had more important matters than their appearances on their minds. "Good evening, Mademoiselle Blum," he said.

"Please, call me Irene."

He scanned the terrace. "Simone is not here?"

"I thought she would be coming with you."

Absently, Louis reached for a chair. "Then you haven't seen her today?"

"Do you think something happened at the police station?" Irene asked, as the fear of what Simone might have revealed to the authorities pushed its way forward again. "Surely we'd know if she'd been detained."

Louis's features were narrow and sharply defined, giving his expression an intensity that made her edgy as his eyes moved from the blue beads of her costume to the solemn set of her mouth. She realized that he was unaffected by how she was dressed. Nor was he distracted by her hair drawn back to emphasize her high cheekbones, or the black crystal earrings she had selected for the way they outlined the curve of her neck. "Would they have any reason to detain her?" he asked.

Irene had to give him credit. Even Mr. Simms could be diverted to a degree by a pretty dress. She studied Louis's angular face, trying to determine if he knew the truth about Roger's death. But his thoughts were inscrutable as he raised his hand to summon the waiter and ordered a Dubonnet for himself and another whiskey for Irene. When she didn't answer, he continued, "Would your worry have anything to do with this temple you think is hidden in the jungles of Stung Treng?"

Irene's hunch was right, Simone *had* done it—given away Irene's secret with complete disregard for her feelings. "I find it interesting that she told you about the temple, but she didn't say a word to me about your meeting us in Saigon." She paused as their drinks arrived, served by a man whose open-topped turban revealed his oiled black hair tied into a Psyche knot. "Why is that, do you suppose?"

"She must have known how you'd respond."

"What do you mean?"

"She told me how upset you became in Cholon yesterday. You don't want me coming with you. I understand, naturally. If this had been my discovery, I wouldn't want to share it either. But it's too late, Simone's already told me. I plan to be there if and when you find this temple."

His presumption was infuriating. "The scrolls are not—"

"Scrolls?" Louis sounded stunned.

"She didn't tell—"

"What scrolls?"

"I thought—" Irene glanced around, flustered, and caught sight of Simone coming past the far side of the theater into Garnier Square, a sailor hooked on each arm. Her silver dress shivered with glacial strands of crystal beads. Her jeweled headband formed a fallen halo around her hair, and her boots flashed their polished buckles. As she shed the sailors, Louis leaned forward, drawn by the tether of her approach. Though his eyes were on Simone, he said to Irene, "I am going to want to know all about these scrolls of yours before the night is through."

Simone did not look like a woman who had spent the day at a police station being questioned about her husband's murder. She cast a haughty gaze around the terrace before settling it on Louis and declaring, "I met the most wonderful Yugoslavian couple down from Shanghai at the gaming tables. They invited me to go dancing with them later at the Cascades. You'd better be on your best behavior, or I'll join them."

Louis was already up and holding out a chair for her. "I've ordered a bottle of Moët."

Simone smiled. "That's an admirable start."

With the informality that comes from a lifetime of knowing a person, he reached out to smooth a tendril of hair that had come loose from her headband, but she pulled away and snapped at Irene. "Do you know what the *commissaire* had the nerve to say to me? *A snake is powerless without its fangs.* As if I have done nothing for the cause. As if I was a puppet. As if I was not as capable as Roger—no, *more* capable—of leading the revolution."

"Forget about that," Louis said. "It's in the past. Simone, why didn't you mention the scrolls to me?"

"You told him?" Simone asked Irene, astonished.

Irene felt sickened by her sloppiness in assuming Louis knew. "I thought you'd already—"

"Of course not." Simone was offended. "I saved that for you."

"What's going on?" Louis asked.

Simone grasped the bottle of champagne, poured a glass, and raised it.

"We're going to change history," she laughed. "We're going to *make* history."

Louis looked at Irene, waiting for an explanation. In any other circumstance, this would have been a thrill, telling Louis Lafont, assistant curator of the Conservation d'Angkor, that she had information about the location of the history of the ancient Khmer. She should have been the one lifting a glass of champagne to toast, but all she could think was: Two against one, them against me.

"It's taken all of my willpower not to tell you everything, Louis. And you know how little willpower I have. But now! Oh, Irene, I knew you'd see things my way." Eagerly Simone told Louis, "Irene's father found a diary. It belonged to a missionary. There's a map, Louis, a map to a temple up near Stung Treng. He saw it—"

"Your father?" Louis asked Irene.

Irene shook her head. She was trying to corral her thoughts, but she couldn't concentrate amid the noise of clattering silverware and the whine of an addict peddling a matted tiger pelt just beyond the railing. Behind it all, the restaurant's orchestra scored the night with a tango whose fiery pace was meant for a much later hour.

"The missionary saw the temple," Simone corrected Louis. "He saw a scroll. A copper scroll! You've heard the rumors. The history. He used that exact word in the diary. *History.*"

"Have you seen this diary?" Louis asked her.

She nodded.

"And the map?"

"Yes, oh yes, it's amazing." Simone's eyes gleamed, and champagne spilled from her glass as she drank. Irene wondered if she had taken some of her pills. Her enthusiasm was too out of character as she announced, "It's real, Louis. This is real."

Still, Louis remained impassive. "That's not an area associated with the Khmer," he said. "With or without this map, you're making quite a leap, assuming there is anything of significance up there."

Irene thought of all the times that she had stayed silent about her skills, and how her silence had eventually been her downfall. She may have been filled with dread, but she would not let Louis Lafont think she was an amateur.

"Have you spent any time studying Simone's father's research on Khmer trade routes?" she asked. "If you follow the patterns he laid out toward Laos, you'll find a network of trails that ends abruptly north of Kratie, right at the river. At the Brooke, I came across letters from a botanist who found stone markers in Ratanakiri province. When I connected his findings with Simone's father's and the steles that were discovered by Garnier's expedition, the path went directly through the location where the missionary claims he found the scrolls."

Irene now had Louis's full attention. The realization that she might know what she was talking about was visible on his face. He said, "Truffaut spent months in that area. He didn't come across a temple."

"I examined his maps. He didn't visit Kha Seng. That's where the temple is said to be."

"I have been working toward this discovery my entire career," Louis told her as he lit a Gauloise. "You've never been to Cambodia, and somehow you claim to have figured it out. How can such a thing be possible?"

"Henry Simms's greed," Simone said. "That's how it's possible."

"Henry Simms? What do you mean?" Louis asked.

"He's financing my expedition," Irene said. There was no point in hiding this fact.

Louis frowned. "That explains what he's doing in Phnom Penh."

It was as if a charge had been detonated, and Irene could hear only a ringing in her ears. "What are you talking about?" she asked as sound slowly returned—the orchestra, the shouting newspaper boys, the neighboring conversations.

"He arrived two weeks ago."

Above the tables, webs of cigarette smoke drifted in a stench of stale liquor and overcooked meats. "No, he didn't," she said.

Louis was confused. "I saw him."

"I knew it, Irene." With alarming speed, Simone's elation contorted into anger, and she hissed, "I knew you and Simms were plotting something."

"You didn't know he was here?" Louis asked Irene.

"He's sick," Irene said, staring into her empty glass as if it were a lens onto the day she had left for Shanghai. She could see Mr. Simms in his car on the dock, a moment when he had not known she was watching, his expression unguarded and grim from the disease that was devouring him. "He's too sick to travel. He wouldn't come all this way unless something was wrong."

"What could be wrong?" Louis asked.

"Who else did you tell?" Irene demanded of Simone. "You told Louis. Who else? This is your fault, I know it is."

"Irene, calm down," Louis said. "Besides the three of us and Henry Simms, does anyone else know about this temple?"

Irene watched a crowd erupting from the Municipal Theater, men in white suits and women in white gowns, tripping like ghosts down the stairs. She saw a flicker of blue, a flash of green—a fan of peacock feathers in the hair of an olive-skinned young woman. She remembered that night in Shanghai, the night she had felt so alone. "Yes," she said, getting up from the table. "Someone else knows."

Chapter 11

The Butterfly Garden

Through a high wrought-iron gate, Irene saw a watchman lying in a hammock strung between the trunks of two young magnolia trees. She raised the latch and opened the gate slowly. Despite her care, it creaked, but the man did not stir. Carefully skirting past him, she knocked lightly on the front door of the bungalow belonging to Marc Rafferty's aunt. No one answered. She knocked a bit louder. Still no answer. She could have woken the watchman and asked him to fetch Marc, but she was afraid he would shoo her away at this late hour and tell her to come back in the morning. She tried the door. It was unlocked.

The front room was decorated with oil paintings, delftware, and lace, mementos of a Europe that had been left behind, but when Irene inhaled, she smelled the same musty undercurrent that lingered in every other building she'd been inside in Shanghai and Saigon. She stepped into the hall and peered past its closed doors. A light was on at the end, and she made her way to the back of the house, to a closed verandah that was misted over by a mesh screen to keep out mosquitoes. Beyond, in the garden, Marc emerged from a shadowed pathway. She saw by the glow of lanterns strung through the trees that he was dressed like a Hindu, in loose white trousers and a collarless kurta shirt.

If he was surprised to see her, he didn't show it, pausing at the head of the path, framed in the smoke wafting off a bamboo torch. Irene had come here impulsively, walked in uninvited, and as she stood at the open door of the verandah, she could think of only one thing: She wanted nothing more than to take shelter in this stranger. She did not like that she had to remind herself why she had sought him out.

"The local style suits you," Marc said. "You look lovely."

Before her thoughts could stray any further, she asked, "Did you know that Mr. Simms is in Phnom Penh?"

"Yes."

"How?"

Puzzled, he took one of his hand-rolled cigarettes from his shirt pocket and lit it. "When Henry Simms is in Indochina, it's not a secret."

"It was to me."

"What do you mean?"

"I found out tonight from Louis Lafont."

"I assumed you knew when we met in Shanghai. I assumed you planned to meet him in Cambodia. What's wrong? Come down here and tell me what's happened."

Although Irene was keeping her distance, as she reached the bottom of the porch steps, she was close enough to see the dark flecks in the green of Marc's eyes, shining in the lantern light filtering down through the branches. He was even more handsome than she remembered, looking relaxed now that he was far from Shanghai, and she had to force herself to stay on track. "Are you after the scrolls?"

He laughed. "Why would you ask that?"

"Someone else must be hunting for them. There's no other reason for

Mr. Simms to come all this way. Not in his condition. You know the Orient. If there's a threat to my expedition, what do *you* think it is?"

Marc drew on his cigarette. "I must admit, it is odd that Murat Stanić has showed up in Saigon. The last I heard he was in South America. He could be reason to worry. But if I had to place a bet? I'd put my money on Simone."

Irene had a strange feeling he was telling her something she should already have known. "Why?"

An errant palm frond bowed over the eave of the verandah. It scraped against the silk panel of one of the Japanese lanterns, and Marc's eyes darted around at the sound. From the quickness of his reaction, Irene could tell that he was always on the alert. Tossing his cigarette to the ground, he walked back into the felt shadows of the garden. As Irene caught up to him along the pathway of rippled paving stones, he said, "The first thing Simone did the morning after you met her at Anne's party was send a telegram to Lafont."

"What did it say?"

"That she would be in Cambodia soon. That her time had come. That history was hers for the taking."

Irene's stomach buckled at the thought of Simone's carelessness. "Did she mention the temple?"

"No, not directly, but after I met you, I figured that was what she was talking about."

"Marc, how were you able to read her telegrams?"

"That was my life in Shanghai. I watched, I listened, I kept track—of letters, telegrams, telephone calls. Comings and goings. Only in the Orient can a man make a career, gain respect even, from such activities. Nothing happened in Shanghai that I didn't know about. Love affairs could have been my stock-in-trade if I had any interest in ruining lives that way, but my specialty was politics, the back alley dealings. The Communists' infiltration of the Municipal Government. The government's infiltration of the Communists. That sort of thing."

"What did you do with all of it?"

"Bartered with it. But mainly I sold it."

Marc stopped walking, staring into the dark contours at the far end of the garden, while beside him Irene thought about how similar they were, using the currency of illicit knowledge to build their lives. But he had been given recognition and even acclaim for his skill, while she had been rewarded with nothing at all. "Why would Simone write something that incriminating to her former lover in a telegram? Surely Roger was having her watched."

"I was the one he paid to watch her."

"You too?"

"I take it you met Boisselier on the ship?"

Irene nodded. "Why didn't you tell Roger about the telegram?"

"Roger Merlin didn't deserve to be handed his wife that easily. But the truth is that I have protected her for years for what she could give me: insight about the party. I rarely used it. It would have been traced right back to her. But I needed it, I needed to know everything so that what I did use had currency. And it wasn't *one* telegram. She sent four the week she met you. She was in a frenzy. I remember one sentence in particular. 'We must protect what is rightfully ours.' She must know that you're going to take the scrolls back to America."

"So she contacted Louis to help her stop me." Irene glanced down at a wooden worktable piled with clusters of cut wisteria. "I don't blame them. I'd do the same." Picking up a branch, she dug her thumbnail into its soft bark, peeling its leaves. "Do you think Mr. Simms found out about her telegrams? Do you think that's why he's here?"

"You told Simone about the temple not even three weeks ago, but to reach Cambodia by now, he would have had to leave Seattle long before that." Removing the bare stem from Irene's hands, he placed it back on the worktable. "You do present me with quite a mystery."

"It's my fault he's come all this way. He would do anything to help me. He knows what this means to me."

"You trust him completely, don't you? You trust he doesn't have plans for the scrolls that you don't know about."

It was painful, this constant expanding of her uncertainties. "I would be a fool to say I'm sure of anything at this point."

"You don't seem like a fool to me."

"Do you think I'm a match for Simone and Louis?"

He lifted her wrist and laid it over his open palm, as if testing its strength. He pressed gently, his thumb resting against her pulse. "I don't know."

As her gaze took refuge on the glimmer of a lantern hanging in the trees, she let her fingers close over his. "Ask me to stay the night."

He stepped back. "I'll do what I can to help you figure this out, but you need to go."

Mortified by her miscalculation, she said, "I didn't . . . I thought—"

"I don't want you to be sorry, and if you stay . . ."

She could feel the weight of her hands, set free from his, hanging at her sides. "I'm not a girl. I won't expect anything from you."

"I wish it were that easy."

That night as Irene tried to sleep, the thin cotton sheet felt like rough canvas, but when she kicked it off, the breeze from the fan became a thousand moths fluttering across her body. Staggering out of bed, she switched off the fan. The humidity expanded, pressing her down into the mattress and leaving her in a damp web of fatigue. For a few precious moments she nearly fell asleep, only to be roused by the graze of one leg against the other. As dawn came with the whir of passing rickshaws, she felt raw with humiliation, not only from Marc's rejection but from an inescapable understanding—she was not as cunning as she had always believed herself to be.

She would confront Simone about the telegrams, but it was too early, and besides, before she did so, there was one other thing she must do. Marc was right. Murat Stanić should have been in Bolivia. His interest in pre-Columbian civilizations was as predatory as his passion for the Khmer. Irene had heard that the moment news surfaced about a series of stone idols unearthed from the Akapana pyramid dig, Stanić had headed to the Southern Hemisphere. If anyone was going to raid that site, it would be him. Yet now he was in Indochina, arriving at the same time as Mr. Simms. In the insular world of treasure hunters, there were no coincidences. She should have been suspicious the moment she heard Stanić was in Saigon. She had to make up for this misstep. Before leaving for

Cambodia with Simone and Louis, she would talk to him. She knew better than to ask outright if he knew about her temple, but she could prompt him and read between the lines.

Irene made the short walk back to the terrace of the Continental, where men of importance in Saigon took their morning coffee and newspaper. Predictably, Stanić was among them, his plump, balding head bowed over the day's edition of *Le Courrier Saigonnais*. She stood beside his table, wearing her best naïve smile. When he noticed her, she said, "I believe we've met. You probably don't remember, but—"

"Pasadena," he said. "Huntington's estate. The night Isadora Duncan danced on the lawn." Even though his interest was in very young Oriental girls, he regarded her sleeveless dress with appreciation, as she had known he would. She had chosen the straight sheath to emphasize the slightness of her figure, and had pulled her hair back into a plait, as an adolescent girl might. She was not wearing lip rouge.

"How could I forget Henry Simms's secret weapon?" he asked.

"What do you mean?"

He grinned. His back teeth were capped in gold. "The ring you wanted. The empress dowager's ring that you traded me for the location of Caesar's Ruby. You said you were an intermediary, but I keep track of people. I know what you've been doing at the Brooke."

Despite her distaste for Stanić, Irene was flattered.

"Please, join me," he said.

Stanić was a revolting man, with his perverse predilections, but none of this could be allowed to matter right now. Irene sat down. She had no appetite, but she ordered coffee and a croissant. At least the air was not yet laden with heat, even though the nighttime hues of the terrace's amber lamplight had been replaced by the bright morning sun.

"So," he said, "let me guess. Simone Merlin is searching for something, and you and Simms want it."

Irene was unsurprised that he had made the first move. Catching an opponent unawares was essential, and she was pleased that he considered her one, for this meant his intentions—or at least the fact that he had intentions—were out in the open. She could deny or she could feint. Denial would be the easy way out, but it was a novice's move. And what better opportunity to perfect her lie? To parry with Monsieur Boisselier had been satisfying, but to dupe Stanić would be an achievement.

"Simone and I have been collaborating on Khmer trading routes," she said. "We're hoping to find a road through Tonkin into China, a path that connects Angkor Wat directly to the Forbidden City. But a few months back, I began to suspect that she's using our studies for other means. Some of her routes are off the probable paths we've determined," Irene said, purposely vague. "It's as if she's looking for something else." Having edged her way toward an accusation that might nudge him into divulging what, if anything, he was scheming, she went on, "I've been told that you came to Saigon to make a deal with Simone."

His hand twitched on the table. He frowned as he asked, "A deal for what?"

The coffee had invigorated Irene, pulling her out of the groggy aftermath of her sleepless night. "That's what I'm trying to find out."

In Stanić's line of work, it was essential that a man keep his composure. He regained his quickly. "What makes you think that I'm interested in anything Simone Merlin has?"

Irene looked out at the barefoot Annamite soldiers drilling in the square in front of the theater. "Something lured you here. You should be in Bolivia right now."

With a frankness that was necessary for entrapment, Stanić explained, "You had never left the country, Irene. When my people told me that you *and* Henry Simms were on your way to Indochina, the possibilities were too intriguing for me to ignore."

How degrading. Even Stanić had known about Mr. Simms's travel plans. Irene could feel a stalemate brewing, and she decided to try a different tack. "Since you know so much about me, you must have heard that the Brooke decided it no longer needs me. That it could replace me simply because I don't have a Ph.D. behind my name. I want them to regret that decision, and for that I need a discovery valuable enough to make them acknowledge my worth. If Simone does happen to find something that could help me achieve this goal, keep in mind that I would pay a great deal for it."

"Why don't you deal directly with her?"

It seemed that he believed her bluff, but Irene knew it was never smart to feel sure of oneself with such men, whose lives revolved on an axis of deceit. His question may have been innocent, or he may have been trying to trip her up, and she had already stumbled too many times on this journey. Carefully, she answered, "I plan to, but I am sure she will want to sell to the highest bidder."

"And you don't think you can outbid me?"

"With money, maybe not. But I have many other things you might want."

From the way he appraised her, Irene saw why he had earned his lecherous reputation. "And what would they be?" he asked.

She closed her mind to what he might be thinking about her and forged ahead, steeling herself against the fact she was about to reveal. "Henry Simms is very sick. Soon I will inherit his entire estate." There was no way for Stanić to know that this was a lie. She had inventoried Mr. Simms's treasures for dispersal to museums, galleries, and rival collectors around the world. It would be his beyond-the-grave coup, exposing the extent of his illicit acquisitions. "I might be willing to give you the pick of his collection."

"Such as?" Stanić asked, sounding almost bored. His show of indifference at the pending death of one of his greatest competitors was impressive.

"The tsar's treasures," Irene said.

"There's more where Caesar's Ruby came from?"

After Lenin had nationalized the Romanov palaces, imperial possessions began to filter into the collecting underworld. Then the Soviets started plundering relics from churches, museums, and private homes, with Trotsky calling it famine relief to avoid criticism. Irene had followed this rupture in history with fascination, for she could not help comparing the House of Romanov to the kingdom of the ancient Khmer. So this was how an entire civilization's treasures could vanish completely.

"What do you want?" she asked. "Raphael's *Alba Madonna*? The Wedgwood dinner service commissioned for Catherine the Great?"

"This is all quite interesting." Stanić called for the bill, and while he paid for their breakfast, he asked, "Tell me, why has Henry Simms come all this way to die?"

The question jolted Irene, and she turned her attention to the street, where the morning's commerce was well under way. Rice, fish sauce, and egg sellers made their rounds, baskets atop their heads, clay jars hanging from bamboo poles over their shoulders. At the surrounding tables, businessmen began folding their newspapers, preparing to ease into another day of work. Irene sought an answer, but there was nothing she could say that would not cause a hitch in her voice. She had no choice but to remain silent.

"Apparently, I've gone too far," Stanić said, but without apology. As he stood and returned his wallet to his jacket pocket, he once again studied Irene, but this time his look was not prurient. If she had not known of his ego, if she had not been on guard, she could have let herself believe that he considered the two of them equals. Nodding at the touring car that had pulled up to the terrace, he said, "I'm off to Phnom Penh. It would not do for me to be in the area and not pay my respects to Henry. Please stay in touch, Irene."

Getting to her feet, she said, "Naturally."

"And my dear, once Henry is gone, you can always work for me." His gaze roved the length of her body. "After all, I am not a half-wit like those men at the Brooke. I do appreciate what you are able to do."

Although Irene had learned nothing concrete from Stanić, she felt it had been worthwhile to go to him. He needed to know that she was aware of him, and that she would be keeping her eye on him, just as he would be keeping his on her. She was still concerned by how much he might know that he was not telling her, but she had to set this worry aside for the time being. When she arrived back at the hotel, she asked the concierge if Simone and Louis had come down for breakfast yet.

The burly Frenchwoman glowered. Her fleshy forearms lay as if wearily abandoned on the counter behind which she stood. "There was a ferocious argument last night," she reported, with the vicious pleasure that a certain type of person takes in gossip. "You did not hear it? I nearly called the authorities, but Madame Merlin left. She has not come back."

"Did she take her luggage?"

The concierge shook her head.

Irene climbed the steps two at a time, running down the hall to her room, but the diary and her maps were locked in the bureau where she had left them. The bedsheets were on the floor where she had kicked them during her restless night, and her new outfit was in a heap on the arm-chair. Relieved, she pushed at the shutters to let in air, balmy with the syrup of tropical flowers. Stepping out onto her balcony, she caught sight of Louis below, slumped on a stone bench among the rosebushes in the garden. He did not seem to see her as he blinked up into the sunlight crest-ing over the roof of the hotel.

She was down in the garden as quickly as she had been up to her room. Standing over him, she asked, "What's wrong?"

"She's sleeping." His voice was hoarse. "After they pumped her stom-ach, the doctor gave her a sedative."

"Pumped her stomach?"

As Irene said this, she realized that minus the jacket, Louis was still wearing his suit from the night before. His eyes were bloodshot, his shirt was untucked, and he was scarcely recognizable as the man she'd had drinks with at the Continental. He massaged the bridge of his nose with his thumb and forefinger, and when he replied, it was as if saying the words took all of his effort. "Simone overdosed on phenobarbital last night."

Overdosed? "What . . . how?" Irene stammered, afraid to know what he meant by this. "Is she going to be all right?"

Louis reached for Irene's hand. Whether to calm her or steady him-self, she couldn't have said. "The doctor assured me she will be fine."

Around the base of a rosebush, fallen petals lay like pink snow. Above, the magnolias were swollen with heat and light. "A person who overdoses on pills is not fine."

"I know." His eyes filled with tears, and he did not attempt to hide them as Irene would have.

She released his hand and sat down on the bench beside him. Their shoulders touched, and she felt him shudder as he caught his breath. "What happened?" she asked.

"We had a fight," he said.

"About what?"

"We used to want the same things, but now . . . I didn't know how much she'd changed. I didn't know how much it all really means to her."

"What are you talking about? The temple?"

Louis shook his head. "We fought, and she left. She must have gone straight to the Majestic and checked in to a room there. Sometime during the night a porter saw water trickling out from under her door. They found her in the bathtub. She was unconscious." His words faded. "She could have drowned."

Nausea pressed into the back of Irene's throat. "She didn't." She said this as if it were a command. She lit a cigarette. "Do you think it was an accident?"

"Do you think it was deliberate?" Louis asked, startled.

Irene recalled the Luminal she'd found in Simone's desk in Shanghai. "I don't know."

"There was a time when she wanted to find the Khmer's history more than anything else, when the history would have been enough for her. When we were young, we talked about it endlessly. To hell with Sherlock Holmes. The Khmer were the greatest mystery story we'd ever been told. But a mystery without an ending. We were half-crazed by it. Everywhere we went, we wondered about it. Was the maid at the governor-general's residence the descendant of a princess? Was the debonair old man who repaired shoes at the market a descendant of the last king? They were all out there among us, they had to be. Their world was our entire life. I don't know if you can understand such a thing as this, Irene, but—"

"I can." Envy rushed through her. To have someone who shared your past. "I do."

"Did Simone tell you how I fell in love with her?"

"No, she didn't."

"I was nine years old. She was only six."

As he stared straight ahead, Irene observed the outline of his thin nose, the light brown shading of stubble along his tensed jaw.

"We'd ridden out to Ta Prohm with Monsieur Commaille, and while we were climbing around the ruins, we found a grove of pansy butterflies. Hundreds of them filled the air. If you stood perfectly still, they would land on you. I can see Simone, her entire body fluttering with blue and green. Even Monsieur Commaille had never seen such a thing. He called it *extraordinaire*. As a man whose life was shaped around the Khmer temples, he did not use this word lightly. A week later, she gave it to me for my birthday. The entire grove, as if it was hers to give. Think of it, at six years old. She even painted a sign: LOUIS LAFONT BUTTERFLY GARDEN. Sometimes when I missed her, I would drive out to the grove and spend the night."

"Are you still in love with her?"

"We had always known that we were going to be married. Then her parents died." He lifted his shoulders, rising out of his reminiscence. "It was terrible for everyone. She did the only thing that made sense to her at the time."

"You're generous."

"I'm realistic. I have to be. I know that I alone am not enough anymore to make her happy. I know that if you hadn't come along with the temple, she never would have left him. She couldn't have. But I never imagined that she wanted to leave him for . . ."

"What?" Irene asked, her thoughts turning to Monsieur Boisselier's cryptic comment about Simone's first love. If it wasn't Louis, she was baffled as to what it could be. "Please, tell me what she wants."

But Louis began to cry again, not the undone weeping of a woman but the stifled, resistant sadness particular to men. Irene let him take her hand once more, let him trust her so he might keep on trusting her, as the moist warmth of the garden spun around them like a cocoon.

Chapter 12

The Compass Rose

Plane trees flanked the pathway leading from the road to the hospital, their branches joining to form a vault of flickering sea green leaves overhead. Irene and Louis followed Simone's physician, the grizzled Dr. Kessler, through a shadowed corridor. Although the sun was as potent as usual at this mid-morning hour, the passage delivered them into the protection of a large courtyard, surrounded by a gallery of patios, all shielded by latticed partitions. Irene tread cautiously over the raised roots snarled between two camphor trees. As they walked, Dr. Kessler said, "She's been asking for you." He could have been speaking to either of them. He nodded to the patio in the farthest corner. As they started toward it, he put a hand on Louis's shoulder. "May I speak with you for a moment?"

Reluctantly, Louis stopped. Irene wanted to hear what the doctor had to say, but the moment she had stepped into the hospital, the horror of what had nearly happened convulsed through her. Struck by how thankful she was that Simone was alive, she left Louis with the doctor and hurried across the courtyard to the open doorway of Simone's room.

Glossy green shutters hugged the tall windows. Above the bed, a rosewood cross hung askew, while on a chest of drawers, a tin image of the Buddha resided on an areca wood altar. Simone was sitting up, her narrow shoulders engulfed by pillows. She wore a nightdress with a crocheted collar that was the same sickly beige color as the walls. A thin blanket was pulled over her lap. Her skin was more pallid than usual, and deep lines of exhaustion pursed the corners of her mouth.

She blinked at Irene, and Irene stared back, unblinking, afraid to speak. She did not understand the fury that was enveloping her.

"I like my doctor," Simone said. "He's a German. The French go about things in a roundabout way, but the Germans, they know how to be direct."

"How dare you . . . We killed your husband." Irene was appalled by her inability to stop the words. "I didn't do that, I didn't save you, I didn't help you escape from Shanghai, for this, this . . . I don't even know what this is!"

"Are you through with me?"

"What are you talking about?"

"Now that Simms is here." Simone's voice shrank to a pitiful whisper. "You don't need me anymore, do you?"

"You're crazy. After all the time I spent getting you out of Shanghai. After all the time I've lost because of you. My God, Simone, I already told you, I didn't know he was coming."

"Stop shouting at me. This was devastating. Worse than I imagined."

A new fear came over Irene. Simone's contradiction, to be so frail and yet to have survived so much, had once been interesting. Now it felt only dangerous. "What kind of person *imagines* something like this?"

"It was an accident, Irene. An accident. I couldn't sleep. I haven't been sleeping since we left Shanghai. And Louis and I, we fought. He's so selfish! I had a drink and took some pills, and then I couldn't remember if I'd taken any pills, and I was wide awake, it was making me crazy, the thoughts, such awful thoughts, so I took more, but two, only two, I swear to you, I was careful, I was." A fan stirred the air from above, but Simone's face was slick with sweat; even the roots of her hair were wet.

Irene's gaze rose up the wall to the ceiling, where dark patches of mold made the room look as if it had been scorched. After everything Simone had been through, Irene wanted to feel sympathy for her. She wanted to believe that the closeness they'd shared on the steamer had not been part of a con. But she just couldn't be sure how much of Simone's despair was genuine, and how much was calculated. "Are you deliberately making this journey difficult for me?" she asked.

"Dr. Kessler said the bottles were empty, the pills and the wine too, but I don't remember drinking all the wine. Why would I do that? Even when Roger was at his worst, I never wanted to die."

Or maybe Simone did not intend anything she did, and the real risk she posed was in the unconsciousness of her actions. "But you just told me you imagined it," Irene said.

"That's different from wanting it. You don't know what it's like, not to be able to sleep."

Irene could still feel those hollow hours, two o'clock and three and then four, the sky gradually lightening outside her window. "Don't tell me what I don't know. Stop presuming that I don't know anything, who's following us, the threats to us. That I don't know about your telegrams to Louis."

"What are you talking about?"

"You decided the moment I told you about the temple that you'd find a way to escape from Roger. You probably even knew you were going to kill him. The minute I opened my big mouth at Anne's party, you started planning how you'd take the scrolls for yourself with Louis's help."

"That's not true. That's not at all what I want."

"Then why didn't you tell me about Louis when we were in Shanghai?"

"What if the scrolls have been found?" Simone's eyes were glassy, and her face was even paler than when Irene had arrived. "What if that's why Simms is here? What if that's why Stanić is here? Maybe, even, what if they've made some kind of deal? Between the two of them they can make the scrolls vanish, and that will ruin everything. The scrolls are our only hope. Don't you see, Irene, I couldn't let you take them back to America."

So, Simone had known this all along. "Of course you couldn't. *If* that's what I was going to do, which it wasn't." Holding fast to her lie, Irene sat on the edge of the bed. "Besides, Mr. Simms isn't making any deals with Stanić. His deal is with me, to help me, and that's that."

"I wasn't always like this," Simone murmured. "I wasn't always desperate. In the beginning, it was obvious to me what was necessary. And I wanted to trust you, Irene, I really did. I wanted to believe that ultimately you would see that we wanted the same thing from the scrolls. But now Henry Simms is here. You understand, don't you?"

Troubled, Irene said, "No, I don't."

Simone turned her head away. "I should have known."

As Irene and Louis sat vigil with Simone, the late afternoon swelled with sunlight thick and golden as honey. Then the light paled and night collapsed over Saigon. The sudden absence of daylight deflated the hospital room.

It was six o'clock, that hour of demarcation peculiar to the equator. A young nurse arrived with broth and rice. Irene noted her starched white gown and bare, flat feet. Nothing, not a single thing, was congruous on this side of the world. Dr. Kessler followed with a sedative, saying, "Madame Merlin will sleep well through the night."

"I'll stay with her," Louis said.

"It's not allowed."

"I will stay anyway."

Dr. Kessler did not protest further. He had stated the hospital's policy. Apparently, enforcing it was not his job. He bid them good night, and Irene said to Louis, "I'll be back first thing in the morning." Although she wanted to stay and keep an eye on Simone, she could no longer bear being in the room, frustrated as she was with having lost another day and with Simone's irresponsibility. That Simone and Louis had scarcely spoken to one another did not help Irene's discomfort. She could feel the pressure of their need to follow their argument through to its end. Maybe, if they made their peace, Irene could glean some information from Louis, since it didn't seem worth it to try with Simone anymore. "I'll be at the hotel," she told him.

In the calm of the courtyard, Irene allowed herself to deflate. Above the rustling trees, the sky was held in place by a trellis of stars. She stood for a moment, inhaling deeply, as if she could find rejuvenation in the scent coming from the eucalyptus that grew in ceramic containers against the sides of the building. As if, simply by breathing in, she could clear her head. She couldn't. Clarity would never again be as simple as a few deep breaths.

In the near dark, Irene carefully navigated the channel of trees back out to the road. When she reached the sidewalk, she saw Marc leaning against a streetlamp. After last night, she had thought she would never see him again. Hurrying toward him, she blurted, "You came," as if he had climbed the Himalayas to reach her. Dropping her gaze, she saw half a dozen boot-crushed cigarette stubs on the ground around him.

"When I first heard the news," he said, "I thought it was you. I thought the two of them had done something to you."

Irene was pleased that he would care about this. "Instead, it was Simone being an idiot," she replied.

"Are you okay?"

She nodded, glancing away from him, up the street to where a dozen rickshaw drivers huddled in a semicircle tossing dice against the curb. "How did you find out?"

"It's the gossip in every café on the Rue Catinat." He moved away from the lamppost, held out his hand, and took hers. "I'm sorry I asked you to leave last night."

"There's no need to—"

"I am uncomfortable with uncertainty." He turned away and led her into a narrow, canopied lane.

As Irene passed rough wooden walls, the faint lamplight from the road faded and then disappeared altogether, and sight was replaced by sound—the scrape of their shoes over the uneven path. To speak in such a darkness was to speak as if her words would evaporate the moment they touched the still air. As if they could never be retrieved and held against her in a moment of vulnerability.

"There was nothing uncertain in my asking to stay last night," she said.

"I have never met anyone like you. I have never met a woman who knows so clearly what she wants." The day's heat had recoiled into the trapped hollows of the city, settling into this fugitive lane. "Who isn't afraid of wanting."

They emerged into the lamplit boulevard across from the Petit Hotel du Cap-Ferrat. The tall shutters of Irene's room were open behind the branches of the mango tree, and she saw the gauze drapery of the canopy bed tumbling down. Marc's face was flushed above the pale linen of his shirt. She touched her lips to the wisp of a scar on his cheekbone. "There is nothing uncertain about this either," she said, and her mouth traveled over the lids of his closed eyes. He pulled her closer, and his eyelashes grazed her temple. Her hand traveled across his face, the uncharted territory of him. Her lips met his, and it was like reaching a still harbor at a journey's end.

Rain trampled over the slope of the roof, waking Irene. Her skin flickered in the golden glow of candles burning down. Wax dripped into stalactites beneath the windowsill. Marc lay on his stomach, his long, muscled legs tangled in the white sheets, his back exposed. A dark circle on his shoulder caught her attention, and she examined the tattoo, a sharply etched compass rose. Pointing north, the spine of its emerald needle looked as if it pierced his skin. "What does it mean?" she asked.

He woke into the whisper of her question. "I killed the man who killed my wife."

"You're having a nightmare," she said.

But as he shifted onto his side, his voice had the precision of one who is wide awake. "I would spend all day doing nothing but sitting in the garden staring into the windows at the back of our house. It was like an abandoned stage. I could see the bassinet. And Lara's dressing gown over a chair. That was why I killed him. For my daughter, who never slept in that wicker basket. For Lara, who never put that gown on again. For my life. A new life I was ready to begin once my daughter was born. And the sun kept rising, but there was never any heat. Just the white winter light of Shanghai and air as cold as it was that night when I found that bastard sucking on a pipe in an opium den on Soochow Creek."

Irene laid her hand over the uneven beating of his heart, as if she could touch his grief and ease it. But even as he wrapped his fingers around hers, accepting her gesture of solace, his sorrow was inaccessible. She, of all people, understood this.

"I knew that I'd lost my way," he said, each word a hard stone polished with bitterness. "Not when I pulled the trigger. That I took pleasure in. No, I lost my way long before, to have reached a place where I could take pleasure in doing such a brutal thing. After it was over, I got drunk. One day I woke up and realized that I'd been drunk for more than a year. I realized that I needed to be either dead or sober. I wasn't ready to stop remembering them, so I quit drinking and discovered how empty a man's life can be. Then one night I passed a tattoo parlor in Blood Alley. I thought, There must be a way to draw the poison out of my body. I chose a compass to help me stay my course. I'm lucky I'm not covered in tattoos. The pain was unambiguous. I wanted it to last forever."

He was sitting up, and Irene leaned toward him, resting her forehead against his. "Is this the reason I will be sorry for being with you? Because you've killed a man?"

"No," he said, quietly. "Irene, Henry Simms is my father."

She opened her mouth to say *I don't understand,* but that would not have been true.

"Whenever he was away from Shanghai, he sent letters," Marc continued, "and when he was in Seattle he wrote about a girl who lived in a museum. She crept around his house searching for hidden treasures and danced like a young goddess when she thought no one was looking. I thought he just wanted to entertain me, and I was young myself. I didn't understand that the girl was real. Of course, I knew about you later, but it was still disconcerting when we met, as if a fable from my childhood had come to life. And when you told me that he loved you because he'd never had a child of his own, it was as if I was being told that I had never existed. You hadn't heard of me, but I knew so much about you. I've been trying to figure out why."

Irene slid her legs over the side of the bed and stared at Marc's body cast in wavering shadow on the wall. It was as if with his confession a darkness within him had been freed and taken a shape of its own. "Have you? Figured it out?"

"No. We've never been close, but why would he keep me a secret from you?"

. "He acquired priceless works of art and never told anyone."

"He told you. He told you everything. Except about me."

At the resentment in Marc's voice, apprehension swept through Irene. "Is that why you came for me? If you can find a way to hurt me, then you can hurt him too?"

He shook his head. "When I heard about the overdose, when I thought something had happened to you, I realized that I want to keep knowing you." He drew her in to him, his heartbeat soft against her back. "You're a part of me." He kissed the arc of her shoulder. "For some reason, he made sure that you've always been a part of me."

In the scant middle-of-the-night light, Irene left Marc asleep in the bed and put on her dressing gown. Kneeling on the floor, she opened her satchel and piled her maps of Cambodia, all but the one drawn by Reverend Garland, beside her. Each of her maps was unique, not in the way the cartographer had shaped the country, or the locations of villages and mountains and rivers, but because it was its own adventure that she had undertaken as a girl. She had brought them with her because she thought she would need her childhood quests to help her find her way. How wrong she was. There was no trace of this new journey in the countless journeys she had taken so long ago.

She lifted the top map from the pile. The contours of its topography were faint over the countryside, and she was able to locate the smallest of towns only because she had memorized their positions long before time faded the cinnamon ink. It was the map her father gave her right after her mother died. She rubbed her thumb along the threadbare border, where Cambodia washed into the Gulf of Siam.

She struck a match. Flame burst from the matchstick, and she watched as it burned down to the tip of her thumb and forefinger. She blew on the dart of fire, and it vanished, then reappeared as a fleur-de-lis of smoke. Behind her, Marc stirred. She lit another match. It faltered and expired. She lit a third.

She moved the flame in a circle beneath the map, and the paper grew translucent. Then she held the match still, until a brown stain flowered beneath Siem Reap. The dusty, chicory odor of the paper seeped into the air. Her hand trembled, and the map tilted precariously close to the fire. The paper split apart along the road that led to Angkor Wat. She shook the match out and dropped it to the floor.

As Marc sat beside her, his fingers grazed the bare skin between her neck and shoulder where the collar of her robe had slipped down. He asked, "What are you doing?"

"This is my past," she said, whisking the flame of a new match against the edge of the map. An ember spread, and a hood of fire rose above the page. "I've drawn it so tightly around myself that I can't see where I'm going. I can't see that there might be a different path to take, other than the one I started out on." She watched as an orange river flowed toward Stung Treng, and Cambodia's shadowed gray countryside shimmered beneath the fire. "At least I thought this was my past. Now it seems I was part of a past I didn't even know about." She carried the blazing paper to the washbowl beside the bed and dropped it into the water. It hissed, leaving a scroll of black ash.

"Do you wish I hadn't told you?"

"I wish he'd told me years ago. All that time I could have known about you, the way you've known about me." Feeling the loss of this chance she'd never had, she took the next map and continued to light the limitations of her history on fire. She burned another, and another, until all of her maps except one were gone, and the room reeked of scorched paper.

——

As morning broke over Saigon, Irene began to pack. She unstrapped her map case from its hiding place in the bureau and tossed it on the bed. The buckle wasn't secured, and the flap fell open, displaying Reverend Garland's diary, her mother's watercolor tablet, and Anne's gun. Its coral handle shrank in Marc's grip. "I didn't take you for the type to carry a weapon."

They had spoken only a few words to one another since she had destroyed her maps, and she felt dazed as she told him, "I don't even know how to shoot the thing. Anne gave it to me after Simone and I killed Roger."

"I suspected that it was the two of you."

"He was going to shoot me, and she stabbed him, and then I hit him with a car." The room smelled of smoke, and Irene opened the window. Rain slunk through, relieving the sticky, closed heat. "We didn't mean to do any of it," she said, savoring the dampness on her skin. "Or maybe we did." After last night, the murder and its motives seemed more distant than ever.

"Why is this expedition so important to you, Irene? You say it's about your reputation, but I've checked around. You may have been cut out at the Brooke Museum, but you're well-regarded. You already have what you need to claim a new place for yourself—a good place—in the art world. You don't need the scrolls."

She turned to him. "What are you talking about?"

"Tell me the real reason, for both of you, you and Simone."

"The reason we share?" She gathered up the costume she had bought to impress Louis. "It's where we're from," she said, running her fingers over the blue buttons. "It's what shaped us. Finding the history of the Khmer is like finding a missing part of our own histories. It's a way of making ourselves complete."

"And this is why you don't leave her behind?"

"I wish I could, I do, even though it would be against Mr. Simms's wishes. She's made such a mess of everything." Irene could not help but laugh at how absurd the situation had become. "But that's not it. No, I was foolish enough to show her the map. She knows where the scrolls are. There's no way I can outrun her, not with Louis on her side. They could easily beat me to the temple. Or they could send off a telegram. That's all it would take to have every official in the country after me."

As Marc reflected on this, he searched for his shirt among the sheets. His tattoo was dark and unforgiving on his shoulder. "It seems to me you need someone on your side."

"Are you . . . do you want to come to Cambodia with me?"

"Do you want me to?" he asked.

She was listening for a trace of the desire they had shared, but she sensed, instead, caution. As he dressed, she watched him. Tall and fair, Marc was the closest Irene would have to family once Mr. Simms died. The closest she would have to being known without having to explain where she'd come from, who she was. She trailed her fingers through the slush of ash in the washbowl. She could see the remains of her blackened country, the daub of a charred village bereft of its surrounding landscape. "Yes," she said. "I do."

Part 3

CAMBODIA

I do not know if many men have from childhood, as I have had, a presentiment of their
whole life. Nothing has happened to me that
I have not dimly foreseen from my earliest
years.

PIERRE LOTI,
A Pilgrimage to Angkor

Chapter 13

Not a Mirage

Beside Marc, in the front of the Pierce-Arrow sedan he had borrowed from his aunt, Irene tucked her feet up onto the seat, her bare toes resting against his leg. She gazed out at the sunrise brushing the morning chill from the leaves of rubber trees, planted in even rows along the newly paved highway heading west toward Cambodia. Light welled on the horizon, and the radiant green of an occasional rice paddy emerged from beneath shawls of white mist. Rolling down her window, she let the wind cool her face, still warm from Marc's lingering touch in her hotel room hours before.

Simone sat in the backseat with Louis. They had taken her from the hospital against her doctor's orders, and although she was drowsy and silent,

Irene was aware of her attention as Marc lowered his hand from the steering wheel and traced his finger over her ankle. Always such a private person, Irene scarcely recognized herself as she laid her hand over his, not caring that she was being observed, while the landscape around them brightened and opened wide, the coconut and rubber plantations giving way to the flat, exposed countryside monotonous with rice fields. She didn't care about anything right now except the memory of the previous night and the reddened highway leading her toward the home of the ancient Khmer.

Sitting next to Marc, Irene noticed the way he listened to every word spoken to him with undivided attention, and how he was not self-conscious when she caught him watching her, and her attraction for him flared like the incandescent blue kingfishers startled to flight with the passing of the car. She thought about her feelings for the Khmer and how she had nurtured them so diligently over the years. She had not known that passion could take root without being sown, and the discovery was intoxicating. She laid her head back on the seat and gazed out at a flock of egrets, their silky wings dragging feathered shadows over the surface of the fields. The sun burned her wrist, exposed over the edge of the door. She knew she should pull her hand inside, but she was engrossed by the deepening color, as if she were being shaped at that very moment, like an unformed piece of clay.

"I should be drinking Pernod over ice on the terrace at the Manolis by now," Simone declared, waving her Gitane with one hand and a rice-paper fan with the other, to whisk the smoke from the car.

Ice. Irene's mouth watered for it as she sat in the front seat watching Marc, who was drinking coffee in one of the *nipa* stalls, beneath strings of drying cuttlefish. They had been stopped for almost an hour along the low shore of a delta tributary, waiting for the ferry. It was nearly noon, and the sun was a flat white haze, as if it had smoldered into the molten pallor of the sky. Irene knew it was dangerous, the compulsion to give parts of herself to Simone, but she could not resist the urge to talk about her feelings for Marc. And Simone of all people would not judge her for what she was going to say. "I don't know why, but I always chose men I could live without. Men I wouldn't miss when they were gone." She confessed, "I was engaged once, and when he wrote from the Somme to tell me that he had fallen in love with a Parisian girl, I was overwhelmed by how relieved I felt—that I wouldn't have to be the one to call off our marriage."

Having yet to ask why Marc was with them, Simone nodded and said, "It can ruin you, wanting someone too much."

The car's doors were open in the vain hope of a breeze stirring through, but the air was too heavy to move. The muddy brown river was as motionless as the landscape. Irene thought about how tenderly Louis had helped Simone from the hospital to the car, and how she had slept for a while with her head on his shoulder. But there was also a coolness between them. If they had reconciled, they had not done a tidy job of it, and the effect this problem could have on the expedition concerned Irene. "Is that how you feel about Louis?" she asked.

Simone gazed up the road, where he stood in front of a stall displaying bottles of sun-warmed cola. "That was how I felt about Roger."

"You loved him more than you loved Louis?"

"It was different. Roger came along when I needed him to. He rescued me from the heartache of my parents' death. He gave shape to my longing. He taught me how to understand my country in an entirely new way."

"He beat you."

"Yes, he did that too. But he had strength. He had conviction. He never would have let me go. But Louis did. I don't know if I'll ever be able to forgive him for that."

Seeing no advantage in arguing against Simone's logic, Irene watched Marc. He was close enough for her to see the dusting of crumbs that had fallen onto his shirt from the baguette he was eating with his coffee, but still, in the newness of her craving for him, he was too far away. She asked, "Was there ever a time with Roger when you didn't feel fragile?"

"Not a moment. And I'll be honest with you, Irene, I never felt more alive." Squinting, Simone cast her gaze out across the river. "*Merde,* if that ferry doesn't arrive soon, I'm going to crawl out of my skin."

———

Out in the open of the ferry landing, Irene could not touch Marc the way she wanted to. She could not even look at him the way she wanted to, and she certainly could not ask the things she wanted to ask with Simone and Louis around. The restraint was making her edgy. "It's hot as hell out here. I have to do something besides smoke. Teach me how to shoot the gun."

"At anyone in particular?" he asked, tossing a piastre coin beside his empty coffee cup. He surveyed their surroundings, beyond planks of fly-infested boar fat, past a group of women, half-asleep, having abandoned their bamboo poles festooned with trussed, listless chickens. He led her around these obstacles toward the ridgeline of dried mud that ran along the bluff above the sluggish river. His loose shirt and trousers could have been bought in the Chinese quarter in Shanghai. They were so unlike the tailored suits favored by Mr. Simms, and she wondered if this was deliberate, or if he was simply that unlike his father. *His father*. Strange, how easy this was to accept.

As the food shacks fell into the distance, their soft drinks and baskets of shriveled vegetables growing indistinguishable on their counters, Marc put his back to the river and scrutinized a dehydrated sea of low, wiry trees and tufts of woolen scrub. His eyes settled on a lone banana palm a few dozen yards away. "That will be your target. Give me your gun. Do you see the blossom?" he asked, using the pistol to point it out, as if shooting was the only reason they had walked so far from the others.

Irene had not expected him to take her in his arms, but she had hoped, once they were beyond being overheard, that he would say something about last night. Just a word, to bind it securely to this morning. As she spotted the blossom, hanging like a purple pendant from its corrugated vine, she felt herself withdrawing from his nonchalance, and she fought the impulse. She did not want to retreat, not from this man. The day was hot, they were both tired, and they had already declared much to one another, simply by leaving Saigon together. She took the gun back and raised it, surprised by how shaky her grip was.

"You can use both hands," Marc said.

She laced her fingers tightly and peered over the apex of her clenched fists. The blossom seemed to perch on the tip of the barrel. She asked, "Why don't you have the same last name?"

Marc wiped his brow with a handkerchief. "You can't wait until we're at least beneath a fan?"

"I can't help myself. You say you know so much about me. I'd like to know about you."

The caution she had heard in her hotel room crept back into his voice. "You mean about Henry and me?"

"Yes, that's part of it."

He tilted Irene's hands, straightening her aim. "I didn't even meet Henry until I was six years old."

The banana blossom quivered over the tip of the pistol. "Why not?"

"Up until then I hadn't known about my mother's affair with him. I thought a man named William Rafferty was my father. Then he died, and it turned out he'd gambled everything away. The debt was too much for her. She had no choice, she had to tell Henry about me."

Irene lowered the gun. "What if she needed Mr. Simms to believe—"

"My mother had her weaknesses. Henry was one of them. Honesty was another. She couldn't tell a lie."

"Didn't she lie to William Rafferty?"

Marc ran his fingers through his hair, and the cuff of his sleeve fell open, drawing her eyes to his tan wrist. "I don't think she did," he said.

"But she lied to you?"

"She never called him *your father.* She always said, *Tell William it's time for supper. Run down to the factory and take William his lunch.* After he died, she told me the truth. She didn't weep to gain my sympathy, and she didn't apologize. I respected her for that. I even respected Henry for taking responsibility. He was a lousy father, but he never hurt my mother. He gave her a good job and bought her house back. He could have humiliated her, but he never demanded that I take his name or even told anyone that I was his son, although by the time I was eighteen all of Shanghai had figured it out. There was a brief time when I looked just like him."

With each new loss—her father, her job, and soon Mr. Simms—Irene's world crumbled a bit more. Now, with Marc's revelations, she could feel it being shored up. She felt it straining within her to take on a new shape. He started to speak again, but she stopped him. It was too much for her, the realization of how her understanding of her own life was going to change with every word he spoke. Slowly, she must do this slowly. She tugged at the neckline of her blouse. It really was too hot out here. She raised the gun again and took aim. She tried to focus on the banana palm rippling in the heat. Marc was studying her expectantly, the way he had before she kissed him in the street in Saigon. The gun slipped against the sweat of her hands.

"Shoot the damn thing," he said.

The gunshot cleaved the torpid hush from the day. A hurricane of panicked birds' wings beat the air. Then came a dazzling silence.

"Did that help?" he asked.

"What do you mean?"

Marc stared across the field of low sumac, at Simone and Louis leaning against the car, looking back. She in a white cotton dress and he in his white linen suit, they were brushstrokes of light on the brown canvas of the day. Marc's laugh was low and brief. "Where the hell's a hotel when you need one?"

They had been driving steadily for hours through the Cambodian countryside when Irene said, "Stop the car."

"Is something wrong?" Marc asked.

She had made out a shape in the darkness. "Stop, now."

Marc pulled over to the side of the road and cut the engine. Irene walked through the translucent rays of the headlights to the bridge ahead of them. At the front of each of its balustrades the stone hood of a cobra surged toward her, like a cape flung into the sky. "The *naga*," she said, telling the night what it already knew, that these were the mythical serpents that protected Cambodia's rivers. They guarded the Khmer temples and this highway into Phnom Penh, its lights shining on the black horizon. In the galleries of the Brooke Museum, she had held *nagas*, creatures of cast bronze and rosewood that had been brought from this very country, serpents whose arched bodies were still gritty with the iron red dirt of

Cambodia. But it was a different thing to touch one here, in the land where it was born.

When they'd crossed the border, the landscape had not changed, and although Irene knew they were in Cambodia, she had not felt it. Until now. She laid her hand flat against the cobra's stone heart. The half-moon hung askew over the river, and beneath the bridge, a fluorescence of green traced the path of the curving shoreline.

Simone walked up behind her. "This *naga* was built by the French. An attempt at cultural understanding designed by urban planners with a romantic streak."

"I've waited all my life to come here. Let me have this moment. Please."

"They're good at convincing themselves they care. They think a few statues are all it takes. They don't understand. They can't, they're too caught up in their version of progress. But you, I don't know why, but somehow I still think there's hope for you." Simone removed Irene's hand from the statue and steered her back toward the car. "I know what you're thinking, Irene, but this isn't your moment. Not on this bridge with this chunk of cement. This isn't the moment when you realize you're in Cambodia, but I can give that to you." She asked Marc, "Are you tired?"

He waved an empty thermos. "I've had enough coffee to keep an elephant awake until Christmas."

"Angkor Wat is always spoken of in comparison," Simone said. "To the Taj Mahal or the lost cities of the Incas. I've heard it compared to Versailles and the Egyptian pyramids. But I've been to Versailles. I've been to Egypt. There is nothing else like Angkor." Simone leaned into the car. "Can you drive through the night?"

Marc said to Irene, "If you want me to."

"You want to go now?" Irene asked Simone, amazed by her audacity at even suggesting such a delay after what she had done in Saigon.

"Simone," Louis said, "don't be rash."

But even while Irene knew all of the reasons she should not spare an extra day, she looked with longing beyond the bridge, at the road that led through Phnom Penh to Angkor Wat, less than two hundred miles away.

"We can be back here by early tomorrow afternoon," Simone said. "What do you think?"

"I think this isn't the time," Louis admonished.

"I'm not asking you," Simone said.

"We have to find out what Simms is up to. It will take at least two days for gathering the permits and requisitions, and you'll need time to organize the supplies. You know the steamer only leaves on Sundays," Louis reminded her. "If we miss it, we'll lose a week."

Irene tipped her head toward a sound in the distance, the urgent thud of a drumbeat, discordant against a breaking-glass xylophone chime. She had been so focused on her lost temple in the far northeastern jungle that she had forgotten how close they would be to the center of Khmer civilization. It was only five hours away. Simone was watching Irene expectantly. How easy it would be for Irene to tell herself that they should go in order to pacify Simone, as an attempt to keep her from falling to pieces again. But the truth was that Angkor Wat was the ultimate reason Irene had come to Cambodia—the reason she was searching for the scrolls. The scrolls mattered only because they would tell her what had happened to the ancient temple city that she had yearned to visit for as long as she could remember. "Actually, Louis, this *is* the time. Now, right now."

Dawn lay in wait, and the world was clasped in purple shadow. The moon was falling behind Irene, casting its light over her shoulders, skimming the waters of the moat. Beyond the stone wall, far down the causeway, the silhouettes of three peaks stood like mountains in the pale, starry garden of the dying night. Marc started walking toward them. Irene touched his sleeve. "Wait," she said. "Not yet. There's something we need to see."

She guided him through the shadows of the entry tower to the head of the causeway that stretched across the many-acred grounds of Angkor Wat. He sat down, and she tucked herself in front of him, her back settling against his chest, his chin resting on her shoulder as he listened to the chanting of Buddhist monks. "It's as if we're in a church," he said.

Except for the unseen monks, they were alone. They had left Louis at his office in Siem Reap to gather survey maps of Stung Treng province, and Simone to sleep in one of the rest houses outside the temple walls. Having had only a day in the hospital, she was still weak.

"Angkor wasn't built like most Khmer temples," Irene told Marc. "That shadow ahead of us, that's the entrance. It faces west."

"Why does that matter?"

"Watch."

The morning was windless, and the violet sky quiet and flat as the moat. Marc's arms enclosed her as they looked out to the base of the temple, where mist lifted its curtain off the lower galleries, uncovering the hazy robed figures of monks walking where dancing girls and warriors once served a king. Shadows shifted from gray to gold. Out of sight, sunlight scaled the temple's back walls, curving up from the east. Light traced the massive bud-shaped towers. Simone had been right, this was Irene's arrival in Cambodia, her entire being narrowed to a single pinpoint of expectation as the pinnacles atop the towers sparked and burst into flame. She leaned forward, watching a city rise from the depths of the planet. In an instant the fire was extinguished and the sun owned the sky. Angkor Wat exposed its colossal sandstone expanse, revealing itself for what it was—the largest temple in the world.

"I've never seen anything like it," Marc said. "I've never dreamed of anything like it." He studied the towers and terraces. The temple was like a Russian nesting doll, its highest, third-level central sanctuary within the ring of the second level within the ring of the first, all of it enclosed within the outlying walls and the moat. "How big is this place?"

"Five hundred acres," Irene said. "This causeway is more than a thousand feet long. Inside, on the first level alone, there are thirteen thousand square feet of bas-reliefs." She knew every measurement of this temple. Every gallery, every sanctuary, every sculpture, if it had been chronicled or sketched or photographed. As a teenager, she had sat in the professor's office late at night in the museum while her father made his rounds; through tracing paper, her pencil had re-created the image of a fly whisk or sword, until she knew each detail, each rosette twined like scrimshaw over the vaulted ceilings, as if she had created it herself. Her eyes rose to the temple's crimped summit, the towers obscured in the vaporous sunlight. "They were gilded. Can you picture anything that large covered in gold? And there was lacquer and brass and wood, so much wood, but it's all gone, disintegrated over time."

"You lived halfway around the world. How did it happen, the way you feel about this place?"

This was essentially the same question Simone had asked her on the ship out of Shanghai. It felt good to be among people who cared about what was most important to her. Irene eased out of Marc's embrace in order to retrieve a leather-bound tablet from her map case. How well she knew the thickness of the paper, the slight roughness to the surfaces that seized the sheer liquid shape of watercolor paint. Her mother's name, Sarah Blum, was written inside the cover. Irene opened it and showed Marc a painting of white flowers on an altar set before a bodhisattva, the deity seated in the traditional lotus pose of meditation. "My mother," she said. "She gave it to me."

"This is all Angkor Wat?" he asked, as she turned the pages.

"Some of it. These galleries. And this peak. But Angkor Wat was originally Hindu, you'll see that in the carvings, and a lot of what she painted are Buddhist images. I'm guessing the rest of these are from other Khmer temples along the Petit or Grand Circuit. Maybe even farther out on the Royal Road. She loved to explore." Irene closed the tablet. "It's something else to look forward to. Walking into a temple one day and recognizing it from my mother's paintings."

"So it wasn't Henry who ignited your passion?" This seemed to give Marc some kind of satisfaction.

"He kept it alive after she died."

"And how do the scrolls fit into Angkor?"

Irene luxuriated in the view of the temple's peaks, the simple grace of the central tower, dedicated to the god Vishnu, perforating the sky. "Scholars have managed to decipher hundreds of inscriptions on the temples," she told him, "and we still know so little. They figured out the genealogy of more than thirty Khmer kings, and they deciphered the gods the temples were dedicated to. But nothing about why the capital moved around so often after Angkor was abandoned. Nothing about *why* it was abandoned. As for what it was like to live here, there's only one eyewitness account—the journals of a Chinese envoy. The details are invaluable. He wrote that twice a day the king would come out from his palace and sit on a lion's skin, wearing a garland of jasmine wrapped around his head like a crown. He took his audience with commoners as well as functionaries. This was highly unusual for a king. Can you imagine Louis the Fourteenth doing such a thing? And whenever he left Angkor, the blast of a conch shell announced his coming, and hundreds of girls lined the way. They all held candles, even if it was light out. His royal wives followed in chariots carrying parasols coated with gold." Irene dropped her gaze to the expanse of grass spread out before them, with its water buffalo, egrets, and two boys prodding sticks into the lily pads in one of the marshy ponds. "Somehow, it all changed drastically. No more god-kings, no more stone palaces, no more roadways and waterworks."

"Civilizations end," Marc said as he rolled a cigarette. "What's different about this one?"

"If you take a look at modern Cambodian court life, everything from the syntax of the official language to the style of murals painted on the palace walls, it's as if Khmer culture never existed. It hasn't influenced anything. Rome fell, but Italy continued to create incredible works of art. Think about the Renaissance. But the Khmer fell—then nothing. This country has created nothing of value since. Why not?" Frustration contracted her voice. It exhausted her, every time she tried to make sense of this. "What happened to deplete Cambodia of its talent so completely? That's what I want to know."

"This place is like the skeleton of some prehistoric animal. The dinosaur that takes its last breath and in an instant its entire species is extinct." He took hold of her wrist, rolling the carnelian bracelet that she always wore between his fingers. "You say people have been seeking answers for decades. What makes you positive an answer is even out there?"

Irene heard something deeper than just curiosity in his question. She felt a current passing between them as Marc listened to her. "After Angkor Wat fell," she said, "it became a mythical place. In the fifteen hundreds there were vague tales of European missionaries who saw a hidden city of vaulted towers. One Portuguese writer described how a Cambodian king came across 'a wonderland' while hunting for elephants. But even though the rumors were passed along by Spanish soldiers and Dutch merchants, no one believed them. If such a place existed, wouldn't the world know about it? And anyone who saw the bush village that Phnom Penh was before the French arrived was especially skeptical. Then, in 1860, Henri Mouhot came along."

While she dug through her map case again, Irene was aware of Marc observing her. She unfolded a paper scored with words that she had copied down when she was a girl. "This is what Mouhot wrote: *The region in which we are now traveling is rich in floral and faunal specimens. A superstitious dread of the jungle has kept it free from natives. The story of the district is quite like that of other regions of Indo-China. The forest is haunted by a million ghosts and it is bristling with enchanted cities. But that fact seems hardly worth recording inasmuch as any uninhabited place will be bristling with enchanted cities as long as men have the fecund imaginations necessary to construct them out of moonshine and stardust. One hears these reports so frequently that he begins to doubt his own common sense. It seems a concession to ignorance that I should be wasting this much time and space in recording a fable that is so lacking in originality of plot and refinement of expression.*"

Irene looked up, and the temple was still in front of her. Not a fantasy, not a mirage, it soared into the sky. "Three days after he wrote that, Mouhot discovered Angkor Wat." She took Marc's hand and held it to her cheek. She could smell the sweetness of tobacco on his skin. "It didn't exist, and then it did. One day it wasn't, and then the next day it was. That is how I can believe the history is out there."

Chapter 14

The Revolution

Irene rolled over on the mattress, the humidity trapped within the mosquito net clinging to her skin. The ceiling fan revolved lethargically, which was its most energetic speed, and she could not even feel a ripple through the gauze. Not quite awake, she blinked and saw Marc, hazy in the open doorway of their room at the Manolis Hotel.

"What time is it?" she asked.

"Almost seven."

They had arrived in Phnom Penh from Angkor Wat the previous afternoon and fallen asleep before dinnertime, so tired that when Irene tossed awake from the heat in the middle of the night, one of her shoes was still on, and Marc, sprawled beside her, was wearing his shirt, which he had managed to unbutton but not take off.

Now he was clean-shaven and dressed in fresh clothes, and she asked, "Where are you going at this hour?"

"I've already been out," he said. "I've been asking around. Henry has a villa on the road to Siem Reap. He's been out there for almost two weeks, but he's booked on the *Alouette* for the day after tomorrow."

This was the same steamer they planned to be on, if Louis could organize their permits in time. "Did you see him?"

"No," Marc replied.

Irene raised the mosquito net and tied it to the front post of the tester bed, a scarred, hulking piece of mahogany furniture that looked as if it had been dragged all the way to Cambodia from a mountain lodge in Europe. "I know he's here, but I hate to think about it," she said, wishing for a cup of coffee to clear the debris of her long, heavy sleep from her mind. "I hate thinking about him crossing the ocean. It's so cold on the water at night. I keep imagining the sea air, what it must have felt like, aching in his bones."

"I'll go with you."

She was touched by the offer, aware of how reluctant Marc was to see his father. She shook her head. "I'm not ready."

"Don't you want to know what he's up to?"

"You all know such a different man than I do. He's not *up to* anything, Marc. I know exactly why he's here. I knew the second I heard, but I couldn't admit it to myself. He's too close to risk waiting for me back in Seattle."

"Too close to what?" Marc asked, reaching behind him to shut the door, as if he already knew the answer and did not want it to be over-heard.

"His death. And I'm not ready to face that, Marc. Not yet, not after yesterday. Yesterday was perfect. I want to hold on to it for a while longer." She stared up at the fan and wondered why she couldn't feel even the slightest breeze as it paddled against the incoming tide of already warm air through the open window. "Do you think that makes me a terrible person?"

"You tell me you helped kill a man, and it doesn't occur to you that I might judge you for that. But this is why I would think you are terrible? Because you want one more day?"

Irene lowered her head into her hands. She felt the floorboards shift as Marc crossed the room. He knelt in front of her and said, "I hope he knows how lucky he is to be loved by someone as terrible as you."

"I've read the accounts, I know what the French say—that the Cambodians have no ambition. But really, hasn't that always been what colonials say about the natives?" Irene asked. "I just thought the French were envious because this was the one place they knew they could never get the upper hand. How could they, given what the Cambodians have come from? But I never expected it to be like this. I truly didn't expect to see so many people like her."

Sitting over lunch with Simone and Marc in an arcaded café on the Quai de Vernéville, a drowsy boulevard that ran alongside the torpid canal that encased the European quarter, Irene watched a young Cambodian woman walk past. Her gait was slow and without purpose in the looseness of her *sampot,* a piece of fabric that was neither trousers nor skirt, wound around her waist and drawn up between her legs. With her wide features and shorn black hair, which stood as stiff as a bristle above her forehead, she could have been male or female. Only her blouse gave her gender away.

"It's as if she doesn't even see a point in lifting her feet." Irene examined the woman's expression, the deadness in her eyes, as she stared straight ahead, avoiding the foreigners. "She looks tired. And unhappy. They all do. It's as if they have no idea that they're descendants of such nobility."

Simone and Irene had spent the morning at the customs warehouse, sorting through the crates Irene had shipped from Seattle, and now Simone was cross-referencing those supplies with her own list of benzene, gaiters, and mackintosh water bags. "Most of them know what the government wants them to know, and it gets worse every year," she said, annoyed, drawing a dark black line through "wicks." "Unfair land taxes and random punishments for crimes that can't be anticipated. The under-mining of traditions. And that's the least of it. Unhappy? Of course they're unhappy!"

Simone had been irritable all morning, and Irene, still a bit woozy from her visit to Angkor Wat, as if the temple were a particularly strong drink she'd had one too many of, was trying to ignore her mood. "You sound as if I'm faulting them, Simone, but I'm not. That's the last thing I want to do. In fact, I want the opposite. The scrolls have the potential to bring them the kind of recognition they deserve, not just from the outside but from within too. By knowing how their story ended, they can know how to start over. The scrolls could turn out to be just the thing to show the Cambodians how they can be capable of it all again. The art. The architecture. Just imagine it." Stirring her asparagus soup, Irene looked across the street, where flame trees spread their carmine branches above the shore of the canal. Three Cambodian men were squatting on the deck of a sampan, halfheartedly playing cards. A clay jug that had been full of rice whiskey was now discarded next to an ugly yellow dog passed out at their bare, splayed feet. "Honestly, though, Simone, don't you wonder at all how the French have been able to take their pride away from them so thoroughly?"

"You're being naïve, Irene," Marc said. "The French have bigger guns."

"They *have* guns," Simone said, so sharply that Marc observed her with wariness as he continued. "They would kill every last Cambodian if they sensed a hint of resistance. I saw it too often in China. It's disgust-ing, how many excuses a colonial government can come up with for a massacre. The Cambodians wouldn't stand a chance."

"But what about Angkor Wat? There's no reason they shouldn't live there. Why not reclaim it?" Irene asked, even though, as she was speak-ing, she knew exactly why not. She understood that what you wanted, no matter how badly you wanted it, did not mean anything if it was also wanted by someone more powerful than you. "There's no point in them living here! A hill, that's all the Cambodians have of a heritage in Phnom Penh. A hill with a Siamese-style stupa guarded by Chinese Fu dogs on a spot where a woman buried some sacred Buddhist relics in the fourteenth century. Not to mention a tinfoil royal palace for a puppet king that may as well have been built in Bangkok. They're heirs to the Khmer, and the only evidence of that is the king's dancers."

"Angkor Wat is too symbolic," Simone said. "The government would never let them have that kind of foothold." She scowled. "What could possibly be wrong this time?" She was being summoned by a Cambodian man in a blue button-down dress shirt and matching *sampot,* who was standing beyond the low whitewashed wall of the café terrace. Irene had already seen him twice that morning, coming and going at the warehouse. He was helping with the final arrangements for the equipment they still needed for the expedition—more axes and an elaborate first aid kit and what seemed like miles of sturdy rope—but every time he ambled up to Simone, she became more exasperated and he more sullen. Now she hissed, "On the surface, yes, the Cambodians are no longer impressive, but essentially, they're no different than they have always been. That's what gives them more strength than they receive credit for. If only people would see their possibility in that. The problem with you, Irene, is that you can't stop focusing on the least important part of what they used to be."

Marc watched Simone stride away. "I liked her better in the car. She was amiable."

"She was doped on Luminal," Irene said, growing concerned about more than just Simone's disposition. Given her evident displeasure as she spoke rapidly with the man in Khmer, Irene added to her list of growing worries that there might be trouble with the last supplies needed for travel into the uplands, or that Simone was on the verge of doing something reckless again that might cause them to miss the steamer. With these concerns compounded by the issue of getting permits on time and the possibility that Louis would tell one of his colleagues about the temple now that he and Simone had had a falling-out, Irene was completely drained. "Louis found the bottle when they were unpacking at the hotel," she said. "She must have stolen it from the hospital."

"So she's going to be this temperamental for the rest of the trip?"

"Probably, if Louis keeps her clean."

"How pleasant for us in the middle of the jungle." Marc stirred his sugarcane juice, watery with melted ice. "But you know, Irene, I think I know what she means."

"What are you talking about?" she asked.

"Their history, their past, whatever you want to call it." He turned from Simone to the fishermen. "It's in the way they're sitting, and how their hair is pulled back at their necks. It's fascinating. Take away that bottle of rice whiskey and give them fishing poles, and I'd swear they were one of the carvings we saw at the Bayon."

After leaving Angkor Wat, Irene had taken Marc to the nearby Bayon temple, where the galleries were wrapped in bas-reliefs of Khmer daily life. But rather than warriors and kings, these were detailed depictions of women cooking over charcoal braziers and men carrying loaves of palm sugar to market. As her eyes roamed from Marc to the men on the boat, Irene was able to see what he did: their bony figures transformed into sculpted stone.

Irene had not expected Marc's growing interest in the Khmer. To share a past was one kind of intimacy, and more than she had hoped for. To share a passion was a good fortune beyond her belief, and she felt a thrill at this prospect, as he pointed out a matron at her wooden-wheeled cart, roasting scrawny fish over cinders, and said, thoughtfully, "Look at the style of her *sampot*. Did you see the looms beneath the huts as we were driving back from Siem Reap? Just like on the sculptures at the Bayon. I doubt the techniques or patterns have changed over the centuries." He rose in his chair to acknowledge Simone's return and said to her, "Their strength lies in the way their past is still present in their day-to-day lives. That's what you mean, isn't it? Despite what's been taken from them, and what's been inflicted on them, they've persisted in living the way they have always lived."

Simone's annoyance appeared to lessen, and she nodded.

But this did not appease the anger Irene felt about how little regard the colonial system had for what the Cambodians should still be. "Managing to hold on to the minutiae of their daily lives hasn't given them any advantage. Their kingdom, their ability to create such a kingdom, surely that's where any remaining power lies."

"The Egyptians, the Mayans—civilizations disappear. It's the law of nature," Marc asserted, slipping back into their discussion from the previous day. "There's always a time to let go. A time to move on."

What Irene was beginning to feel at discovering the position the Cambodians had been forced into by the French was something greater than disappointment. It was sadness that her beloved Khmer had been reduced to this, and a growing fear that what she might in fact end up learning from the scrolls was that the Cambodians had fallen so hard centuries ago that their defeat had become a trait, like hair color or height, inherited and passed down and accepted without question throughout the generations, so that when colonization arrived, it did not come as a surprise, and fighting back was not a consideration. Sickened by the thought of their being so beaten down, she asked, "Do you really think that fate has that much influence on the rise and fall of a culture?"

"It's hardly fate," Marc said. "History has its natural rhythms. Maybe, somehow, the Cambodians know this. Have accepted it, even. Their time for distinction has come and gone."

Simone slapped her notebook shut. "I let you see Angkor Wat, and this is what the two of you conclude? That the Khmer are so confined by one aspect of their heritage that they don't have any other way of rising out of this? How can you claim to care about the Khmer, Irene, if you can't conceive that their time could come again? Their time *will* come again."

"I'm sorry, Simone, I want to, I do, but—"

"*Mon Dieu,* that man is a nuisance!"

The Cambodian had returned to the railing, curling his fingers in a downward wave, beckoning. Simone went back to him. Marc and Irene looked uneasily at one another, like chastened schoolchildren. "I hope Louis sorts out our paperwork," Marc said. "If this is what we're in for, I don't think I have the stamina for another week of waiting for the steamer to come around again."

Irene watched a rickshaw sluggishly approaching Simone and the Cambodian. It was laden with the oiled canvas tarpaulins the expedition would need for protection from the rain. Irene was too far away to see what was wrong with them, only that Simone did not approve. "It's frustrating, not having any contacts of my own for the rest of the supplies," she said. "It makes me nervous, having to rely on her so completely right now."

"The way she's behaving, it seems as if it's about more than having a few pills taken away," Marc said. "What else do you think is wrong?"

"Welcome to the rabbit hole. I could sit here guessing for a year and the only thing I'd know for sure is that whatever I concluded, if Simone is involved, I wouldn't be right."

Irene and Marc did not have to wait long to learn the reason for Simone's ill temper. Halfway through dinner, in the middle of a discussion about the difficulties of river travel because of the lateness of the monsoons this season, Simone shushed Louis—"I think we've heard enough about rapids for tonight"—and leaned toward Irene. "I've been waiting all day for you to mention his name," she said, her voice smudged by the two glasses of Bordeaux she'd had with her cassoulet. "In Saigon, when you learned that Henry Simms was here, I thought you were going to run all the way to Cambodia to find out what is going on. Now we've been here an entire day, he's living in a villa less than a mile outside of town, and my contacts tell me you haven't gone to see him."

Instinctively, Irene scanned the dining room, but the Cambodian in the blue dress shirt was not skulking in one of the corners. "What else have your contacts told you?"

"That he's nearly dead."

Marc's leg braced against Irene's beneath the table. Her wariness slipped from the room's depths to the open terrace doors, where large winged insects soared in, drawn to the apricot burn of the electric lamps. Light flickered with the shadows of thick, flapping moths and the uneven swing of the electric fans. A storm was approaching, and waiters dashed around the patio, bringing in cushions, candleholders, and plants.

"He has cancer," Irene said.

Tonight, Simone had chosen to resemble an American flapper, in a dress that swayed with beaded fringe every time she moved. She had even found time to oil her hair into pin curls, and she twisted a lock around her finger as she said, "When you and I first met, Irene, I assumed you and

Henry simply had a business arrangement. Two people in the same circle whose paths crossed at the right time and who made a deal for the scrolls. Then you showed up in my hospital room with his son."

"I've been waiting for you to bring that up," Irene said.

Coolly, Simone appraised Marc. "In love, of all things, with Henry Simms's son."

Heat rushed to Irene's face, and her eyes darted away from Marc's. She had not been hiding her feelings for him—they were sharing the same hotel room, after all—but still she felt exposed. She held out her after-dinner cigarette to Louis, the only one she could face without embarrassment. "What do you want from me?" she asked Simone.

"Clarification. Let's start with the story behind you and Henry Simms."

There was obviously more to Simone's challenge than finding out how Irene and Mr. Simms were bound to one another. Irene could hear her digging for something deeper. Watching Simone take a third glass of wine, thinking about how argumentative she had been all day, and knowing how distrustful she was of Mr. Simms, Irene felt her instincts tell her to make peace. And to tread cautiously. *My contacts.* They were in new territory. Simone's territory. "All right," she said, "if that's what you need from me tonight." She wished she had ordered something stronger than the Cointreau digestif in the tiny cordial glass before her. She drank the citrus-flavored liqueur in one gulp, as if it were a shot of whiskey. "I was kidnapped before I was born."

Outside, beyond the patio, clouds approached low and fast, and the moonlight was obscured. The gramophone crackled with the wet electricity in the air. *Ain't nobody's business if I do.* There was a shift around the table, a collective movement toward Irene, who had never told this story to anyone. She had never had anyone to tell it to who would not be shocked or, more likely, horrified. But these people—Marc, Simone, and Louis—they might not even find it unusual.

"My parents were living in Manila," she told them. "Whenever my father was away in a port, he scoured curio shops. He bought porcelain vases, terra-cotta statues, wood-block prints, whatever caught his eye, and sold it to dealers." As thunder rumbled its deep-throated imitation of the world's end, she had to raise her voice to explain. "But he wasn't an expert. He never wanted to be. He called himself a scavenger, and that was what he loved most about the hunt. The element of surprise."

As Irene sifted through the details of her parents' story, the rain fell, a thick wall toppling against the hotel. Although it lapped onto the terrace, threatening to flood the dining room, the louvered doors remained open. Waiters served wine, the front-desk madame worked the gramophone beside the dance floor, and the hotel's Greek owner inhaled snuff with a turbaned guest. Despite the distraction of drunken conversations and raucous laughter competing with the storm, Marc, Simone, and Louis were intent on only one thing.

"Go on," Marc urged.

"My father was on shore leave in Borneo when he learned about the death of a missionary who was said to collect tribal artwork. He asked to view it. There wasn't much, some crude carvings of Jesus, the usual shrunken heads and bone pipes. But he did find a trunk of botanical drawings, a catalog of the flora of Sarawak. He thought it might be of interest to a university. When he got the trunk back to Manila, he discovered a false panel. He removed it and—"

The sky splintered, and thunder exploded through. A roar of approval flew up from the men and women in the dining room.

"He removed it and he found—"

The ground seemed to open deep beneath them, releasing a detonation from the earth's core. The hotel shook. The lights went out. Through the pounding rain, the colonials cheered louder.

Irene felt a hand on hers. It was Louis, asking, "What did he find?"

Irene whispered, "What if it was Reverend Garland's diary?"

Around the room, matches flared, and candles began to flutter. Kerosene lamps were lit, and as a waiter set one in the center of their table, their faces took on an eerie, quavering orange pallor.

"What are you talking about?" Simone asked.

With the fans stilled, the air grew heavy. Lightning stripped darkness from the sky. "The diary. What if that's what my father found in the missionary's trunk? He told me it was a book."

"What kind of book?"

"I don't know. *That damn book*. That's all I ever heard him call it. I'd forgotten that it had belonged to a missionary." Her mind raced, calculating. "If that missionary was Reverend Garland, that would mean my father found the diary before I was born. It could mean that Mr. Simms knew about it all the way back then, and not just after my father died."

"Why would he have known?" Marc asked.

"And what does any of this have to do with the kidnapping?" Louis asked.

"Mr. Simms was also living in Manila then. That's when he became friends with my parents," Irene explained. "There was a gangster there too. An Englishman named Lawrence Fear."

Simone sat forward. "Fear?"

"I know. A criminal named Fear. It sounds like something from a dime novel, doesn't it?"

"What happened?" Simone asked, urgently. "What did he do?"

"My father had shown the book to one of the dealers he worked with, to find out what it was worth, and he figured the dealer must have told Fear. Fear had people fishing for information for him all over the Orient. When he learned of the book, he waited until my father was out of the house and sent his men for my mother. She was eight months pregnant with me, but that didn't matter to them. They locked her up in a warehouse on one of the wharves. My father brought the book immediately, but something went wrong and Fear shot my mother. I remember the scar, above her breast."

"Simms," Louis prodded. "How does Simms fit in?"

"He went with my father to help. They knew they'd be searched, so they weren't carrying guns. Mr. Simms killed Fear with an iron bar he'd found, and another man with Fear's own gun before the rest ran away."

"Everything he's told me about you," Marc said, dazed as he absorbed this loose scrap of his father's history, "but he never said anything about this."

"I was told that the book disappeared," Irene said, "but what if that's not true? What if my father kept it all those years until his death?"

"Why would he take it and not tell anyone?" Louis asked.

"I don't know," Irene said.

"Lawrence Fear." Simone repeated the name, as if it were a foreign term she was trying to interpret.

As swiftly as it had blown into the city, the squall was moving on. The growl of thunder began to fade, and Irene contemplated the possibility that Reverend Garland's diary and the book her father had found in the missionary's trunk were one and the same. It didn't make sense: If they'd had the diary, her father and Mr. Simms would have gone after the lost temple back then, and she could think of no reason why Mr. Simms would have her hunt for it again. Still, she could not shake the thought.

"I took you to Angkor Wat," Simone murmured, fidgeting with the fringe of her dress. "I let you have that, because I really did think that, deep in your heart, you're one of us."

"Simone," Louis said, with warning.

"Once she sees it, I thought, then I won't have to convince her." Simone drained her wineglass. "She'll know. She'll want their resurrection as much as I do. But I didn't understand. This goes too far back for you. In the womb! Of course you're like Henry Simms. Of course the opinions of men like him matter to you. You can't help yourself. I knew this was going to be a struggle, but . . . And my mother. My mother! How does she even fit into this?"

Marc and Louis looked to Irene for an explanation, but Irene shook her head, silently letting them know that she had no idea why Simone was talking about her mother. Speechless, the three of them watched Simone as she began to whisper, "No." Her head tipped from side to side, her dress shimmying as she repeated herself. "No!" she shouted, shearing conversation from the room.

"Simone?" Louis said, tentatively this time.

"What did she take?" Marc held up his hand, dismissing the rapidly approaching front-desk madame. "Simone, did you take anything tonight?"

"You're still not well," Louis said to her. "You shouldn't have had so much to drink."

The madame crossed her arms over her brick-house torso and planted herself a few feet away.

One of us—it rustled into Irene's thoughts.

"My mother, of all things," Simone muttered.

"What about your mother?" Marc asked. When Simone did not respond, he said to Louis, "She's almost delirious. This is more than too much to drink."

Defiantly, Simone said, "They know they can trust me. They told me about . . . I know Simms intends to leave a fortune to L'École Française d'Extrême-Orient." Breathing heavily, she turned to Louis. "You promised you wouldn't tell her, and you did. Now you think you can trick me, as if this revolution—"

Louis caught Simone by the arm and lifted her from her chair. "It's time to go."

The agitation in Irene's thoughts amplified as Simone's words from the night on the steamer when they were sailing out of Hong Kong broke through. *There are reasons a revolution is necessary, Irene. I didn't believe in it solely because he told me to. . . . I knew what I was doing. I have always known what I am doing.*

Simone mumbled, "If you think you can trick me into giving up the scrolls by funneling Simms's money to me through some lackey pretending to work for the government—"

"Enough!" Louis pulled Simone away from the table.

The front-desk madame looked worriedly at the hotel owner, but the Brillo-haired Greek shrugged and took another whiff of his snuff.

Irene remembered Simone berating the official in the customs shed back in Saigon. *People like you are the reason I joined the Communists. You are the reason the French are going to lose Indochina.*

Simone struggled against Louis, and Marc stood. "Let me help you."

"No." Louis was much stronger than he appeared to be. Already, he had Simone halfway across the room.

Then there was today in the café. *Their time* will *come again.* Irene reached for a drink, but her hand was shaking, and the glass shattered as it hit the tile floor. "Shit."

"What?" Marc asked. "What in the hell is going on?"

Incredulously, Irene said, "I think Simone wants the scrolls for the Communists."

Chapter 15

A Great Cambodian Adventure

For her confrontation with Simone, Irene chose the one kind of place where she had always felt sure of herself. As she heaved open the front door of the Musée Albert Sarraut, she pressed her palms against the carvings on its surface, the same floral pattern found on stone pillars and lintels throughout the Khmer temples. Inside, a Cambodian slouched in a hammock. He opened one eye, halfway. It was not yet 7:00 A.M. Her stare dared him to turn her away. He could not be bothered to confront a wild-eyed white woman at such an early hour and retreated back into his sleep.

Although the morning was already liquid with heat, the rose-hued vestibule was cool. Irene had never been inside a museum that was not cool, and she savored the familiar subterranean atmosphere.

She crossed the hall to the opposite door, and when she pushed it back, a reflection of sunlight pooled at her feet. It was as if someone had poured warm water over her sandals. She entered the courtyard. Simone had not yet arrived, and Irene was both relieved and amazed as she studied the galleries that framed the lotus ponds, four dark green water gardens that fanned out from a central gazebo. Unlike any museum she had ever been in, there was not a single interior wall to protect the centuries-old statues of Siva and Brahma, nor even screens to pull closed against the elements.

Irene waited on a wooden bench in a well of shade, where she watched sunlight crawl across the red-tile roof, lifting a vaporous film from the air. Pillars showed their sharp angles, and as morning levered the sun farther into the sky, light billowed around pedestals scattered like pilings in a shallow stone sea. It rose like a tide over the bare feet of Vishnu, easing up his polished calves to the smooth hem of his *sampot*. Simone's yellow dress seemed to glow when she arrived from the entry hall, clutching the note Irene had slipped under her hotel room door. The paper said only "Musée Albert Sarraut."

Too tired to accuse, Irene simply asked, "You still want a revolution, don't you?"

"You should know that I'm through with the Communists," Simone announced rapidly, as if she too had been up all night and still did not know how to begin. "They're as bad as the colonial government. Everything is politics to them. Everything is about power. About who has the power. Not only over the country but within the party too. Roger spent as much time battling Voitinsky as he did the Municipal Government."

"If this isn't about Communism, then I don't understand what happened last night."

Making her way through the statues, Simone stopped to lay the back of her hand against the cool cheek of the goddess Lakshmi. "I've never cared about power, but I've always cared about Cambodia, even when I was a girl, even before I met Roger and understood what my feelings could accomplish. After I came back from my first trip to France, I would think about the architecture here, the wrought-iron balconies and forest green shutters, and I could never figure it out. Why would a person come this far and then make every effort to feel as if he had never left Marseilles? What purpose could there be in taking a ship halfway around the globe only to eat crème brûlée in a café where the tables were covered in bobbin lace from Normandy? The French have done a remarkable job of paving their culture right over the top of the Khmer's."

Irene could not remember if Simone had always talked like this. *The French. Their culture.* As if she belonged to an entirely different nationality. Despite how Irene felt about the way colonialism was stifling the Cambodians, she said, "They're restoring temples. Surely there's value in that."

Tracing her finger along the engraved braid that framed Lakshmi's high brow, Simone said, "I'm not talking about their pretentious efforts at archaeology to bolster the soiled reputation of the French Empire. I'm talking about the present day. Give them another generation of *mission civilisatrice,* and any last trace of Khmer culture will be erased. All that will be left is this museum and an amusement park called Angkor Wat with one of your Coney Island roller coasters swooping over the lotus ponds."

"And how do you think the scrolls can change that?"

"Shouldn't the Cambodians be the ones to decide what kind of life they're going to live? What kind of future their country will have?" Simone tipped her head in thought, and it was as if she were consulting the sculpted goddess beside her rather than Irene when she asked, "Shouldn't they be the ones to choose if they're going to replace *amok* with bouillabaisse? *Sampots* with Brooks Brothers suits? Shouldn't their history— their own history—belong to them, to do with as they please?"

"And what is that?"

"Start a nationalist party and take their country back."

It was such an unprotected, unrepentant statement; Irene had to force herself to hold Simone's gaze. She felt an immediate shame that any of this came as a surprise. She thought about everything Simone had told her in Shanghai: how she had organized arms shipments with the gunrunner Borodin, and had helped found the workers' *Shanghai Chronicle,* and was the confidante of the wife of Chiang Kai-shek, but mostly her declaration, "I am valuable." In retrospect, Irene could too easily see that this had not been said to soothe Simone's wounded ego. Searching for something to say that might encourage answers without provoking Simone, Irene said, "I had such idealistic ideas about what I was going to find over here, what I would discover about the Cambodians that no one else had. I didn't realize how inadequate a decade of study could be compared to a single day in the streets."

"That's exactly it, Irene. The Cambodians are more than they're given credit for. They care about traditions, and they're willing to work hard to feed their children. How different is that from any of the Europeans over here? But there's no point in hard work, since everything they earn is taken away from them. The government sees them as nothing but the labor they provide the rubber plantations. The colonials are doing everything they can to drain the Cambodians of any last excellence they might have in them. It's because they know. Given a pittance of their old superiority, the first thing the Cambodians would do is kick the French out of their country."

Irene stood. "You still haven't explained how the scrolls fit into any of this."

Simone crossed her arms. "And you still haven't explained how Lawrence Fear and my mother fit in."

Again, this reference to her mother. And what could Lawrence Fear possibly have to do with anything? "I have no idea what you're talking about," Irene said.

"You're honestly telling me that you don't know about Madeleine and Sarah and their great Cambodian adventure?"

Irene's eyes jumped from Simone to the impassive statue beside her to the red hibiscus flickering in the cloud shadows of the courtyard—trying to comprehend. Why had Simone Merlin, hell-bent on taking the scrolls to start a nationalist party, just said *Sarah*, Irene's mother's name?

"Oh," Simone gasped. "You really don't know, do you?"

Irene shook her head.

"Fear. It's a name you've never forgotten. Well, I can't forget it either, although I didn't know it was a name until last night. When my mother died, I found a letter among her belongings, from a woman named Sarah in America. Do you remember how it was when your mother died? How you gathered everything you could? The memory of her perfume. The way she kissed your forehead when she put you to bed. Her smile. You fought to keep her alive."

"I remember."

"I memorized this." Simone unfolded a worn sheet of paper, glanced at it, and then recited from memory. *"My dearest Madeleine. I have learned of the tragic loss of your son. I am so sorry. Some days the thought of what might have happened to my unborn daughter is too much to bear, and I cannot fathom the pain you are now suffering. There is no greater loss than that of a child. I will never be able to thank you enough for helping to save us from Fear in Manila."*

Irene tried to shut out the scratching noise of the bats in the rafters, but as Simone held out the letter, their shuffling grew louder. She noticed Simone's nails, bitten down to the raw red quick. Her body did not know what to do, tense or wilt, as she recognized her mother's handwriting on the same oyster-colored stationery she had used for all of her correspondence, even notes left for the milkman or tucked into Irene's lunch pail.

Simone said, "I remember thinking that it was such a strange thing to write. *For helping to save us from Fear.* Especially since *Fear* was capitalized. Do you see how it's capitalized? I thought that was a mistake."

"But it wasn't."

"No, it wasn't. *I will always treasure our great adventure in Cambodia. I cannot know why you agreed to keep the secret, but I know why I did, and I am not sorry. I hope you still feel the same. Patrik sends his love, as do I. Your devoted friend, Sarah.* Do you see the date, Irene? 1897. This was written two years before my parents were married." She scanned the letter, as if searching for hidden answers. "I've never understood it, Irene. My mother never told me about having a son who died."

"I was told that Mr. Simms saved our lives. He's the one who killed Fear. How could your mother have saved us? What could she have done?"

Simone thought this over. "She served as a nurse during the Franco-Chinoise War. She was at the hospital night and day during the uprisings in Siem Reap. You said your mother was shot. Mine could have treated the wound."

"What would she have been doing in Manila?"

"The same thing your parents were doing. Traveling," Simone speculated. "Exploring new places. It's not an unrealistic thought, Irene. Do you understand what this could mean? If my mother was in Manila, if she was with them for some reason, and if she helped your mother, then she must have known Henry Simms. If you're right, what you said last night, if your father had Reverend Garland's diary before you were born—"

"I don't know if that's true." In the bright daylight, without the urging of a storm, Irene was reluctant to jump to this conclusion.

"But if it is. If it is!" Whatever politics Simone believed in, whatever larger-than-life hopes she had for the revival of the Khmer Empire, they were forgotten for an instant as she said, excitedly, "A great Cambodian adventure. Irene, promise me that you'll tell me if you find out what that means."

"A Cambodian nationalist party?" Marc whistled. "Did she tell you how she plans on doing this?"

Irene stood inside the closed door of their hotel room. The yellowing glass lamps were not turned on, as if dimness could equal coolness. It couldn't. She peeled off her blouse, but her camisole was still too warm for the sticky late-morning heat. "We didn't make it that far. We were interrupted by the discovery that our mothers might have had some kind of Cambodian adventure together. A *great* Cambodian adventure. Possibly with your father. Possibly having to do with the diary."

Marc pushed away from the mahogany desk, where he had been reading through the small collection of books about the Khmer that Irene had brought with her. Around the books and tucked into them, his notes were scribbled on letter paper provided by the hotel. "I didn't know your families knew one another."

"Like everything else, neither did I." She unlatched the tall slatted doors that opened onto the balcony. A downy rain had started as she was walking back from the museum, and the rattan furniture outside was slick with a fine mist, despite the awning above. She retrieved her packet of cigarettes from where she had tucked it into a pot of withering marigolds.

Marc said, "I know it doesn't make sense, but do you think there's any way Henry could have something to do with this nationalist party of hers?"

"At this point anything is likely, but I don't think so. My guess now is that Simone is part of this expedition because of some relationship Mr. Simms had with her mother. Something happened over here, before we were born, presumably to do with the temple we're after. It could be why he wanted me to get her out of Shanghai."

"Why wouldn't he tell you that?"

"I'm not sure. He's always been a manipulator. I just didn't see any of this coming because he's never manipulated me." Irene should have been angered. Instead she felt honored, at being at the heart of this mechanism Mr. Simms had set in motion. "As for Simone's politics, I have a feeling that they're an unlucky coincidence. It all seems to be tangled together because we're all tangled together." Tipping ashes onto the dead moths in the flowerpot, she sighed. "A revolution to call her own. Who would have guessed that *that's* what she really wants from this? I still can't quite believe it."

Marc joined Irene on the balcony. Leaning against the railing, they looked down at the French tricolors hanging damp and limp from iron posts dotted along the riverfront promenade on the opposite side of the wide Quai Lagrandiere boulevard. "If it makes you feel any better, I was Shanghai's watchdog, and I didn't know Simone was planning anything."

The worst part of this for Irene was that she knew the exact cause of her blindness. "Simone told me what I needed to know to see this coming, and I didn't listen because I wanted to hear something else. I wanted someone who understood me. Who desired what I desired. I felt unmoored after everything that happened in Seattle." She traced his shoulder, searching for direction as her finger circled the compass that showed beneath the cotton of his white shirt. "I thought that once we found the scrolls, we could reach some kind of compromise. I thought she was homesick and defeated. I felt sorry for her. I thought I was saving her. But Marc, she killed her husband. She saved *me* that night. It's unforgivable, how wrong I allowed myself to be about her."

"You weren't wrong. She does share your desire. Both of you plan to use the scrolls to fulfill a dream. The problem is that you have such different dreams." He caught her hand and stilled it, and while she was comforted by his closeness, it unsettled her too. He asked, "What are you going to do now?"

"She does love her sedatives. Maybe I can drug her and make a run for it."

He nodded appreciatively. "Good girl. Never lose your sense of humor, especially here in the gallows."

"If I could figure out her reasons for thinking it will do any good to hand the scrolls over to the Cambodians, if I could understand how the scrolls can make a difference in what the revolutionaries are trying to accomplish, then I'd have a better chance of knowing if there's any validity in what she wants to do. Of knowing what I'm truly up against."

Marc was thoughtful as he looked out at the leather brown Tonle Sap River. Although the day was well under way, there was no commerce on the docks, only vacant fishing boats and a Cambodian boy sprawled in a canoe. Finally, he said, "When Angkorian society began, Paris and London were not much more than elaborate villages. Europe was crawling with barbarians, and here were the Khmer engineering sophisticated irrigation systems and constructing the biggest temple in the world. I didn't know about any of this until I started reading." He waved inside, at the books on the desk. "I've lived in the Orient all my life, I've lived under a colonial government all my life, and I've never questioned one empire usurping another. It's the way of the world. But when we were walking through Angkor Wat, I found myself wondering about what is lost when one culture is systematically annihilated so another can thrive in the name of progress. Think about it, what might have happened if Cambodia hadn't eventually been taken over by Siam and then France—what the Cambodians could offer the world if they're given the opportunity to follow through with what they're meant to become."

This was counter to everything Marc had said about inevitability, and Irene struggled against disbelief as she asked, "Do you think she's right? Do you think the scrolls should be given to the Cambodians?"

He was momentarily puzzled by her question. "I didn't know this had anything to do with right and wrong. As for what I think, I've already told you, history has its course, and there's not much to be done about it. I'm simply trying to help you find your way through that minefield of a brain of hers. I thought that's what you wanted."

"But what if it's possible?"

"What?" he asked.

"That this is about opportunity. That the Cambodians might create something of value again if only they're given the chance. Can you imagine how glorious that would be? Can you imagine being part of such a resurrection? Theoretically, what you're saying has logic. And I don't know, maybe what Simone is saying does too."

"Don't tell me you're planning on becoming a revolutionary?"

Irene wished she could find this funny. "The more rational her argument becomes, the more legitimate her threat becomes."

"So you think she's sincere?" Marc frowned, as if this had not occurred to him. "This isn't just a melodramatic reaction to Roger's death?"

Irene snuffed out her cigarette in the marigold pot. "That's what I plan to find out."

Down at the end of the waterfront, the customs warehouse was dark and smelled of stale lager, cigarette butts, and river-soaked wood. Irene walked through it quickly, holding her breath. On the wharf outside the rolling doors, next to a bearded customs agent, Louis stood with a manifest in one hand. He was barking at two coolies who struggled to haul a crate into the hold of the *Alouette*. The words BROOKE EXPEDITION, SEATTLE, USA bobbed with their effort. Irene had ordered this stamped on each of the containers she'd sent over, since association with the museum would add credibility. She stepped between the two men. "Excuse me. Louis, I need to talk with you."

They had not seen one another since he dragged Simone from the hotel restaurant the previous night. He glanced from the coolies to the list, and when she saw "tinned provisions" on the paper, she knew exactly what the crate contained—peaches and applesauce, Van Camp's pork and beans, and Campbell's oxtail soup. She had bought it all from a grocer who supplied Alaska mining camps in Seattle. "I'll meet you back here in half an hour," he said to the agent.

As soon as the man was out of sight, Irene accosted Louis. "How long have the two of you been planning this?"

"What *this*?" he asked, guiding her to the side of the warehouse, not for privacy but for shade.

"A revolution."

Louis laughed. "What in God's name would I want with a revolution?"

"Why else would you be—"

He cut her off. "I'll tell you what, Irene. Let's not talk around this. You admit what you're going to do with the scrolls, and I'll be frank with you."

Across the quay, balconied French villas dozed in the heat. Down the cobbled embankment, sun-bleached sampans had collected like driftwood in the muddy shallows of the boat landing. One view belonged to a world Simone intended to topple. Another to a world she hoped to raise from the ashes. How peacefully they seemed to reside together. How dangerously easy such an illusion was to believe. Irene had nothing to lose by conceding to Louis. "I'm going to take them to America and use them to buy a curatorship. New York is the obvious choice, but I've been thinking about San Francisco. The Ethier Museum. It's competed with the Brooke for years, but it never stood a chance. It didn't have me. But with the scrolls and me, within five years I will transform it into the most notable museum of Oriental art in the world. In ten I'll have filled its galleries with at least half the Khmer relics now in the halls of the Guimet, not to mention everything I acquired for the Brooke. I will give the Khmer the prominence they deserve."

"So you do have a solid plan." Louis folded the list of supplies still in his hand and tucked it into his pocket. "Simone thinks she is going to sell them for the money she needs for a revolution here in Cambodia."

"Money? She wants money? But I've offered her fifty thousand dollars for helping me."

"You know those scrolls could be valued at up to a million."

"Fine. I'll talk to Mr. Simms." Irene had negotiated acquisitions worth a king's ransom before. "I'll get her whatever she wants. Money." Relief washed over her. "Why didn't she tell me? Or did she really think she could persuade me to join her cause?"

"She thinks she can persuade both of us," Louis said, removing his straw hat. He rubbed his fingers over the red crease of the band's imprint along his forehead. The rest of his face was ruddy from heat, sweat darkened the rim of his collar, and his string tie had come loose from its knot. He looked as worn down as Irene felt. "She thinks it's only a matter of time before we come to our senses. As for your generous offer, she's refusing to sell them to just anyone. She plans to sell them to the government."

Squinting up the promenade, where two foreigners in rumpled suits stood smoking in the shelter of a magnolia tree, Irene said, "But the French are the last people she'd want to get their hands on them."

"You're not thinking like Simone. When they look at those scrolls, she wants them to think about how they financed the downfall of their colony."

Irene had no patience for Freud or any other psychoanalytic fad chasing socialites around America, but she knew the terminology. "Is she delusional?"

"Does it matter?"

"But if she's selling them to the government for spite? It's shortsighted. It's—"

"What, Irene? It's what? The same as you thrusting them in the faces of the trustees who wronged you? To shame them into regretting how they underestimated you?" Coolly, he said, "I believe therein you will find the definition of spite." He straightened his jacket, securing an undone button, and then he began to fix the knot in his tie, as if by putting himself to rights he could banish his annoyance. But when he spoke again, his voice was still sharp. "What in the hell is wrong with the two of you? If these scrolls exist, they're a greater understanding, not only of the Khmer, but of civilization, its evolution, and you're treating them like cheap glass beads. As if they're worth nothing more in trade than a chunk of your petty pride."

Louis was no longer the lovesick satellite that Irene had watched tearfully orbiting Simone in Saigon. He was his own man, with his own convictions. There was danger in this, but at the same time Irene liked him the better for it. "The government won't pay her," she said. "They'll demand she hand them over. You know the laws."

Late in the previous year, after another bodhisattva from Angkor Wat had showed up at the Fogg Museum in Cambridge, the governor-general of Indochina had issued a decree: All ancient edifices found in the French-controlled provinces of Cambodia were now "monuments of public interest." Anyone caught trying to take even a stone from one of the temples out of the country would risk imprisonment. Simone would have to make her deal from another country, where French law did not apply, and even then, the trade-off, exchanging the scrolls for the money, would be a gamble. "Although now that I think about it," Irene added, "if she does manage to sell them to the government, how ideal that would be for you, since the Conservation d'Angkor is under their control."

"It wouldn't do me any good," Louis said. "They'd send the scrolls back to France."

Given all that she had been through in Seattle, Irene could understand his grievance. "It must be demoralizing, having them take everything of value away." She glanced toward a fishing boat drifting past the end of the dock, distracted by the red and aqua gloss of its reflection wavering in the dark brown water. When she looked back, Louis was examining her in a way that made her feel as if he were reevaluating his opinion of her.

"Have you read Marchal on the subject of in situ?" he asked. " 'Angkor's admirable sculptures receive their full values only from their situation. Detached or broken they lose all meaning and are nothing but insignificant fragments.' All of the experts determined this years ago. La Jonquière with his inventory of Khmer monuments. Aymonier with his rubbings of Sanskrit inscriptions. Carpeaux with his photographs of Angkor Wat. But this administration has never been able to understand the irreparable damage of archaeological diaspora."

"Then you *do* want this government overthrown."

"I want this government to stick with governing and leave Angkor to us. Leave the monuments for us to study and decide what is best for them. There is no reason for a single artifact ever to have left this country."

"That's not true," Irene protested.

"Naturally you would say that, raised by Henry Simms."

"That's not what I mean. If nothing left Cambodia, I wouldn't know the Khmer. If people hadn't taken statues, if my own father hadn't brought back *apsaras* for the Brooke Museum, my mother would never have been able to give me their remarkable world." The shadow narrowed with the passage of the sun, and Irene stepped closer to the warehouse. "That was how I survived as a girl. I would not have survived."

"We are not talking about *your* survival, Irene. If I had the money you're so casually willing to give Simone, I'd have a good chance of keeping the scrolls here. That kind of money buys control over an object."

"I don't know why you'd want that. You've seen the museum. It doesn't even have walls. They wouldn't be safe."

"I wouldn't put them in the museum. I would establish an institute, a place where I would be more than just the assistant curator of a poor relation outpost of L'École Française d'Extrême-Orient. What does a government school of research based out of Hanoi know about the best interests of the archaeology of Cambodia? I should have taken you to the conservation depot at Angkor Wat. It's like a salvage yard. But right now I don't have the authority to do anything about it. If I were the director of a privately funded foundation, however, that would change matters. With enough money, I could keep the remains of the Khmer Empire intact. It's such a shame that you're so, what was that word you used? Short-sighted. You can't see what a good life you could have for yourself here. A life with me on your side." He brushed at a streak of dust on his sleeve, frowning when he realized the effort was useless. "As it is, I intend to make sure that neither you nor Simone gets your way."

Based on the story Irene had crafted about a search for ancient Khmer trade routes, the travel permits were approved, which meant the expedition, fractured as it was, would depart the next day. She was ready to leave

Phnom Penh, and not just because she was eager to hunt for the temple. As she made her way from the warehouse back to the hotel, she was once again painfully aware of the bleak demeanor of the Cambodians she passed. Perhaps they smiled and laughed when they were alone, but in the European quarter, they eyed her warily, with hostility even. She had never dreamed she could feel unwelcome among these people when they meant so much to her. All she wanted was to find a way to rescue and preserve the best of what they had been. She was going to build an entire museum around their history. She was going to bring their culture prestige, and still they eyed her as if she, like the French, was responsible for their poverty and subjugation.

In the refuge of her room, she found a note from Marc, who had gone to visit the museum. She took a nap, which offered meager deliverance from the midday heat. Waking, she lay in bed, waiting for the rest of the day to pass. She hadn't had an appetite since the previous night, but when the odors of garlic and grilled shrimp wafted through her open window from a food cart in the street, her sudden hunger drew her downstairs.

Beyond the wide doorway of the hotel lobby, colonials passed in open motorcars. Drawn outdoors by the cooling sway of late-afternoon air, Buddhist priests trailed orange robes as they walked by deep in conversation. It had rained again, and indistinct voices were punctuated by the *tcho-kay* cry of the gecko lizard. Irene made her way to the dining terrace, where florid Frenchmen were getting a head start on the night's drinking. As a waiter approached to take her to a table, she saw Murat Stanić in the far corner.

It was that time right before tropical nightfall, when details sparked like fireflies—the filigree of wrought iron on lampposts on the promenade, the sage green ankle-strap shoes worn by the woman sitting beside Stanić. Although the woman's face was lowered, hidden by a cloche hat the same color as the shoes, Irene could tell from her sleek black hair that she was an Oriental. They were talking intently with their heads close together, keeping their conversation safe between them. Preoccupied with Simone's overdose, Angkor Wat, her feelings for Marc, the arrival of Mr. Simms, and now, of all things, a revolution and the stated opposition of Louis Lafont, Irene could hardly fault herself for forgetting that Stanić was coming to Phnom Penh. But there he was on the terrace of her hotel, reminding her that even if she, Simone, and Louis could miraculously find common ground, her journey was still burdened with more complications than she dared to consider.

Chapter 16

The *Alouette*

As Irene came around the stern of the upper deck, she hesitated at the sight of Mr. Simms. Hunched outside his cabin door in a canvas chair, he looked as if he was doing nothing more than taking in the clean dawn air, but she knew that he was waiting for her. Her stomach churned as she walked toward him. For the first time in her life, she was unsure of what to say to him. Nervously, she readjusted the traditional *krama* scarf wrapped around her head to keep her hair from whipping in the wind stirred by the forward motion of the *Alouette*.

He smiled up at her, and she saw in his expression how much he had missed her. "My sweet girl," he said.

His desiccated voice was scarcely capable of competing with the steamer's graveled engines, but the endearment touched her deeply. Kneeling in front of him, she took his hands. She'd thought she had prepared herself for the inevitable changes in his appearance, but she was not ready for *this*. His leonine features were crumpled behind parched wrinkles. His skin had become sallow. And he was unshaven. Irene had never seen Mr. Simms unshaven. The man she loved like a father was there but he was not, his body concealed within the shroud of a winter coat, making it hard to tell how much of him was left. She bowed her head, blinking back tears.

He withdrew his trembling fingers from hers and lightly caressed her checked scarf as he whispered, "You have always been strong, Irene. You will recover from this too."

Traces of a midnight chill clung to the warming air as she drew up a chair beside him. Together, they watched the first of the sunlight extinguish the gleam of the lamps in the sampans along the riverbank. She wanted to know why he had come, but there would be time to ask that later. They would have at least five days on the *Alouette*, depending on the rapids and the monsoon rains. Right now she just wanted to pretend that he was not dying. From the instant she boarded the steamer, she'd craved only this—for things between them to feel as they once had. "Simone is planning to sell the scrolls to start a new nationalist party in Cambodia," she told him, as if she was curled up in the leather club chair in his study, coming to him as she so often had for the analysis that was the currency of their island nation.

Mr. Simms considered this revelation before asking, "What does she want for them?"

"The government's coffers. Nothing less than the French Empire's total humiliation."

He chuckled. "I can't say I was expecting to hear that."

Mr. Simms was never amused when he felt threatened, and his humor lightened Irene's spirits. "What *were* you expecting? She's the most irrational person I've ever met. She takes pills as if they're candy. Most of the time she's a liability."

"I know all of that, Irene." This was said with unexpected compassion.

"You know?" Although Irene had considered this possibility, it still made no sense. "Then why include her in this? Do you also know that I was nearly killed by her madman of a husband?"

"I was right about you. I knew that if anyone could do it, you could."

"Do what?"

"Get her away from him. It was only a matter of time before he completely destroyed her, but what could I do? She would never have believed that I cared about her welfare. Then this opportunity came along."

"Why *do* you care?"

"Good Lord, after what she's been through, she still wants a revolution. The girl puts me to shame. And I thought bringing all of us back together one last time was ambitious."

Irene glanced up and saw the wind pushing at wisps of his thinning hair, revealing the translucent, age-mottled skin beneath. Although his attention had wandered beyond the railing, he did not seem to see the flotilla of Cambodians paddling past in crude dugout canoes. She had no experience with cancer. She did not know what it took from a man at this stage, or how it seized his mind.

"Who is *all of us?*" she asked, reluctantly. "What do you mean?"

"Us?" he asked. He seemed confused, searching Irene's face as if he did not recognize her.

A rash of panic warmed Irene's skin. She could force herself to bear Mr. Simms's physical decay. He was thin and small-boned, with a bantam physique. His body had never been a part of his power. But his mind. He was not just smart, he was razor sharp. If his infirmity took his mind, it would take away everything she understood about him. Everything she loved about him.

"Mr. Simms," she said, tentatively.

He coughed, a withered hawking. "I'm sorry, my dear. My thoughts, they stray so easily these days." Hoarsely, he asked, "How is Marc?"

The mist was breaking apart, but despite the rising sun and porcelain blue sky, there was no color on the river. "Why didn't you tell me about him?"

"There was a time when it seemed for the best, keeping the two of you separate. You were each such a different part of my life," he answered, sounding in control of his thoughts once again. "I remember after your mother died. I have never seen a man so grief-stricken as your father was. And then he asked for my help to raise you. Me, of all people. I suppose he knew he could trust me, after the business of your mother's kidnapping. And if something were to happen to him, you had no other family." Fumbling with the top button of his coat, Mr. Simms said, "He had to be sure that someone would take care of you."

"Let me." Irene leaned in to help with the button, noticing the loose, crepelike skin of his throat.

"I didn't understand then why I agreed to be your guardian, but I have come to believe that few men understand anything they are doing while it is happening. That is what deathbeds are for—reflection. And that's why I can see my reasons so clearly now. After so many mistakes, you were the chance to do something right in my life. Unfortunately, I realized too late the harm I was doing to Marc." His voice slowed and trailed off.

Irene wasn't sure if she was ready to hear Mr. Simms confess the damage he had done to his son, so instead she asked, "Why do you want me to know about Marc now?"

Along the shore, manufacture was giving way to nature as factories were replaced by lean-to shacks on lanky stilts that grew like reeds out of the embankments. Mr. Simms's eyes dipped with a flock of white birds as they swerved over the river. "My son deserves happiness. And you, my dear, have always given me such great happiness."

"There was a moment when he seemed confused," Irene said. "Seconds later, he was fine. But in those few seconds, I felt a flash of dread, as if everything I knew about myself had gone missing."

Squinting at the silhouette of Irene's body in the sun-framed doorway of his cabin, Marc rolled onto his side on his narrow bunk. "I've been down to check the hold. He brought a crate full of medicine with him. Morphine and laudanum. Bricks of Chinese pastes. There's an entire box of needles, enough to stock a small hospital. Or better yet, sedate all of northeast Cambodia while we hunt for this temple. It's a wonder he can even speak coherently."

Irene sat on the side of the bed. "He is the last person who knew me as a child, as a daughter. Once he dies, that part of my life will disappear."

"I can't say I will be sorry when *that* part of my life is gone," Marc said.

The shutters were closed, and through their slats, daylight carved the floor into a chessboard of warped wood planks. Overhead the fan negotiated with the musty air. Marc's expression grew hard, as if he were waiting for her rebuke. But Irene simply asked, "Was he really that miserable of a father to you?"

"He had moments when he could be kind enough, if that's what you need to hear."

The rhythmic pulse of the steamer felt to Irene like the beating of her own heart. "I need to hear the truth."

"The truth?" he whispered, sitting forward and drawing her into the warmth of his chest, wrapping his arms around her, containing her so that there could be no space between her body and his, no room for his words to stir desolately between them. "I figure Henry spent three to four months out of every year in Shanghai, and in that time, he would see me once or twice, at the most. I would be invited to his house for dinner, and he would ask me about school and my mother. Then, one visit when I was seventeen, he asked if I wanted to work for him. I did, I couldn't help myself. I scarcely knew him, but he was my father, and I wanted to please him. I took on odd jobs at first, easy work, but gradually he gave me assignments he would trust to no one else."

"What kinds of assignments?" Irene asked.

"They don't matter. Or I should say, only one of them still matters. Eventually, Henry asked me to set up some burglaries." Marc said this with force, as if he were about to share something that he had kept a secret for too long. "The targets were specific, city officials *and* Communists. He was selling guns to the nationalists as well as to the French navy at that time. This was not unusual for him. Henry was willing to negotiate with anyone, and he was aware that conflict is good for business. I think in a way he *enjoyed* putting his interests at risk. He always wanted more than money. He liked a challenge, even if he had to create it for himself. Even if it meant peddling weapons to the opposition. But there had been some double-crossing behind his back, price-fixing and then reselling at a profit. He decided to make a statement. Make it known that he was in charge. Let his enemies know that no matter how invulnerable they felt, they had nowhere to hide, not even in their own homes."

Marc was sweating now, and the dampness seeped through Irene's blouse as he confessed, "This all made sense to me then. I was his son, and I was a son of Shanghai, so naturally it made sense. It took years for me to realize that other cities aren't like this one. Corrupt, yes, a city can't function if it's not corrupt on some level. But there are degrees of corruption, and Shanghai sets the bar. The burglaries worked. The right people took heed. The Shanghailanders are well-versed in warnings, and they knew what his next step would be. He would cut them off completely. These men, these profiteers, they couldn't afford to be cut off by Henry Simms. Around this time he sent me to Formosa to do a job any one of his lackeys could have done. While I was gone my house was broken into, and my wife was shot. 'A tragic accident,' the *Post* called it." His voice was rough. "Murder is not an accident. I knew it was retaliation."

"And you think it was Mr. Simms's fault?"

"What kind of man brings his son into a world where something like that can happen?"

"He's sorry," Irene said.

"I understand what you want. You want me to forget the man I know. You want me to replace him with the man you know." Marc trailed his finger along the sun-browned skin beneath the open collar of her blouse. "I can become a different person, Irene. I'm ready to try. But I can't change who he was to me. I'm not sure that I even want to. And my fear is that you won't be able to live with that version of him as a part of your life."

The *Alouette* was a modest-size river steamer, and after dinner that night, the crew shifted tables and chairs to convert the dining room into a salon. Moroccan sailors in fiery West Indies bandannas played backgammon on the baize tops of folding game tables, and military officers drank cognac and smoked Dominican cigars. Retreating to a chaise in the corner, Simone produced Roger's memoir from a bag and studied its loose pages. She scribbled notes in a tablet like a dutiful schoolgirl, while on the far side of the room, Louis and Marc fell into conversation, discussing timber hitches versus bowlines. Marc had been reading Irene's copy of *The Art of Travel,* and he wanted to know more about whirling to start a fire and bivouacking in wet weather. "In Shanghai I knew the back alleys to avoid," he told Louis, "and every two-bit hatchet man with a derringer inside his coat pocket. But I wouldn't last a day in the jungle."

Irene could have joined the men, but reluctance held her back. Dinner had been awkward. They had waited for Mr. Simms, who did not come. Halfway through the meal, Irene sent a steward to check on him, and the steward informed her that he was sleeping. In his absence, Simone prattled on about her revolution. Louis, meanwhile, seemed to have decided that the best way to deal with Simone was to ignore her. Added to this, Marc was unusually quiet, and when Louis invited him for cigarettes and digestifs after dinner, he accepted quickly. Irene suspected that he needed some distance from her, and instinct told her to let him be for a while.

As she watched him talk with Louis about the expedition, admiring the way he was making her world his own, she was aware of an ache growing within her. It was true, what Marc had said. She did not want her own memories of Mr. Simms tainted by his. Needing air, she went outside and walked along the deck until she was beyond the voices in the makeshift salon. Her thoughts swayed with the motion of the water. Eventually, passengers and crew began to return to their cabins, everyone on the same deck, except for the Cambodians confined to the level below, since the steamer was too small to be divided into classes. Unsure if she would be welcome in Marc's cabin tonight, Irene made her way around the deck so she could pass Mr. Simms's door. It was open.

Propped on his side, his head resting on the concave surface of a lacquer pillow, Mr. Simms lay on his bed. A lantern hung in one corner of the dim room, and Irene was able to see a pipe on a tray that matched the pillow. Its stem was made of black-stained bamboo, and its white metal mount was inlaid with green stones. The tray also contained an opium kit, the needle arranged beside an ivory opium paste container carved with herons, their wings spread in flight. There was a bowl scraper and a dish for collecting ashes, and inside the glass cone of a spirit lamp, a wick flicked the air with its spur of heat. The cabin smelled of the Chinese districts in Shanghai and Saigon, of *fumeries* awash in the odors of burnt molasses and old men.

A woman sat on a straight-backed chair beside Mr. Simms. Irene tensed as she recognized the sage green, ankle-strap shoes. She was the Cambodian who had been with Murat Stanić at her hotel's terrace restaurant in Phnom Penh.

"Who are you?" Irene asked, remaining just inside the doorway.

"My name is Clothilde."

"That's not what I mean."

"I take care of Henry."

At the sound of his name, Mr. Simms attempted to speak, but his words slurred into silence. His eyes, although open, saw nothing beyond the pall of his intoxication. His chin was still rough with stubble, and this upset Irene. He was not a bum. He was a mandarin, wearing a padded robe of Qing silk, patterned with waves of gold thread. She said, "You're not doing a very good job. He hasn't even been shaved today. Are you a nurse?"

Clothilde appeared to be in her late twenties, close to Irene's age. She wore a simple but expensive blouse and trousers, and on the ring finger of her right hand, an enormous emerald that could not be ignored. She smiled a spare, polite smile. "He can tell you all about me tomorrow, after he's had a chance to rest."

Irene could not admit to this stranger how afraid she was that Mr. Simms might die in the night. How worried she was about everything she might not have the chance to know. "I want you to tell me all about you right now."

Clothilde bobbed her chin toward the end of the bed. It was only then that Irene noticed Simone on the floor, lying on a sheet, flat on her back. Dressed in a long white nightgown, with her eyes closed and her arms at her sides, she looked as if she had been laid out in a funeral parlor for viewing. Unable to picture Simone trekking day after arduous day through the jungle, Irene felt weary from the burden the other woman had become.

"How long has she been here?" Irene asked.

"About an hour."

"Did she speak to him?"

"No. She handed me her pipe and lay down."

Irene watched the sluggish rise and fall of Simone's rib cage, listening to the moan in her breathing. "She's an addict."

"I know. I was one too, before Henry saved me."

Clothilde's affection for Mr. Simms stung Irene. Coolly, she said, "She's unconscious, and even if she isn't, I doubt she'll remember a thing you say."

"I don't think it's my place—" Clothilde focused on the tray and dipped the needle into the opium paste, scooping out a soft brown pill. Then, for some reason, she changed her mind and began to talk. "My daughter has tuberculosis. It's an expensive disease, if she's to be kept comfortable, and especially if she's to be kept alive. I would go to bars to . . . Well, I'm sure I don't have to explain. Six years ago I was in a bar in Phnom Penh, and I met Henry. We became close, and when he learned about my girl, he sent us to California. He paid for her to live in a sanatorium there, one of the best, and he would come down to see us whenever he could. In that way, we have been with one another ever since."

Another secret world of Mr. Simms. "Do you know why he's here?"

Clothilde held the sticky bead over the flame and watched it simmer. "I'm from Kha Seng."

This was the village written about in Reverend Garland's diary. Irene glanced at Simone, but she was still comatose.

"And the temple?" The question tumbled out before Irene had a chance to collect her thoughts.

"I used to pray there on holy days when I was a girl."

Irene spoke through the thickening in her throat. "Then it does exist."

"Yes," Clothilde said, giving no indication whether or not she knew how much this meant to Irene.

Barely able to take in what she was being told, Irene kept her eyes on

Clothilde's hand. One second of inattention and the opium would burn, but Clothilde held the needle's tip motionless over the flame. "What about the history of the Khmer? Have you seen that too?"

Slowly, Clothilde turned the bead. It swelled, turning golden in the low heat. As if she were performing a religious ritual, she set it in the bowl of the pipe. "I'd never heard about the history until Henry mentioned it a few months ago. That was also when he told me the reason I'd interested him in the first place was because I'm from Kha Seng. I was stunned. I hadn't known until then what my village meant to him."

"Has he been to the temple?"

"He gave me a house in Santa Barbara near my daughter, and he's going to leave me enough money to live on for the rest of my life." She raised the pipe to Mr. Simms's lips. Fitfully, he inhaled. The opium glowed like a shard of melted amber, and a loamy odor coiled through the still air. "He tells me what he chooses to tell me, and I don't ask for any more than that. I'm not sure if he's been or not."

"Does Murat Stanić know about the temple?"

Clothilde looked up at Irene, as if uncertain about how much she should admit. She said, "Henry is proud of how clever you are."

"You were sitting with him in plain sight on the terrace of my hotel, and I happened to see you. That hardly makes me clever." Irene wanted to ask Clothilde what she had revealed to Stanić, and how much he already knew. But if Clothilde was working with him, there was no reason for her to tell Irene the truth. "How much did he offer you to watch me?"

"Enough to make it worth my while. But there are some men a woman never wants to be associated with. Don't let this trouble you, though. Henry knows all about it."

Although Clothilde sounded sincere, it was too soon for Irene to decide if she was trustworthy. She asked, "Do you know how long Mr. Simms had been planning on coming over here?"

"As I said, he summoned me a few months back. He told me about the history and asked me to accompany him to Cambodia."

This confirmed that Mr. Simms had intended to join the expedition all along. "But he's not strong enough to go into the jungle with us, is he?"

"No," Clothilde said. "He will wait in Stung Treng."

"How do I know Stanić isn't on his way? How do I know that once he gets here, you won't tell him where we've gone?"

"I can hardly tell him when I'll be with you. I'm going to guide you in, Irene." Gently, Clothilde lifted one of Mr. Simms's hands from where it had slipped over the edge of the bed. With great care, she moved it to a comfortable position and straightened the sleeve of his robe. "The reason I didn't shave him today is that it was one of those days when even the touch of his razor would have been torture. Irene, my father died of cancer, in the middle of the jungle without a single pill. I still remember the constant agony of it. I couldn't bear for Henry to be in that kind of pain. This is the kind of sickness that takes away a man's control over every part of his being. I try different combinations of medicines every day, hoping one will have mercy on his body *and* his mind."

As if to respond, Mr. Simms let out a low groan, but when he spoke, it was only to murmur, "Othello's drowsy syrup."

"Alouette, gentille alouette, alouette, je te plumerai." Simone had worked her way to semiconsciousness and was singing the song of Canadian fur traders, softly in her opium sleep.

"You might feel better if you join them," Clothilde suggested to Irene.

"Je te plumerai la tête . . ."

After all that Mr. Simms had done for Irene, she wanted to be the one to rescue him, to ease his misery, but there was only one thing that could save him tonight, and Clothilde was its master. As for Clothilde's offer, Irene declined, feeling the sudden need to be alone with the staggering revelation: The temple did exist.

She left the cabin and leaned against the railing. *It exists.* This fact— not a theory, not a guess, not a hope, but a fact!—swept over her, stronger than any drug Clothilde could have offered her. Irene scarcely remembered returning to her cabin, and the next thing she knew, it was dawn, and she was shivering in her bunk, having slept as if dead with the door wide open to the night's storm.

She blinked at the sunlight that seemed to be rising out of the earth, emanating from the unbroken green fringe of the banyan trees. Cormorants flapped through the mist. *The temple exists.* But panic gripped Irene as she realized it was not elation she felt at this thought. It was fear.

Yes, the temple was a fact, but the history was not even known to those who lived closest to it, if she were to believe Clothilde. As the Midas touch of a tropical day turned the river to gold, Irene fought visions of rich men and follies and wild-goose chases. Mr. Simms had never been such a man, but after seeing him last night, she could not help but question what his illness was turning him into.

Chapter 17

Second Chances

"If we have another night of hard rain, the captain thinks we can clear the rapids at Sambor without being towed and reach Stung Treng by late afternoon the day after tomorrow," Irene said. "Once we arrive, there might not be any time to talk to him before we go. We'll be starting into the jungle as soon as we finalize supplies. We need to do it here. I told Clothilde we'd come at four. She's not going to give him anything. She says he should be lucid."

"You don't need me for this," Marc said.

"He wants to see you." Before Marc could protest, Irene held up her hand. "He hasn't said it, but he does. Can't you at least let your father have this?"

Marc propped his forearms on the railing, his

hands hanging over the rippling, waterlogged tops of the *cam xe* trees floating in the river's silver foam. It was the same submerged landscape as the day before, and the day before that. "I don't want you to expect too much from me," he said.

They were four days out of Phnom Penh, and Marc had still not been to see his father. He had not asked a single question about him, even though Irene sat with Mr. Simms for hours each day as he dozed. After a while the steamer had begun to feel like a hospital waiting room, but Irene no longer had time to wait. If all went well, the expedition would enter the jungle in just a few days. And before they did, Irene needed to know why Mr. Simms had brought her together with Simone and Marc, and how her mother and Simone's fitted into the picture. She also wanted to see Marc with his father, to gauge, like the guide perched in the makeshift crow's nest of the *Alouette,* what obstacles might lie ahead.

"I'd rather you expect more from yourself," she said, unable to hold back her frustration. She tossed her cigarette into the Mekong River and led him to Mr. Simms's cabin.

Unlike the previous days, the curtains were drawn back and the room bloomed with light. Mr. Simms was sitting up, not in bed but in a rattan armchair that Irene recognized from the captain's quarters. He was shaven, and Clothilde had dressed him in a fresh linen suit, which matched the blue of his eyes. On the tray table where she usually laid out his opium kit, she had set a pitcher of *citron pressé* glistening over ice, as if this were nothing more than a typical afternoon social visit. Kissing his cheek, Irene observed him looking past her.

"Hello, Son. Thank you for coming," he said. There was a vulnerability in his voice that Irene had never heard before.

Marc merely nodded, his expression firmly impassive. As Irene joined him on a settee that had been brought in from the dining room, Clothilde whispered to her, "Without the drugs he's going to tire easily. Whatever you are here to do, please be quick about it."

Clothilde was no longer wearing her green shoes. She was barefoot, and a lapis lazuli strand gleamed against her bare ankle. Irene wanted to resent her, but instead she felt nothing but gratitude as she recalled stumbling upon Clothilde bowed over a bucket outside Mr. Simms's room, washing vomit from his pajamas in the middle of the night so no one would see. On deck, so that he would not see.

"Mr. Simms," Irene said, "I need to ask you some questions."

"It's about time." He grinned.

She wanted to joke with him, to enjoy his good humor, but she knew she shouldn't keep him from his painkillers any longer than was necessary. "The book Lawrence Fear kidnapped my mother for. Was it Reverend Garland's diary?"

"Yes," he answered, his eyes returning to his son.

"And you knew about the diary all along. When you found it in the box my father left you, you weren't surprised to see it, were you?"

"No, Irene, about that you are wrong. It was a tremendous surprise." He flinched as he spoke, as if the utterance of each coherent sentence caused its own sharp pang. "I thought the diary had disappeared the night we rescued your mother, taken by one of Fear's men as they fled. I had no idea your father still had it."

"Did you go looking for the scrolls? Before the kidnapping, I mean. With my parents and Simone's mother?"

Mr. Simms fluttered his hand toward Clothilde, and she removed a thin twist of a cigarette from her pocket. As the sweet odor of hemp slipped onto the draft from the window, Irene was aware of the nauseating, underlying sickroom smell of menthol, musty sheets, and old age. Mr. Simms may have been costumed to resemble his old self, with his bespoke-tailored Savile Row suit and Patek Philippe pocket watch, but his palsied hands gave him away, as did the greediness with which he drew on the cigarette. The pain must have been excruciating for him to ask for relief in front of others, particularly in front of the girl he had always protected and the son he had not seen in years.

Marc placed his hand over Irene's on the cushion between them, but she scarcely felt his touch. She was so afraid of losing Mr. Simms and not being able to reach him again. "What did you find at the temple?" she asked him.

"Not yet, Irene, not yet," he murmured. "That is not where this story begins." He smiled with appreciation as he inhaled. "I was still young when I fell in love with Katrin. I'd just set up my first factory in Shanghai."

Irene asked, "Who's Katrin?"

"My mother," Marc said.

"It took me years to accept that she would never leave her husband," Mr. Simms said. "She knew the disgrace of a scandal would have killed him, and her sense of duty was too great. I may have known my way around the business world, but I was inexperienced enough with women to believe that my heart was irreparably broken, so I left Shanghai. I traveled for a while and eventually settled in Manila. As you know, Irene, that's where I met your parents. What you don't know is that I moved there with a woman I'd met in Cambodia. Madeleine." His gaze fell away from Marc, and Irene followed it to Simone, standing in the doorway.

"*My* mother." Simone's face was as stony as Marc's as she asked, "You had a son with her, didn't you?"

"It was too easy to lose a child back then. Fever, smallpox, polio," Mr. Simms told Simone. "Nicolas went quickly, and I couldn't look at Madeleine without wishing I were dead too. This time I truly did know the meaning of a broken heart, and for the second time in my life, I had to leave a woman in order to save myself. But I still loved her. And even though it wasn't my fault, I felt guilty about Nicolas's death. If I had never come into her life, she would never have had to experience the death of a child. When you were born, Simone, I began to send your mother money, as if that could keep you safe and make up for what had happened."

"Are you . . ." Simone could not bring herself to finish the sentence.

"No, I'm not your father. After Nicolas died, your mother went back to her family in Cambodia, where she got married and had you. There was no longer anything left for me in Manila. The kidnapping frightened your parents, Irene, and they returned to Seattle. They were shaken by what could have happened, and they were ready to leave the Orient. I arranged for your father to be given a job at the museum, so he could still spend his time among the treasures he loved. And I made my way back to Shanghai. I had more than a dozen factories there by then. My business was thriving. I thought that because of my new grief, Katrin would no longer matter to me. But I can still remember what it felt like to open my door so many years later and find her back in my life, telling me that her husband was dead and holding the hand of a six-year-old boy."

Mr. Simms's attention moved back to Marc. "I knew you were my son the instant I saw you. You were like Nicolas in many ways. The color of your eyes, the shape of your smile. The way you would not say a word but instead clenched your fists when you wanted something badly. Second chances," he declared. "Nonsense, that is what I had always thought of second chances. What is done is done. Then your father left me the diary, Irene. When I realized what had happened, my feelings changed. I wasn't afraid of this second chance." Breathing raggedly, he looked from Marc to Irene to Simone. "You are all my second chance."

His skin was turning gray. The cigarette was not enough, and Clothilde anxiously fingered a brown bottle. Irene reached out for a pill and knelt in front of Mr. Simms. The neediness with which he took the dark bead grieved her. She smoothed the sparse hair away from his flushed brow.

"My girl," he whispered, "my dear, dear girl. You are so good to me."

Behind her, Irene heard the crack of glass against wood as Marc set his drink down too hard on the table, and she thought, This is what it is really about for us. It is not about whether I can live with his version of Mr. Simms but about if he can live with mine. This loving version that should have been his.

Again, she asked Mr. Simms, "Tell me one thing. What did you find at the temple?"

The old man leaned forward. "Nothing," he said, gravely. "I found absolutely nothing."

"A ruse?" Irene asked in disbelief.

"Yes, a ruse," Simone said.

After leaving Mr. Simms's cabin, Irene and Marc had followed Simone to the salon, where she had angrily relayed the situation to Louis before making her accusation. Irene said, "I suppose you think his story about our mothers is a ruse too."

"What I think is that he's trying to make me doubt the scrolls' existence, so if you find them and tell me you didn't, I will be more likely to believe you. But I know better. Just as I know you're all opposed to me. Even you." She glowered at Louis, who had yet to look up from the survey compass he was repairing with his penknife. "Simms is crafty, incredibly crafty."

Irene was so tired of Simone. "You're only here because Mr. Simms wanted to rescue you from Roger. He didn't have to include you. You should feel grateful to him."

"It's all part of his plan," Simone insisted.

"He's on his deathbed."

"I'm not certain of that."

For a moment Irene thought, She can't be serious, and then she saw that Simone was. She looked away, out the open window. Along the shoreline, brown water flowed uninterrupted over the muddy, root-tangled earth, corralling the steamer's floating world. She felt trapped. Needing to establish some kind of logic, she said, "I know it must be a shock, finding out that he had a child with your mother, but you don't *really* think he's not sick. You can't. All you have to do is look at him—"

"He's not as sick as he wants us to think he is. And bringing that girl with him, as if having her here feeding him opium is enough to give his story credence."

"Henry Simms is clearly dying," Louis said, as if to himself, "and *that girl* is here because she knows her way around Stung Treng province. We're lucky he brought her. She can take us straight to the temple."

"Guiding you to the temple is my role," Simone declared.

"Your role? *Your* role?" Louis's voice was tight with restraint. "You are a drug addict, Simone, and the only role an addict has is to make life worse for everyone around her."

Recently, Louis's silences toward Simone had begun to feel ominous, and Irene had been wondering if he would eventually erupt. Now that moment was closing in, like the sudden approach of a monsoon.

"I don't care what you think of me, what any of you think of me," Simone said. "I'm here because my revolution is right, and right will have its justice in the end."

"For God's sake, Simone, I've had enough of your ideological rhetoric. You sound like an automaton." Louis moved toward her, his knife clenched in one fist.

Marc stepped closer, ready to intervene.

But Louis stopped before he reached Simone. "No, that's incorrect. You sound like your dead husband. And we both know the value of everything *he* had to say."

"And you're so much nobler than me," Simone accused, "chasing Irene around this boat with your architectural sketches for your institute at Angkor Wat. Babbling on about scholarship and the greater good of humanity, when we both know this is all about your career—"

"That's enough," Marc interrupted. "Irene, take Simone outside."

But Louis persisted. "You used to be the most intelligent girl I knew. I never thought I would say this, but you're the last thing the Cambodians need now. You can't control your emotions. You're dangerous to them." Although he was furious with Simone, Irene could still hear the longing he felt, for the girl he had known before she'd been twisted by her parents' deaths and Roger's cruelties. "Selling the scrolls to the government? That's the most idiotic idea you've ever had. I wish I could understand what happened to you."

"I grew up."

"It's useless talking to you." Louis snapped the penknife shut and shoved it into his pocket. "Rafferty, what's your take on Simms's story? Do you think the scrolls are up there?"

Caught off guard by the abrupt change of subject, Marc took out his rolling papers and worked a pinch of tobacco into a cigarette. As he smoked, he gave the room time to cool. A minute passed, and then another. Finally, he asked Irene, "How ill was Henry when your father died? Was he like this? In this degree of pain? Do you know how much morphine he was using?"

Irene shook her head. "None that I knew of. He tired more easily than usual, and he had moments when he clearly wasn't feeling well, but he was nothing like he is now."

"He's sending us up here to finish some romantic quest, but I don't believe he's doing it just for sentimentality's sake." As Marc said this, defiance flashed across his face. "My best guess, based on what I know about him? When he launched you on this trip, Irene, he didn't know how fast he was going to deteriorate, and he had a good reason to believe the scrolls are still up here."

During the final day of the voyage, the sky was claustrophobically low, and the river, though rising from the monsoon rains, remained thick with boulders and marsh. Irene could not fathom how the captain would steer the steamer, but as late morning passed into early afternoon, he negotiated the braided waters at the frenzied direction of the pilot until at last she saw it, the confluence of the Mekong River with its sleek bronze tributary the Sekong. It was just past this junction that the colonial outpost of Stung Treng had been built, on the foundation of a primitive hill tribe village, on a passage between India and China.

This was one of the few legitimate sections of an ancient Khmer trade route that Irene had incorporated into her bluff about the purpose of the expedition, a still-used byway through which gold, ivory, kingfisher feathers, and rhinoceros horn had once traveled. Otherwise, this no-man's-land was considered to be as lacking in Khmer heritage as the European continent. It was easy for Irene to appreciate this belief as Stung Treng came into view. The town's strand of shabby stucco buildings showed their dirt in the afternoon sun, and at the end of the unimpressive main street, shacks were propped up on crooked stilts within groves of tall, taut sugar palm trees.

Locals in odd combinations of Oriental and Occidental attire began to gather on the embankment, hazy in the reflection of sunlight off the water. As the steamer approached, Irene made out a white pith helmet worn by a large, bulky European, who was using a cane to whack his way through the crowd. Coolies dropped into the river with thick mooring lines tight between their teeth, while the man in the helmet loomed above them. He wore a white dinner jacket, unbuttoned with nothing beneath it, revealing the flab of his chest coated in a moss of rust-colored hair. He had tied a maroon sarong around his fat waist, and on his feet Irene saw that he wore two-toned, wingtip dress shoes.

"Benoit Ormond," Simone said, coming up behind Irene.

"The *commissaire?*"

Observing him press a finger to his nostril and blow snot to the ground, Simone said, "You can see how fortunate the natives are to have his civilizing influence."

The *commissaire* for each district in Indochina was its gatekeeper, and this one would fulfill the expedition's requisitions for oxcarts, horses, porters, and a camp cook, as well as give final approval for the travel permits issued in Phnom Penh. Irene had been worried that the *commissaire* of Stung Treng would find their arrival suspicious. After all, they were not the usual assembly of explorers. But looking at Ormond, who had transferred his attention to scratching his buttocks with his cane, she felt that he would not find much out of the ordinary. This should have eased her mind, but instead she wondered what it meant, that the French saw no need to entrust the guardianship of this territory to someone more serious.

"Fine, fine, this is all in order. I'll put the boys to work on the oxcarts in the morning." Ormond waved the expedition's documents at a Cambodian youth whose reddish mop of hair matched his. "They'll be loaded and ready to go with the horses and oxen by nightfall. And you can take my guide, Xa. The best in the region." He leaned back in his chair and held out his empty glass. "Boy, bring me another bottle. Three weeks without wine waiting for the *Alouette*. Damn the rains. A Frenchman without his *vin rouge*. Is there any greater tragedy?"

Ormond had invited the expedition for dinner at his mildewing villa at the far end of Stung Treng, on a bluff hanging over the Sekong River. Having made their way through spicy fish stew, too much wine, and a gummy rice pudding, they were now settling into the screened verandah. Mr. Simms and Clothilde were not with them, but they had been joined by a middle-aged anthropologist named Lisette, who had been living in the province *for longer than I care to remember, darlings, how delightful to have fresh faces in our little settlement.* After nearly a week on the river, Irene welcomed how firm the earth felt beneath her. She was relaxed, or as relaxed as one could feel on the brink of what might turn out to be the most important archaeological discovery of the century.

As Irene passed Marc to take a seat in the circle of chairs that Ormond had haphazardly arranged, she brushed her fingers along his upper arm. She was wearing an amethyst sheath, clinging to her beneath a sheer mantle of the same glassy color. She'd had it especially made for museum receptions, modeled after one of her favorite paintings, Erté's *Moonlight*. On the steamer Simone had warned her that after a few days in the jungle, her feet would be septic, her face a rash of insect bites, and her dignity, along with her modesty, all but gone. Irene wanted to be beautiful for Marc tonight, so he would have something to envision once the jungle took hold of her.

Irene was not the only one wearing formal clothes. Louis and Marc were also dressed, each in his own style, as if for an evening in Shanghai, and Simone's maroon, velvet-lined robe matched her low boots. Perhaps these efforts to appear civilized were an instinctive attempt to foster peace. Irene hoped so, for they could not afford an argument in front of Ormond like the one that had occurred on the steamer.

"Shall we listen to music?" Lisette asked. She had used kohl to give herself the eyes of an Asiatic, and with her salt-and-pepper hair, she looked like a Siamese cat.

"Mmm, indeed, I am in the mood for Ravel," Ormond said. And then to the room in general, "I hope you will pardon my ignorance, but I'm still not quite clear on what you're doing up here."

"We're investigating Khmer trade routes," Louis said in a professional tone, as he began to explain the pretext Irene had invented to justify their journey. "Particularly from the periods of Suryavarman the Second and Jayavarman the Seventh. We hope to give scholars a new way of understanding the region's historic mercantile systems."

"We have photographs we'd like you to look at," Irene added. "Markers from the Royal Road."

How ideal it would be if there were similar stones in this area. How tedious it was to have to sit through this evening. Catching Marc watching her, Irene wished they could go to their room, a real room in Ormond's villa with a real bed—a luxury after the discomfort of the steamer's hard, narrow berths. She wished they were already deep into the jungle. She wished she knew if the scrolls existed. She was a bit light-headed from eagerness and anxiety and alcohol. She set her glass aside.

"Fascinating stuff," Ormond said, without interest. "There's always someone up here chasing after something. Glow-in-the-dark centipedes. Savages to study. Did you see the article in *National Geographic* on the Moi? Why do Americans have such a fascination with bare breasts?" He threw a half-eaten dinner roll at another young houseboy, who had fallen asleep in the corner. With a start, the boy resumed operating the punkah, tugging the rope back and forth so that the wide sailcloth fan swept the air overhead. "The real point of my question is that I don't understand what the assistant curator of the Angkor Wat temples, Henry Simms's son, Roger Merlin's widow, and a young lady from the Brooke Museum are doing in my province." He uncorked a bottle and took a whiff. "Bah, piss of cat! Another one spoiled!"

Irene did not have to look at the others to know that they were instantly alert.

"And that girl," Ormond said, "the Cambodian. I remember when Clothilde was a penny prostitute working the Chinese traders here in Stung Treng."

Attempting nonchalance, Irene said, "She doesn't work for pennies anymore."

In his sea captain's jacket and a sarong that was possibly made from damask curtains, Ormond—no fool, it turned out, despite his appearance—looked around, expectantly. "And for the pièce de résis-tance, you plan to leave a dying man in my house while you go in search of these trade routes of yours. And not any dying man. The notorious Henry Simms."

Irene's mind raced. Murat Stanić? Clothilde? How else would a *com-missaire* in one of the farthest regions in the country know who they all were?

All of a sudden, Lisette laughed, a throaty, cigarette-singed trill. "Don't let him bully you," she said, as she removed a black record from its paper sleeve. "He knows you're hunting for the temple. That's all any-one comes up here hunting for. Bugs and that temple."

The henna light from the oil lamps twitched against the gauze walls of the mosquito netting. Marc's foot shifted slightly against Irene's. From across the room, she felt Simone flinch. She forced herself not to panic while Louis asked, "A temple? There's a temple around here?" His surprise sounded pathetically false. "What kind of temple? Is it worth looking for?"

Ormond guffawed, rubbing at a liver spot on his forearm. He pulled another bottle of wine from a box, where it had been packed in cloth embroidered with dainty English lavender. "Don't you think if there was anything of value up here, it would already have been exploited? This isn't the moon."

Irene thought back to the thatched Stung Treng market that they had walked through on their way to Ormond's. Along with typical local goods, such as palm oil and tight tubes of betel leaves, she had seen cheap Japanese fans and tins of Chinese pastes used to color a woman's lips. Inhaling the reek of fermented fish, she had watched a matron bargain over a container of Joncaire Paris face powder, the round box patterned in aqua and gold, with the words *Un peu d'Orient* in coy, slanted script. A carton of Hatamen cigarettes, made in British factories in Shanghai, had lain near the trader's feet. All of these goods came through from Laos, Siam, Vietnam, and Burma, as well as China, India, and Malaya.

Clothilde had known about the temple since she was a girl. This cat-eyed anthropologist knew about it. Ormond wasn't admitting it, but he knew too, Irene was sure of it. And he was right. Stung Treng may have been a poor backwater, but how could anything of significance stay a secret when it lay so close to a crossroads such as this?

While Louis offered many assets to the expedition, lying on the spot was not one of them. Marc stepped in, taking control of the conversation. "I suppose there's no harm in us having a look around while we're here."

Ormond eyed him with distrust. Then, so casually it was laughable, he said, "Do as you please. It doesn't matter. You won't make it past Leh. If you try, I can't guarantee your safety. Tell them, Lisette," he said, sternly.

The woman seemed confused. In coming to Ormond's, she could not have been expecting anything more than a break in the monotony of

Stung Treng's meager social life. "I've been studying Mon-Khmer dialects for almost a decade. I've traveled all over these provinces, but recently the village of Leh has become a fortress," she explained with little conviction. Setting the gramophone record on the felt surface of the turntable, she continued, "There are rumors that the natives have discovered mineral deposits and are selling them to the Chinese. Gold, yes, I believe that's what it is. Gold. The military is still trying to figure out what to do about the situation."

"There's nothing *to* do," Simone said, quickly. "The deposits are theirs. They can sell them to whomever they like."

Louis scowled at her. Now was not the time for proselytizing. But Irene had a feeling Simone was doing something different. If there was gold in these jungles, the government would not spend any time at all thinking about what it should do. It would swarm over the area, and Simone knew it. "With enough money, they could shift the power in this region." She was diverting as only she could divert. "That would certainly affect your position, Monsieur Ormond." Muddling as only she could muddle.

As if she had just remembered, Lisette added, "The villagers have guns."

Raised in Shanghai, Marc knew how to steer a man. "As long as we're talking clarity, Ormond, there's something *I'm* not clear on. Have you even looked? If there's a Khmer temple somewhere around here, wouldn't that be prestigious for your district? For you? Isn't this the sort of thing a man in your position hopes for?"

"One wonders if such a thing is feasible: a tribal council based on a unification of principles," Simone expounded, distracting Ormond as he attempted to concentrate on Marc.

Irritably, Ormond said, "Yes, such glory for me and my forests. But what would my forests become? Every fortnight when the *Alouette* arrived, it would dump off more archaeologists, more fortune hunters. And tourists! Loud, insatiable tourists." With undisguised fondness, he gazed out through the screen, where locals had gathered in the tall grass to watch the visiting foreigners. Or was it to admire their redheaded leader? Through the mosquito netting, the dark, hunched figures wavered like figments of one's imagination. "I have heard about what is happening at Angkor Wat," he said. "The schoolmistress spinsters from Iowa and Lyons riding through the ruins on the backs of elephants. Phhttt."

Interested to see what they could lead Ormond to reveal, Irene feinted around Marc to fuel his growing temper from another angle. She called upon the cheap but consistently surefire act of girlish innocence. "I'd be too curious," she said, enthusiastically. "Aren't you even a bit curious? After all, a Khmer temple all the way up here would be quite a find."

Simone leaned toward Ormond and said with the tiresome vagueness that Irene continued to suspect was intentional, "It's a fascinating thought, don't you agree, a government system that combines the various local tribal principles?"

Regaining his composure and making his best effort to enter the game, Louis said to Irene, "To hell with old trade routes. This could be the discovery of the century. Do you realize what this could mean for us?"

"That's what I'm think—"

"I know exactly what it could mean," Ormond interrupted, violently tugging the cork from a bottle. "The last lost temple of Cambodia. The next Angkor Wat." He waved the open bottle, and wine splashed to the floor. "Some say it's deep in the Damrek Mountains, and others that it's hidden in the Cardamom foothills. Well, well, what do you know, it's right here in my own backyard. Ha! Why can't people keep their grubby hands off this country!"

"That's my feeling too," Simone announced.

With a look of regret, Lisette turned up the gramophone, as if it could drown out the damage she had done by mentioning the temple. But as Ravel's sad birds soared into the margins of the verandah, Ormond shouted over the music, panting, his expression stricken, "Why can't you people leave my territory be!"

No one spoke. There was no need to. Ormond had given himself away. He was the reason no one got past Leh. Not because he greedily wanted the temple for himself, but because he wanted his remote kingdom left alone. It was this, Irene now knew, that explained how the scrolls could have been kept a secret for so long.

Chapter 18

Crossing the Line

From the back porch of Ormond's villa, where she was sitting with Mr. Simms, Irene watched the heat leaving the day in scalloped waves. Lapwings raced across sandbars, their velvet heads as dark as ravens', and in the distance, the fawn shadows of women bathed in the river's edge, flanked by a bank of mud and purple iris. With her departure only a few hours away, he had asked her to meet him alone. Now, he held out a brass pocket watch.

"I have already set it for you," he said, in a rare state, drugged *and* comprehending. "I want you to wind it in the mornings and keep it with you at all times."

Ready for the rest of the story, for the final pieces of the puzzle he was assembling, she examined the etching on the back of the watch, a ferocious tiger swallowing a terrified horse. The blood that sprayed from the wounded animal was made of excellent-quality Chinese glass. "Didn't I see this in the market yesterday?" she asked.

He smiled, sheepishly, as if he had rounded the corner of his old age and careened back into his younger self, caught with his hand dipping into a cookie jar or the collection of his old rival-pal Henry Huntington. "Today has been one of my better days. Clothilde had the boys fashion a palanquin for me. I looked quite regal riding through town."

Even in a remote jungle trading post, on the threshold of death's door, he could not resist the hunt for a treasure. They were physically wrenching, these blunt realizations of how much she was going to miss him. Irene felt a foreboding sense of grief at the thought of leaving him, even though he would be well taken care of while she was away. Clothilde had already consulted with the town doctor and chosen two local women to keep vigil. Lisette, the anthropologist, had offered to help as well.

"These are also for you," Mr. Simms said, pressing a pair of keys into her palm.

"From the market too?"

"No, these I brought with me." Strung like charms on a gold chain that could be worn around one's neck, they were not door keys but keys to something much smaller, a jewelry or safe-deposit box perhaps. His withered fingers strayed from her palm to the carnelian bracelet on her wrist, the one that he had given her from the box her father left for him. "I'm glad you wear this. It might be helpful. In fact, I think it could be very helpful. Don't take it off," he instructed. "Oh, my sweet girl, I am putting all of my faith in you." As twilight descended and the air grew thick with the odor of sodden roots trapped in the mudflats, Mr. Simms became pensive. "Tell me the truth, Irene, are you going to find them?"

"Am I going to . . . ?" She'd thought he had summoned her to tell her at last what she was going to find. She had thought that was what he was leading to with his gifts. But he now appealed to her with a look of anticipation, his tone disconcertingly beseeching, as if she was the one who had possessed and withheld the answer all along. Dismayed, she laid her hand over his. "I am," she said, for what was the point in expressing her doubts? She did not know how much longer Mr. Simms could fend off death. In case she did not make it back in time, she would not be able to live with herself if she let him spend his last days without hope.

It seemed to take all of his effort simply to hold his head up, and as she looked at his shrunken posture, she understood that it was finally time to stop waiting for him to get better. It was time to stop believing that he was going to make everything clear, and to accept the situation as it was. Even if he lived until she returned, he might never again be lucid enough to explain himself, or to understand the outcome of her journey, whatever that might be. Now that the moment to embark had arrived, after all he had put her through, it turned out he was sending her into the jungle armed with nothing more than a bracelet, a watch, and a set of toy-box keys. As for the at-odds team he had assembled for her, their only unified act had been their half-baked manipulation of Ormond, which had resulted not in accord but instead in a new disagreement: How were they going to deal with the village of Leh?

"Like hell I'm going into that village without a gun," Marc declared. "I didn't leave a city filled with professional assassins to be killed by natives in loincloths. If they so much as snap an arrow at me, I'm defending myself."

"We can't just start shooting," Simone argued. "It's not ethical. They're only protecting what's theirs."

"Ethical?" Irene asked, as she attempted to pull her boot out of a suction of mud on the side of the trail. "You stabbed your husband, and now you're using his manifesto to start your own rival political party. And if we do make it past the village, you plan on taking the scrolls and selling them to the enemy. But now you're telling me you're concerned about ethics!"

They were three hours out of Stung Treng, beneath a moon so bright and high that Irene could see how bloodshot Simone's eyes were from whatever pills she had taken, and from waking in the middle of the night. They'd had to leave at such an early hour because at this phase of the monsoon season, the storms were heaviest during the day. Nights were generally free from rain, and they were also cooler, so the plan was to walk during the four or five hours before the sun ignited the morning. By eight it would already be too warm to continue. As it was, at this ungodly hour, the damp air was merely uncomfortable.

"For the Cambodians!" Simone said. "In the long run, I'm doing all of this for the Cambodians."

"And nobody's going to *just start shooting*," Louis admonished, although as he said this his hand unconsciously touched the pistol in the holster at his hip. "All we're saying is that we need to be armed and ready."

"As for protecting what's theirs," Marc said, "according to our helpfully indiscreet anthropologist in Stung Treng, the villagers in Leh are members of the Brau tribe. Isn't that right, Clothilde?"

Studying her, Simone said, "I'd be interested to know what you think their ethnicity has to do with any of this."

Irene sensed that Simone was challenging the Cambodian woman, but Clothilde replied as if she thought Simone's interest was genuine. "For the most part, the tribes in this district can understand one another. Our dialects are similar enough. Even someone who speaks fluent Khmer like you should be able to understand. But otherwise, there's not much unity in this part of the country. Ormond's coolies have no relation to the villagers in Leh. Xa comes from a distant Kreung village. Like most tribes in this region, if the Brau had any relationship with the ancient Khmer, they were probably captured as slaves."

"If the villagers try to stop us, chances are it won't be about the Brau protecting their own," Marc added. "It will be about them following orders from Ormond."

"But if any one of us is shot by a native," Louis said, "there will be repercussions."

"That's what I've been thinking," Marc said. "If the villagers do have guns, it can only be because Ormond armed them. Most likely he did it so they can scare people off, since if they kill a European, he'll have to punish them—the government will demand it, and if he won't do it, they'll send someone up here who will. Surely the village chief understands this. And Ormond's not stupid. He must know that if he's forced to punish them for following orders he gave them, there will be some kind of retaliation against him. I think they might take a few potshots at us, but I doubt they'll go all the way." He paused and looked around, but beyond a fringe of trees, the surrounding wilderness was in shadows, and one could only guess at the dangers they masked. "This is getting tiresome. Irene, you need to decide. Let's turn around, or let's make a plan that we can all agree on and stop standing here like tiger bait."

"Why is Irene making the decision?" Simone asked.

"The next time you find a treasure map, you can be the leader," Marc said.

"You're absolutely certain there's no way around Leh?" Irene asked Clothilde, eyeing her simple shift and thin-skinned moccasins with envy. The cuffs of Irene's own many-pocketed drill shirt were snapped tightly around her wrists, and her collar was snug at her throat. She had tucked her pants into her boots, securing them with straps that made her feel like an overheated Houdini wrapped up for a straitjacket escape. "No other trails in this area?"

"If there were one or two of us, maybe. We could have the coolies clear one of the old hunting paths. But not with the horses and oxcarts," Clothilde said, indicating the pack of native porters waiting with the lanterns and supply carts.

"And Xa agrees?" Irene nodded toward their guide, a wiry, weathered Cambodian who had planted his torch into a bed of moss on the trail. Although he was at least sixty, he'd brought along his five-year-old son. Both wore the brown sarongs common among highland Cambodians.

"Xa? Xa! He works for Ormond," Simone said. "Of course he's going to say there's no other path. And why are you all so willing to trust *her*?"

Clothilde wisely ignored Simone.

Staring resolutely at the trail ahead, Irene said, "We're going to Leh."

"And why should we take that risk?" Louis's eyes settled on her with disapproval.

Clouds of high-pitched mosquitoes whined around Irene's face, which was slicked with a protective Chinese ointment. Encased in her body's own clammy humidity, she resented the need for her oppressive clothing. Such insistent physical distractions were new to her, making it a struggle to hold on to the scheme she had begun to work on once she realized that Mr. Simms was not going to hand her a solution. When she realized, truly, for the first time, that the outcome of this expedition was up to her. She said, "We're going to walk into the village and out the other side because we know they won't stop us."

"Why do we know that?" Marc was intrigued.

As Irene sorted her thoughts, low brush crackled to their right, a reminder of the lethal vipers it sheltered. The matte brown Sekong River was deceptively hushed to their left, its stagnant pools a hazard of leeches, Siamese crocodiles, and dengue fever. She watched Xa's son, Kiri, playing a one-sided game of tag with the gibbon that was his pet. He needed only a coating of saffron paste as defense against the deadly mosquitoes, while her ears were ringing from the quinine tablets she had taken in Stung Treng. "Because we've been sent by Ormond," she said.

"What do you have in mind?" Louis asked, his censure relenting.

The mosquitoes were crawling into the eyelets of Irene's boots and somehow even managing to get inside her shirt. They were absolutely maddening, but she still felt the old thrill making its way back to her. A thrill that had once been a part of her everyday life, as she found a way to achieve what others had not. Marc, Louis, Simone—none of them had a plan. She had a plan.

"We're going to tell the villagers that Commissaire Ormond has been informed that the colonial government will be sending a mission to the northeast provinces," she announced. "There is to be a formal mapping. Not an inch of this region will go unexplored. He's done his best to keep the area autonomous, but there's nothing he can do about this. Soldiers will accompany the surveyors to put down any local resistance. New administrative outposts will be established. They will find the temple, since there's no way to keep something like that hidden, but Ormond wants to save the history. If the villagers of Leh will help him with this, he will save them too."

Fascinated, as if what Irene was saying was true, Simone asked, "From what?"

"The same thing that empires have wanted from their so-called savages for centuries. The French are building roads and factories in the lowlands, and what's the one thing they need?" She glanced at Clothilde, whose sidebar on the historic relationship between the Brau and Khmer had given her the final bolt she needed to secure her idea into place. "Cheap labor. Essentially, slaves. We will tell them that Ormond will keep them from being taken as slaves."

Through the remainder of the night, on the just-wide-enough, northeast-bound trail that traveled from Stung Treng to Siem Pang near the Lao border, the expedition continued toward Leh, which Clothilde estimated they could reach as early as the following evening if they kept up their pace. They walked steadily on the rutted path, accompanied by eight coolies, six horses, and two oxen dragging carts carrying food and supplies. The dirt trail had been tamped down over the years by the callused bare feet of boar hunters and dry rice farmers, and as the sun came up, Irene saw that it was framed not in lush foliage, as she had expected, but in a low, tattered forest and the occasional thicket of purple thistle. Her leg muscles were already sore from the strain of walking on soggy ground in heavy-soled boots, and she wondered how the others were feeling. So far, no one had complained, not even Simone, who looked as if she was going to faint most of the time.

In the sympathetic air of the daybreak hour, they stopped in a sheltered clearing for breakfast. Through ribbons of chiffon light, wiry apes scrambled out of the sparse scrub and ran down to the river to scold the horses drinking in the shallows. Bouncing on Simone's shoulders, Kiri's gibbon—May-ling, Simone had named it, after the wife of Chiang Kai-shek—chattered at her fellow beasts. The cook served warm porridge lumpy with tinned peaches, while they all sat on a tarp spread out above the riverbank and talked through their plan, which they agreed was as solid as they could hope for, given the circumstances, with one exception.

"There's no reason for him to believe us," Louis said to Clothilde, speaking of Xa, who was squatting at the river's edge, smoking one of the Gauloises that were part of his salary as he watched his son digging in the sandbank. His graying hair was pulled into a knot at the nape of his neck, and his back was adorned with a tattoo of two snakes, fangs bared, looking as if they had crawled out of the jungle to writhe up his spine. Little did he know, he was about to hear the story that would be presented to the chief of Leh: The "French chiefs" planned to take over northeast Cambodia, and Commissaire Ormond's benevolent leadership was coming to its end. "Ormond is the one who sent Xa to watch us," Louis added. "Why wouldn't he have told Xa about this himself? And what's to stop Xa from running straight back to tell Ormond what we're doing? I think we should leave him out of this."

A phantom breeze sounded like rushing water in the tops of sugar palm trees. Gazing beyond Xa at the slow-moving river, Irene said, "We can't pull this off without him. If he's not a part of it, the chief will never believe us."

Because they had decided to show deference by following local custom, the women would not participate in the meeting with the chief. Instead, it made sense for Xa to take the lead. Since Xa did not speak English or French, translation would take place through the chief's eldest son, who Clothilde had learned was one of the students of a short-lived program in which the French had taken a boy from each village to "civilize" him in Phnom Penh, then had sent him back to train the rest. Still reluctant, Louis said, "I've worked with these people all of my life. Xa doesn't know us. He has no reason to trust us. I don't see how we can convince him."

"Any ideas?" Marc asked the others, as he refilled tin cups with a second round of tea.

With her hair in tangles and her arms scored with scratches, Simone appeared wasted by their long walk. Even food and drink had not revived her, and her drooping carriage did nothing to alleviate the impression that she would not have the stamina for three or four more nights on the trail. Scowling down, her attention focused on a red ant marching across the tarp, she said, "Yes, Clothilde, any ideas? Why do I have a feeling that you might have some suggestions about how to use Xa after all that chatting you and he were doing on the trail last night?"

Beside Simone, Clothilde sat with her legs folded up to her chest. Wrapping her arms around her shins, she rested her chin on her bare knees. She thought for a moment before saying, "Like every man, Xa has a vulnerable spot."

"Which is?" Marc asked, amused.

"Kiri is Xa's only son. A late-in-life miracle from a now dead wife. Whenever it's among your choices," she declared, with a coolness that was impressive, if not a bit disturbing, "always choose the child. A parent will do anything for his child."

They all stared at Kiri, whose skin was still scruffy with saffron paste. Both he and his father were staring into the air, studying something the others could not see.

Clothilde said, "We should talk to Xa as soon as possible. He will need some time to think about our story, to understand the benefits of accepting it as true."

Kiri's giggle scampered up the riverbank, and Irene's thoughts swam from Marc to Simone to Mr. Simms—the damage each had suffered from the loss of a child. She spoke not from reflection but from reflex, surprising herself with her vehemence. "I don't want to use the boy."

"So that's your line?" Simone asked, looking up.

"What do you mean?" Irene asked.

"The line you won't cross. We can shoot back. We can threaten the villagers with the fear of slavery. But we can't threaten Xa with—"

"Nothing that's not real," Clothilde interrupted, in the placating tone Irene had heard her use with Mr. Simms.

"Real?" Irene shook her head. "What real threats could there be to his son?"

"Actually," Louis said, "it's unfortunate, but the threats to a boy like Kiri are plenty, with or without us. For example, the government could start rounding up native children for their experimental programs again. Have any of you heard about what's going on in Kep? There are rumors of medical testing. Doctors are infecting locals with viruses and trying various cures. It's shameful."

"And still no one wants my revolution," Simone muttered with disdain, as she crushed the red ant now crawling across her ankle.

From the shore, Kiri screamed in delight, dancing from one foot to the other as he stared at the leathered mitt of his father's hand. On it was balanced an enormous butterfly, its wings spotted turquoise, emerald, and black, lustrous as peacock feathers.

"Besides, we're not going to threaten anyone," Clothilde said, standing and slipping one foot and then the other into her moccasins. "All we need to do is plant a seed of doubt. Let him know what *could* happen if our story about a French takeover of the region does turn out to be true. Then we simply assure Xa that no matter what happens, his son will be taken care of."

Above, sunlight moved through a lattice of knobby branches, reminding Irene that the morning was passing quickly. She could feel the rinds of dirt embedded beneath her clipped fingernails, the dried sweat crusted at the base of her spine, and she longed to strip off her dirty clothing and bathe in the river. But there was no time for that. They had to keep moving, to get in a few more hours before the heat became unbearable. Confused by the resistance she felt to Clothilde's idea, she got to her feet and said, "I don't know, if you really think this is the best way to go about it . . ."

No one spoke, and the decision was made.

The men stood. Marc held out his hand to help Simone up, and as she gripped it, she said, "If you're feeling shabby about doing this, Irene, don't bother. One of these days you'll see that you're no better than the rest of us when it comes to compromising principles."

"What happened at breakfast? What was that all about?" Marc asked, when he and Irene had a chance to step away from the others. "Are you all right?"

"The way it washed over me, it was so strange."

"What?"

Irene watched the coolies setting up a shelter for the hammocks. The expedition had stopped once again, this time for the day's rest, and everyone would try to sleep until right before sundown, gathering new energy from the cool brought on by the rain. "Guilt," she said.

Concerned, he asked, "Are you having second thoughts about taking the scrolls?"

"No, it's not about that." She arched her shoulders and stretched her arms toward the treetops, but she could not loosen her sore muscles. As she shifted her weight, her feet oozed inside her boots, and she could feel her neck and wrists, chafed from the constant rubbing of damp fabric against her skin. "I outmaneuver people, Marc. That's what I know how to do. It's what I love to do—with collectors, dealers, men who would deceive me as happily as I'd deceive them. I was ready for the colonial government. I was even looking forward to opponents like Ormond and the ferocious Cambodian tribesmen," she said with a dry laugh. "But Xa and his son. An old man and a little boy. Listening to them laughing over a butterfly while we sat there plotting how we could use them." The viscous air made her feel as if she was drowning. She blinked back the sweat burning into her eyes. "I've never felt that kind of guilt before, at least not when I'm pursuing something I want. Why now? Why them?"

"The minute we walked into this jungle, we walked out of our known worlds." To emphasize his point, Marc raised his head, and her eyes followed his upward. Woven into the lianas, at least ten feet wide, a frayed web caught prisms of glinting sunlight.

As she stood looking up at the spider in the center of the web, its body as big and fat as a fist, Marc smoothed back the loose hair clinging to her forehead. It was the first time he had touched her with such intimacy since they had entered the jungle, and she leaned toward the comfort of his hand as he said, "There are probably going to be more times like this morning when you won't recognize your reactions, and for people like us, who do what we do, that might not be a bad thing. However capable I was in my job, or you were in yours, there were feelings we had to keep at bay to make sure we succeeded. Guilt was certainly one of them. Compassion, another.

"I can't say for certain, I don't know you well enough, Irene, I can only speak for what I know about myself, but maybe you're tired of having to harden your heart to get what you want. Maybe you're finally afraid there will come a day when you'll go too far."

"But what if I don't realize it until it's too late?"

Fashioning a headband from the bandanna he carried in his back pocket, Marc arranged it beneath her hat, to soak up the sweat dripping over her brow. "Whatever you decide to do, don't change tonight. Not if you really want to find this temple. We're walking into an armed village operating under the orders of a man who dresses like a circus clown and seems to be using 'Heart of Darkness' as his manifesto. It's no place for feeling guilty, because I can promise you, the villagers won't feel guilt over anything they do to you."

Chapter 19

Complete Certainty

As the moon returned, it felt to Irene as if they had walked full circle, right back into the previous night. The same slow brown river flowed to their left. The same vague patterns of leaves swayed in stands of tall bamboo to their right. But they must have made progress, if only because of the searing pain in her calves and the stinging, swelling, red bramble scratches on the backs of her hands. Still, she was not entirely convinced until she smelled burning wood and saw blue-gray smoke spiraling above the distant trees.

One of the coolies had been sent ahead to announce the expedition's arrival. As they approached, the village of Leh trembled in a glow of torches that filled the air with the smell of scorched resin. Flanked by half-clad men, women wrapped in sarongs, and clusters of naked children, an old man stood in a dirt clearing in front of a shack that sagged on its stilts. It was as rudimentary as every other shack in the impoverished compound, with the exception of a totem pole of boar skulls stacked beside its bamboo ladder and an arsenal of muskets stockpiled beneath it.

"The chief," Clothilde whispered to Irene.

There were too many guns to count in the dark, arranged within a large wooden frame, but Irene saw that each was strategically angled, accessible in an instant. Behind the frame, a shadow moved, and she made out the shape of a sentinel with a rifle pointed in their direction. She shivered with cold terror and exhilaration.

In the wavering torchlight, Irene could tell that as Louis and Marc walked toward the village, Marc was keeping back, although he was not as far back as the women. She had helped him fasten one holster inside his shirt, and she knew that he carried another revolver in the baggy thigh pocket of his trousers. Her own pistol was tucked into her belt, the steel muzzle pressing against her hip bone. Marc looked back at her and mouthed, *Are you ready?*

She noted Clothilde, dutifully vigilant, earning her keep. Nearby, Simone held Kiri's hand, while in his other arm the boy cradled his gibbon. Both she and the child were bleary-eyed. Positioned in front of his son, Xa surveyed the scene. Irene could not guess what he was thinking. That morning, his response to the lie about Ormond had been unreadable, and he had not said a word to anyone as he led the expedition onward. If he had managed to warn the coolies, there was no way of knowing, since they remained with the oxcarts, silently watching from afar.

"If there's shooting and Xa is hit," Irene said quietly to Simone, "take the boy and run for the forest." Then, to Marc, she nodded, *yes.*

He made a clicking sound with his tongue, as if spurring on a horse, and Louis stepped forward and approached the chief. Although the light was poor, Irene could see the chief's face well enough, dark and wrinkled as a walnut shell. Four village men, two on each side, moved closer to their leader, but he remained still.

Having cleaned himself up as best he could given the circumstances,

Louis was moderately presentable as he performed the expected honorific greeting, genuflecting with his hands folded together as if in prayer. With his head lowered before the chief, he waited for Xa, who also performed the traditional *sampeah* while he introduced the two men to one another. Although Irene did not take her eyes off the chief, she was listening carefully to Xa for any hint of worry or warning, but she was unable to read the unfamiliar tone of the tribe's dialect and didn't want to draw the chief's attention toward her by asking Clothilde.

After a moment Xa stepped aside, and Louis presented the chief with an offering of English snuff in an oak box. The chief examined the finely worked gold lid, and although he ran his fingers appreciatively over it, his only response was a noncommittal grunt that revealed a glinting gold tooth framed by dark, toothless gaps. Then he turned his gaze on the women.

His eyes shone like onyx, and Irene was mesmerized, staring into the stern face of this man who had been charged with standing in her way.

"What in the hell are you doing?" Clothilde whispered, urgently. "Irene, Simone, bow your heads."

"I know what to do," Simone hissed back, while Irene, immediately realizing her impudence, did as instructed, listening to the men communicate in a stop-and-start of French and the Brau's tribal language until she heard footsteps scuffling away through the dirt. This was followed by the creak of the ladder up to the chief's home. When Clothilde motioned for her to look up, the men were gone.

This was going to be the hardest part for Irene, to behave as if she was not waiting—for an argument to erupt and even the sound of a gunshot, or for the men to bring word of the chief's approval to let the expedition continue on.

In Irene's profession, there had often been a need to blend in, and she had perfected the art of seeming invisible in the middle of a crowd when she wanted to. But as she was shuffled toward a wood fire beneath one of the huts, the curiosity that followed her was inescapable. Village women swarmed around her, peering so intently it felt as if they were trying to see inside her. They were so close that she could smell the coconut oil they used to style their cropped black hair. An older woman scrutinized her throbbing cheek, with its discharge of blood and pus where Marc had burned away a leech, and around the fire, women continually glanced up at her as they squatted on the ground, mincing pork and stringy forest greens with cleavers on slabs of tree trunks.

"The chief's wife has invited us for dinner," Clothilde said, referring to the eldest of the women, whose breasts, unlike those of the younger women, were not covered in cloth. Instead, they hung exposed, low and pendulous on her chest.

Despite the exoticism of her surroundings, Irene could not stop thinking about Xa and Marc's guns and the lie being told in the chief's bungalow. "I'm not hungry."

"You should eat anyway," Clothilde said, and Simone interrupted, "It's nearly ten. Do you think these women are cooking for themselves at this hour, Irene? It's a sign of goodwill to offer a meal." She gave Clothilde a frown that declared her understanding of the customs. "It's an insult if you don't accept."

"And it's not going to be an insult if they tell us to go back and we refuse?" Irene asked.

Ignoring her, Simone leaned against the ladder that led to the women's communal hut and took off her mud-encrusted boots. Under the ever-watchful gaze of the women at work, Irene followed her example, struggling with laces that felt as if they were bound with glue. She peeled off her clammy socks. Released, her feet expanded, puckered and red, like overripe fruit. With an easy flick of her toes, Clothilde slipped out of her moccasins, and after conferring briefly with the chief's wife, she led the way up the ladder. Irene came after Simone, followed by nearly every female in the village, with the exception of those doing the cooking. Along with the rest, she sat Indian-style on the bamboo floor, since there was no furniture, only reed sleeping mats folded in one corner.

As the Brau women encircled their visitors, and Irene shifted with the discomfort of being so tightly and thoroughly surrounded, the flimsy floor vibrated. While giggling girls took turns sneaking up from behind to graze their fingers against her sun-lightened hair, the women clucked and whispered among themselves. They were the descendants of the women her own mother would have encountered if she had in fact made this journey to the temple. Perhaps Sarah Blum had sat even with some of the eldest, who were now tucked into the corners of the room, gnawing on betel leaves, crimson saliva glistening at the edges of their pursed mouths. Irene felt sick with wanting Clothilde to ask if any of them had met her mother. But she kept quiet, giving Clothilde the opportunity to interpret their muttering, in case any of it revealed what could happen if the expedition tried to proceed.

Instead, Clothilde leaned toward her and said, "I was raised in a room exactly like this one. It had palm-leaf walls that were alive with roaches and spiders. The interesting thing about the story you've made up, Irene, is how true parts of it are. It *is* only a matter of time before the government swoops in and all of this is gone."

"Not if I can help it," Simone said, caressing the gibbon in her lap. Xa's son, because he was male, had gone to the chief's hut.

"Why would you want anyone to keep living like this?" Clothilde asked.

"Why do you want them to change?"

"If by change you mean why should they have electricity? Why should they have vaccines or clean water or Monet? Are you really going to insult me by asking that?" Clothilde's voice rose, and although they did not understand the language she was speaking, the children perked up and the women inched closer, fascinated by one of their own arguing in a foreign tongue. Clothilde neatened her pretty shift over her knees and adjusted her emerald ring, as if to confirm that she had not somehow been transformed back into her past self upon entering the village. "I was malnourished my entire childhood," she told Simone. "Four of my brothers and sisters were dead by the time I was born. Idealists! You're certain you know what's best for the natives. You think there's nothing more romantic than living in a grass shack. Try living in one during monsoon season."

"My parents were born here," Simone said. "This is my country as much as it is yours. I know what the Cambodians want."

"You were born into the privilege of French citizenship. That may give you many rights, but not the right to think you know who these women are."

"Stop it, both of you," Irene said, softly. "This isn't the time or place."

But Clothilde, who had been so dispassionate up until now, was not finished. "I remember the first time I saw a book. I didn't recognize what it was, but somehow I knew it meant *more*, it meant *better*, and I wanted it. The first time I heard Mozart, I was outside Ormond's porch like the poor wretches you saw the other night, and I wanted nothing more than to find the source of that beautiful sound. Not the phonograph but the village. That's what it was like for me then. A world so confined and pitiful that I could only conceive of it in terms of villages. They should know that living like this, living in complete poverty and isolation, is not all there is."

Slowly, deliberately, Simone focused on Clothilde's flamboyant ring, which unawares, Clothilde was still twisting round and round. "Clearly," she said, "the life you have chosen is a much better alternative."

"Simone!" Irene was fed up with her hostility. "Stop being such an ass."

Clothilde blinked around at the village women, who were warily eyeing the threesome, tigers loose in their midst. "How awful," she spat out, "being put in a position to have to defend yourself with those decrepit muskets down there. What I'm trying to say is that when I was one of these people, when this was my life, I would have wanted to know I had other choices than to follow Ormond's suicidal orders or believe the ludicrous lie your men are telling the chief right now."

It was nearly dawn, and the torches that had illuminated the expedition's arrival were burned down to char. The orchid glow of the sky was growing visible through the gaps in the clouds as Irene, Simone, and Clothilde climbed down from the women's hut to join the men, who were gathered in the bare patch of earth that served as a village square. Having been roused unceremoniously by one of the Brau girls, Irene heard Simone whisper to Louis, "What's going on?"

"We tried," he said, his voice graveled with lack of sleep. His jacket was not even buttoned, and one of his boots was untied. In his fatigue, he seemed to have forgotten his unhappiness with Simone, and Irene could hear the echo of his old intimacy with her as he said, "We've been up all night trying to convince the chief that Ormond sent us to protect what's left in the temple, but he still wants us to leave."

"Now?"

"Right now."

Irene sought further explanation from Marc, but his face was grim as he kept watch on something behind her. She turned, and she shivered.

She had envisioned opposition, of course she had, but still she was not prepared for the rank of Brau men lining the trail that led out of the village in the direction of the temple. There were at least fifty of them, a small militia, all armed with the exception of the chief, who stood at the head of the dragon their dark bodies formed, observing the small expedition with no doubt in his expression that it would retreat.

Looking around, Irene saw that he had no reason to believe otherwise. Of their own accord, the coolies had gathered the horses and oxcarts at the start of the trail back to Stung Treng. Xa was with them, standing protectively in front of his son, who was peeking around him. Simone's face was taut, and she concentrated on the rhythmic stroking of the gibbon's head with her forefinger. Her eyebrows drawn together, Clothilde did not try to hide her worry, even as she held on to her Mauser, which she claimed to be able to sight to the centimeter at fifty yards. Although Marc and Louis appeared intent on holding their ground, revolvers firmly in hand, this could only be for show, for they were outnumbered. What the Brau lacked in the quality of their old firearms they made up for in manpower.

"Once the first shot is fired," Marc whispered to Irene, "there's no turning back."

His warning jarred her. Despite his experience in the underworld of Shanghai, and his words of caution the previous day, even he had not expected the situation to go this far. But she felt that it could only have come to this, so that she could know with complete certainty that she wanted the scrolls no matter what.

The village men stood before Irene in the cloudy gloom, narrow waists wrapped in sarongs, chests bare, muskets held at the ready. Cords of white mist spiraled over the dense olive green of the Sekong River. Dew dripped off the fog-soaked trees, tapping from leaf to leaf. She took a step toward the chief, and the muskets were raised. She took another step, and they were aimed. The irregularity of her heartbeat pounded in her ears. The village women were gawking out at her from the doorways and windows of the surrounding huts, but when she stood before the chief, looking once again into his dark eyes, his old face was like a mask. Marc was right. This was not her known world. How confident she had been of her skills at manipulation. How transparent and irrelevant those skills now seemed. A *ludicrous lie*, Clothilde had called it. As Irene accepted this—the insult it was to both the chief and herself, the ways she had turned this into a game—she could feel something within herself being set free.

She reached into her pocket and took out her pistol. The forest's sounds gave way to the staccato ticking of muskets being cocked. She sank to her knees. With her face lowered, hidden from view, she blinked back tears of pure fear. Holding the gun flat between her shaking palms while she drew her hands to her forehead, she bowed to the ground three times, a *sampeah* to show her respect. She set the gun at the chief's gnarled bare feet. She slowly stood. His countenance had not changed.

She had always operated from behind the impervious shield of her strategies. This morning she would be unarmored. She persisted across the impossibly fluid ground, through the village square, toward the trail that led to the temple. She was staring straight ahead, but she could see that none of the Brau were focused on her. Their gazes were fixed on the impenetrable border of forest behind her, as if it contained a repository of hidden strengths.

The men stood side by side, forming a chain along the rim of the path. They were close enough to strike her down with the wooden stocks of their guns, but she could not even hear their breathing. With each man she passed, her back felt broader, more exposed, but she kept walking, despite the melted rubber of her knees, until she reached the last of them. Finally, her eyes could not stay away. In the single instant of her glance, she saw him as if he were standing in a spotlight, the serrated puffs of ritual scars on his arms and cheeks, the resoluteness of his posture. She felt the potency of his waiting for instruction from his chief.

She lifted one leaden boot and forced it forward, and lifted the other and forced that one ahead too. If the man were to lower his musket, he would shoot point-blank. He could not miss. Bats tore at the cindered sky, and the village men began to murmur. The jungle ahead was a frayed green wall. She was as terrified of backing down and never knowing what lay ahead as she was of defying the chief and being shot. So she kept going, one step at a time, into the turbulent discord of frogs and cicadas, growing so loud that eventually she could hear nothing else, not even her own footsteps. She walked blindly into the first rays of sunlight, for how long she didn't know. She did not pause until a hand reached into her trance, touching her shoulder.

Irene expected it to be a Brau, and longed for it to be Marc so she could collapse into him, but it was Clothilde, still holding her gun. "I think your courage impressed even the chief," she whispered. "Here, have some water, you've been walking for more than an hour."

As Irene took Clothilde's canteen and drank, she looked back down the path. Adrift a few yards away, Simone stood with May-ling curled head to tail on her shoulder, watching Irene and Clothilde with bewilderment on her face. Next came Xa and Kiri, and beyond them, Marc and Louis, holding their rifles to their chests in positions of readiness, still on guard, for farther on, in the morning's smoky blue light, Irene could make out a group of ten armed Brau villagers in a somber file behind the coolies and the oxcarts.

Chapter 20

The Sacrifice

"This is a good sign," Louis said and then added with a resigned smile, "or at least as good a sign as we could hope for in such a situation. Not that I've ever been in such a situation." He waved the spark of his cigarette toward their Brau escorts, who were standing at a distance down the path, watching the members of the expedition as they gathered around Irene. "If the chief was positive we were lying to him about Ormond sending us up here to retrieve the scrolls from the temple, or if he's protecting that temple for himself, he would have stopped you, Irene. And he never would have let us follow you. Don't you agree, Clothilde?"

"Based on what the chief told Xa, the village doesn't have any interest in the temple," Clothilde said. "He's under orders from Ormond. He couldn't risk trying to detain you, in case your story is true. Plus, he couldn't be sure of what a band of greedy foreigners with guns might do if provoked. So his men are going to keep an eye on us while he sends someone to Stung Treng to consult with Ormond and find out what's really going on."

"Even if the scout travels alone and on foot," Louis interrupted, "it will still take him more than a full day to go there and back, and another to catch up with us. By then we should have reached the temple, if your estimate is correct."

Kiri was asleep on Clothilde's hip, and with one hand cradling his head, she said, "It's not an estimate. I visited the temple half a dozen times for holy festivals when I was a girl, and I made annual visits to Kha Seng to see my aunties when I was living in Stung Treng. Same road, same number of days."

Louis said, "That will give us a bit of time to look for the scrolls."

"Irene?" Simone said. "I should have been at your side."

"Not now, Simone," Irene said and then asked Clothilde, "If the scrolls are up at the temple and Ormond sends someone to stop us, what do you suggest we do?"

"You should be asking me," Simone whispered, gnawing on a ball of sticky rice she had taken from her knapsack.

The group had become adept at paying no attention to Simone's mutterings, and Louis said, "We can deal with that later. All I know is that I want to keep going. Hell, Irene, that was incredible!"

Irene noticed the speckles of blood on her sleeves from smashed mosquitoes. She didn't feel incredible. She felt cold to the bone, and she was grateful when Marc took her hands, rubbing them between his palms, melting the deep chill of her residual fear. "And you?" she asked him. "Do you still want to go through with this?"

He studied her with a questioning look. "I'm still here, aren't I?"

Sensation was returning to her numb limbs, a tingling in her calves and upper arms. "Too many things could go wrong," she said. "If you're doing this just for me—"

"That's a part of it," he said, kneading her fingertips. "But we all have more than one motive, when it comes down to it. If we didn't, this jaunt would be a hell of a lot easier."

"I think we should talk to the Brau." Simone forced her way into the conversation. "We should find out what they really want."

"The chief told us he wants to ride in a motorcar," Marc said.

"And to see a skyscraper before he dies," Louis added.

"That's not what I mean," Simone said, swatting at May-ling as she grabbed at the rice with her black paw.

"We know what you mean," Irene said, once again looking down the path at the Brau, standing in an orderly row, one behind the other, their expressions impossible to decipher, their presence—and their muskets—impossible to ignore.

Clothilde rolled her eyes. "I'll tell you what they really want. They *really* want to chew their hemp and be anywhere other than here right now."

Annoyed, Simone said, "You would know best, wouldn't you?"

Within the jungle's deepening heat, with the Brau men watching the expedition's every move and Ormond's coolies warily watching the Brau, the hours seemed to leapfrog and backtrack, intermingling like the liana vines that climbed the banyan trees from the forest floor. Was it on the second day of the trek, or the third, or the first, that sunburn singed the exposed backs of Irene's hands? She could not remember a time when they were not submerged in flame, a time when she did not wince as she walked on blistered feet. Edging her way past the spiraling blades of pandanus trees, she felt her fatigue as if it were a weight she had been ordered to carry on her back.

As for the others, Marc was physically fit and emotionally tough, an ideal combination for the jungle. Clothilde did not tire as easily as Irene did, despite all of the time she had been away in America, and Louis was clearly accustomed to trudging about in swampy heat. He, of all of them, had the strongest instinct for what a situation required. He knew when to hand a canteen to someone, and when to stop for a break. He was attentive to their surroundings and individual needs, even Simone's—especially Simone's—despite his shattered feelings for her.

Although Irene had given up hope that Simone might prove useful, she came to admire the woman's incredible stamina, especially when the group woke from their day of rest after leaving the village of Leh and discovered that Simone was not well. All of them were sweating all the time, but there was a strange grayness to the sheen on her skin, and she was shaking. Louis suspected malaria, but when he tried to talk to her about the symptoms, or convince her to drink one of the teas she had brought from the Chinese pharmacy in Saigon, she refused and insisted it was the mild flulike malaise that was typical in overly humid weather. If she suspected that the expedition was taking a break for her sake, she would forge ahead.

Three days into the pilgrimage, with one more day's walk to the temple, they were still using the narrow hunting and trading path. But it was much less traveled than the section that had skirted the river. The horses whinnied in protest as they were prodded through the entangled leaves of giant ferns. The leather gloves that Louis had given Irene were too thin, and the pads of her palms were bruised and constantly bleeding from grabbing vines to pull herself along the most overgrown portions of the trail. The coolies had to force the oxen and carts through brush so dense that it was inconceivable to imagine the ancient Khmer dragging thousand-pound stones across such terrain.

Hoisting herself over shoulder-high, moss-glazed logs, Irene understood how Cambodia's first travelers could have believed that Angkor Wat was built by gods or monsters. The woolly trees screeched and scratched like living beasts. The only signs of humanity were the occasional villages, scruffy and as unsettling in their indifference as Leh was in its watchfulness. With their aging chiefs and tall bamboo towers for keeping lookout for tigers, each cluster of huts was more primitive than the last. It felt as if, in their approach to the temple, they were traveling back in time—a journey made even more disorienting by the restless truce between the expedition and its Brau keepers, as each group waited to see what the other was going to do.

———

"How much hashish could they have brought with them?" Marc asked, unable to hide his fascination with the Brau. "There's not a minute in the day when they're not chewing on it. And where the hell do they store it? They don't have a single pocket among them. They're starting to unnerve me. They're high all the time, and yet they still manage to keep an eye on us. I was watched in Shanghai, but never like this. They don't even blink."

"At least Ormond's coolies chat among themselves. I haven't heard the Brau speak since we left Leh," Louis said. "Have you?"

"Not a word," confirmed Marc, who was perched with Louis and Irene on fallen logs in an open space on the side of the trail.

They had stopped so that antiseptic could be applied to the morning's newest injury, a bloody gash on one of the coolie's shoulders from the unanticipated whip of a vine. While Xa spread a melting cream over the man's torn skin, Irene wriggled her toes inside her boots, her feet sticky with sweat and antifungal powder. As Marc and Louis discussed the enigmatic demeanor of their Brau wardens, she looked around for the man on guard duty, for there was always one taking a turn, while the rest gnawed on hashish, sharpened knives, dozed, or skinned the squirrels they caught in the woods, giving the fuzzy brown tails to Kiri, to add to the collection tied to a leather strap draped over his shoulder. Watching the assigned guard was a way for Irene to remind herself of what she had done in Leh. Of what she was capable of doing.

She located the day's watchman, his cheeks speckled with tattoos. He was standing on the trail behind Kiri, who was passing the time batting at leaves, sucking nectar from flowers, and shaking a string of cans to scare off tigers and ghosts. She told Marc and Louis, "I try to put myself in their heads. I try to imagine what they could be thinking—"

But before she could pursue this train of thought, Clothilde approached and said, "Irene, could you come with me for a moment?"

"What is it?"

"There's something I want to show you."

The men continued with their discussion while Irene followed

Clothilde into the forest off the opposite side of the path. Behind the im-mense trunk of an evergreen tree, Simone was on her hands and knees, vomit pooled in the scrub in front of her. Instantly, Irene thought of her overdose in Saigon. "Simone, what have you taken today?"

"No pills, Irene." Her voice was feeble. "I promise."

"She was sick last night too," Clothilde said.

Simone scowled at her.

Taking a handkerchief from her pocket, Clothilde asked, "Can you sit up? Here, let me help you."

But as Simone scooted back from the evidence of her suffering and leaned against the tree, she pushed the cloth away and snapped, "Don't touch me."

"Clothilde," Irene said, "ask the cook to make some rice. And a pot of weak black tea."

As Clothilde rushed away, she passed Marc and Louis, who were wan-dering over to see what was going on. The moment Louis saw Simone, he crouched in front of her, laying the back of his hand over her forehead, as if she were a child. They sat together like this for a minute, each of them looking miserable, until Louis said, "You have a fever. I knew it, I knew this would be too much for you. Simone, what am I going to do with you?"

Simone lowered her head, and if Irene had not known her better, she would have thought she saw shame on her face. Nearly inaudible, she said, "This is her fault."

"What are you talking about?" Louis asked.

Simone eyed Clothilde already hurrying back, carrying a wet towel and a tin of crackers. "This is your fault. You're ruining everything. If you weren't here, I'd be in charge."

"No, Simone," Louis said, with resolve, "you can't blame Clothilde for this."

Rather than lash out, Simone stared up at him, her eyes sunk into their sockets. She wiped her mouth with the back of her wrist, and with this defeated gesture Irene realized that it was more than dislike, what Simone felt for Clothilde. It was jealousy, and Irene understood it, because it was warranted. With her knowledge and her loyalty, with the mere fact of her stability, Clothilde had taken the place that Simone had hoped to occupy—a place Irene had wanted Simone to occupy when they first met. Irene was saddened by Simone's disgrace, but she did not know how to mend the situation, for Simone was in no shape to take charge of anything, not even herself.

Morosely, Simone said to Clothilde, "I still don't even understand why you're here. This has nothing to do with you."

Clothilde examined each person in the group in turn before handing the towel to Louis. For a moment it seemed that she was going to walk away. Then, with her eyes on no one, she said, "Do you think I want to be here? I'm doing this for him, because he saved my daughter. He saved me. He gave me a normal life, or as normal a life as a woman like me can expect. Do you *really* think I'm taking pleasure in any of this? Do you think I enjoy watching the way you treat my country? I should leave you to fend for yourselves."

With this outburst, Irene recalled the beginning of the expedition and how coolly Clothilde had talked of using Kiri. That indifference was such a contrast to her words in the hut in Leh, and to her anger right now. "Please," Irene said, "we need you, don't go."

"I can't." Clothilde looked beaten. "Everything he's promised me, everything I need for my daughter, it's all in your hands."

"What do you mean?"

"You'll find out soon enough. It's in his will. He's left me a trust, with you in charge of it. It's up to you to pay me if I follow through with his plans."

"And what are his plans?" Irene asked.

Drumming her thumb against the lid on the tin of crackers still in her hand, Clothilde did not appear to have heard Irene's question. "He warned me that you would all be difficult, but I didn't realize how serious he was." Her gaze cleared a boneyard of toppled tree trunks, settling on the sentinel Brau who had followed them into the woods. He had lowered his musket and aimed it, as he always did when he was the one on duty, idly sighting them down the barrel. "I never imagined the jungle would be the least of my worries."

Louis wanted Simone to ride on one of the oxcarts, but she refused, saying, "I *need* to walk." Finally, he accepted that she was going to have her way, and the expedition started off again. But they had made it no more than another hour up the trail when Xa raised his machete.

Somehow Irene knew, they all knew, simply by the way he motioned, carving into the air with the blade of his knife, not to move, not to make a single noise.

The cobra glided onto the path in front of them.

The *naga* spirit of the Khmer, the serpent gatekeeper of Angkor, slithered out of the myths only three feet from Xa's son. It rose, its fan unfolding slowly, its hood flaring until its sloped eyes gazed out from a brown cape. Kiri's scrawny target of a chest was bare. The snake was nearly his height.

With a single snap of its venomous fangs, the cobra could kill an elephant. Blood rushed to Irene's head, blurring her vision, but still she saw the muscles tense in Xa's mahogany arms and the tattooed serpents strain up his back. His grip tightened around the handle of his machete, and for once Irene was able to interpret what he was thinking. Could he act fast enough? Was there any such thing as fast enough? She would have looked away, but it felt as if the slightest movement could kill the boy, and even blinking seemed a dangerous thing to do.

"Oh," Clothilde gasped.

Beyond the cobra stood one of the Brau, a bony man with the face of an ascetic. His body was still as death. Irene had not heard him, she had not felt him, but he had bypassed all of them and was behind the snake, within reach of it, his own machete lifted. His eyes were ferocious, and she shut her own as the snake lunged and metal slashed the air. The thud was blunt and sickening. Kiri shrieked. Simone screamed, and Irene saw her kneeling on the ground holding the child tightly in her lap.

"What do we do?" Irene asked, seeing the despair on Xa's face.

"The first aid kit!" Louis shouted.

Marc was already running back to the oxcarts.

But Kiri was struggling to free himself from Simone, and the stunned adults realized that what could have happened had not. The relief would take hours to sink in. Scooping up the two pieces of the dead snake, the Brau carried them back to his fellow villagers. Clothilde dug out the thermos of lukewarm tea and passed it around, everyone drinking from the same cup as they waited for Xa to regain his composure. But he was in shock, staring blankly at the ground where the snake had been.

As Clothilde started toward him, Simone touched her arm. "Let me. Please."

Clothilde nodded.

Simone went to Xa, whispering, soothing. He whispered back.

"What's he saying?" Irene asked.

"If we're serious about keeping Kiri safe, then we'll take him out of the jungle with us when we go." Although Simone appeared to be weaker than ever, there was a steadiness to her words, as if by being sick she had purged herself of some degree of instability. "And if we do that, Xa will continue to play our game and pretend to believe our story."

That Xa understood the situation did not surprise Irene. She watched the boy dancing after the Brau, hissing triumphantly at the severed snake. "Tell him we want to do whatever we can for his son."

"Do you mean that?" Simone asked.

Xa was looking at Irene expectantly, and she saw in the old man's expression the same helplessness that had been in her father's face during the months after her mother died. She understood for the first time not only the burden that had been accepted by Mr. Simms but the relief that her father must have felt in being able to count on his help. "Yes," she said. "I do."

Early that evening, as the sun descended, clouds dispersed into a metallic froth over the darkening sky, and wind whipped the treetops into a frenzy. An unseasonable night storm was coming in, and it would be imprudent to try to take on the ever-narrowing trail in a downpour. In an overgrown resting area, the coolies cut away long grasses and tramped on the remains before setting up camp. The day had been tiring in more than just the usual ways. It had been emotionally punishing, and the group was worn down, all but Simone, who had miraculously improved. Though she was not well, she was not incapacitated, which was the state Irene had expected her to be in. She had even managed to make a batch of gin-tonics and was carrying the glasses around on a tray.

Sitting in a canvas chair, as Marc applied Unguentine to the crosshatch of scratches on her cheek and neck, Irene watched the Brau. They had started their own fire in a clearing behind the tents. Ragged strips of the cobra's skin were strung on forked branches over the flames. As usual, one of the men stood sentry, squatting on an oxcart with a musket in his arms, his eyes fixed on the foreigners.

"What are they doing with the snake?" Irene asked Clothilde, declining the drink Simone offered.

"They're preparing to make a sacrifice," Clothilde answered, taking a glass.

Irene had bathed as best she could in a makeshift tin-bowl sink. She had changed into clean clothes and loose canvas shoes to relieve her swollen feet, but none of this tempered the foreboding that came with Clothilde's answer, swift as the snake that had crossed their path. According to Clothilde, they could reach the temple by tomorrow afternoon. In less than twenty-four hours they would, or would not, discover the scrolls, and with them the entire time would be these Brau, who could sneak up silently behind a rearing cobra and strike it dead.

"What is the sacrifice for?" she asked.

"I have seen a child bitten by a cobra. I held him through the seizures. I watched him take his last breath. Still, it's not the snake that frightens me. It's the snake's spirit that I respect and fear," explained Clothilde. "It's the same for these Brau. The one who saved the boy, he will eat the snake's heart and pray it will give him strength to fight off the *naga*'s spirit when it comes for him tonight."

Intent on maintaining the minutiae of the expedition, Louis looked up from the screwdriver he was using to tighten the eyepiece on a pair of field glasses. "Superstition has always fascinated me, how half of the world has found a way past it—the advanced half, I might add—and the other half is still dominated by it."

"I have lived in both worlds, and I have yet to find reason to stop believing in the spirits," Clothilde said.

Carefully massaging the antiseptic into Irene's skin, Marc asked, "What are they going to sacrifice?"

Clothilde motioned to May-ling, perched in Simone's lap. "They caught a gibbon about an hour ago."

At that instant Irene heard the first agitated cry of a wild animal. The air smelled deceptively civilized, of citronella and the leather boots drying in front of the flames, but the Brau had circled their own rising fire, chanting softly, stirring the night with a rhythmic moan that was echoed by stalks of bamboo groaning together against the storm. "I wish they'd chosen a place out of sight," she said. Any curiosity she might have had about the ritual was overpowered by its eeriness and her growing apprehension.

Chuckling as he polished the lenses of the glasses, Louis glanced at Marc. "Maybe it's biology that makes women more susceptible to hocus-pocus than men."

The Brau tramped in a back and forth pattern around their fire, while the coolies sat in the brush and watched. The wind picked up, adding a restless clacking to the plaint of the bamboo. "My daughter came to me once in Shanghai," Marc said, the reflection of flame wavering in his eyes. "Ghosts only appear when something isn't finished."

"Hell, Rafferty," Louis chided, "how much opium did you smoke that night?"

Irene flinched as Marc's fingers dug into her skin, roughly rubbing buffalo tallow over the inflamed blister that cupped her palm.

There was silence around the campfire, and it took a moment for Louis to realize the harshness of what he had said. "That was unnecessary." He set his glasses aside. "This has been quite the day. Simone, I'll take one of those drinks, if you're still offering."

Simone handed him a gin-tonic, then sat back in her chair and pulled her velvet jacket tighter around her. "The fact is, Louis," she said, "human beings all need superstition to some degree. Without anything to believe in, life is simply too hard. Even you worship the Angkor temples. The secular direction the world is headed, it's dangerous, don't you think?"

She sounded so logical that everyone stared at her as if she were speaking in tongues.

The Brau's chants grew louder, coarser, casting a haunting baritone over the campsite. A dagger of lightning stabbed the forest yards from the encampment, and the chanting intensified. The expedition's stallion stamped its hooves, and the mares brayed in frightened reply.

"Too close for comfort," Marc muttered toward the sky.

"The French have taken all of the Cambodians' power," Simone said. "The government has taken almost everything, except this—their beliefs. Why shouldn't they cling to their so-called hocus-pocus?" She faltered and her eyes widened as an inhuman shriek splintered the night.

The Brau who had saved Kiri's life seemed to be rising out of the fire. His brown skin dripped sweat as he clutched a knife in one hand and a limp gibbon in the other. Its throat was slit. The rush of its blood gleamed in the firelight. The Brau's tribesmen undulated around him, propelled by hemp and the wind. He threw the hemorrhaging ape to the ground and raised an earthenware jug to his lips.

Simone sheltered May-ling inside her coat.

Transfixed, Clothilde whispered, "Rice wine mixed with the snake's blood."

Lightning flared again, and the floodgates were ruptured. The rain struck fast and hard, and everyone scrambled to their feet to run for shelter. The stallion had broken loose, galloping toward the camp chairs with two coolies stumbling behind it. Marc and Louis darted forward to cut off the spooked horse. With Simone gripping one arm and Clothilde grabbing for the other, Irene ducked to rescue her map case from the ground beside her chair and barely dodged out of the animal's way. As she skidded through the mud, the mares ran free around her, bawling as lightning shattered the dark, illuminating the entirety of the night so that for an instant Irene saw the Brau racing toward the camp, machetes and axes raised.

Her breath came in short, petrified gasps as the Brau surged through a frenzy of coolies and horses, a sable riot tearing saddlebags, slashing tents, smashing crates.

"Get down!" Clothilde screamed, and over this Simone shouted in

French for Xa, having forgotten in the madness that he did not speak the language. *"Qu'est-ce qui se passe? Qu'est-ce qui se passe?"* But Xa and Kiri had vanished, and everyone knew exactly what was happening. Knew finally why the chief had sent his men: to prevent the foreigners from reaching the temple. But how far would they go, fueled by drugs and blood sacrifice and the storm?

The shadows of two Brau found the shadows of the expedition's rifles and beat them against the trunk of a tree. Simone clambered through the mud, calling frantically, "May-ling! I can't find May-ling!" Marc caught hold of a horse. His fingers tore at its mane, but he could not tame its panic. If Louis was out there, he was not visible, and Irene could see less and less as the rain drenched her vision. Clothilde forced her into the swampy grass, hissing, "Stay down," but Irene struggled against her. She had to defend what she'd come all this way to do. She had to drive the Brau the hell out of there before someone was hurt. She crawled toward Marc, shouting, "Your gun! Give me your gun!"

The pistol flew into the air. The horse kicked out. Marc fell. Squinting through the thundering rage of the storm, Irene saw Simone slumped on her side. She saw crumpled tents and the Brau swinging their machetes. Swiping water from her eyes, she dug the gun from the mud, but she was not fast enough. Beside her Clothilde fired her Mauser. One shot, two, three, four, then rapidly five and six, exploding into the camp until the chambers were empty and the Brau and horses had fled and one body lay motionless on the ground.

Chapter 21

The Bullet Wound

Through the steady current of the rain, Irene could barely see Marc as he bent down to pick up one end of a makeshift stretcher, which had been hastily cobbled from a broken folding cot. Louis carried the other end, and they shuffled toward the shelter they had jury-rigged out of a damaged tent. Although the worst of the storm had passed, a thick rain remained. Using a flashlight she had salvaged, Irene searched the debris around the oxcarts for the black leather satchel that contained the first aid kit. Xa and his son were nowhere in sight, and the few coolies who had not run away were talking in distraught tones nearby. If the Brau were still out there, they would make sure she did not hear them, and she kept her eye on the cracked lantern that hung within the flimsy tent, to keep from straying too far and getting lost.

"Hurry," Clothilde said, coming up behind Irene, the raw nerve of hysteria in her voice. "He's going to bleed to death."

"Whose fault is that?" Irene said, shielding her eyes from the rain with the visor of her hand as she caught sight of a dark object half-hidden in the undergrowth.

"You gave me no choice. I'm being paid to protect you."

"I thought you were being paid to guide me."

"This history, Irene, why does it mean so much to you? My God, how much is it really worth?"

"Now's not the time for pretending you don't know the answer to that question." Setting her flashlight aside, Irene plunged her hands into the scrub. Thorny branches tore through the dirty bandage around her finger. Although it had been flung into the night, the satchel containing the first aid kit was miraculously intact. "I found it!" she shouted.

Marc and Louis had propped the stretcher on two battered trunks retrieved from the muddy chaos of the campsite. The only remaining Brau lay on his stomach, unmoving. Louis had found a vial of morphine tablets and had forced one of the large pills down his throat. Still, the man groaned, low and anguished. As Marc took the medical bag from Irene, he winced. The horse's kick had broken one of his ribs. Louis insisted they needed to be wrapped immediately, while Marc argued that the Brau's blood-soaked gunshot wound was more urgent.

"Take his leg and keep it elevated," he ordered Irene. "Clothilde, start a fire and heat some water. Louis, you're going to have to hold him. See if you can find any rope. If we can tie his arms down, that will help."

As for Simone, she was useless. Trampled in the bedlam, her wrist had snapped like a dry branch, yet another injury to be treated in due time. She was lying semiconscious on a tarp on the ground, her velvet jacket slushy with mud, the right side of her face scraped from chin to brow, her wrist askew.

Irene scooped one hand beneath the Brau's ankle. The skin was nearly hairless and pocked with bluish scars from a lifetime of walking barelegged in the jungle. As she raised his leg, she felt his numbed resistance, and she was sorry for the poor man, abandoned by his own, bleeding among the strangers who had maimed him. The bullet had gone through the back of his calf, and Marc grimaced against his own traumatized ribs as he pushed pads of gauze into the black, oozing holes. The Brau kicked, and even though Louis had tied his hands, he still needed all of his weight on the injured man's back to hold his shoulders down. Irene steeled her entire body to keep the damaged leg from flailing.

"Take this," Marc said, giving her a roll of gauze, "and keep pressure on it."

Using the wedge of her knee to prop up the Brau's leg, she bore down. Her touch seemed to go straight to his lungs, driving the air from his body in a vicious exhalation of pain. His jaw tensed as he gritted his teeth, and when he turned his face toward Irene, it was contorted, but she still recognized him. He was the one who had saved Kiri's life. "Is he going to be all right?" she asked.

Blinking against the rain leaking into the shelter, Louis said, "The bullet went clean through. He's lucky for that. Who knows? We might pull this off."

Marc doused a cloth in antiseptic, and Irene felt light-headed from the sharp odor of alcohol. "Hold on to him as tightly as you can," he said, peeling the gauze away from the bullet's entry hole and squeezing the cloth into it. The cloth absorbed the blood, which continued to flow, and the Brau, his eyes wide open, rigid with pain, strained against Irene, two combatants in their own private battle. From the corner of her eye, Irene saw Clothilde take an object from the first aid kit, something metal attached to a wooden handle. "I heat it?" Clothilde asked Marc, nervously.

"Yes, but don't let it turn red. If it turns red, it's too hot."

"What are you going to do?" Irene asked.

"Cauterize," Marc explained. "We need to stop this bleeding. Now be ready to hold him down. He's about to feel a kind of pain unlike any he's felt before."

With Irene, Louis, and Clothilde gripping the Brau, Marc pressed the scalding cautery against the wound. The man's skin sizzled. His howl ripped into the night.

It was over quickly, but when Irene relaxed, Marc said, "We're not finished. I can only apply pressure for a few seconds at a time. Otherwise I'll burn healthy tissue."

As he reheated the shield and stamped the welting skin again, her throat convulsed against the meaty smell of seared flesh. And she found herself thinking, Who else in this world would not find it strange that this is what is being asked of him in the name of love? How many men would even know how to do what I need done? Today, treat a bullet wound. Tomorrow, who knows what? Yet she had faith that Marc would be ready for any of it.

But now was not the time for such thoughts. She returned her focus to the Brau. She owed this man her full concentration, as he continued to weaken, sapped by his struggle against the wrenching pain.

In the middle of making tea, exhaustion overtook Clothilde. She fell asleep slouched against a carpetbag, with four mugs of hot water steaming on the tarp in front of her and four muslin bags of Ceylon tea held loosely in her hand. A combination of distress and sleeping powder from the medical kit had knocked the Brau out cold. Having offered Simone morphine, which she inexplicably refused, Marc set her wrist while she held her breath against the agony of bones being crushed back into place. Within minutes, she too succumbed to a comatose sleep. Then it was Marc's turn.

As he stood in the center of the shelter in the waning kerosene light, Irene peeled his shirt away from his skin. The left side of his torso was dingy and swollen with bruises, and she wanted desperately to be alone with him, to take care of him. Since leaving Leh, they'd had no privacy, no chance at all to talk. There was only one tent each for the men and women, and Irene and Marc could not slip into the night. It was too dangerous. She knew how unattractive she had become, greasy and scabbed and florid, but his few intimacies toward her, even though they happened while surrounded by the others, meant more to her than any they had shared in the seclusion of a hotel room. Their bodies were a matching patchwork of scrapes. He had seen the raw flesh of her wounds. He burned leeches from her skin as tenderly as he had held her their first night together in Saigon.

The rain continued, but halfheartedly, as if even it had grown tired of itself. Louis reached into the black medical bag, and like a magician pulling a rabbit from a hat, he revealed an item that looked somewhat like a woman's corset. "This is going to hurt like hell," he said, matter-of-factly.

Marc raised his arms gingerly, high enough for Louis to bind his ribs. As Louis tied the laces, Marc sucked at the air in short, tight breaths. "This will ease some of the pain," Louis said, "but take it off every few hours and breathe for as long as you can without it. It's compressing your lungs. You could easily catch pneumonia with the moisture in the air up here. Do you have a preference?" He showed Marc the first aid kit's collection of sedatives and painkillers.

Marc shook his head at the pills and said, "I'm old-fashioned. I suppose they smashed the whiskey?"

Louis dipped again into his bag of tricks, this time producing a flask. "Emergency rations. Irene, would you like anything?"

"Please."

He emptied the mugs of hot water and dashed alcohol into them. While Marc undertook the difficult work of simply sitting down beside Irene, Louis perched on one of the salvaged trunks and looked into the night. "I'll stay awake and keep an eye out," he said.

They all knew how easily the tribesmen from Leh could maintain their surveillance of the campsite in this dark. "I'll stay up with you," Irene offered.

Marc drank his whiskey in one gulp and turned his body so that he lay on his back with his head resting in the pillow of Irene's lap. As he fell asleep, she could feel the labor of his breathing. Unconsciously, he tipped to one side, favoring his damaged ribs.

While she and Louis kept watch, the vision of the Brau raging through the campsite played over and over again before Irene's eyes. Were they obeying Ormond? Obeying their chief? What, she wondered, did the villagers really want? She asked, "How could Simone's revolution help these people living up here? Do you think it's what's best for them?"

Louis contemplated the passed-out Brau before returning his guardian gaze to the forest. "If we give their country back to them right now, it
will be a disaster. They're not ready for the modern world, but at the
same time they can't go back to living in the past. The West progressed
gradually, organically, but that's not possible over here anymore. Colonization guaranteed that. There would always be a gap between what they
were and what they had no choice in becoming."

Simone was asleep on a second rescued cot, her bandaged wrist curled
up to her side like a wounded wing. "So a revolution is useless," Irene
asked, "but not because she's the one who wants to lead it?"

"I don't think she would make matters any better." Louis grinned.

Irene had gotten used to the emotion that slipped into his tone when he
talked about Simone, and she wondered, after all that had happened, if he
was still in love with his childhood sweetheart. She had asked him this
once, in the hotel garden in Saigon, but he hadn't answered. She was not
comfortable trying again. Instead, she said, "You must have an opinion:
What do *you* think is best for the Cambodians?"

"Do you care?"

She considered Xa's wishes for his son, the danger the wounded Brau
had been forced into, and the unhappiness of the Cambodians she had
seen in Phnom Penh. She thought about Seattle and the museum's board
of trustees, and how far away she felt from what she had wanted there.
Brushing her fingers over the scratches on Marc's temple, she said, "I've
always cared. It's just never mattered before."

Louis nodded with appreciation. "I believe there's much to be gained
by letting the Khmer examine their own history. Their perspective will be
entirely different from ours. Who knows, if we give them a chance, what
will come to light? What they will see that only they can see from their
point of view. At the same time, perhaps they can use what they learn
about their past to at least bolster some kind of position for themselves,
precarious as that might be. As it is now, they're not even interested. They
don't know what good it could do them, and why should they, since the
government has done everything to separate them from their heritage."

"I assume your institute would play a part in their enlightenment?"

A branch snapped and Louis glanced around, but the lamplight had burned down, and it was impossible to see more than a few feet beyond the tent. As he stood to scout, he asked, "Is this conversation even worth having?"

Irene too peered into the forest, even though she could see nothing. "I'll let you know once I find the scrolls."

The instant Irene saw the devastation of the campsite in the gray dawn light, the seriousness of what could have happened convulsed through her in waves of nausea. She left the others asleep in the improvised tent, to take stock. The damage was thorough, and although no one in the expedition had been deliberately assaulted, it was violent and clearly calculated to terrify them. The men's tent was shredded, hacked with axes taken from their provisions. Tins of oysters, olives, and spaghetti were strewn in the shrubs as if by a tornado. The broken leather body of a camera hung by its strap in a bush, and the horses had all fled. As the heat of the coming day steamed against the retreat of the night, she found her trunk, the one specially made to hide the scrolls, smashed beneath a tree. It was so utterly destroyed that it was nearly unrecognizable.

"It's like a battlefield."

Irene had stooped down to examine the pulverized travel case. Looking up, she saw Simone gazing around the disheveled camp. She was holding her wrist to her chest, and May-ling sat on her shoulder, wide-eyed and alert. "We need to leave now," Irene announced. "They're serious about keeping us away from the temple."

"You're only just realizing this?" Simone asked.

Scowling, Irene stood. "Who knows what they have planned next?"

"It's a shame about your trunk." Simone jabbed the toe of her soggy slipper against a cracked slat that was once part of the lid. "Whoever made it did a good job. I was impressed. I never would have suspected."

"You knew about it?"

"If the cabin locks on the *Lumière* weren't so flimsy, you might have sneaked it past me."

"You searched my cabin?"

"Naturally," Simone said, petting May-ling's long tail with her good hand. "Haven't you searched my things?"

Irene admitted, "I went through your office."

"As you should have. I hope you know I don't fault you for not trusting me. I still find it surprising that you didn't leave me behind. I wouldn't have been as persistent if I were dealing with someone like me."

Once again, Simone sounded uncharacteristically reasonable, and Irene scrutinized her. Her hair was caked with mud, her bandage streaked with dirt, and her trousers torn at both knees. She looked completely broken, but although she reminded Irene of the woman she had been in Anne's office back in Shanghai—with her jaw bruised again in exactly the same place—there was something different about her now. Her eyes were clear. Irene's thoughts skipped back to the day before, when Simone had been sick in the forest, and to her refusal of morphine last night. "You've stopped taking pills, haven't you?"

"I'm trying," Simone said, the words coming out like a sigh of relief.

"Since when?"

"After we left Leh."

"Why?"

"Roger never would have replaced me, no matter how big a handicap I became. But you didn't even think twice about it. You let her step right in and then behaved as if I didn't exist. I exist, Irene."

Irene started as footsteps crackled in the forest, setting off a warning *chit-chit-chit* in May-ling's throat. But the sound was too loud to be the Brau villagers. Having disappeared into the night, Xa and Kiri emerged from the jungle, the boy toting a dented can of Folgers coffee. Xa looked around at the state of the camp. His expression was disturbed as he began the work of digging out the swampy fire pit.

Simone's addiction had become one of Irene's greatest advantages in the contest over who would end up with the scrolls. Irene could not guess what kind of threat Simone's sobriety was going to pose to the expedition. As she watched Xa and Kiri, she thought, These are the very people she is determined to help. Wondering if Simone's feelings about how to help them were shifting as she became clearheaded, Irene asked the question she had put to Louis last night: "What is your revolution going to give the people up here that Ormond isn't already giving them? He may be self-serving and probably insane, but he does seem to have protected them. At least he's keeping the worst of what the government could do to them at bay."

"I'm not unrealistic, Irene. I know the Khmer Empire yesterday was the same as the French Empire today. A handful of despotic leaders, a privileged upper class, and millions of subjugated citizens. It's dispiriting, how similar they are. But at least during the time of Angkor, their country belonged to them." Sinking to rest on a fallen log, Simone gazed across the campsite at Kiri, who was bowed over the slaughtered gibbon near the Brau's doused fire pit, poking at it with a stick. A scarf of singed snake-skin was wrapped around his neck. "People deserve to do things their own way. Even if it's the wrong way."

"So you don't think your revolution will bring equality?" Irene asked.

"There is no such thing as equality."

"Please, Simone, just let me give you the money you need, and I'll take the scrolls."

Simone sniffed the air as it filled with the smell of brewing coffee. "This country is my country. Its history is my history. But its blood has never been my blood. How can I be trusted to save it if I don't have its blood to shed?" she asked, her eyes roaming over the campsite. "The scrolls can be that blood, Irene. Don't you see? I want them more than I have ever wanted anything. They're the only sacrifice I can make. I have nothing else to offer." She frowned as she caught sight of the oxcarts. Although the oxen had not run away, two wheels were detached, and the leather yokes had been cut to tatters by a determined assault of machetes. "The Brau were smart, making sure we lose at least a day."

Reminded of the urgency of their situation, Irene said, "Go wake the men. They can fix the carts and yokes while Clothilde salvages what's left of the tents. We'll repair the rest of what we can when we make camp tonight. You and I are going to gather anything that hasn't been de-stroyed." She pointed at items she had already found: a box of Louis's surveying equipment, two rifles, and three bottles of Glenlivet. "I want to be out of here in an hour."

"That's not possible."

"You of all people should know that nothing is impossible. We've made it this far, haven't we?" Irene took the mug of thick, black coffee that Xa pressed into her hands. "I've had it with this gauntlet of Ormond's. I'm ready. I want to see the temple today."

Chapter 22

The Ravine

"At least twenty meters across," Louis estimated, after stepping back far enough to peer down the length of his outstretched arm and use his raised thumb to calculate the width of the ravine. Irene, Marc, and Simone remained at the edge of the chasm, gazing skeptically at the bridge that spanned it. Constructed from bamboo slats, it was woven so loosely that gaps of green light shone between the shiny flat stalks. It seemed no more substantial than the torn and ragged spiderwebs that clung to the roof of the jungle. At each end, nets of vines were attached to cables made out of much larger vines, nearly six inches in diameter and buried in waist-high stacks of rocks to hold the bridge secure. The rocks were massive too, but they looked precariously piled. If just one came loose, the heap would surely collapse and the bridge would swing away from its mooring. Irene could not gauge the full depth of the ravine because far below, the shaggy tops of thousand-year-old trees blocked the ground from view.

The expedition had left the ravaged camp by ten that morning and had walked through the full heat of the day with hardly a pause to rest. Even with his broken ribs, Marc was determined and stoic, and Simone, though clearly recovering from her habit of gulping pills to get herself through each day, had managed to persevere. It was now after four, less than two hours until nightfall. There was no way to get the oxcart across this bridge. Provisions would have to be carried item by item, and then what? Irene had been determined to reach the temple today, and she was upset. "How much farther to Kha Seng?" she asked Clothilde.

Clothilde knelt down to help Kiri unwrap a sweet that Simone had given him. "We passed my village an hour ago," she explained.

"I don't understand," Irene said. They had not seen a single hamlet all afternoon.

"The fork in the trail. If we had gone to the left, that's the road into Kha Seng. This is the way to the temple. Once we're on the other side of the ravine, it's about ten minutes away if the path isn't completely over-grown." She was concentrating on the candy wrapper, picking at it with her thumbnail, which was manicured and clean, as was everything else about her. "We can set up camp here. I will show you the temple first thing in the morning."

Irene was not the only one staring at Clothilde in disbelief. "Ten minutes?" Irene asked.

"Unless the Brau have sabotaged the bridge," Clothilde said.

A vigilant awareness of the vanished Brau tribesmen had traveled with them throughout the day, on a trail that grew narrower and less tra-versable with each bruising footstep.

"How can we tell?" Irene asked.

Marc provided the obvious answer. "One of us will have to cross it."

Irene felt as if her body was being held together by cuts and soreness and a thousand points of fire where red ants had crawled beneath her clothing. Inhaling and exhaling raggedly, she bent down stiffly to study the bridge. Compromised or not, it looked deadly.

Louis offered a crushed packet of Gauloises, the cigarettes poking out as if the group were going to draw straws to see who would risk his life to test the bridge. Everyone except Clothilde took one. Their intent smoking was a puny ritual, but necessary, as they absorbed what she had told them. Wreathed in smoke, Irene thought, I will do it. I must do it. And then it sank in, as if it had been dawdling on the trail and just now caught up with her—the temple was minutes away. To hell with waiting until tomorrow. To hell with waiting another second.

But as she threw her cigarette to the ground and stamped it out with her boot heel, Kiri and the nimble gibbon took off over the swaying bridge. Simone darted after them, followed by Louis and Clothilde. The bamboo slats rocked with their every step, but the boulders did not tumble and the cables did not yank free. Their startling swiftness reminded Irene of the Brau killing the cobra.

"Go on," Marc urged. "I'll be right behind you."

Gripping the railing of woven vines that was strung between two distant trees, Irene walked as quickly as she could, though she felt she was moving much more slowly than the others. She stepped carefully, the leather soles of her boots too smooth from days of scraping over tree stumps and rocky trails. But although the slats tilted and tipped, the structure was remarkably steady. Knowing not to look down, she focused on the end of the bridge.

She was halfway across when a stuttering movement caught her eye. Simone had turned and was running into the jungle. "Louis, stop her!" Irene screamed and in her alarm, lost her footing, skidding as the bridge slipped out from under her.

Clinging to the railing, her legs dangling below the walkway high above the trees, she winced as the roughly hacked side of the bridge dug into her chest. The vine rail cut the flesh of her palms. Marc was making his way toward her, and even though he was walking carefully, his heavy tread rocked the bridge. She held on tighter, waiting for him, but when he reached her, he couldn't pull her up because of his broken ribs. "Your leg!" he directed, crouching over her. "Swing it up!"

She could hear the fear in his voice, and as she tried futilely to see if Louis had gone after Simone, she kicked up at the same time. The motion pushed the bridge away. She kicked again. The bridge pitched, and Marc lost his balance, falling to his knees. She could hear Louis and Clothilde calling out, but their words were lost in the disorienting cries of birdsong rising out of the trees below. "Where's Simone?" she panted.

"To hell with Simone. Let go," Marc instructed. "Let go of the vine and grab onto the bridge."

The bridge was a foot wide. She might be able to wrap her arms around it. But if she missed she may as well plummet from a ten-story building. The gnarled treetops would not cushion her fall.

"You can do it," Marc promised.

She tried one last time to lift herself with the strength of her arms, but her muscles were too sore, and the gain she did make failed to raise her body and only pulled the railing down.

"Back up," Louis yelled to Marc. "I'm coming out. I'll try to lift her."

"Damn it, tell him to go after Simone," Irene ordered and gasped. Her shoulder sockets blazed. She could feel the weight of her heavy clothes and boots pulling her down. Every second hanging there was another second Simone had to reach the temple before Irene. "Lie down," she called up to Marc, "and hang on tight."

There was no way Irene was going to let it end here. She released the railing and took flight, flailing her arms and strapping them around the bridge. It bucked, and the crudely cut ends of the slats tore through the thin fabric of her shirt, slashing the skin beneath her arms. But she was holding on. She was hoisting herself up. She was stabilizing herself on the walkway and miraculously crawling across with Marc behind her, then lying in the moss on the other side, laughing. Hysterical, she could not stop laughing. When she opened her eyes, Simone was bent over her on her hands and knees, with Clothilde clutching her by the collar.

One side of Simone's face was the color of jaundice where she had treated her scrapes with smears of iodine. Panting, she said, "What's about to happen, it's not about our mothers or a revolution or a museum in America. That's all going to matter, of course it's going to matter, but not now, not right now."

Sticky, warm blood pasted Irene's torn shirt to her burning wounds.

She looked for traces of sanity in the lunatic wideness of Simone's eyes but found none. "I know."

Simone lowered her face even closer to Irene's, her gaze trembling from one side of Irene's head to the other, seeking something. Her pupils withdrew to black pinpoints. Her breathing was frantic. Irene felt as if she was watching Simone being possessed, and she thought about the spirits that haunted the forest. Had they decided to come for Simone?

"Move!" Simone gasped. Roughly, she shoved Irene aside and clawed into the lichen with her tattered fingernails.

Irene rolled up onto her knees and saw that she had been lying on a flat slab of sandstone. Carvings of lotus flowers scrolled around a latticework of script. "What is it?" she asked.

Simone was kneeling over the stone as if in prayer. "A dedication," she whispered. "To Avalokiteshvara."

Marc asked Louis, "What does that mean?"

Louis said, "Every Khmer king dedicated his temple to a deity."

But Marc had no chance to ask more as Irene jumped up and started to run.

She couldn't gain speed in the coiling thickets of roots and vines, but she stumbled and careened as fast as the landscape would allow. The ground sucked at her boots, and she jerked them free. Branches whipped her cheeks, but she felt nothing. Tripping, she fell against a rotting tree stump. As she struggled to her feet, she saw a henna wall threading through the jungle. She could hear the others stamping and cracking through the scrub behind her as she approached it. When she raised her eyes, they met those of the *naga,* the mythical cobra, carved on the twin pillars of a high stone gateway. She pulled herself up atop a pile of rubble in front of the arched structure. She searched frantically through the foliage, and in the distance, through the mantle of the trees, she made out the soaring bud shape of a temple's top—nearly identical to the central pinnacle at Angkor Wat.

Jumping down, she grabbed a stick and hacked at the valance of lianas that hung across the gateway. Pushing her way through, she found herself at the head of a short causeway running across a marsh that must once have been a moat. The marsh surrounded the giant building blocks of an outer wall, patches of which she glimpsed through the grasp of fromager trees that had taken root along its top edge. The flowing trees held the masonry in their talon grip as if to keep it from escaping.

Made with stones aged to the color of burnt incense, the causeway led to a *gopura*, a tall, towered entrance pavilion built into the middle of a second, interior wall. The enclosed area between the sets of walls was scattered with vines, scrub, bamboo, and prehistoric ferns taller than a man, and as Irene staggered her way up the root-bound causeway, she could not see the others behind her but she could hear them. She knew that Simone was doing exactly what she was doing—seeking the fastest way to the temple at the heart of the grounds. Trying to get her bearings, Irene focused on what she knew about Khmer architecture. If this place was at all like Angkor Wat, the *gopura* would open at the back onto an enclosed field, at the center of which would be the temple.

Climbing over the ivory root of a banyan tree growing across the end of the causeway, Irene tore through a gray sheen of cobwebs that veiled the *gopura*'s open door. Strands of sticky gossamer clung to her eyelashes as she entered the pitch-black interior. She'd left her flashlight in one of the crates on the oxcarts. She would have to feel her way through.

Stepping inside, she was struck by the stench of bats, which instantly made her eyes burn. The smell was so ripe, it felt as if the walls were made of it. With the dirty, bloodstained cotton of her sleeve, she covered her mouth, and with her other hand, she groped through the air in front of her, slowly walking forward. She had taken only two steps when her fingers jammed against stone. Something had collapsed, which explained why she could not see the opposite doorway at the far side of the *gopura*. She backed out and inhaled the green peat of the jungle.

Determined, she propelled herself up and over the wall to the left of the *gopura*, tipping headfirst onto the ground on the other side. She managed to catch her balance only by landing painfully on her wrists. As she stood, she saw that the inner field was enormous, acres sprawling beneath the encroachment of the forest. Although still thick with foliage, these grounds were not as unruly as the outer area, and there was a central causeway, this one much longer and cleared of debris, that led to a free-standing, covered terrace. Beyond this low structure the temple rose stories high, and Irene stared with amazement at its five towers depicting the peaks of the mythical Mount Meru. The temple was so much bigger than she had expected it would be. As her eyes dropped to the lowest level, she made out the open arcades that encased it, and she knew what lay beyond them. Layers of alcoves and nooks, and at the core, a sanctuary—the obvious place to contain the scrolls described in Reverend Garland's diary.

She hurried toward the temple but froze when she reached the covered terrace. It was the kind of traditional dance stage used by kings for royal ceremonies, and through crusts of black lichen, the foundation that supported it revealed a garnish of upturned hands and coy smiles. Wrapped in vines, dozens of *apsaras* mimed their forgotten dance around the base of the platform. They caught Irene unawares. These figures had existed for centuries, surviving against all odds in this improbable, far-off temple. And yet she had seen them before. They were replicated exactly in her mother's watercolor tablet, which Irene was carrying at that moment in her map case.

Although the late-afternoon sun was obscured by the high, overlapping fronds of rattan palms, the air was hot and insufferably stuffy, and Irene squatted down, to steady herself and to absorb this proof that her mother had been here. With her head tucked to her knees, she heard Simone's voice—"This must be it"—and the sound of running, boot soles slapping quickly against stone.

Irene turned in time to see Louis racing through the trees, no doubt sprinting after Simone. Irene bounded after him, around the terrace and along a side pathway, to a set of steep stairs. They led up to a small entryway into the temple, this one cleared and opening onto an alfresco gallery that ran the length of the building. Within the arcade, the green daylight did not penetrate more than a few yards, and Irene could barely distinguish the shadowed Buddhas cut into the walls.

Spotting Louis ahead of her in the corridor, she overtook him, snatching his flashlight as she darted past and into an open-ceilinged room that took her deeper into the temple. She caught up with Simone in a courtyard, and together they reached the threshold of the central hall. Like the *gopura,* the vast chamber was as black as a moonless night inside. Irene ran the beam up a wall, whose false stone windows let in no light. Entering, she felt the mossy cushion of the floor beneath her feet. Water dripped from what sounded like a very high ceiling. The flashlight's humming battery accompanied the squeak of bats overhead. Side by side, Irene and Simone took one careful step at a time. As they walked ten feet, then twenty, and then more, the air grew dank, as if they were in the far reaches of a cave.

"Do you smell that?" Simone asked.

"Incense," Irene whispered. Even through the stink of bats, she could detect the spiced ceremonial perfume that was burning somewhere within the space. She moved the light slowly through the darkness, and as it advanced over a knee-high upheaval of stones, Simone said, "Stop. Go back. No, more to the left."

"What is that?" Marc had tracked them down, the dim passages of an overgrown temple probably not much different to him from Shanghai's lightless back alleys.

Irene shoved the flashlight into Simone's hands and cautiously started to climb the fallen stones.

"It looks like a door," Louis said.

Irene dug her boots into the crevices and made her way up the pile and down the other side. "A wooden door!" she said in a reverent whisper, as Simone steadied the light on a pattern of flower petals wrapped within a geometry of intertwining circles. Irene ran her hands along the ruffled carvings.

"This is it!" Simone gasped. "*Mon Dieu,* this is really it! A wooden door."

Irene patted the sculpted timber, feeling for a handle.

"The Khmer used wood," Louis explained to Marc, his disembodied voice husky with emotion. "Window frames, shutters, ceiling beams, doors like this."

Simone clambered over the stones behind Irene, methodically steering the orb of light.

"But it was all destroyed by time or in the fires set by the Siamese," Louis continued. "There aren't any traces of it left, let alone a piece as large and as intact as this. Nothing like this has been found in a temple before."

"I've got it," Irene said triumphantly, wrapping her fingers around a thick iron ring.

The hall was as wet as a sauna, and sweat made her hands slippery. She had to pull the handle with her entire weight, while Simone leaned against the edge of the door and pried it with the lever of her own body. The door groaned, resisted by the uneven floor. As they managed to open it, an orange glow slowly emerged through the widening entryway, until they could all see into a windowless chamber, where Kiri was sitting in a corner, holding an oil lamp. From the light it cast, a second door was visible in the opposite wall of the small, enclosed space. The boy must have entered through a back passageway. Following his stare, Irene saw that he was watching Clothilde, transfixed.

In the center of the room, Clothilde stood before a wide pedestal with her eyes closed. She did not acknowledge them as they pushed their way through the narrow opening, filling the doorway with their awe. Holding three sticks of burning incense between her palms, she touched her hands to her forehead three times and then planted the incense in a ceramic dish on the altar that had been built on the top of the stone base.

Irene clenched her fists, one wrapped tightly inside the other, and held them to her lips, afraid that if she opened her mouth she would scream. Afraid she would erupt after all these weeks—no, all the years—of wanting something that was now, finally, within her grasp. This room had to be the sanctuary written about in Reverend Garland's diary. Its walls and ceiling were made of copper that quivered in the lamplight, setting ablaze the offerings of coconut milk, rice, and jasmine set out on a tray on the pedestal beneath the object of Clothilde's worship.

Walking slowly around the sculpture, Irene examined it from all sides. The sloping flatness of the face in profile. The shadows beneath the closed eyes. The high brow, with a fine scoring that drew the hair back into a topknot. Pendants were carved into the long lobes of the ears, and a faint mustache skimmed the upper lip. The rose-hued stone was nearly the color of human flesh. The mouth was serene in a smile of rest and meditation.

Tenderly, Simone touched her fingers to the sculpture's firm cheek. "You know who it is, don't you?" she asked.

"Jayavarman the Seventh," Irene whispered.

She knelt, not to pray to the last great king of the Khmer Empire but to look more closely at the ledges that protruded from the stone base. An inch in depth, they were much like the gallery ledges used to display paintings on the walls of museums. She circled the platform, counting rows of three ledges on each of the wide sides and rows of two on each of the narrow sides. Ten in total. The quantity matched the description in Reverend Garland's diary, as did the measurements of the ledges. Each was ideal for holding an unrolled scroll the size of a sheet of writing paper. Irene lingered over the vision of the scrolls wrapped around the statue, mooring it in place. She did not have to light incense and ask Jayavarman for a blessing, for the blessing was being given to her right now. "Where are they kept?" she asked Clothilde.

So deep within the temple, protected from the jungle shrill of insects and birds, the sanctuary was as silent as a crypt. Perhaps it was the deadness of the air that made it so Irene did not feel Simone's presence right behind her. Or perhaps, at Irene's question, Simone had simply stopped breathing. Irene would not have known that Louis and Marc were there if they had not been within her line of sight. Even Kiri's usual chatter was silenced.

"Henry asked me to bring you to this temple, and I've done that," Clothilde answered, bending down and feeling the ledges with her fingertips, as if discovering them for the first time. "As I told you, I came here to make offerings for the lunar new year when I was a girl. But I have never seen any scrolls."

Chapter 23

Midnight

In its persistent, stone-tumbled, thirteenth-century voice, the King's Temple called to Irene, its summons edging through the spongy heat of too many bodies asleep in the confined space of the one tent the group had managed to repair. It sidestepped Louis and Marc, unconscious on reed mats on the floor. It moved cautiously past Clothilde, curled in a corner like a cat, and crept around Simone, sprawled on a cot, cradling her bound-up wrist. It wanted only Irene.

Sometime during the night, while she had tossed and turned with fitful sleeplessness, a window flap had been tied back, but the tent still stank of sweat and rot. There was not a piece of clothing among them that was not mildewing. Through the window's white netting, she could see the first tendrils of dawn. Taking her clothes outside and dressing quietly so she would not wake the others, she heeded the temple's whispered invitation.

As if in a dream, she passed the tarpaulin lean-to where Xa, Kiri, and the coolies slept with the wounded Brau and followed the path that led to the ravine. To her great relief, she found that she had not imagined the bridge. Glossy with dew, it was real, just as the cuts on her hands and the sides of her body were real, set ablaze as she began to sweat. She crossed the bridge easily this time, taking long, careful strides so the bamboo strand did not swing with the shift of her weight.

She bypassed the *gopura* and made her way to the central yard. With the fever of first discovery behind her, she stood and savored the grace of the temple's crumbled architecture, the solitary outline of each tower against the sky. It felt lonesome as a place can feel only when light has crested the horizon but the sun has yet to appear. White shadows of mist were like the invisible ghosts of pilgrims centuries gone. Chanting echoed over the damp grasses, through the fog that skimmed the courtyards— the prayers of the small community of monks who tended the temple and lived at the back of its grounds.

Wanting to take in as much of it as she could, Irene walked to a stone bungalow built up against a wall. It overlooked the dance pavilion and behind that, the temple. The scrolls are in there somewhere, she thought, as she sat on the steps. They are lost behind a fallen stone or safeguarded in another room, but they are there. Although their search of the sanctuary had been fruitless the afternoon before, her faith in the scrolls' existence was stronger than it had ever been.

Her muscles ached, and the cuts from the bridge throbbed, but she felt contentment. Until now, she had known herself only as a person who yearned. A woman who had what she wanted was a stranger to her. But here, in this faraway temple, that stranger was finally within sight.

Wrapping her arms around her knees for warmth, she watched a deer wander into the pavilion, grazing on weeds growing up through the stones. Its spotted coat was silver in the dawn light. Insects scratched noisily at the leaves in the depths of the jungle, and birds clamored all around her, but still she heard Marc's footsteps. Like hers, his hair was matted, and his clothes were creased and stained. As he approached, the

deer lifted its head. Its dark brown eyes were wide, but it was not wary.
Marc sat beside Irene and took her hand.

"By the end of the twelfth century, the Cham had overtaken Angkor,"
Irene began, needing to explain exactly what this place meant to her.
"Jayavarman the Seventh was a prince in exile. He was nearly sixty when
he led his armies to the capital and took back the Khmer Empire. There
are records of the naval battle on the Great Lake. They say its waters
flowed with blood. He ruled for forty years, and there was no reason during that time for him to build a temple here. The hill tribes were his enemies. There's no accessible water route, no major land route, but . . ." She
hesitated. She knew how irrational she was going to sound, but if she
could not trust him with her small madnesses, what was the point in letting him into her life? She said, "If this temple was anywhere else in
Cambodia, if it was in the boundaries of the known Khmer Empire, it
would have been found by now. It would not have been here waiting for
me. I know that's not what happened. I know that seven hundred years
ago a king didn't build this temple for me to find, but that's how it feels."

"If you didn't want the scrolls, this temple would be enough for you,
wouldn't it?"

"More than enough."

"And if you don't find them?" Marc asked.

Irene refused that possibility. "Once I find them, I'll know what to do
with them, and once I know what I'm going to do with them, I'll know
how my old life ends and how this new one begins."

"Are you thinking about *not* taking them back to America?"

Irene was still adjusting to her new and fluctuating feelings for Cambodia. This country that she had thought she knew so well from afar was
a place of contradictions and uncertainties, fresh challenges and possibilities, now that she was here. The Brooke Museum, that awful day when
she had stood in front of the board of trustees—it all seemed like such a
distant memory, cold and faded when compared to this lush, overheated
part of the world. "I'm not sure what I'm thinking anymore," she said.
"All I know is that when you've wanted one thing for so long, it feels as if
you're betraying yourself to even consider changing your mind."

"I understand that," Marc said, brushing his lips over her sunburned forehead. "I had never wanted to meet you. Then you walked into my bar. After we talked that first night, I knew I was going to betray myself. I was going to betray the promise I'd made to turn my back on you if you ever appeared in my world. Somehow I felt it would be worth any pain that would come with having you in my life." Carefully, he wrapped his arm around her and held her to him. "I was right."

Irene knew he would always struggle with his feelings about her relationship with Mr. Simms, but at this moment, his confession assured her that they could overcome them. She rested against him, and beneath the roughness of his shirt, she could feel the laces that bound his ribs. His hand lay softly over the bandages clinging to her sides. The jungle had encroached upon the two of them, as it had on the temple's ruins, and she was aware of how their wounds had become an abiding part of who they were.

While the fog thinned in the growing heat, light rose in the sky. With it came a deep thundering, and Irene and Marc watched as the auburn flash of gibbons stampeded through the canopy of the trees, swinging from branch to branch, howling their exhilaration to the sun as it slowly emerged.

Louis and Simone met Irene and Marc at the dance pavilion at eight o'clock, the time they had agreed upon when discussing a plan of action over the campfire the night before. From what they had been able to discern before darkness fell, the temple grounds encompassed acres, and the temple itself consisted of dozens of structures. Aside from the sanctuary, there was no single logical place to look for the scrolls. If there had been, Irene would have started searching at dawn. But since it would be a waste of time to approach this randomly, they decided to begin their reconnaissance, and assess the situation, by paying their respects to the temple abbot.

The abbot's presence in this remote place had come as a surprise to Marc, but Irene and the others knew that long before Jayavarman VII reclaimed the Khmer Empire for its people, he had been influenced by his wife's devout Mahayana Buddhist beliefs. It was not unusual to find an active monastery in a temple that bore the Buddha's image, no matter how far-flung that temple was. Even Angkor Wat had been inhabited by monks when Henri Mouhot discovered it.

Leaving one coolie in camp to watch over the Brau, whose leg was slowly healing, Xa had joined the other remaining porters, supervising the transfer of equipment over the bridge to the temple. Clothilde had gone with Kiri and May-ling in tow to visit her aunties in Kha Seng. And so it was that their meager, dirty, bloody, and broken-boned foursome carried the offerings of tobacco and gold-leafed Buddhist images to the back of the temple's walled property, where huts of wood and palm thatch were built among stone pavilions. As they waited for the abbot, novitiates in topaz robes loitered in twos and threes, holding taffeta parasols aloft to protect themselves from the sun. The boys studied the foreigners openly, while out of the corner of her eye Irene noted the *chedi*, a bell-shaped edifice that spiraled toward the sky. She knew it was devoted to religious relics and would be an ideal hiding place for the scrolls. But she couldn't see into it from where she stood, nor could she edge closer to it without every one of the attentive young monks heeding her move.

When the old abbot arrived, *sampeahs* were performed, heads bowing toward the dirt at his bare feet. They were invited to join him in his open-walled *sala*, where he sat cross-legged on a reed mat. They were all tense in their impatience to start hunting for the scrolls, and Simone spoke rapidly through the ritual of asking after the abbot's health and the health of his followers. Irene noticed that a new sense of confidence came across in Simone's demeanor, reflecting the strength that seemed to build in her with every hour she remained sober. Simone was visibly self-assured as she explained, in the formal Khmer used by religious orders, the same story they had told the chief of Leh: They were scholars, and Ormond had enlisted them to retrieve the scrolls and keep them from being exploited by the government.

The abbot was unresponsive.

The four of them had agreed that there were two potential benefits in being straightforward with the abbot about the scrolls. Ideally, though not realistically, he would tell them where to find the temple's treasure. And if he did not do this, they hoped his reaction would at least give something away. But so far he had revealed nothing, and Irene felt as if her nerves were soldered to exposed electrical wires. "He doesn't seem to understand," she said to Simone. "Are you sure you're using the correct words?"

"There is only one way for me to say *copper scrolls* in Khmer," Simone said. "I can't be any more precise."

The abbot's malarial skin drooped from his scrawny upper arms. His head looked scuffed with bristles of shorn gray hair. The only things about him that did not appear ancient were his eyes, and they gleamed as he spoke to Simone. "I don't know of these scrolls Monsieur Ormond has sent you to protect. I have not heard of this history of the Khmer people. Perhaps you have come to the wrong temple."

While Simone translated, any contrition Irene had felt about trying to con a monk was banished; she was certain that his apparent candor was as calculated as theirs. "How many white women come this way?" she asked with frustration. "Our mothers? That anthropologist we met at Ormond's? He's not even pretending to be shocked that we're here. None of them are. Not a single one batted an eye when Simone started speaking Khmer, and no one's the least bit insulted that the abbot is being addressed by a woman. They've been prepared for all of this."

"Did you expect otherwise?" Simone asked.

"But don't you see the real problem?" Irene said. "He doesn't care that we know it. He's that sure of himself. He's not going to give anything away."

"He doesn't need to." Marc kept his tone even and his smile benign, to counter the emotion in Irene's voice, which had caught the abbot's attention. "Now that he knows exactly what we're searching for, he's going to put his effort into keeping it from us. Meanwhile, we'll watch him watch us. No doubt he's sharp enough to keep his composure, but most of his monks are quite young. They're too unworldly not to become careless at some point. It doesn't matter how well they've been trained, boys are boys, and it's these fellows he's going to have trailing around after us."

The abbot was conspicuously unperturbed by this side conversation that he could not follow. "Look at him. He doesn't have anything to worry about," Irene said. "He has a thousand places to hide the scrolls. We could dig around here for years and never find them."

"Unfortunately, this is true," Louis agreed, tugging at his string tie. It was the worse for wear, but he had still put it on out of courtesy to the abbot.

"That's why we need to keep an eye on the boys," Marc said. He plucked a cigarette from the lacquer tray being passed around by a novice. "If we're vigilant, my bet is that one of them will lead us right to the last place they want us to find."

"Let's begin here," Louis said, standing in the cleared doorway of the *gopura*, gazing at the innermost yard. He was armed with metal stakes and balls of twine, and surrounded by the rest of his surveying equipment, as well as the rescued crate that had contained it. Near him, two monks were investigating the remaining contents of the crate—a brass protractor with a lead plumb line, a Jacob's staff for supporting a compass, and a clinometer for measuring elevation angles—touching each item with the universal curiosity of teenage boys.

"We'll use ten-by-ten grids in these open areas and smaller grids inside," Louis explained to Marc as he tossed him a stub of chalk. "I'll measure the distances, and you mark them off. Simone, tell the boys we want them to run the string. You're right, Rafferty, if we keep them close, we might be able to get something out of them." He dug into the crate. "We should be able to grid this entire area by nightfall. Here, Irene, take this notebook. I want you to map our findings."

"What are you doing?" Irene stared at the notebook as if it offended her. "We need to search for the scrolls!"

"We *are* searching for the scrolls. But my way. Not yours." Louis spoke with the authority that his lifetime's work in the Khmer temples had earned him. He handed the compass to Marc, who took it while looking questioningly at Irene. She knew he would put the compass down if she asked him to, but she was not interested in picking that kind of fight with Louis. She studied his face, dark and chapped from the sun. He had been tidy when they started out. He looked like a madman in comparison now, with unruly coils of brown hair springing out around his head. But he was in his element, with this unexplored temple awaiting him.

He continued, "Once we've charted the property, we'll have a complete inventory of every place we've searched and every place that still needs searching. We'll know what parts we can work at with crowbars and what will require elephants and pulleys. If we're systematic, there won't be an inch of this temple untouched."

"If we're systematic," Irene said hotly, "we'll be here for weeks plotting out the main complex. Ormond's men will be here in days, if that. They might have even beaten us here, or the Brau could have warned the abbot after they ruined our camp. That would explain why the scrolls aren't in the sanctuary. *And* why he's so blasé."

As she spoke, she could not stop thinking about what she had seen of the temple. Tree roots had taken hold of even the central structure's substantial foundation. An entire hall was blocked by the fall of its corbeled doorway and a courtyard by the collapse of its own walls. For days she had been able to keep Mr. Simms's deterioration in the back of her thoughts. There had been so much to distract her, but now, standing in this impossible temple in the bright light of day, she could think of nothing else. She simply did not have the kind of time Louis was asking for. A man's will, no matter how determined, could hold out for only so long over a body that had already made its final decision.

She was aware of the keys hanging from the chain around her neck, the bracelet clinging to her wrist, and the watch in her pocket, diligently ticking each minute away. She had no argument with Louis's methods. They were sound. But they served only his needs. "What if I never know what he sent me here to find?" she asked. "What if I don't get the scrolls back to him before he dies?"

No one said what they were all surely thinking: *If he isn't already dead.*

Instead, Louis said, "I don't know what you want me to do, Irene. We know where the scrolls were, but they're not there anymore. Either they've been carefully hidden, in which case we might never find them, or they're stranded among all this stone, and we need to search inch by inch."

"The monastery," Simone blurted. "We need to figure out a way into the monastery. We should check the *vihara* and the *chedi*, and the abbot's residence too."

Adjusting the lens of Louis's brass-trimmed Leica, Marc said, "I can do that if you want, Irene. I once searched the British consul's home while he thought I was in my wine cellar hunting for an 1846 Meursault Charmes." He did not say this proudly. His skill was merely one fact of many about his life. "I found what I was looking for too."

Irene watched one of the teenage monks inspect a protractor, turning its arc of incised numbers around in the sunlight. How far away and impossible it seemed, the effort of calculating her way to the scrolls. Even though calculation was what she had always excelled at, it paled right now in the face of her instinct—not the rational instinct she had relied on in her past but an instinct that came on so quickly it poured a metal chill down her spine. "Look wherever you think you should," she said. "Here, the monastery, I don't care. I'm going back to the sanctuary."

With sore, raw fingertips, Irene meticulously examined every polished inch of the pedestal that supported the bust of Jayavarman VII, but it was made from a solid block of rose-hued stone. She was hunting for anything they might have missed the day before, but with no luck. "I can't find any hidden panels or recesses," she said to Simone, who was standing in the center of the sanctuary, hands on her hips, studying the floor-to-ceiling copper sheets layered over the high walls.

"I was hoping they were made up of smaller pieces," Simone said, "but they're not. It's incredible. They're single sheets. Far too big to fit the description of the scrolls. Besides," she added, peering at the hammered fretwork of interlacing circles and foliage, "this isn't script."

A lantern hung from the ceiling, and in the light that fluttered like a golden breeze above their heads, Irene recognized the pattern that was typical of Khmer design. Hopefully, she asked, "Could it contain some kind of code?"

"I don't see any irregularities."

Marc had offered to come with Irene rather than snoop around the monastery, but she had decided in the end to have him stay with Louis, in case Louis happened to get lucky and stumble across the scrolls. In truth, as much as she wanted Marc at her side, she knew that if anyone was going to be with her when she found the scrolls, it should be Simone, no matter what her motives were. This journey had begun with her. It must end with her too—and perhaps, also, with the monk hunched outside the sanctuary door watching them. Resigned to the boy's presence, Irene turned to Jayavarman VII as if he could provide counsel, but his eyes were closed, his internal gaze given over to the contemplation of eternity.

"Do you think the reverend misunderstood what he saw?" Irene asked, her patience shrinking.

"Let me see the diary again," Simone said.

As if they were the allies Irene had hoped they would be the night they met in Anne's apartment, they sat shoulder to shoulder on the stone-paved floor. With their backs against the pedestal and the book on Irene's knees, they read:

> *The lantern's flame rebounded inside the sanctuary, and I discerned a metallic glow. Svai plunged into the temple and returned with a flat metal scroll no larger than a sheet of writing paper, scored with the elaborate hybrid cuneiform of Sanskrit and Chinese characters I had seen on stone steles at Ang Cor. Svai said what I can only crudely translate as "the king's temple" and then proudly declared that this temple contained the history of his savage people on ten copper scrolls.*

Simone crawled forward, toward the copper wall in front of them. She pried her fingers into the seam between its bottom edge and the floor. The panel was half an inch thick and at least four yards high. She rapped the crowbar she had brought against one of the bolts that was driven through the copper and secured between the stacked stones of the wall. "There's no way to misunderstand that."

"I have to find them," Irene whispered. "I have to—"

"Don't!" Simone clipped the word so that it did not even echo off the walls.

The monk's eyes widened, and he shifted into the darkness of the out-lying room.

"I'll tell you what you have to do," Simone declared. "Stop thinking about him. No matter how soon you find the scrolls, you aren't going to save his life. He *is* going to die. Pay attention to where we are right now, Irene. We're overlooking something. Something obvious, I know it." She stared at Irene, expectantly.

It unsettled Irene, to feel so muddled while Simone was acting so levelheaded. Her mind began to churn, trying to fit the pieces together and fill in the blanks. "My mother's watercolor tablet," she finally said, taking it from her map case. "There are paintings in it of this temple."

Slowly, Simone turned the pages, passing images of Phnom Penh's Royal Palace and Angkor Wat until she came to a rendering of the *chedi* from the monastery out back. She studied it, then continued through the book. She stopped again at the last page. "What's this?" she asked.

A tall white building stood out against the yellowed tint that age had inflicted on the warped sheet of paper. Its roof was paved in green tiles, and its door was flanked by pedestals that upheld a pair of *apsaras* as tall as humans. It could have been an illustration for a children's story. "My mother used to say this was where we would live if we were rich," Irene explained. "It's her dream house."

Holding out a packet of Gitanes, Simone muttered, "My mother's dream house was a tea plantation in the highlands of Java."

Irene watched the shine from her cigarette pirouette on the copper walls. "At least three of these watercolors come from somewhere in this temple. I say we check each one." Since the *chedi* would be the hardest to search and the dance pavilion was out in the heat of the yard, she chose the painting of a bas-relief, which they had seen in the eastern gallery, and said, "Let's start here."

The lower level of the central temple building contained a perimeter of roofed, open-air galleries, similar in their arcaded, wraparound layout to those at Angkor Wat. But instead of containing scenes of battles and myths, their walls were covered with an intricate stone tapestry of Buddhist imagery. Irene and Simone stood before a section depicting the Buddha's enlightenment beneath the *bodhi* tree. It was exactly as Irene's mother had painted it, down to the bedrock shades of purple and gray. Streaming along the wall on either side were more images of the Buddha among vines and gibbons, deer and birds, in an endless variety of classic postures. The details were so refined that the flames of the stone lamps carved around him seemed to catch fire in the late-morning light.

"What do you think?" Irene asked.

"I think we're on the right track if what we're doing is worth six of these little monks," Simone said, watching as the orange-robed sprites emerged from the forest. They spread themselves out, but they were inept at behaving casually, especially the scruffy pair squatting with their backs pressed against the wall. "They're like prisoners waiting for a firing squad. Poor things, stuck here with us women. The others are probably having a terrific time keeping an eye on Louis and Marc."

Irene stepped closer to the seated monks and easily found what they were guarding. A crevice ran from floor to ceiling through a portion of the relief. The sun had edged up over the eave, leaving the gallery in ivory shadows, but as she looked closer she could see that the gap in the wall had been deliberately made, unlike the many ruptures forced by a tree root or fallen stone. The boys stared up at her, as uncertain of her as she was of them. "What do I do?" she asked Simone.

Simone knelt down in front of the boys and spoke, her voice as soft as a feather.

Even though they had heard her in conversation with the abbot, they stared at her incredulously. Between the dark rings around her eyes and the smears of iodine on her face, they must have thought she was a ghoul.

"What are you saying?" Irene asked.

"I'm not threatening them, if that's what you're worried about."

Irene knew beyond a doubt, she could feel it as strongly as the blister of the day's heat, that the temple's treasure was in that crevice. Why else would her mother have chosen to paint this segment of bas-relief and not any of the dozen others that encircled the temple? Fighting her impulse to grab the boys by their robes and fling them aside, she focused on the sculpted Buddha that was next to the monk with the wine-stain birthmark on his cheek.

The Master's hands were held palm-up in his lap, and he was seated on a coiled cobra, which protected him as he meditated. But the Buddha only exacerbated Irene's agitation. He was a reminder that she did not have one iota of his infinite patience. Her hummingbird pulse rapped so urgently against her temples that she could scarcely hear Simone's murmured Khmer entreaties to the boys, who were nodding solemnly, as if in some kind of agreement, even though they appeared puzzled at the same time. She said to Irene, "I'm telling them that we know what they're doing. We know what they're protecting. We know it's their job, but we too have a job, and if they don't move away, we will step over them and go in. We have no choice."

"I don't understand."

"It's bad luck for a Buddhist to be stepped over, and especially for a monk to be stepped over by a woman. I would never do such a thing, but I can't think of anything else to tell them to make them move."

Slowly, Simone approached the older boy, to give him a chance. When she was mere inches from him, he flinched and jumped up. He could not do it. He could not let a woman near him, no matter how important the object was that he had been charged with guarding. Not waiting to be challenged, or worse, tarnished, his fellow sentry scuttled away behind him.

Before the boys could change their minds or another young monk rushed in to take their place, Irene stepped into the space where they had been sitting and shone her flashlight through the gap, using her other hand to swat at the swarm of flies that stirred to life under the light. As the beam hovered in the darkness, she heard all of the boys talking at once, their words overlapping, getting louder until it sounded as if they were surrounding her.

She kept her eyes on the dark, narrow space.

"Can you see anything?" Simone asked.

"No, nothing." But as she pulled the flashlight back, something metallic sparked. Irene probed the light through the gloom once again, but because of the angle, the flicker was elusive. "I need to get in there. Hold this."

Simone took the flashlight, and Irene reached her arm inside and felt the open space behind the wall. Though her mind raced with visions of snakes and spiders and bats, she wedged her shoulder into the opening that any one of these monks could easily fit through. Small and malleable, Simone could probably slip into it as well. But there was no way Irene would let Simone get to the scrolls first if she could help it, so she straightened her spine and exhaled, making her body as narrow as possible. The trick would be to move quickly. Too slowly, and she would be stuck, as well as torture her wounds. With her arm already through, she rocked back and forth, back and forth, steadily shoving herself forward. As she tumbled inside, the monks gasped.

Simone's arm reached in, handing her the flashlight. It took a moment for Irene to make out the dimensions of the compartment, which was no more than three feet wide. Like the other floors inside the temple, this one was slick with moss. The ceiling was so low that her hair grazed along its surface. She used the beam like a searchlight, trailing it slowly along the walls. As she cast it downward, she saw the ground shimmer. "Simone," she whispered.

"What?"

"I've found something."

"It must be the scrolls. The boys are petrified."

Irene saw another hint of golden color. She felt dizzy, and she was terrified she would pass out in the small space and they would not be able to get her out. She pressed one hand against the wall to steady herself. After a moment she was able to crouch and shine the light directly down.

But instead of the scrolls, she found herself looking into a pair of wide, glittering diamond eyes set into the compassionate face of a fallen, four-armed bodhisattva. The Buddhist god was the size of Kiri, its skin glowing, its robe inlaid with pentagons of flat-cut rubies. Devastated, Irene crumpled into the darkness.

"Irene?" Simone called. "Is something wrong?"

"It's not the scrolls," Irene managed to say.

"What is it?"

"A statue," she said, her voice choked. "Solid gold. It must be worth a fortune." She attempted to catch her breath, but there was no oxygen left in the closed space. "Simone, what if the abbot's not hiding the scrolls from us? What if he doesn't know anything about them? He could have thought we were lying to him, and this statue was what we're after."

"That's exactly what he *wants* us to think." But Simone, although consoling, did not sound entirely confident. She sounded as disappointed as Irene felt, as they both realized that it was probably a coincidence that Irene's mother had painted this portion of the temple. And it was dumb luck that they'd begun their search in the exact place the abbot kept this statue hidden, just as it would be dumb luck if they managed to find the scrolls today. Or tomorrow. Or next year.

Nightfall approached, a swift advance marked by a flight of dragonflies, and then swallows, and then the emergence of the bats that creaked like ancient floorboards overhead. Irene and Simone had searched the dance pavilion. They had searched the chamber outside the sanctuary and two of the accessible libraries as best they could. Their foreheads were scraped from peering into dark gulfs, and their arms ached from shoving and dragging stones. Their fingertips bled. They were dirtier than ever. After telling the abbot they had found the gold statue and assuring him it was not what they wanted, they had lost the attention of the young monks. They tried to convince themselves that this was part of the abbot's strategy, to make them think there was nothing else worth looking for, but the absence of the nosy boys only added to their discouragement.

Now that it was nearly dark, it would be futile to continue. It was time to go back to camp, but Irene paused with Simone in the doorway of the temple's main entrance. She watched Louis and Marc, sitting on a low wall at the far end of the yard, sharing a flask and admiring their lattice-work of stakes and string. She knew what Louis was doing, and she did not blame him for it. He was on the lookout for the scrolls, but at the same time, he was claiming as much of this temple as he could for himself before anyone else came along. Just in case. She envied him, that he seemed willing to take a consolation prize.

Earlier, Louis had set up torches, and they shed a thin blush through the low-lying twilight. Above her, bats moved restlessly beneath the eaves that overhung the entry, shifting in anticipation of their nightly departure. Irene said to Simone, "From the description in the diary, I thought we were going to find a memorial or some kind of testimony to a king's passage through the region. Someplace small, the size of Banteay Srei at most. A place we could scour from top to bottom in a day. But this is a whole city." She gazed at the inner grounds, from the dance terrace to the open sweeps of grass, still amazed by the immensity of it all. "We may as well be searching Shanghai."

"We need some rest. We'll have better luck tomorrow. I can feel it."

Irene appreciated Simone's determination. "You really do want us to find the scrolls together, don't you?"

"A part of me even admires you enough that I want you to have them. But I can assure you," Simone said, "I will never let that happen."

Irene watched her stride off to join Louis and Marc. It was the same way she had abruptly walked away at Anne's party the night they met in Shanghai. But Irene was too tired to be annoyed by Simone's rebuff. She was so lost in her own exhaustion that she did not hear Xa approach until he spoke. "Miss? You go."

The thrashing of the bats' wings grew louder, and the stifling air trembled beneath the eaves. "You speak English?" Irene asked, startled.

"Go." He looked at her as if she should know what he meant. "Kiri go."

She'd not had a chance to think about Xa's request to take care of his son since he had made it, and she wished she had the words to explain this to him, to let him know that although she did not yet know how, she would keep her promise. "I'm sorry, Xa, I don't speak Khmer."

In the grainy haze of dusk, Marc started toward Irene, carrying the flask.

Xa shoved a scrap of paper into Irene's hand. "You go."

The eaves whirred as if a fan had been turned on overhead. To keep from stumbling, Marc was watching the uneven ground as he walked. Behind him, Simone rested her head on Louis's shoulder, as if they'd never been at odds. Furtively, Irene glanced into her palm and saw a single word in handwriting that she had known since she was a girl.

Midnight.

Thunder surged down from the eaves. "Go," Xa insisted, grabbing her wrist and dragging her aside as the storm of bats rushed from the entrance and into the night, shattering like black raindrops in the shadows above the trees.

Chapter 24

The Puzzle Lock

As Irene lay in the dark, waiting for midnight, the first of the rain dropped like pebbles onto the bowed canvas roof. The storm that followed shook the tent as if it were a raft in a typhoon on an open sea. She prayed that it would not pass too quickly. If she could hear nothing beneath its thunder, not even Louis's snoring, then maybe they would not hear her leave the tent. The blackness was impenetrable, and each time she looked at the watch that Mr. Simms had given to her in Stung Treng, she was cautious, fixing a shelter under layers of clothing and a blanket before holding her flashlight to the jeweled face. Finally, it was 11:55. For what felt like the hundredth time, she checked that the two keys were around her neck and that the carnelian bracelet circled her wrist.

She felt as large and loud as an elephant as she inched her way blindly around the others, along the edge of the tent. She squeezed through the door flap quickly, before a gust of wet air could wake anyone. She was thankful for the sheer exhaustion they all shared, the debilitating alloy of emotional and physical fatigue. Simone had finished one gin-tonic before passing out on her cot, and Louis and Marc had soon followed. Adrenaline was the only thing keeping Irene awake. She felt punch-drunk as she stood outside, hurriedly dragging on her flannel coat and oilcloth poncho.

As she brushed against the tent, a runnel of water poured over the awning. Instantly, her boots were soaked through. Too late, she remembered her hat. Rain streamed down her face as she shielded her eyes with the flat of her hand, peering into the waterlogged darkness until she was able to see a blurry flickering. Anchored in the tide of rainfall, a small figure held a torch, its flame outlining the shell of an umbrella. Irene stepped into the seabed of the storm, and with the ground sucking at her boots, she plodded toward the light. When she reached it, she found Kiri waiting for her.

Five years old and sent out alone into the night. His bare, scrawny arms were goose-bumped with cold, but he was grinning, the impish, ecstatic grin of a boy who has at last been invited to play with the older children. His torch was crafted from burning pitch stuck to the end of a stalk of bamboo. He handed Irene an umbrella of her own. It was slick with a thick coat of oil to keep water from leaking through. The sound of raindrops bounding off it made her feel as if she were inside a tom-tom. She offered the boy her flashlight, and he snatched it from her. Flinging his torch into the mud, he started toward the ravine.

The center of the bridge was indiscernible in the torrent. For a moment she thought he might try to cross it. Horrified, she grabbed his arm to jerk him back, but he was only squinting around. Squirming free, he squatted on his haunches beneath the canopy of a tree. He patted the ground. She joined him to wait out the deafening rain. She had been grateful for it in the tent, but she now cursed it for causing yet another delay.

Beneath her poncho, she twisted out of her coat, which she discovered was not hers but Louis's. After emptying its pockets of bent cigarettes and a sterling hip flask, she gave it to Kiri. He put it on eagerly, although she had a feeling it was more for novelty than for warmth. He looked tinier than ever, sunk within the collar, his arms lost in the sleeves.

As Irene sat with Kiri, she wondered if the child had been sent by his father, to prove that he could be useful to her. She wondered what Kiri knew about his mission, what Xa had told him and what Xa knew, and if either could even comprehend the whole fantastic story if she were able to articulate it to them. There was a man, very old and sick, who'd sent her halfway around the world in order to give her this night. A night that had somehow become entrusted to a five-year-old. She let Kiri hold the pocket watch, and his eyes widened at the fierceness of the tiger and the terror of the horse. Marc had taught him to whistle lively military tunes, and as they waited out the storm, he accompanied it with a reedy version of Sousa's *Gladiator* march.

Gradually, the rain eased. When it was penetrable, Irene stood. The flashlight's battery was winding down, its shine little more than a flush of light, but the landscape was growing visible as the clouds drifted downwind. A clear, pale nocturnal light laid a course over the slats of the bridge. Kiri giggled as he slipped and slid across. With the shimmering treetops below her, Irene walked on the edge of the night.

Beneath the star-filled sky, the temple was no longer a ruin. It was not destroyed by nature or trampled down by time. Dusted in a fine talc of moonlight, the guardian *nagas* arched proudly toward the sky. There was a sugared luster to the rain-soaked surface of the walls and the molten roots of the strangler figs. But as she stopped at the end of the causeway, it was the flames that entranced her, torches blazing around the open platform of the dance pavilion. The *apsaras* seemed to have come to life, their arms swaying with the motion of some long-ago song. The smell of burning eucalyptus filled the air, mingling with the grassy aftermath of the rain. At the bottom of the pavilion's stairs, Kiri stared up at Clothilde waiting on a stone bench, wrapped in a thick blanket.

Irene approached and sat down beside her. She asked, "Are you going to take me to the scrolls?"

"I presume so, but I don't know for sure. This is for you." Clothilde held out a cloth bag. "He must love you very much to go to all this effort."

How loyal Clothilde had been. Irene said, "He must love you very much to trust you with this."

"I happened to be a woman for sale at the right time at the right price." This was said without bitterness. "I still have more left to do tonight. I will see you soon." Before Irene could ask any more questions, Clothilde walked away, farther into the temple's tree-shrouded shadows, beyond the torches' tenuous reach.

Kiri's eyes moved back and forth between the women. Should he follow Clothilde, or should he stay with Irene and see what was in the bag made of green Chinese brocade? Irene unhooked the buffalo bone toggle, and as she reached in, the boy's curiosity trapped him. He came to her side and watched eagerly as she took out a metal box. It was too small to contain the scrolls, but it made her smile. "I remember this," she said, running her fingers over the pair of overlapping brass locks. "He showed it to me when I was a girl."

Indifferent to the language barrier, Kiri nodded intently.

"This is called a puzzle lock." From around her neck she removed the chain that contained the two keys. "Here, hold this for me." She gave the box to the boy, who took it solemnly, as if he understood how important this moment was. "These are pin tumbler locks, but they're special. The keys won't work unless you know the code. What a risk! What faith! He told it to me almost twenty years ago. What if I'd forgotten? But I haven't forgotten. He knew I wouldn't."

Her chest tightened with happiness. She rolled the dials into position. 1. 8. 5. 7. The year of Mr. Simms's birth. She fitted the first key into its keyhole, and the second into the other. With Kiri gripping the box to hold it steady, she rotated both keys at the same time. The lock clicked. The shackle snapped free.

Unable to resist, Kiri tore back the lid. His eyes moved quizzically from the book inside to Irene. It was no bigger than her hand. It had a cover of watered silk, and in the center "Diary" had been painted in elegant script. A page was marked with a stiff square of paper, and as she opened the book, she realized it was a photograph. She saw the back of it first. Penned in Mr. Simms's hand, the same hand that had written "Midnight" on the note from Xa, were the words "Sarah and Irene, 1901."

Turning it over, she whispered to Kiri, "I was the same age in this picture as you are now."

But when he found that the box contained no genie or king's crown, or any of the other magical things he might have hoped were inside, Kiri's quicksilver attention strayed, back to the pocket watch, which he began to dismantle into a pile of springs and metal bits.

Irene had not seen her mother's face in such a long time, and she was stunned by how fresh the shock of death could feel, decades after the fact of it. Sarah had been nearing thirty when Irene was born, and so in this photograph she was only a few years older than Irene was now. The girl—*me,* Irene thought, disoriented by this new and unexpected vision of her past self—clung to her mother's skirt as if she would never let go.

Sadness rose within Irene, filling her, and she knew that to read the diary would be to drown in heartache. She also knew that she had no choice. She wanted no other choice. Steeling herself, she looked at the page marked by the photograph. At the top left was half a paragraph continued from the previous page.

> *searched the entire day. We found a magnificent gold deity hidden in a stone closet but nothing that resembled our scroll.*

It was not "our scroll" that caught Irene off guard. After everything she had been through on her journey, after everything she had discovered, this—her mother's involvement with the history of the Khmer—felt fated. It was her mother's voice that unnerved her, the voice that had always sounded hoarse, *from talking so much,* Irene's father used to tease. As her eyes moved over the sentences, Irene was not reading her mother's tale but rather listening to it, the words so distinct it seemed inconceivable that Kiri did not hear them too.

> *We were all disappointed and on the second day looked with less enthusiasm. There were many places where stones had fallen and a sheet of copper might be crushed beneath, but Patrik and Henry are not the kind of men to give up easily. We had no success in the morning, and it was after lunch that the strange event occurred. Now that I am back in Ma-*

nila it seems a dream and I wonder if I am foolish to even write it down, but I feel I must make sense of it, especially since I cannot bring myself to tell Patrik about it.

The men had gone off to explore the upper level of the temple and Madeleine and I were at the back of it when a stout old woman brought an unconscious girl to us. We determined from our guide that the child had eaten some kind of poisonous plant. The old woman seemed to be calling for nuns but we could not quite understand because she was hysterical and our guide spoke such atrocious French and the temple was home only to monks. Madeleine is a nurse and explained to me that the girl needed to vomit the poison but we could not communicate that to the woman. The child was motionless and I felt the terrifying presence of the shadow that precedes death.

All of a sudden Madeleine ordered me to fetch a kettle and heat water. I could see in her eyes that she had determined to save the girl. She extracted a charge of gunpowder from her pistol and mixed it with a cup of warm water and forced the girl to drink it. She turned the girl over her knee and pushed her finger into her throat. The mother was screaming and the girl was vomiting and the monks were silent as the temple's stones. They must have thought we were trying to kill the child.

This occurrence was unusual but it is not the strange event of which I am compelled to write. It was what followed that haunts me. The old woman wanted to take us to the girl's home and thank us properly for saving her life. We did not travel for long from the back of the temple before we reached a set of stairs cut into a hillside. At the top we walked through a small orchard until we came to an opening that revealed the most incredible sight. A great white house was set on a green lawn. Another woman emerged, a Cambodian sister of some kind of religious order. Her head was shaved and she wore a robe that was a beautiful shade of gray. She looked at us as if we were ghosts and spoke to the old woman. Her tone did not sound angry but we knew something was wrong. Then to our astonishment she spoke to us in perfect lyrical French. She thanked us and Madeleine told her the girl's mother should have her drink water. The nun said the girl had no mother.

This is where my tale departs into the realm of fantasy. The sister told us that her convent is the keeper of the history of the king's reign recorded in a library of palm-leaf books. Because the books are perishable they are copied every fifty years during a period of twelve lunar months known as the new kingdom. They are not copied by the sisters but by one child who is always a girl and an orphan. The girl is trained in Sanskrit and Khmer for this purpose. When she turns eighteen, the period of the new kingdom begins, and at the end of the twelve months the documents she has written are examined against the old for accuracy. In a ceremony that lasts three days the old books are burned and the girl becomes the new keeper of the library.

Irene was startled by Kiri impatiently tapping on her boot. He was grinning at a precarious tower he had built out of the watch pieces, eager for her approval. She smiled back at him and then looked out at the temple yard, half-expecting to see her mother walking across the grass. But the spell of her mother's story had been broken, and only the shadows of old stones inhabited the grounds. Irene was confused, but scanning back through the words she had just read did not help clarify the mystery her mother's story presented. She had written about a library filled with palm-leaf books, not a sanctuary containing ten copper scrolls. Irene did not understand and anxiously resumed reading.

I wanted to race back to the temple to tell Patrik this fabulous story but the sister was not finished. She gave each of us a bracelet made of red stones. She told us they were from the king's treasure house.

Irene glanced from the diary to the strand of carnelian beads around her own wrist and then quickly read on.

She wanted to know if there was anything more she could do to thank us. Madeleine has always been bolder than I and she declared we wanted to see the scrolls. Why she believed the scrolls were at the convent I still do not know.
The sister escorted us to a large room and held up a lamp. A lacquer

shelf hung on the wall. It displayed nine flat rectangular segments of unrolled copper identical in shape and size to the scroll we had left hidden in our cellar in Manila. I knew as I looked at Madeleine that she had spoken recklessly. She had not expected this and neither of us could guess why the sister was showing them to us.

I knew how much Patrik wanted to find the scrolls. I knew the information they contained and how valuable they were, but I also knew I was carrying a child. I am six months along as I write this. I have never known why Madeleine agreed to my request to leave the scrolls and never speak of them even to Henry, but I know why I wanted this. As soon as I saw them, as soon as they became real, I realized how they would change everything for Patrik and me and for our new family. We would spend the rest of our lives searching and always wanting more. I want to be happy with our life as it is.

It was here that the diary ended, the rest of its age-yellowed pages blank, but Irene did not need to read any more to finally put the entire story together from the beginning, the moment when her father had bought a trunk from a missionary's estate in Borneo, a trunk with a secret compartment containing Reverend Garland's diary. What had not occurred to her, until reading her mother's story, was that in the trunk her father might also have found a copper scroll taken from the temple—only one scroll out of ten. The reverend could have stolen it and not written about the theft!

As the torches nuzzled Irene with their fragrant heat, she thought about her father, her mother, Mr. Simms, and the woman who would become Simone's mother traveling to this very temple, using the reverend's diary as their guide to search for the other nine scrolls. Her father must have been greatly disappointed when they did not find them, never supposing that his wife *had* discovered them and left them behind.

Upon returning to Manila, Irene guessed, he took the diary and the original scroll to be appraised. Word somehow reached the gangster named Fear, who then kidnapped Sarah Blum and held her for ransom. Fear was killed by Mr. Simms, and Irene's mother was saved. But in the chaos of that night, Mr. Simms believed the artifacts were lost, stolen by one of Fear's men who got away. There would have been no reason for him to suspect they were taken and hidden by his closest friend.

Irene could understand why her father had done such a thing; the diary had come to represent danger to him. She could also imagine his shock, after his wife died, when he came across a second diary, this one belonging to her, describing how she had turned her back on the scrolls at the temple. How difficult it must have been for her father to keep this secret from Mr. Simms, the man to whom he owed so much.

Now, clutching her mother's diary in her lap, Irene mulled over the original scroll—Reverend Garland's scroll—the one that had started this entire quest. If the reverend's diary had been in the box that her father left to Mr. Simms when he died, it was logical to assume that the scroll was there too. Mr. Simms could even have brought it with him to Stung Treng. Standing up, she motioned to Kiri to gather the bits of the watch, certain she had only to follow her mother's words in order to find the other nine scrolls, which would bring this journey to its end.

Chapter 25

The Last Orphan

Leaving the puzzle-lock box on the bench in the dance pavilion, Irene tucked her mother's diary into her pocket and rushed up the slippery causeway toward a yellow flame that fluttered on the bottom of the temple steps. She stooped to inspect the dish of burning oil and caught her breath as she recognized it—a black-glazed Jian tea bowl, one of a set that she had once inventoried for Mr. Simms. Ascending the steps to where a second Jian vessel sat, also filled with fire, she marveled that Clothilde had managed to keep such fragile objects safe from the attack by the Brau.

With Kiri behind her, Irene ran toward another bowl shining at the far end of the east gallery, guiding her down the length of the arcade, past the Buddha, enlightened beneath the *bodhi* tree. A pottery lamp illuminated a path out the back of the temple and through the sleeping silence of the monastery grounds, to a gate where a lantern hung from a metal pole.

Irene saw a dish of flame in the distance, burning in a bed of moss, and then a second lantern swimming in a snarl of branches. As she chased this stammering light into the forest, Kiri sprinted ahead of her, leaping the snares of banyan roots and creepers that crawled across the ground. Insects clicked in the trees. The base of a hillside emerged, its overgrown stairway edged with two glowing cups of oil. Clambering up the slick steps, Irene tried to ignore the blades of pain sliding into her sides.

Kiri reached the top first. Silently, pounding his fist against his thigh, he urged her on. On the muddy landing beneath him, she bent forward with her hands braced on her knees to catch her breath. When she stood up, Cambodia had spread itself at her feet. The storm had moved on, the moon was bare of clouds, and she saw the immensity of the temple below. The King's Temple. *Her* temple.

She panted up the last of the steps. A narrow path pushed through a grove of jackfruit trees, and with Kiri she bounded out of the darkness and onto the edge of an open ground. His hand reached for hers, and her fingers tightened around his as she looked across the muddy grass at her mother's dream house.

Afraid the great white building might vanish like a mirage if she took her eyes from it, Irene concentrated on its details as they walked toward it. Even from a distance she could see the *apsaras* dancing on the pedestals that flanked the imposing front doors. It was not the human fluidity of their gold-leafed bodies that amazed her, or the jewels that shone in their diadems. It was that they were as tall as she was. In the iridescent light of moonbeam, they leapt in a life-size ballet, just as she had danced among their sisters in the museum when she was a girl.

Reaching the porch, she let go of Kiri's hot fingers and laid her palms against the doors. Like those at the sanctuary below, they were carved in a floral crochet, within a hardwood frame that was more than twice her height. As she stood before their sculpted surface, they opened. Clothilde stood in the space behind them. Silently, she motioned Irene inside.

Glazed floor tiles the color of marigolds filled Irene's vision as she entered the foyer. The hall was cavernous, rising into a coffered ceiling. Kiri tried to scamper past Clothilde, but she caught him by the arm. He squeaked in protest as she pushed him outside. When she turned to Irene, she looked dazed, as if she had not quite expected this moment to come, despite how long she must have been preparing for it with Mr. Simms. She had shed the blanket she'd been wearing earlier to keep herself warm, revealing a deep blue dress that fell all the way to the floor. Her feet were bare, and she gestured to Irene to remove her boots.

As Irene knelt to untie her laces, and also took off her poncho, Clothilde regained her self-assurance. Laughing, she admitted, "I did my damnedest to open that box, but I couldn't force it without breaking it."

Skeptical, Irene said, "Don't tell me you've done all of this tonight just because he asked you to. You must know why."

"I know it has to do with the history you're looking for."

Before Irene could question her further, she was stunned into silence.

A woman was gliding into the foyer. She was exactly like the nun Sarah Blum had described in her diary, a Cambodian with a shaved head, wearing a powder gray gown. But she could not have been the same one that Irene's mother had met, for she did not appear to be much older than Irene. She studied Irene uneasily, her brown eyes roaming from head to toe, seeking some kind of recognition that she did not seem to find. In French she asked Clothilde, "This is the one you were instructed to bring to me?"

Clothilde nodded.

How awful Irene must have looked to this woman. Her grimy clothes were beyond salvaging, and the stinging wound from the leech was so inflamed that it would no doubt leave a scar on her cheek. Although she knew it would make no difference, Irene instinctively smoothed her hair, bedraggled from the storm. "Do you know who I am?" she asked the nun.

The woman glanced at Clothilde. "Should I?"

Irene had already used the pair of keys. Kiri had taken the watch apart. All she had left was the carnelian bracelet. She slipped it from her wrist and held out the string of stones. "Does this mean anything to you?" she asked.

The nun was startled. "Where did you get that?"

"It was among my mother's belongings when she died."

"Who was your mother?"

"Sarah Blum."

"How long has she been dead?" the nun asked, lowering her eyes.

"She died when I was a girl."

The nun took the bracelet. "I'm sorry to hear that."

"My name is Irene."

"I am Loung." Her fingers closed around the stones. "I have heard the story. Your mother told the abbess she was with child and asked for her blessing." She smiled at Irene, but there was a sadness in her expression, as if they were sharing a melancholy secret. "You pursue knowledge and have a strong sense of planning. You are sober-minded too."

"What are you talking about?" Irene asked.

"You were born in the Year of the Monkey. 1896."

A powerful feeling of déjà vu washed over Irene. But she actually *had* been to this temple before, although in her mother's womb. She asked, "How do you know these things about me?"

"Your mother and her friend saved my life."

"You're the chosen one," Irene uttered.

"What does that mean?" Clothilde asked, spellbound by their exchange.

Irene had forgotten that Clothilde was there, and her voice prodded Irene back to the present. "Extinguish the lamps," she ordered Clothilde. "Take down the lanterns. If Simone wakes up and sees that I'm gone, she'll go to the temple—she'll find her way here. Do it now! I'll explain later."

Clothilde clearly wanted to stay, but she was doing a job, and she had not finished. If she wanted the money Mr. Simms had promised her, then she would obey Irene. "I'll come back as soon as I can," she said.

The moment the door closed behind her, Irene whirled to Loung and said, "You're the one who transcribes the history."

"So that *is* it. The history. That's why you have come."

"Where is it?"

Loung could have stalled Irene, or simply lied. But without hesitation the nun walked directly toward one side of the foyer, to a timber door overlaid with silver panels adorned with tendril script. Still clutching Irene's bracelet, she unlocked it and stepped aside.

Irene could not get past Loung and down the long hallway quickly enough. Reaching a second door, she groped for the handle, but her sweaty fingers slipped around the metal knob. The door was heavy. She shoved with all of her strength, until it gave way, pitching her into a black room.

"Loung?" she whispered.

The nun did not reply, but Irene could hear the chafe of her feet on the tile floor. There was a sulfurous hiss, and Loung emerged beside a lantern mounted in a sconce. In front of her, Irene made out what seemed to be a stack of palm fronds on a table. Loung lit a second lantern, and the fronds became palm-leaf books. With a third lamp, volumes made of mulberry paper appeared upon shelves. A fourth and final lamp, and the library was revealed.

Irene stared in amazement. Books covered the trestle table and filled the hardwood shelves against the walls. In those that were open she recognized the arabesque text, not carved on stone doorjambs, not inscribed on stone steles, but handwritten on pages made of palm leaves and lavender-hued paper. Not a single such volume was known to have survived from the time of Angkor Wat. Standing before the table, she drew her finger across the tip of a metal stylus. A wisp of black ink clung to her skin. She said, "Read something to me."

"What would you like to know about?" Loung asked. "His childhood? His exile in Vijaya? Even his record keeping is poetry." She plucked a volume from one of the shelves and spread its accordion pages onto the table. "This inventory is from a storehouse in his royal treasury. Honey and beeswax and camphor," she recited, as if the words were verse. "Parasols and silk bedding and kingfisher feathers."

"So everything in this room is about Jayavarman the Seventh?"

"Yes."

Captivated by the thought of finding more than she had anticipated, so much more than only the scrolls, Irene asked, "The other kings, where are their libraries?"

"What other kings?"

"All of them."

"I'm not sure what you mean," Loung said. "There are only records for Jayavarman here."

"But there were more than thirty Khmer kings. They ruled for hundreds of years. Jayavarman doesn't even account for fifty." Irene's gaze darted from corner to corner, scanning the spaces between the bookshelves and beneath the table. She had been so astounded by all of the books that she had not immediately noticed what was missing from the room: the lacquer shelf described in her mother's diary. The shelf that held the scrolls. "The history of the empire, the whole empire, not just one king. Where is it?"

"Is that what your mother told you that you would find?"

"I know she saw the scrolls. They were in this room, nine of them. I believe my parents had the tenth. That's why they came here, to find the rest."

"And you think you are the first person to come looking for them since then?"

Irene was distressed by the condolence in Loung's voice. "Aren't I?"

"I'm sorry, Irene, if that's what you thought you would find. You're too late."

Was it possible that Stanić had gotten here first? Or Ormond? Irene's body prickled with heat. Cold sweat ran down her spine. Grasping the corner of the table, she lowered herself to the floor. "No," she whispered, laying her head back against the wall. "Please, no."

"Your mother didn't want them," Loung said, coming closer, watching Irene intently. "Why do *you* want them so badly?"

Irene murmured, "I'm never going to know what they say."

"No, Irene," Loung said, "you didn't come all this way just to know what they say. No one has ever come all this way *just* to know what they say."

"I was going to take them back to America," Irene confessed. "I was going to steal the scrolls and use them to cement my reputation. It used to be the only thing I could think about, but I can't even imagine why I wanted that anymore." She closed her eyes, as if shutting out the room could shut out the deep wave of disappointment that was rolling in with the awareness of what she had really lost. "I don't want to go back to Seattle. I don't belong there anymore. I belong here. I want to be a part of this."

"A part of what?" Loung asked.

"There was so much I didn't understand about the Cambodians," Irene said, still hiding behind the reddened shelter of her closed eyes. "I couldn't understand it until I came over here and saw them for myself. I'd been told how far removed they are from their own history, but it was a revelation to see how much of that was forced on them by colonialism. It was also a revelation to discover that they're not as far removed from who they once were as it may at first seem. No one wants to admit it, I haven't wanted to admit it, but it's careless, not to mention arrogant, to try to understand how they were able to achieve what they did in the past without understanding who they are today. Their day-to-day life could be as important in reviving their culture as how their royalty lived. Maybe even more important, since that's what has lasted. Not the gold spires. Not the god-king hierarchies." She sighed. "Keep them safe."

"Keep what safe?"

"That's what I would do with the scrolls. I would keep them safe. I would keep them from being exploited by people like me. But I'm too late."

As Irene sat on the floor, this realization sank in, and she bowed her head into her arms, listening to the rustle of Loung's gown as the nun walked about the room. Papers were being shuffled, and something made a clicking noise on the table. Then Loung said, "Jayavarman the Seventh was an extravagant king. His lifestyle was too opulent."

Shaken by her defeat, Irene remained quiet.

"He exhausted resources and manpower building his cities," Loung went on. "He emptied what was left of the empire's coffers to build this temple. It was to be his refuge if he was ever forced to flee."

How is it possible that I did all of this for nothing?

"When Jayavarman died, his successor had nothing to work with."

How is it possible that Mr. Simms could have been so wrong? That the scrolls have been taken and he and I have no idea where they are now?

"By the fifteenth century, the Orient's prosperity relied on the sea," Loung said, persisting with her scholarly monologue, as if duty-bound. "Angkor Wat was too far inland, and the Khmer couldn't conduct this kind of trade. Meanwhile the Siamese continued to invade, and the Khmer population continued to grow. The people needed more food, but too much cultivation cleared the lower slopes. Erosion caused floods, and the *barays* and canals silted over. There was also the gradual adoption of Buddhism across Cambodia, and there is no place in the Buddhist religion for a god-king." She paused, and when Irene did not respond, she asked, "Am I wrong in assuming that this is the story you've come here to find? How the kingdom came to its end?"

At least Loung had memorized the empire's history before the scrolls were taken from this place. Perhaps she had even written it down on some of these palm-leaf pages and kept it safe among the accounts of Jayavarman. *That should be enough. That is what you told her you wanted, nothing more than to know what the scrolls revealed.* But it wasn't enough. Of course it wasn't. Irene wanted to see the scrolls for herself, to touch them, to discover them, even though she no longer needed to possess them. Unable to rouse herself from her position on the floor, she could only murmur, "Thank you for telling me."

"Irene, open your eyes."

Irene raised her head and squinted up at the nun, whose gray robe filled her vision. Loung was holding something out, and as Irene gripped the object in her hands, it took a moment for her to apprehend that she was holding a copper scroll.

Made of metal, the thin sheet was slightly curved, as if it had been unrolled from a longer piece. Reverently, Irene ran her fingers over and around it. Its sides were smooth, but at the top and bottom, the edges were ragged. At one time the scrolls must have been of a single piece, but they had been broken into sections upon being opened. She examined the script, engraved into the back so the letters were raised on the front, and even though she knew what they said from Loung's telling, she still longed to read them for herself.

The polished scroll had been well cared for, showing not a trace of verdigris. Reluctantly taking her eyes from it, Irene looked at Loung and asked, "Why did you want me to think they'd been taken?"

"I had to see your face when I told you the scrolls were gone. I had to hear your reasons for wanting them. I had to be sure."

"Are you?"

"I could take the scrolls and run deeper into the trees, but one day there won't be anywhere left to run. The earth is round. I will simply end up where I began. Ever since the French took control of our country, we have been preparing ourselves for this. It is inevitable, isn't it? That the world will discover us." Loung's eyes were wet as she set a flat wooden box at Irene's feet. She knew that it was over. She was a vestige of an extinct civilization. A king's scribe. The last of her kind. Once the library was given over to the twentieth century, she and her successors would not be needed. Louis's Leica could do her entire job in less time than it would take her to transcribe a single book. "We know it's only a matter of time. We have been waiting and hoping for the right person. But you. I never dreamed it would be you."

Irene was still incredulous. Not only was it actually happening—she was claiming the written history of the Khmer—but also she had found the entire chronicle of the Khmer's most important king. A lifetime's calling, the justification of her hopes, all contained within this room. Cradling the scroll to her chest and picking up the box, Irene stood and said, "The people I'm with, they all want something different. They all think they know best. I want to protect the scrolls, but I don't know what's best for them. Not yet."

"That's a chance I must be willing to take." As Loung watched Irene put the box on the table, she said, "Open it."

Carefully, Irene undid the latches and lifted the lid, and there they were, eight more scrolls separated by layers of cloth.

"You should know, Irene, there is more," Loung explained. "Woven throughout the scrolls' script is a cryptogram. All of the pieces fitted together form a map to the king's last treasure. During the Burmese assaults on the Khmer regions taken over by Siam, the scrolls were brought to our library by Jayavarman's heirs for safekeeping. To be hidden away, like this temple, with the hope that the empire would one day rise again. When I first heard you were coming, that's what I thought you were looking for. The treasure map."

"I've never even heard of it. Where is the treasure?"

"We don't know."

Irene remembered her mother's diary. *We would spend the rest of our lives searching and always wanting more.* Her mother and the others must have had their one scroll translated. They must have discovered hints of the map, and they came here hoping to find the rest of it. She said, "You don't know because there's a missing piece. Is that right?"

Loung nodded. "If you have the last scroll . . ."

"If I have the last scroll . . ."

Clasping and unclasping her hands, Loung whispered, "Now that the world has changed, now that it has become such a different place, what if you are meant to be my successor?"

Always a girl and an orphan.

Irene had lost an hour to the storm and had spent nearly another reading her mother's diary. She didn't know how long she had been in this room with Loung. But what she was suddenly aware of was that most of the night was gone and dawn came early at this latitude. She tucked the ninth scroll into the box and secured the lid. The case had a leather strap for carrying, and she lifted it over her shoulder. "I need to make it back to camp before it's light out. I need to figure out a place to hide this before anyone wakes up."

Wordlessly, Loung led Irene back to the foyer, its periphery studded with the pebbled glow of oil lanterns burning down. Still wearing Louis's flannel coat, Kiri stood beside the open doorway that led out to the front porch, his body tucked against the wall as he peered around its frame. He did not move as Irene and Loung came up behind him. Irene leaned out to look past him. She saw Clothilde standing on the porch with her back to the façade of the white house. Her gun, the Mauser she claimed to be able to sight at fifty yards, was drawn.

"Clothilde," Irene whispered, envisioning the return of the Brau tribesmen. "Who's out there?"

"Your friends," Clothilde said.

"All of them?"

"Yes."

"Are you talking to Irene?" Simone called to Clothilde from outside, beyond Irene's line of sight.

Irene asked Loung, "Is there another way out of the building?"

But as Irene listened to the nun explain where the pathway out the back door led, she thought, And then what? She could run, but where would she go? Beyond the frontier of this Cambodian night there was impenetrable jungle, and then more jungle. She would have to cross the ravine. She did not know the way back to Stung Treng. She had no supplies, no weapon. And what about Marc? Thinking rapidly through every possibility, she realized that even if she could hide the scrolls somewhere out back and return for them, Simone would not let her out of sight for a second. Irene had no options, and she was surprised by how relieved this made her feel.

"Clothilde," she said, "put down the gun."

"I can't."

"Why not?" Irene asked.

"I'm afraid she's going to shoot me."

Warily, Irene leaned farther out so that she could see past Clothilde. Beyond the steps, Marc and Louis were standing in the soggy grass, none too happy about their position, caught between Clothilde and Simone. Clothilde's Mauser was aimed in their direction at Simone, who stood behind them in the yard, her pistol pointing back, having situated herself in order to use the men as shields.

Irene chided herself for ever thinking that Simone might become a rational person merely because she was no longer adrift on Luminal. Knowing too well what Simone was capable of doing if pushed too far, she stepped onto the porch. Despite the distance between them, she was aware of Simone staring at the box that lay against her hip. Its embossing was coated in silver leaf, shining brightly, impossible to ignore. Irene would have to act quickly, before Simone did something rash. "This is a library," she said. "The history of Jayavarman the Seventh. There's an entire room of palm-leaf books. Come and see."

"Tell her to put down her gun," Simone said.

"She has to put hers down first," Clothilde said.

The men remained motionless as Irene begged, "Simone, please."

Insistently, Simone said, "The second I put this down she'll grab that box from you and disappear. You've heard her. She hates us, she hates what we're doing here. She was born here. She can vanish into the trees, and we'll never see the scrolls again."

"I would find them," Irene assured her.

"The world's too big," Simone declared.

"Don't underestimate me. I've found everything I've ever gone hunting for so far." To prove her point, Irene lifted the box.

It was then Irene noted that Clothilde was unusually silent for a woman who should have been defending herself. She saw, suddenly, Clothilde sitting with Murat Stanić in the hotel café in Phnom Penh, their heads bowed together. It was not the posture of a woman who did not want to be associated with a man, as Clothilde had said of Stanić. But Irene remembered other words of hers, as well. *Whenever it's among your choices, always choose the child. A parent will do anything for his child.*

Observing Clothilde closely, Irene said to Simone, "In any case, it's not in Clothilde's best interests to cross us. I know where her daughter is." It was a weak bluff, but it was all Irene had.

Clothilde must have been wondering how she had gotten herself into this bizarre situation. Despite all that had happened, could she ever have guessed that her pact with Mr. Simms would come to anything like this? Her tone sharp, she said to Irene, "What if I came all this way, what if I did everything I was told to do, but for whatever reason, through no mistake of my own, I didn't fulfill my end of the bargain? Or what if I *did* fulfill it and you decided not to pay me?" She kept her eyes and gun trained on Simone as she spoke. "This has been a gamble for me. If you were me, Irene, if you were a Cambodian woman with no other options, you would have listened to what Stanić had to say. You can't fault me for that. You would have played all of the odds too."

"And what specific odds did you play?" Irene asked. "Did you tell him what we're looking for?"

"No."

"But you did let him think you might bring him whatever we found," Irene accused.

Defiantly, Clothilde confessed, "He's waiting for me back in Kratie, just in case I have a change of heart."

Irene noticed the trembling of the gun in her hand, could feel her desperation. "If Mr. Simms made a deal with you, Clothilde, I will honor it. You have my word."

Although the Cambodian woman did not seem reassured by this promise, she shoved the Mauser into Irene's hands. "Don't ever speak of my daughter again."

Irene was not pleased about having to push Clothilde in such a way, but right now Simone was her main concern. She examined Clothilde's gun, its blunt muzzle, its heft. She appreciated the confidence it gave her, but the last thing she wanted to do was hurt Simone, and she did not believe Simone wanted to hurt her. She dropped the gun into the grass and looked at Loung, who had drawn Clothilde and Kiri to her. Irene thought about their world, intact for centuries until people like her and Simone came along. But she knew there was nothing to be done to stop the forward motion.

Irene began walking toward Simone. The ground was a slush of dirt and weeds beneath her bare feet, and as she neared Marc, he whispered, "Keep talking. If you can distract her—"

Irene passed him, refusing to acknowledge him, afraid that her feelings for him, her feelings about the two of them, would make her weak. She approached Simone, whose face was dark with scrapes and still stained orange from iodine. Her heart pounded with fear. "Tell me why you want them," Irene said to Simone. "The real reason."

Holding the pistol with its barrel pointed toward Irene's stomach, Simone said, "You know why I want them."

"Yes, but do you?"

"What do you mean?"

"I know something now." Irene's fingers slid across the cover of the box, drawing Simone's attention downward. Her mind was racing, excavating. She unearthed her conversation with Monsieur Boisselier about how Roger had said Simone would betray him for her first love. Irene had thought this was Louis, and then she had thought it was the revolution. But no. It was the Khmer, their legacy—the desire to be a part of it. Just as it always had been for Irene. *Holy,* Simone had called Angkor Wat, before Irene had uttered one word about the scrolls at Anne's party. Irene said, "You can't know what you really want from them until you've seen them."

Envy stiffened Simone's expression. "Why do *you* want them?"

"I'm not going to make it that easy for you." Irene bowed forward as if she were going to *sampeah* to Simone. "Hold the gun to my head."

"What?" Simone asked.

With calm certainty, Irene repeated, "Hold the gun to my head."

"You're trying to trick me," Simone said.

"Do it."

"Irene, don't test her," Louis called out. "Simone, please, there's no reason for it to come to this."

"If what she really wants is her revolution," Irene said, "I'm the least of her obstacles. If she can't shoot me, then she's not going to get very far."

Marc did not protest, and Irene loved him more for not preventing her from doing what she had to do.

She said, "I won't give you the scrolls, Simone. I will fight you for them, and you will have to shoot me. Prove it. Prove that *this* is what you want more than anything else. More than even my life. Try to take the scrolls from me."

Despite her broken wrist, Simone clutched the pistol's handle in both hands and raised it. Her voice was deep with anger. "You can't talk me out of them."

The muzzle brushed Irene's forehead like a kiss.

Shivering, Irene did her best to keep steady. "I don't intend to talk you out of anything. I'm not that stupid. Or that clever." Keenly aware of Simone's finger resting unreliably against the trigger, Irene reached for the box. She was terrified, and yet somehow this made her even more determined. She unfastened the latches and reached inside.

She watched Simone's face behind the pistol's gray silhouette as she removed a scroll from the box and bolted the lid once again. Simone must have tried to ready herself for this moment, but she had craved it for too long; she was incapable of stifling the elation in her eyes. Irene held out the sheet of copper. Simone did not move. Gripping the pistol tightly with her arms raised, she could not take the scroll without making herself vulnerable.

"Put it on the ground," Simone ordered.

"No."

"Now!"

"No," Irene said. "Not until you tell me what you really want. Say it, Simone, admit it."

Simone pressed the gun so hard into Irene's forehead that Irene felt it bruising the bone. Simone's face was red with anger as she hissed, "You don't think I have it in me."

Fighting the urge to draw back, Irene said, "I don't think you're like your husband, if that's what you mean."

"This is different."

"That's exactly what we said when we killed him, to absolve ourselves of what we'd done."

Simone's fury shook the gun, and the muzzle slid sideways.

Irene dodged in the other direction.

Fumbling, Simone's hands sought to right the gun, and in that moment Irene swung the scroll as hard as she could into the side of Simone's face. The pistol fired into the starlit sky. Marc and Louis leapt forward to hold Simone down, but there was no need. She collapsed to the ground, lying perfectly still, just as her husband had in the tall grass of the Chinese countryside.

Irene knew the scroll was not heavy enough to have really hurt Simone. The death that was taking place before them was not physical. Still, she pressed her thumb against Simone's throat. The pulse was quick and very much alive. Irene whispered, "No one wants to give the Khmer their pride back more than you do. No one will ever want that more than you do. But it's not selfish, Simone, to want the scrolls for yourself too."

Simone opened her eyes, and as she stared toward the Southern Cross, Irene watched her armor fade away.

Irene slipped the strap of the box from her shoulder. She was thinking about how naturally Marc had immersed himself in studying the Khmer since he had met her. She was thinking about Louis's sincere desire to give the Cambodians access to their own history. She was thinking that there was no guarantee any of them could protect the scrolls from the government, or looters, or the museums of Paris and Seattle. But with enough money, Mr. Simms's money, as much as she could beg from him, and with the four of them on the scrolls' side, each in his own peculiar way, who better to try?

"Here," she said to Louis, holding out the box.

He stared at it but did not take it.

"A chance for real preservation and scholarship," she said. "That is what you want, isn't it?"

He nodded, his expression revealing his amazement.

Kiri had crept down from the porch, followed by Clothilde and Loung. They stood at the edge of the yard, where moonlight filtered through the lace of lime trees. A cotton batting of clouds drifted over the sky. Irene reached for Marc's hand. She said, "I'm ready to want that too."

Chapter 26

The Coming Night

The expedition set off on its return to Stung Treng with a new sense of purpose, and Irene with a new urgency. All she could concentrate on with each step was her hope that Mr. Simms was still alive. Walking through the cool breach of dawn and into each day, they stopped only when the heat became too intense or the rains too hard, and they made good time, despite Marc's broken ribs and Simone's diminished emotional state.

Although Simone seemed to accept the decision that the scrolls were going to be used to anchor a new type of study of Khmer history, she was withdrawn as plans were being made. With her broken wrist tied up in a sling, she would gaze off into the trees, silent while the others discussed how they would deal with their discoveries in stages, beginning with the official claiming and cataloging of the King's Temple and the library.

As they talked, Irene could picture the coming months—the massive levers and pulleys being transported deep into the jungle, the recruiting of highland villagers for labor and the corralling of elephants for brute strength, the temple's yards filling with plane tables and bearded scholars in khaki trousers, trailing measuring tapes. Louis would supervise, Marc would follow Louis's lead, and on the hill above them, Irene would work with Simone and Loung to translate and index Jayavarman VII's history. It would be the first full accounting of a Khmer king's life, from birth to death. There was nothing else like it, and only one thing more valuable: the scrolls. As for these, the group felt it necessary to keep them hidden for the time being, until they could figure out a way to prevent them from being confiscated by the government.

The box with the nine scrolls was packed into a trunk and secured to the oxcart with a chain and three padlocks. Irene had one key, Louis the second, and Simone the third. Someday they might trust one another fully, but for now, hacksaws and any other tools that could break the chains or undo the locks were inside the trunk with the scrolls. Their goal, while they undertook their work at the temple, was also to attempt to solve the treasure map, despite the missing piece.

Irene had told no one, not even Marc, the extent of what her mother's diary had revealed or about her hunch that Mr. Simms was in possession of the last scroll. She wasn't sure why, but a part of her still needed to hold on to this last secret, even if it was only for a little while longer.

As they approached the village of Leh once again, they braced themselves for the worst, hiding the trunk in a copse off the trail, chained to a tree. But when they delivered the wounded Brau with his slowly healing leg, the chief greeted them stoically, as if he had never seen them before. Departing unharmed, intact, they could only guess that a village scout had told Ormond how the expedition had defied the chief's orders, and Ormond in response had sent word back to leave them alone—accepting, as Loung had, the inevitable.

This assumption was confirmed when they reached Ormond's villa, four days after leaving the temple. He was waiting for them at his front gate, watching through a pair of tinted spectacles as they plodded up the road from town. His brocade sarong seemed to have faded in their absence, and his torso was flabbier than ever. "How long before the stampede begins?" he asked.

The noon sun blistered the earth, drawing the suffocating smell of wild lilac into the air. Roasting inside her filthy clothing, Irene cast this question aside. "Is he still alive?"

"He's a tough old man."

At this brusque reassurance, Irene felt as if she might break down. Quickly, she changed the subject. "Do you know what's up there?"

Ormond regarded the worse-for-wear trunk bound to the oxcart, surrounded by Louis, Simone, Marc, Clothilde, and even Xa and Kiri. Surely he noticed Clothilde's hand resting on the gun at her hip. "I never cared about what was up there." He looked toward his villa, where his two red-haired houseboys sat on the verandah playing chess. Watching them, Ormond's eyes showed his understanding of how aggressively his realm was under siege, as the world around it shrank with the production of every new wireless telegraph, steamship, and assembly-line car. Sweeping his arm out to encompass the life he had made for himself, he said, "I only cared about protecting what is mine."

Despite how impatient Irene was to see Mr. Simms, it did not feel right to barge in on him when he was not prepared for her. Because none of the women who had been left to take care of him would know how to give him the dignity he needed this day, Clothilde offered to get him ready for Irene.

After bathing in a thatched stall beside the villa, Irene made her way to an upstairs bedroom, where she opened a satchel she had left in Stung Treng for safekeeping. Behind the dressing screen, beneath the beady black glare of a Cambodian rhino whose head hung on the wall, she pressed the Annamite costume she had bought in Saigon, and then slipped it on. The lotus-bud sleeves caped her sunburned arms, and as she fastened the Chinese button knots up the sides of the tunic, her cuts stung from having been washed and freshly bandaged. Still, it felt wonderful to be wearing clean clothes.

Stepping out into the room, she was startled to see Simone in the window seat, her wet hair dripping onto her shoulders. Simone's wrist was wrapped in a strip of new cotton, and she had changed into a white blouse and denim trousers. She would have looked completely recovered were it not for the red marks on one side of her face from the blow of the scroll. Irene peered over her shoulder and saw that Simone was gazing down at Marc and Louis, seated in chairs near the river. On the shore in front of them, black-bellied terns nested on rocks, and golden weavers foraged in the reeds. Through the stipple of sunlight and shadow, the men seemed to be watching a storm roll across the treetops in the distance. Irene could easily imagine what they were talking about. For these past few days, Louis had spoken of nothing other than what would be needed for studying the temple. As he worked on his lists of trundle wheels and Gunter's chains, he would be muttering to Marc, "Caproni, yes, definitely a few of Caproni's men for the plaster casts."

Marc and Louis were not alone. One of them must have fashioned a hat out of a palm leaf, because Kiri was attempting to force May-ling to wear it. As Simone observed the boy chasing the poor gibbon into a stand of gaunt trees, she asked, "What do you plan to do with him, once he's yours?"

Irene stepped back from the window. "What do you mean?"

"Are you going to adopt him?"

With her good hand, Simone was tapping her fingers against her thigh, and Irene offered her a cigarette to stop the jittering. "He has a father."

"But you *are* going to take care of him?" Simone asked.

"Marc and I have been discussing it, what it could mean, raising him, teaching him about his country's past. It's not much, it's not a revolution, but it could be a start—a young, educated Cambodian man who understands his relationship to his history."

"You've certainly changed." Behind Simone, swollen white clouds hung low in the platinum sky. Her tone was sullen as she asked, "And why not? You're getting what you want. Even Louis's esteem."

"I'm giving up the one thing I came here for."

"Status doesn't matter to you anymore, at least not in the way it used to, so it doesn't count."

Whether or not this was true Irene did not yet know, but she saw no point in trying to discuss it with Simone. She checked the gold-leafed clock on the wall. Clothilde had told her to come to Mr. Simms's room at five. There was still some time left, enough to ask one of the many questions that had amassed in her thoughts on the trek back to Stung Treng. "Simone, how long had you been planning your own revolution?"

Simone flicked ash out the window. "I don't think you're going to like my answer."

"When have I ever liked your answers?"

At this Simone smiled. "I've already told you, eventually I saw that Roger's way of doing things was wrong. More than wrong. Dishonorable. I was involved enough in the party to see how change could be made differently. The process didn't have to be so violent, so damaging. But . . ." She hesitated. "Honestly, more than anything, I wanted out. I wanted to go home. Then we killed Roger, and I had to have done that for something more than simply wanting my life back the way it had been."

"So your idea for a nationalist revolution came after he died?"

"I couldn't have murdered my own husband because I wanted to run back to my childhood sweetheart and spend the rest of my life poking around the temples." Simone stamped out her cigarette and began rolling the stub back and forth between her fingers. "I couldn't have left Louis and given my life to that wretched man, loved such a wretched man, for nothing."

Simone's defiance on the *Lumière,* her harsh words about Louis, her convoluted maneuverings in Saigon and Phnom Penh—it dazed Irene to think that all of this had been to justify the death of her husband. "It wasn't for nothing, Simone. We're going to do something meaningful for Cambodia. I'm going to do something meaningful with all the time I've spent studying the Khmer, and as crazy as it sounds, it's because of you. You forced me to look at this country in a different way." Irene's voice shook as she said, "As for Roger, he was more than just a wretched man. He was dangerous, and not only to you. If he'd managed to get into a position of real power, he could have destroyed thousands of lives."

Simone's voice was barely audible. "I know."

Watching her anxiously crumble the remains of her cigarette, Irene asked, "Do you even want to be a part of what we're planning to do?"

Simone looked away from Irene, back outside, down at Louis and Marc, who were now playing some kind of game with Kiri and the gibbon. Sunlight sparked through the clouds, catching in the outbreaks of orange tiger lilies that burned like wildfires in the green dusk of the banyan trees. "It's going to take me a while to get my bearings, but yes, I do. Or I think I do. I'm still not sure how trustworthy my thoughts are."

Hearing this, Irene could imagine another aspect of their future: the foursome working together at the King's Temple, building a collective reputation, so that when they were ready to reveal the scrolls to the world, their intentions would be taken seriously and their claim would not be denied. She could envision Simone grappling with the guilt she felt about wanting what she had gotten, and herself constantly wondering if Simone was going to come across a bottle of phenobarbital one day and find the temptation too great. Always there would be the fear that Simone would stumble over one of her emotional trip wires and sabotage the group in some unexpected way.

And yet, against all reason, Irene was glad Simone was not going to disappear. They were not the kind of women who would keep in touch, arranging reunions over cups of Earl Grey in the palm-studded courtyards of the Raffles or the Metropole. If they parted ways, chances were Irene would never see Simone again. Simone might never have another chance to salvage herself, and Irene did not want to miss the opportunity, no matter how slim, to know her as the woman she'd once had the potential to be.

The clock chimed. It was time. Irene examined herself in the mirror that stood in a wooden frame in the corner. She hadn't thought to get her hair cut since her father died, and it was longer than it had ever been. Taming its sun-bleached strands into a chignon at the nape of her neck, she considered how far in the past it seemed, when looking attractive had mattered to her as much as it did now.

Mr. Simms had always taken pleasure in how well she kept herself, and although her face was mottled with insect bites, her browned skin emphasized her high cheekbones and the bright blue of her eyes. It pleased her to still be worthy of his admiration. She said to Simone, "I have to go."

Having torn the last of the cigarette to shreds, Simone started to disassemble a new one. "You must suspect he has the missing scroll. Why haven't you said anything about it?"

Irene took a deep breath. "I haven't changed completely," she answered.

"Good," Simone said. "I'm glad to hear that."

Mr. Simms's ground-floor bedroom at the back of Ormond's villa could not be reached from within the house. As Irene walked around on the path outside, a light wind shook the leaves in the mango trees. On Mr. Simms's porch, hanging from a wire, a lantern was already burning, a porous wing of light that was pointless without the backdrop of a black night. When Irene reached the screen door, Clothilde stepped outside. Her eyes were swollen and red, and she stared at Irene like a lost child.

Resisting her own sadness was taking all of Irene's strength. She had nothing remaining for Clothilde. Without speaking, Irene left her on the porch and entered the bedroom. The medicinal odor was sickeningly familiar, immediately bringing to mind the ampoules of morphine split open during the final hours of her father's life. Frail Japanese cranes were etched into a glass lamp, and in the dimness of the room, her eye was first caught by what appeared to be a flock of transparent birds taking flight across the walls. Then she saw the bed. Marooned in its middle was Mr. Simms, propped against a stack of pillows.

To Irene's relief, Clothilde had been able to dress him in his robe of black Qing silk. But as Irene sat down on the edge of the mattress, she was dismayed by how colorless his skin had become. His blue eyes had faded to gray and were lifeless as stones. She brushed her lips over his concave cheek, and she could have been kissing a corpse were it not for his meager, ragged breathing. Forcing herself not to recoil from the musty heat of his withered body, she whispered, "We found the temple *and* the library. All of it is still up there. I can show you the scrolls. Mr. Simms, I know how the story ends!"

He did not respond.

Irene lay down beside him, careful not to touch him, for Clothilde had told her earlier that the arsenal of drugs was no longer enough. His pain was beyond alleviation. Irene had never been so physically close to him, and she was overwhelmed by his presence, despite how diluted it was. Putting her mouth to his ear, she gave him the answers the two of them had sought for so long, murmuring to him about a king's opulent lifestyle, depleted resources, Siamese invasions, and shifts in trade to the sea.

"No massive earthquake?" he mumbled.

"What did you say?"

"No giants thrashing the temples down?" he said with a slight smile.

He wasn't rambling. He was aware. She sat up and leaned over him. "Where is it?" she asked. "Please, tell me where it is."

"No grand finale," he sighed.

"The last scroll. Do you have it? Do you know what it is? There's a map, it's a map to the king's last treasure." She rushed to tell him everything in this split second when he might be able to comprehend it.

"No matter how magnificent the story is, it always ends." A cough shuddered his chest. "No blaze of glory." Phlegm rattled in his throat. "Just a dying light."

"Do you understand what I'm saying?" Irene asked.

But his gaze lit upon her without acknowledgment before jumping onward, searching the trellis of frangipani that climbed the porch, the fire-polished beads of her tunic. His words grew muffled. She turned away, shutting her throat against the sobs. She wanted desperately to share this with him. For him to congratulate her, cherish her, tell her how beautiful she was, live forever. Live long enough at least to see his journey all the way through.

She was so used to the jungle that she could smell how near nightfall was, sweeping against the thick veneer of the day's heat. A sheen of soft light spread its liquid mercury across the room. Irene made herself look again at Mr. Simms, whose attention was drawn to the last of the sun crawling across the floor. Together they watched as the pale yellow trail inched toward the bureau, its top scattered with needles and vials. A bottom drawer was hanging open. The light wound up the bureau's claw foot, prowling into the drawer, and as a flash of copper struck the air, Mr. Simms drew in his breath, fast and sharp. Irene glanced at him, but it did not seem to be pain that had caused his small convulsion. She followed his eyes back to the drawer.

From inside the house, the soft melody of "Clair de Lune" drifted down from an open window. Outside, the landscape was dissolving into the coming night. Mr. Simms's eyes were closed. Irene pressed her lips to his brow, and he did not wince. Whispering "Thank you," she got up and went to the bureau to receive the tenth scroll.

Acknowledgments

In the course of writing this novel, I was fortunate to have received the advice and encouragement of many generous people. I would like to thank the following for their individual contributions: Connie Brooks, for graciously reading countless versions of this novel and providing invaluable moral support. Alexandra Machinist, the most magnificent agent in the world, for finding this novel, believing in it, and pushing me to the finish line. Janet Brown, Beth Branco, Blair Mastbaum, Jen Bergmark, Colette Sartor, Jenny Fumarolo, and Jessica Barksdale Inclan, for reading and offering insights along the way. Susanna Porter, my terrific editor, for providing the perfect balance of give and take, and for giving me the classic editing experience I have dreamed of since childhood. Priyanka

Krishnan and many others at Ballantine/Random House for helping guide this book through its final stages. Suzie Doore at Hodder & Stoughton and Whitney Lee at the Fielding Agency for enthusiastically giving Irene and her cohorts a chance to travel the world. John Rechy, for inspiring me to start this novel. Andy Brouwer, for invaluable advice on jungle exploring and temple hunting. Lisa Okerlund, for beginning this journey with me in the sixth grade with the Shona and April Lewis mysteries. My great aunt, for sharing her name, strength, and spirit with Irene. And my gramps, for telling me my first stories and giving me Shanghai.

I used countless resources for researching this novel, and of those I would like to note: *Angkor*, by Dawn Rooney; *Angkor and the Khmer Civilization*, by Michael D. Coe; *Shanghai*, by Harriet Sergeant; and *Silk Roads*, by Axel Madsen.

With all my love, I would also like to thank: my sister Julie, for cheering me on with every book I've written since I was ten. My mom, for giving me my love of books and for countless readings of *Miss Twiggley's Tree*. My dad, for sharing my passion for books. Both of my parents, for never wavering in their faith in me as a writer. And Jim Vitale, for being the icing on the cake!

ABOUT THE AUTHOR

Born in Seattle and raised throughout the Pacific Northwest, KIM FAY lived in Vietnam for four years and still travels to Southeast Asia frequently. A former bookseller, she is the author of *Communion: A Culinary Journey Through Vietnam,* winner of the World Gourmand Cookbook Awards' Best Asian Cuisine Book in the United States. She is also the creator/editor of a series of guidebooks on Southeast Asia. Fay now lives in Los Angeles. This is her first novel.

www.kimfay.net